Praise for
A Love Through Time

"Brisbin . . . puts a fresh twist on the story [of love]. Appealing adventure."
—*Publishers Weekly*

"A timeless tale of faith and hope that will make you believe in love again."
—Jill Barnett

"Brisbin provides plenty of humor and entertainment in this romp through time."
—*Booklist*

"A very special book, and a time travel with a twist. Fans of Scottish adventures will revel in *A Love Through Time*."
—Bestselling author Christina Skye

"*A Love Through Time* is a light and enjoyable night's read that will sweep readers away to the moors and glens of Scotland."
—*Romantic Times*

"*A Love Through Time* is a mystical, magical adventure you won't want to miss. Terri Brisbin is a welcome new voice."
—Susan Wiggs

Look for previous Highland Fling romances . . .

The Border Bride
by Elizabeth English

and

Laird of the Mist
by Elizabeth English

Once Forbidden

Terri Brisbin

JOVE BOOKS, NEW YORK

ONCE FORBIDDEN

A Jove Book / published by arrangement with the author

PRINTING HISTORY
Jove edition / March 2002

Cover design by Marc Cohen.
Cover art by Leslie Peck.

For information address: The Berkley Publishing Group, a division of Penguin Putnam Inc.,
375 Hudson Street, New York, New York 10014.

Visit our website at
www.penguinputnam.com

ISBN: 0-515-13179-2

A JOVE BOOK®
Jove Books are published by The Berkley Publishing Group, a division of Penguin Putnam Inc.,
375 Hudson Street, New York, New York 10014.
JOVE and the "J" design are trademarks belonging to Penguin Putnam Inc.

PRINTED IN THE UNITED STATES OF AMERICA

10 9 8 7 6 5 4 3 2 1

To those friends who made my RWA 2000 experience so much fun and whose enthusiasm fired me up to write this story—Colleen Admirand, Mary Lou Frank and Susan Stevenson. May you always have chocolate for your bananas and an Irish pub nearby for emergencies!

Acknowledgments

My thanks once again to Jody Allen. Her insight into Scottish culture, her knowledge of Scottish history, and her network of sources were incredibly helpful to me while writing this book and answering the many "what if" questions that arose. Any mistakes are my own.

Prologue

Dunnedin, Scotland
August 1351

If Anice could only make it to the door. Wave after wave of dizziness and pain passed over and through her, making the room spin before her eyes. Step by step she inched her way across the chamber. The door. Safety. Someone would help her, must help her.

The edges of the hand-embroidered nightgown dragged on the floor, soiling them even more than the blood and the spilt wine had. Her mother would not be happy at the condition of her wedding gift. Bare feet crunched on the rushes as she took one step after another; making it to the door was her only clear thought.

As she reached out to touch the knob she noticed that her hands shook. She laughed out loud at her trembling fingers and wobbly legs. If the clan saw her now—the proud (too proud, some would say) Lady Anice MacNab, beaten into begging by her husband of one night—would they look on her with respect? With pity? She would not take pity from anyone. Not even in this condition. Not even because of the monster in that bed.

The rustling of the bedcurtains scared her from her reverie and forced her to make the final step to the door. Taking a deep breath, she squeezed the knob and turned it as quietly as she could, trying to escape the madness of the last hours.

"Going somewhere, my dear *wife*?" Evil dripped from his honey-coated words.

Anice didn't hesitate—she knew her life was at stake. She used the last ounce of her strength and pulled the door open. The look of horror on her maid's face told her how truly bad things really were. Firtha jumped to her feet and ran towards Anice, but Sandy got there first.

"Now, Anice, it is too early on the morn after our wedding night for us to be apart."

He wrapped an arm around her neck and dragged her back into the room. Gasping for breath, she fought their movement back to the bed. His steps slowed and he swayed, tripping on the bedclothes strewn in his path. He released her and she crawled away, seeking safety in the distance between them. She saw Firtha standing at the door, fear and confusion on her face. Sandy saw her, too.

"You are Anice's maid?"

Firtha simply nodded.

"Get her cleaned up while I break my fast in the hall." Sandy sat on the edge of the bed and pulled his trews up and tied them at his waist. He leaned over to pick up his shirt from the floor, but fell to his knees and laughed.

"Too much of your fine honeyed mead, Anice, and too much of you, too, I suspect."

Another drunken laugh and he found his shirt. Regaining his feet, he stumbled in her direction. Still panting from her efforts to escape, she scrambled to her feet. Damn her pride, but she would meet him straight on, not crawling like an animal on the floor before him.

Sandy staggered into her and grabbed her arms for support. Anice fought him, pulling backward, but his grasp grew tighter.

"You still have some fight left in you? Excellent!" Without warning he swung out at her and knocked her to the floor.

"You will await me here, dear wife. Get cleaned up for my return."

She peeked at him from eyes nearly swollen closed and watched him lumber to the door. She thought he was gone when he turned back to her.

"I will be bringing my guests back to visit with us. I plan to show them all the wonderful tricks I taught you during our wedding night."

She felt the darkness swirling around her, trying to claim her. She shook her head, knowing that losing consciousness would endanger her. He must have seen the gesture and misunderstood it, for he charged back into the room.

"You are my wife now, to do with as I please. If you please me in this, I may keep you for myself. Displease me and I will share you with every man I brought here from England."

The blow surprised her—she could see his fist moving through the air towards her. Through the haze of pain and blood she saw it move slowly. She thought she had plenty of time to dodge the blow.

She was wrong.

"*Dear God in heaven!*"

He should have been expecting this. He should not have been surprised. And, as the one who led the clan MacKendimen into many battles, he shouldn't be sickened by blood or injuries. But he was.

From the pallor of her skin, she must have lost more of her blood than she kept. The bedclothes piled at his feet were saturated with it. One eye was swollen closed and her face was bruised and cut. Lying unconscious in the huge bed, she looked much, much younger than her seventeen years.

"The rest of her looks much the same, Struan. Cuts and scratches on her stomach, breasts, and back. Bruises on her arms and legs and back. And torn. . . ." The clan healer looked at him with serious eyes. "She looks as if she was mauled by a beast."

"God forgive me, he is a beast."

As difficult as it was to acknowledge that his own flesh and blood did this, he knew the truth. Sandy, heir to the clan

MacKendimen, was a beast, a depraved monster. And he, Struan, current laird, had unleashed it on this innocent.

"What will ye do?" Moira gently placed another wet cloth on another bleeding and bruised spot and looked at him, through him.

"If Robbie sees his daughter looking like this, marriage or no', there will be war."

"'Tis the morning after. The MacNab and his wife will be here to see their daughter. Ye willna stop them."

Struan ran his hands through his graying hair and looked once more upon the ravaged face of his daughter by marriage. Five years ago, he had taken action against his son for the good of the clan. Now, he faced the same decision again. It was good that his wife, Edana, died four years ago and did not have to learn the truth about their son. The sight before him now would surely have killed her.

"Will she live?"

"That is no' my decision, Struan. But, I will do as much as I can to help her." Moira paused and stared at him, awaiting his words.

He reached down and touched Anice's hand. The lass mumbled and moaned in her stupor. He leaned down nearer to her mouth, trying to understand her words. Hearing them, in the breathless, terrorized whisper, was worse than seeing the damage. Anice was begging . . . pleading with her husband to stop his unspeakable attack.

Struan knew what he had to do. The clan was the most important thing. He would send his son back, now, to England. There he could little damage the honor of the clan MacKendimen. There he could not harm this child more than he already had.

And when the MacNab arrived, Struan would pledge on his honor that no more harm would befall the lass. Mayhap that would forstall any repercussions from Anice's parents.

"As will I, Moira, as will I."

"W*hat do you mean I can not go into my wife's chamber?"*

"Sandy, yer faither asked me to bring ye to him. He waits for ye at the stable."

"Brodie, get out of my way. My wife awaits me here. I'll see to my father later."

The warrior simply blocked the door, keeping his cousin from entering. His uncle, the laird, did not want Anice disturbed. His orders were to bring Sandy as quickly and quietly as possible to the stables where Struan awaited them.

"Yer faither said something about a gift ye maun see for the king."

"Now? Nay, Brodie, he can wait. What awaits me inside here will not."

Sandy took a step towards the door and Brodie nodded his head to the two soldiers across the hall. They took hold of Sandy, who put up a brief struggle. The knock on his head from behind put an end to it. More soldiers took their place before Anice's door.

"What is happening, Brodie?" the younger guard asked as they hauled the laird's unconscious son out of the castle.

Brodie thought a moment before answering. He had a very good idea of what was going on, but it was not his place to talk about it with anyone except the laird. From the look of things, Struan was trying to keep this business with his son quiet.

"I dinna ken, Iain. Just follow the orders ye hiv."

A few minutes later, the heir of the clan lay sprawled at his father's feet on the packed-dirt floor of the stables. Brodie watched the laird circle his son, a stony look on his face. He had never seen his uncle like this and, for a moment, he felt pity for his cousin. It was a short moment.

If only Alex were the heir, he thought. The impostor who had lived and trained with them for months was a better man than this one. 'Twas not meant to be, for Alex was gone and the clan was left with this excuse for a Scot.

"Tie his hands behind him, Brodie." He did so, quickly and efficiently.

"Wake him," Struan ordered.

Brodie scooped up a bucket of water from the horse trough and threw it on his cousin. He grinned as Sandy screamed, coughed, and sputtered. Had poor Anice screamed during the night?

"What the bloody hell do you think you are doing,

Brodie?" Sandy looked at him and Brodie saw the dawning perception of danger on his cousin's face. "Father, tell him to untie me. Now!" Sandy rolled on the floor, trying to gain his balance and get to his feet. With a foot on the heir's shoulder, Brodie pushed him back to the floor.

"Stay!" roared Struan.

Brodie smiled as he saw Sandy finally realize that he was in trouble, deep trouble.

"What ye and yer Sassenach friends did to the whore two nights ago was a disgrace, Sandy," Struan began. "But to treat Anice in this way is an abomination. She was an innocent coming to yer bed and ye injured her terribly."

"You have no right to chastise me about my wife, Father. No right at all."

Sandy's voice rose in pitch, sending waves of revulsion down Brodie's throat. He felt like puking when Sandy acted so . . . *English.* Five years in London with David the Bruce, who was being held hostage there by King Edward III, and he had lost every bit of his Scottish pride. Brodie ached, understanding Struan's pain and disgrace in facing this disappointment for a son and heir.

"I hiv every right, ye lousy bastard. I am yer laird and yer faither and ye will obey me." Struan's voice lowered, his expression more furious than before.

"I can raise my hand to her when she needs correction, Father. Even you used your hand on my mother."

"Aye, Sandy, I did once. And I regretted it every day of my life."

"Anice will learn to please me soon enough. She will learn my ways and obey me. The stupid girl thought to naysay me on my wedding night," Sandy continued, completely unaware that he was driving his father to the brink of his self-control. Brodie thought for a moment about warning him off. Another very short moment.

"She knew she had to prove herself a virgin after her actions with that impostor. She resisted my efforts to see if her maidenhead was intact so I hit her. It is my right."

Sandy never saw the first punch coming. His nose, broken before, spurted blood down his face and into the dirt where he landed. It was followed by several more blows and then a final kick. The very air in the stables sizzled as Struan's fury poured out of him.

"She came here and served our clan faithfully. She waited for ye faithfully. She married ye, doing her duty to our clan and hers. And ye beat her on her wedding night like she was some wild animal. Weel, Sandy, how does it feel to ye?"

Brodie let Struan land two more solid hits before he stepped in to stop him. He knew that Struan wanted to punish Sandy, not kill him. Struan was panting and blowing from the exertion and strain of beating his son.

"His damned English friends wait for him outside the gates. Tie him on the horse if ye maun, but get him out of Dunnedin now." Struan wiped his brow and turned away. No one said another word.

Brodie nodded and with the help of the other guards he did just that—tied the unconscious man over the saddle and led him to the gates. When the iron gate had been raised, Brodie slapped the horse sharply and it skidded through the gate and down the path. The English escort, aware of Struan's intent to rid the clan MacKendimen of its heir once more, galloped after the spooked horse.

Good riddance to bad rubbish, Brodie thought as he watched his cousin leave the clan once more. And this time, in addition to his plea that Sandy was gone for good, Brodie begged one more boon from the Almighty. Surely, He could find a fitting heir to follow after Struan and lead the clan MacKendimen.

Surely.

chapter 1

Six months later

"*Do you think we need more flour, Calum?" Anice counted* as she pointed to the barrels stacked along the wall. "We have but eight left."

"Eight should get us through the worst of the winter, my lady. We can purchase more at the spring festival."

Anice slid her hand down her back, aching now from bending and twisting in the cramped storage room, and straightened up to face the cook. Pulling the edges of her plaid shawl back up onto her shoulders, she wrapped it more tightly around her to keep out the coldness. Normally, she enjoyed the bite of the winter's cold, but this winter was not normal for her in any way.

"Calum, I have told you to call me Anice."

"Forgive me, my . . . Anice. I didna mean to offend ye." The large man stuttered his words, shifted on his feet, and wouldn't look her in the eye.

She knew that she would still see pity there and would rather him look away from her than gift her with that.

"No offense taken. Now, have we checked all the foodstuffs?"

"Aye . . . Anice, we hiv."

"And you have the list I've drawn up?" Some supplies were short and would not last through the winter. She took full blame for the mistake. As chatelaine, she should have kept a better watch during the harvest and the salting times. She could have made arrangements to purchase what they didn't have. But those times were a blur in her mind, a walk through darkness that . . .

Anice shook her head, clearing her thoughts. She would not think about those times; they were past and done and now she would pick up the pieces.

"Did ye forget something . . . Anice?"

She smiled at him, at his discomfort in using her given name. She had the right to be called "my lady." She had it by her birth and by her marriage. But "my lady Anice" was someone else, someone she used to be, someone she would never be again. No, she was just "Anice."

"Nay, Calum, the list is complete. I will speak to Struan to make the arrangements. Oh, good Lord! I forgot that the laird summoned me to the solar. Come, Calum, help me move these boxes back."

"Anice!" Struan's deep voice echoed down the hallway leading to the storage rooms.

"Here, Struan, I am in here." She started pushing a pile of wooden crates out of her way when she saw the laird come through the door.

"Good God, lass, stop where ye are! Calum, move those boxes now. Now!" Struan bellowed when Calum didn't move quick enough.

Anice hesitated, staying where she was until the path was clear. Nodding her thanks to Calum, she walked to the laird.

"I beg your pardon, laird, for keeping you waiting. I got caught up in taking an inventory of the supply rooms."

"And how many times hiv I told ye not to do this?"

She looked at his face and saw the concern under his bluster of not being obeyed. The flash of pity that followed caused her to look away. Fighting back the burning of tears, she tugged on her shawl and wrapped a bit of the old pride around her once again.

"Again, I beg your pardon. The tasks were not done in the

autumn when they should have been and I feared that we would not have enough to make it through the rest of the winter."

"Calum, leave us."

The cook nodded and ran from the room, as fast as his bulky body would carry him. Poor man, he did not want to be in the middle of another battle between the laird and his daughter-by-marriage. The gossip of the last one still made the rounds in the castle and in the village beyond the walls of the keep.

"Sit. Here." Struan pulled out a large cask and ordered her to it. She obeyed without resistance. Her back did ache and her feet were beginning to swell. A short rest before going on to the next room would be a good thing. Anice sat down and straightened her plain gown around her and pushed the loose hairs behind her ears. When she had gathered herself she looked at the laird.

"I hiv told ye more times than I can count, Anice, not to do this work yerself. We hiv more than enough servants and clan here in the castle to do this for ye."

"Struan, I can do this. I feel fine."

"Ye work yerself like a slave when ye are a lady, Anice. There are others who will do these duties."

"I told you when Dougal was taken ill that I could handle it, Struan. Do you have a complaint about the way I do things? About things not getting done?" She allowed herself some measure of pride in her ability to get things done. No one could complain about that.

"Things have changed since then but ye refuse to change wi' them."

"I have told you . . . I am fine." A glance at his face would have warned her about the coming explosion but she hadn't bothered to look.

"Ye are no' fine, Anice. Ye look pale and ye hiv no' been eating as ye should."

She closed her eyes and let his words pass over her. They had been through this before—it was not new ground to them.

"And, ye hivna been sleeping and ye canna fit into yer shoes any longer."

Her eyelids popped open at this newest charge and she tucked her stockinged and wool-wrapped feet under her skirts. Damn that Firtha! The woman should learn her place. The anger must have shown on her face.

"Dinna think to rebuke your maid. No one else can keep a watch on ye as she can." Struan glared at her. Then, taking her hand in his, he continued, "Ye canna ignore that carrying yer babe is causing ye problems. Moira says ye need to try to rest more, off yer feet."

"You have spoken to Moira about this?" Would nothing about her ever remain private? She knew the answer before she asked the question—not while she carried a possible heir of the clan in her belly.

"Aye, I hiv. She wants ye to visit her in the village."

"No, Struan. She may come here but I will not go there." Anice shivered at the thought of her last visit to the village—the furtive glances, the questions on the faces of the clan, the pity in the eyes of those who knew. No, she would not go.

"Ye will, lass, if I hiv to drag ye there myself."

She stopped herself from laughing out loud at his threat. He truly meant well. He cared about her in his own way. But under it all was his soul-deep commitment to the future of the clan. And she may well be carrying that future inside her now. She knew he wouldn't relent in any matter where the clan stood to lose.

She stood and gathered her shawl around her, rubbing her arms to warm them. Taking a deep breath, she faced her father-by-marriage and nodded.

"I will see her, Struan."

"Today. Now." His voice was insistent.

"Aye, Laird, today."

"Now that's a good lass." He took her arm and wrapped it around his to escort her out of the storage room. "Yer maid awaits ye in the hall wi' yer boots and cloak. She will walk wi' ye to the village."

Realizing that she had no choice in this either, she walked without resistance up the stairs and through the kitchen rooms. Without conscious thought, she placed her free hand over her belly and pressed against the movement from inside. Would this babe be a girl or boy? If it was a boy would he carry all of his father's traits? That fear had driven her to Moira the last time. If only there was an answer for her, a resolution to her fears.

"Come in, lass, come in." *The door swung open and* Anice entered the cozy warmth of the healer's cottage. There was a blazing fire in the hearth and it called to her. Warmth, so good for the coldness that lived inside her now. She tugged the leather gloves off and rubbed her hands together near the heat. When she turned back to the door, her maid was gone.

"Where is Firtha?" The woman's presence gave her peace of mind.

"I hiv asked her to run an errand for me to Pol."

"And she went?" Firtha usually held herself separate from the villagers, as Anice had for so long.

"Weel, Pol is at his brother's house." Moira's eyes twinkled. Anice felt she was missing the joke.

"And?"

"Ramsey is a widower wi' three children. His wife died of the fever last year."

"Moira, I still don't see your point." Anice shook her head. She kept to herself, steered away from gossip.

"Ramsey has an eye for Firtha. He is going to ask her to be his wife."

"What? You canna be serious! Firtha and Ramsey? She does no' ken him—she canna be his wife."

The steel-strong hold over her feelings, her dreams, her fears slipped—and her accent did too. Many years of tutoring had rid her of most of her accent. She had wanted to be the perfect wife for the heir of the clan, a man who had spent five years at the English court. She had learned the English customs, English dress, and English speech. If she were ever to be presented at Edward's court by her husband, he would not be embarrassed by her behavior. She slipped only under great stress.

Stress like this. Like the thought of her faithful maid Firtha putting herself under the control and power of a man. Shaking her head, she clasped her hands tightly to keep them from shaking. And such a large and powerful man. Anice remembered watching the two brothers work side by side one day in the village last summer. Huge men, with bulging muscles, wielding the enormous tools of their trade in the overpowering heat of the smithy. They had to be strong to do what they did but the thought of them turning that power against someone else, a woman . . .

"I beg yer pardon, Anice. I didna mean to tell tales about Firtha. I thought ye ken'd aboot her attraction to Ramsey."

Anice struggled for a moment to regain control of her thoughts and fears. She told herself that she would have to trust Firtha in this.

"Come, lass, sit here." Moira dragged a chair to the place where she stood by the fire. "Ye should sit as much as ye can wi' yer feet raised like so." Moira placed a small stool by her feet and lifted them into place. The clan healer knelt by her legs and looked at her. "May I?" Moira pointed to the boots she wore.

After a moment's hesitation and preparation for the onslaught of emotions that accompanied any touch, she closed her eyes and nodded. Moira pushed Anice's skirt to her knees and tugged at the straps holding the boots in place until they were loose enough to remove, leaving only her woolen stockings behind. A sigh of relief escaped from her reluctantly.

"Are ye drinking the water as I suggested?" Moira touched and prodded her swollen feet.

"I try, Moira," she lied smoothly.

"Are ye resting on yer side wi' yer legs drawn up?"

"Mmm-hmmm." Moira's prodding turned pleasant, if touching could be pleasant. Anice felt herself drifting away, into the sleep that never came at night.

Peaceful.

Safe.

"A*nice, 'tis time to return to the keep.*"

She shook herself awake and rubbed her eyes. Looking around, she noticed that Firtha was back. Anice stretched in the chair and wiggled her toes. She could not believe that she had fallen asleep like this. Without warning, it had crept up on her while Moira rubbed her feet.

"Aye, Firtha, it's time to go. Can you help me with my boots?"

"Stay there, lass, I'll get them." Her maid looked to one and all a formidable woman, but she was one of the gentlest creatures in the world. And Anice appreciated every kind act and gesture of concern from her.

"Anice, may I show you something that may help ye to sleep better?"

What could she say—no, but thank you? No one knew the true terror that the night held for her. Nothing Moira showed her could rid her of the fear she carried. But Moira meant well.

"Of course, Moira. What do I have to do?"

"Sit on the edge of yer bed or in a chair and spread yer knees like this." Moira demonstrated on the footstool. "Now, bring yer elbows down onto yer knees." After Anice took that position, Moira called to Firtha, "Stand in front of her, Firtha, and use yer hands like so on her back."

Anice began to pant. She knew not why but a wave of panic raced through her, and what began as a motion of comfort raised every hair on her body. Gooseflesh covered her and she fought the scream that pushed up her throat as well as the bile from her stomach.

The next moment she was looking up from the floor of the cottage. Firtha's face came into focus and Anice grasped the hand held out to her.

"I don't know what happened. Did I pass out?"

"Aye, Anice, that ye did," Moira answered. "Sit here and have a sip of this water."

Anice sat back on the chair and took several deep breaths, trying to calm her rapid heartbeat. The babe kicked and rolled, as agitated as she at the memories dragged to the surface by that position and touch. Moira, with her discerning eyes, watched her closely. She could almost believe that the clan's seer knew the truth of that night.

"I feel fine now. Firtha, let's go back now."

"Wait, lass. Pol is outside and I want him to walk wi' ye

back to the keep. If anything happens to ye, Struan will hiv my head."

"Moira, there is no need for—"

"There is every need, Anice. Ye just fainted dead away in front of me. If it happens again, ye will need someone to help ye. Pol will do that."

A shiver of fear shook her body at the thought of his touch, those big hands on her. . . .

"Pol kens no' to touch ye, lass," Moira whispered in her ear. "He's a good mon and he will protect ye. Trust me, Anice."

She did trust Moira. Moira and Firtha were the only two on this earth who had her trust. The only two who knew her secrets, well, most of her secrets. She worried, too, about the babe. The fainting was becoming more frequent in the last weeks. She would not jeopardize her babe.

"Pol may come with us." Anice nodded at Moira.

"That's a good lass. Now go afore Struan himself charges in here looking for ye."

Anice walked to the door and passed through it. Turning back, she looked Moira over. The woman's long brown hair formed a braid that fell below her hips. Not a wrinkle marred her face, nor could a gray hair be seen among any of those on her head.

"How is it that you make me obey you as I obeyed my mother when I was a child? You use that tone of voice and I believe that you are so much older than me. But you are not, are you?"

"'Tis my natural talent, lass. Ye are right, I am no' much older than ye." Moira laughed as she answered. "Come again and I'll teach ye how to use it so ye can ready yerself for yer bairn."

Anice laughed with Moira and it felt good. She walked the path through the village with Firtha and Pol at her side. She looked at the ground, watching her step among the ruts in the frozen mud. That's what she told herself, but she knew it was to avoid seeing the looks on the faces of the villagers. The pity in their eyes for the once over-proud Anice MacNab.

chapter 2

"*Robert, a messenger awaits ye in the hall.*"

The young boy's voice rang out in the tense quiet of the evening. Guards had been posted around the mill and the northern edge of the clan's holdings and all was in readiness. Let those damned MacNeils try a raid this night!

"Robert, did ye hear me?" The voice grew in strength.

"Aye, Kevin, I heard ye, and so did every mon from Aberdeen to Skye." Deep guffaws added to his own. The laird's page waited on his answer. "Tell the laird I come directly."

Robert Mathieson made his last review of the defenses and strode towards the main door to the keep. He looked down at his filthy plaid and knew the laird would pardon his appearance—once he reported his findings to Duncan MacKillop, laird of the clan MacKillop and ally to the MacKendimens and the MacLarens, he would have time to clean up.

He took the steps two at a time and approached the door. The guard nodded and pulled it open for him. Running up another flight of stairs brought him onto the main floor of the keep and into the entrance of Duncan's great hall. Normally filled with people and food and activity, it was quieting down for the night. Those of the clan who slept within the walls of the main building were rolling out their pallets for the night.

Robert made his way towards the dais where the laird and his son stood talking with the messenger. He pushed his long black hair behind his ears and walked up the steps. A servant came forward immediately with a goblet of ale. He smiled his gratitude at the girl who was so late about her duties and turned his attention to his leader.

"Ah, Robert, 'tis aboot time ye joined us." The laird reached out to clasp his arm and bring him into the conversation. "Why is my castellan running over our lands like a common soldier this night?"

"The damned MacNeils do no' rest so neither can we, Laird." Robert drained the last of the ale and handed the goblet back to the servant. "They attacked the mill on the far side of the village."

"In the middle of winter? Are they daft?" James MacKillop, his friend and heir to the clan, interrupted his report.

"We already ken they're daft, Jamie; they attack when they please. The miller and his family were frightened more than injured. I brought them into the castle until their home can be repaired." He looked to Duncan for approval.

Duncan nodded and pointed to the man who was seated at the table stuffing food into his mouth. "This messenger is for ye, Robert. Sent by the MacKendimen from Dunnedin."

An immobilizing tightness began in the pit of his stomach and spread throughout his body. He clenched his teeth and waited for the news from "home." His parting from the clan had not been pleasant—Struan had insisted that he should train . . . and live . . . elsewhere. Away from the man who raised him, away from his clan. Away.

"Weel, mon, what's the news from Dunnedin?" He was ready for anything now. But if Dougal thought that by making demands he would be successful in forcing Robert's return, he was sorely mistaken.

". . . for some weeks now."

"I didna hear ye, lad. Would ye say that again?" Robert was so busy with his own thoughts he had missed the start of the message.

"The MacKendimen sends his greetings to the MacKillop and asks that this request be considered in light of the dire circumstances. Dougal Mathieson, faithful steward of the clan MacKendimen, was struck down by a seizure of the brain and lies near death."

Robert gasped and the messenger stopped his recitation. Of all the things he'd imagined he'd hear, this was not one of them. He waved his hand to make the man begin again. His chest tightened and would not allow him to breathe. A knot grew in his gut as he listened to the rest of it.

"The illness overtook him some weeks ago but his condition has worsened and the healer fears that he willna recover. Ye, Robert, are bid return to Dunnedin as soon as possible. The laird requests that ye come and take over yer faither's duties since ye are trained in them. The MacKendimen kens this may be a hardship to the clan MacKillop, but begs their indulgence until he can find a suitable replacement."

"Good God, Robert! Yer faither struck down? Ye maun go to him before 'tis too late." Duncan grabbed him by the shoulders and shook him.

The news did not seem real, did not seem possible. His father near death? Not Dougal. He would never make it this easy for Robert to return to Dunnedin. Without recriminations? Without the hatred and accusations? It could not be this easy.

As he forced a ragged breath in and out, the ringing in his ears grew louder. He had to leave before he embarrassed himself before his laird. "I will leave tomorrow. If ye will excuse me, I have arrangements to make."

Robert waited for permission. He saw the quizzical frown on Duncan's face, but refused to acknowledge it—he would not answer questions about . . . home. Duncan finally nodded and Robert walked away from the table, down the steps, and around the sleeping bodies on the floor.

Passing through a smaller side room, Robert followed the smells into the kitchen rooms. A fire still blazed in the huge hearth, giving off heat on this frozen February night. 'Twas weeks past the day of Imbolc, the Celtic feast that Ada celebrated along with the old ones of the clan. He'd not missed it in the eight years that he'd served the MacKillops.

"Robert, yer back from yer search? How goes it?"

Old Ada limped over to him. She was a part of his life here. She had taken him in when he arrived here—no more a child and not yet a man. Her own children had died and she needed someone to tend. He never knew his own mother and needed one to care for him. They served each other's needs and watched each other's backs. It had worked well for years.

"The miller and his family have moved onto the grounds. Their house was damaged by the raid."

"I'll see to them in the morn. Now, I hiv a hot bath ready for ye in the alcove. Come, take off those horrible things ye wear."

"Ah, Ada, I do love the way ye care for me." He followed the old woman through the cooking area to another small room near the laundry room. Robert could see the steam rising from the large tub of water.

"Put yer rags in that basket and I'll get rid of them. Ye smell as if ye hiv been rolling in horse manure."

"And what if I have?" He challenged her, rising up to his full height.

"Makes no difference to me, lad. Ye hiv a way of cleaning up nicely. Climb in afore the water cools."

Robert peeled the sticky, smelly clothes from his sweating body. Winter or not, the long hard ride left him as winded and soaked with sweat as his stallion who was even now being tended in the stables. Ada's look was that of a mother's as he stripped before her. He threw the rags into a basket and stepped into the tub—moaning loudly as the heat slowly crept into his feet, then legs. After a moment, he sat down and submerged as much of his body as he could.

"If ye dinna stop making those noises, people will think more is going on here than really is." Ada picked up a bowl of soap and a washing cloth. "Here now, wet yer head so I can lather ye."

Robert sank below the water for a moment and let the hot water soften the grime in his hair. He did not enjoy the filth, but he did as he must in his duties. As he opened his eyes and saw Ada approach, he knew that telling her the news wouldn't be enjoyable either.

T*he rest of his bath was accomplished in the warm quiet of* the alcove. Over and over in his mind, he hashed out the words he needed to say to Ada. Later, he would need to use them again on the lass who waited in his bed.

"Ye are too quiet, Robert. The news from yer faither is bad?" Ada held out a drying cloth to him as he stepped from the tub.

"'Twas certainly no' what I expected." He rubbed most of the wetness from his body, then his hair. Ada offered a clean shirt to him and he pulled it over his head. It would be sufficient to cover him until he reached his room.

"Weel, open yer mouth and speak. I could only overhear bits and pieces of it from the doorway." She swatted his behind as she spoke.

He smiled at her admission of spying. Ada meddled wherever and whenever she thought she needed to—particularly if it involved him. Robert offered up another quick prayer of thanks to God for placing her here for him. Robert took her by the hand and led her to a bench. Sitting down next to her on it, he took a deep breath and found that the news from Dunnedin came forth from him in a rush of telling.

"Struan has called me back to Dunnedin. Dougal is ill and is no' expected to live."

"Will ye go?" Her voice quivered with fear.

"Aye. He's my laird—I maun follow his command." That was the safest approach—the claim of duty.

"Oh, pish. I ken too much of the sad tale to believe that 'tis the only reason ye go to Dunnedin. Tell me what I dinna ken."

"Since this will be but a temporary stay, I thought . . ." Robert hesitated to put into words his deepest desire.

"Ye thought what, my boy?" Ada looked at his face, looked deep into his eyes, discerning the truth before he spoke it.

"I hoped to get to ken my true faither."

"Nay, Robert, ye hope that yer real faither will acknowledge his natural son afore the clan."

He could only nod at her insight. His eyes and nose burned with the unshed tears of that lost boy. His throat tightened, making it impossible to speak. The feelings of the fifteen-year-old, almost a man but still a boy, confronted with the truth of his birth washed over him again. Disbelief, denial, anger. Pain and humiliation. For himself, for his mother, and for Dougal.

"I canna say how things will go but ye hiv no choice in the return. Please, Robert, do no' set yerself up for disappointment. Go and see what comes yer way."

He nodded agate at her words. The tightness was passing; he swallowed deeply to clear his throat. "I will try, Ada." His voice was low and gruff, filled with more feelings than he would admit.

"Remember, the MacKillop awarded ye the position ye hold because of yer skills. Ye will always hiv a place here."

"Aye, Ada, I will remember that." He paused and looked at her. She was worrying for him and not about herself. "But who will care for ye while I am gone?"

"Ah, my boy"—she reached up and caressed his face—"I was here afore ye came and will be here after ye leave. I, too, hiv a place here that no one will take away. I will wait for yer return."

He stood and helped her to her feet. They walked arm in arm down the hallway that paralleled the great room until they reached the stairs. His room, suitable for the castellan, was on the second floor. Hers, on this lower floor, with the other women of the keep.

"I willna see ye go so I give ye leave now. Send for me if I can be of service to ye in yer duties for the clan MacKendimen. I will await yer return, Robert. Godspeed go wi' ye."

He leaned down to her and pressed his lips to her weather- and age-roughened cheek. Stepping away, their eyes made contact for a moment, and more was said without words. They turned from each other and he ran up the tower steps.

He feared his next farewell would not be as easy.

If this one could be called that.

The fire burned low in the brazier in the corner, casting rippling shadows on the walls. Robert walked to the window and peered through the thick glass. Frosted over by the frigid air outside and the warmer air inside, he slid his finger around in the moistness on the surface. Duncan had spared no expense with this inner tower. Glass filled the windows in the private chambers as well as the large solar. No skins over the openings for the laird of the MacKillops!

Although just as rich, and higher in rank than Duncan was, the laird of the MacKendimens didn't spend his money on his own comfort. Unless he had changed it, Struan's chamber was a plain one—containing only the furniture the laird needed. Struan balked at tapestries on the walls, rich rugs underfoot. The laird used all his riches for the betterment of the clan. None in the village went hungry or cold. A place and a keeping was found for any and all in the clan. Struan saw to the survival of his people first.

Struan was a good leader for his clan, a man to be proud of, to be admired. Struan was . . . his father. Even the thought hurt. The pain of the truth still haunted him, pain made worse by the truth having been kept secret by those who knew. Hated by the father who raised him and denied by the man who fathered him. Mayhap going back into the fray was not the best of ideas. But, as he told Ada, he had no choice. His honor demanded he obey the call from Dunnedin.

A rustling of the bedcovers broke his concentration. He turned back and saw Helena sitting in his bed, her long blond hair flowing over her naked breasts. His body stirred in reaction to the inviting pose she struck.

"Robert, I was waiting for ye but fell asleep. Come, 'tis late." Helena pushed back the covers, exposing more naked limbs to his view.

Pulling his shirt over his head, he accepted her invitation. She settled into his arms and he covered them both with the heavy woolen plaids. He felt her leg slide over his and the warmth of her body spread through his own as she lay curled up at his side.

"Will ye be gone for long?" Her soft voice broke into the comfortable silence of the chamber.

"I dinna ken how long." He would be honest with her; he had always been so.

"Will ye come back?" She tilted her head back, watching his face as he answered.

"I do no' plan to stay in Dunnedin. I will come back."

"Should I wait for ye?"

They had spoken of this before. The miller's son wanted her as his wife, in spite of her sharing the castellan's bed. The young man's presence now in the keep stirred the pot.

"I canna offer ye marriage, lass, ye ken that. Mayhap my leaving will be for the best for ye and . . ."

"Bain."

"Ah, yes, Bain. He willna hold this"—he squeezed her tighter in his embrace—"against ye?"

"Nay, he willna. As long as I am faithful to him once we marry, he has sworn to forget my past."

"Can ye do that? Be faithful to him?"

"Aye, Robert, I can. I will."

"And will ye forget it as weel?" He thought of the many nights they had spent in his bed—talking, fighting, loving. He would regret losing her, but she deserved the happiness that a life with Bain could offer.

"I dinna think I will forget it or ye, but I will make him a good wife."

He made note in his mind to provide her with a small dowry. He earned his own money and owed her at least that for their time together.

"Are ye too tired to love tonight, Robert?"

He was never too tired for a good bout of loveplay, but he found the urge to be inside her heat had disappeared. He would not feel right about lying with another man's wife, or almost wife.

"I would rather just hold ye this night, Lena, if ye do no' mind?"

"I do no' mind, Robert."

She turned on her side and he fit behind her, draping his arm and leg over her body. Her breathing soon deepened and began a steady rhythm. Sleep tried to claim him, but his thoughts were still too strong. It was a long time before he gave in and surrendered to the quiet of the night.

chapter 3

"*I did it for ye, lass.*"

"Oh, Struan, I canna believe ye are replacing me in my duties." Anice's voice rose in pitch and her accent was back. Struan knew she was mightily upset with him and his decision. But she had left him no choice.

"Ye canna continue to drive yerself into the ground, Anice. Ye are a woman breeding and ye maun consider the babe."

Her face drained of all color; she wore the look of a wounded animal. He felt ill at ease hurting her feelings this way but, as laird, he had to step in and stop her. The next generation of the family lay in her belly and he would protect it as he should have protected her.

"I am no' replacing ye, Anice. The new steward will need yer guidance until he finds his way here. Ye will still hiv yer work."

He watched as she approached him. Her eyes darted back and forth, her breathing was irregular, and her skin took on a gray pallor. Fear was overtaking her—he had seen this before. She reached out to take his hand and then stopped cold as she realized what she almost did. She must be desperate—she never tried to touch anyone. Not since . . .

"Please, Struan, dinna do this to me. I hiv been faithful to the clan, to ye. I hiv done my duty weel. Please, I need my work. I need my duties. It keeps me . . . going." He knew the word she stumbled on: *sane*.

"Lass, yer belly is getting bigger by the day and ye canna keep up the pace ye've set yerself to for much longer. The new steward will help ye now that Dougal canna, and he will carry on yer duties when ye are in yer childbed."

She must have realized that he would not back down from this, because her eyes lost their wildness. He could see her regain control over herself bit by bit until the Anice known to the clan was back facing him.

"Who have you chosen for the position, Laird?"

Struan saw that the terrified child was gone and Anice was back in control. He prayed to God nightly that she would rid herself of the paralyzing fear that still ruled her life. That she would begin to enjoy life within the clan again, especially before the babe came. But, so far, the Almighty was ignoring his pleas.

"Robert Mathieson, Dougal's . . . son." It did not matter that eight years had passed since the terrible argument that had revealed the truth. Struan could not allow himself to think of Robert in any other way.

"Dougal has a son? I did not know."

"He left Dunnedin long afore ye came to us, Anice. He went to the MacKillops for training and now serves as their steward." The old excuse still worked; he would make use of it.

"And he will stay on here?"

"Nay, he will no'."

Without meaning to, Struan raised his voice in denial. Robert could not stay here after he fulfilled his duty. Too many problems, too many lies, too many mistakes from the past would lie open. Nay, he could not.

"The MacKillop wants him to return as soon as he is no' needed any longer here. So, ye see, Anice, ye will hiv yer duties back after ye recover from the birth of yer bairn."

With her head bowed, she nodded. "Yes, Laird," she whispered. "I will obey your commands."

Oh, dear God, what he wouldn't give to have the old Anice

back. The one with the noble airs and the infuriating tone of voice. The one who insisted on being addressed as "milady" and who never trembled in fear before any man.

"Robert will arrive in a few days, Anice. Can ye find a suitable chamber for him to use during his stay?"

She smiled at him and nodded, obviously pleased to be given a task, however mundane it was. He watched her turn to leave the room, when she stopped at the door.

"Struan, may I ask a boon?"

"Anything wi'in my power to give ye is yers, Anice." He meant it.

"Can we keep my dealings with your . . . son a private thing?"

"Aye, Anice, there's no need for Robert to be privy to yer private life."

"Thank you, Laird."

One day, long ago, he had waited for the day this lass would finally call him Father. He had waited for the day she would joyfully give him many plump grandchildren to carry and spoil. 'Twas not meant to be. He regretted that more than anything else ruined by his son.

Sandy, the despoiler not only of virgins, but also of dreams. Struan shook his head in regret as Anice turned and left the room.

Anice made her way to Dougal's chamber. The poor man was withering away before their eyes and no one could slow his deterioration down a bit. Moira tried all the potions and herbal concoctions she knew how to brew and it was all for naught. Well, Anice thought, at least his son would see him before he passed over.

The door was open and Moira was tending the dying man, wiping his brow and face. Anice had tolerated Dougal in his role of steward, but she had never liked him, although that thought felt uncharitable as the man lay near death. At least he had lived a long, full life and God had granted him a son.

Her hand moved to her belly as it always did now when she thought about children. Would this be a son for the clan or a daughter for her? If only Moira would share her knowledge.

Instead she always answered that things would work out for best. But whose best? Hers? The babe's? God forbid, Sandy's?

"Does the bairn move inside ye?" Moira's voice broke into her thoughts.

"Aye, he moves much more now than before." She always called the babe "he" as if she knew the matter had already been decided. She rubbed her fingers over the spot that moved.

Moira stood as she approached the bed. The healer reached out towards her belly but paused, waiting for permission. Moira was one of few whose touch she could bear, but the woman always asked first. Anice nodded her consent and Moira's hands encircled the bulge of the babe and spread outward. She pushed lightly against the movements from within.

Anice smiled as Moira continued her poking and prodding. For some reason, Moira's touch soothed her and she felt the tension of the encounter with Struan leave her body. Moira stopped with her hand on top of the mound and smiled, too.

"All is well?" Anice asked, hoping for some small clue.

"All is well. Hiv ye been resting?" Moira met her glance.

"I try."

"Ye are a liar, Anice MacNab, and no' a verra good one at that."

"When the new steward arrives, I will have nothing to do but rest, Moira."

"New steward? Has Struan spoken of him to ye, lass?" The news of the visitor seemed to excite Moira.

"Aye, Moira, Dougal's son is coming home to serve in his faither's place. Until I recover from the birth of the babe."

Moira walked around her and sat by the bedside again, tending to Dougal. Anice could see she was deep in thought about the return of the son. Mayhap she knew this Robert Mathieson and could tell her about him.

"Struan said that Robert left before I came here to live. Did you know him, Moira?" Anice pulled her woolen shawl tighter around her shoulders and sat on a stool next to the window.

"Aye, he grew up here and left for the MacKillop's at the same time I was marrying my first husband Gordon."

Anice shivered at the thought of marriage. If God was merciful, she had seen as much of married life as she would ever see.

"Duncan, the MacKillop, offered to train Robert as a steward."

"But, 'tis so strange. Why did Dougal not train the boy himself?" A father usually trained his own son, unless he was noble born—then he was sent as a foster son to another clan. Even daughters were fostered before their marriage, just as she had been sent to the home of her betrothed. Another shiver rocked her being. That had been another Anice, at another time.

"The two of them fought at every step, as faither and son sometimes do. Struan thought it best to make arrangements wi' Duncan. The plan was always to hiv him back wi' us but it haes never come to pass."

"Until now. He returns within the week, Moira." She stood and walked to the door. "Which reminds me—I must pick out a suitable chamber for him and have it readied."

"Yer a good lass, Anice. Dinna worry, all things hiv a way of working themselves out."

"You are doing that voice again, Moira." She laughed at the frown on Moira's face. "Remember you have promised to teach me that before the bairn comes."

"I will, Anice. Ye hiv plenty of time left afore that happens."

"Do you need anything for Dougal before I go?"

"Nay, I hiv what I need here. Remember to rest, Anice."

"I will, Moira. I promise." Anice left and headed for the second floor and the unused chambers.

"Liar." Moira's voice followed her up the stairs.

When Struan entered the sickroom, he found her kneeling before the hearth, staring into the flames. As in the past, he knew not to interrupt. The room seemed smoky to him, as if the fancy chimney didn't work. More smoke poured into the room than left it through the small opening. Yet, the ailing man on the bed did not seem to be bothered by it. When Struan could fight it no longer, he coughed.

A few minutes later, the smoke began to clear and the flames died down. He shook his head in wonderment—he had watched the seer receive her "wisdom," as she called it, before, but it never ceased to amaze him. She sat back on her heels and opened her eyes, but she still gazed at the hearth.

"Yer habit of sending yer sons away will haunt ye, Struan. Ye maun deal wi' the problems of yer past afore they take over yer life and yer soul and destroy the verra thing ye seek to protect."

"What do ye mean, Moira?"

"Ye maun decide which of yer sons is to lead the clan after ye and ye maun stand by him and teach him. Sending them away just prolongs the trouble to come."

"My sons? I hiv but one son and ye ken he is no' fit to lead the clan."

Moira looked at him—looked *through* him—and smiled. "He haes his maither's eyes, but they are the color of yours. Ye can play out the charade, or acknowledge him afore the clan and gain their acceptance. The decision is yers. Think ye weel upon it."

A momentary flash of silver-gray cat's eyes intruded from his memory. He shook his head, trying in vain to stop the rest of the image from forming in his mind. The black flowing hair, the creamy white skin, the voluptuous figure that first caught his eye.

Glynnis!

He could see her again as she looked the day she arrived for her marriage to Dougal. A marriage arranged by the old laird to his cousin, she was his one true betrayal of Edana. Oh, he had his mistresses, as was his right, but he'd loved Glynnis. She died bearing her . . . their son all those years ago.

He thought that no one had known the truth of it. Dougal had mourned her death and raised the child as his own—until eight years ago. But Edana had known somehow, had always known, she said as she revealed the boy's true parentage in a terrible argument. All in the solar heard it—Struan, Dougal, Sandy, and the boy.

Dougal never suspected, but he'd reacted as any man faced with a son not of his own get—he'd turned from the boy in anger. The steward owed a duty to the laird and could not turn from that, so the boy bore the worst of it. He could still see Robert's face, his expression at the news that he was the natural son of the laird. Struan would regret to his dying day that he did not acknowledge the boy then and there. Robert waited for it, so did the others, but the words caught in his throat. But why?

He sent the boy to the MacKillop for training as a steward. Sandy eventually went to England with King David. Edana was dead four years now. She forgave him his sin against her, she'd told him on her deathbed. But Dougal never did. The man's hatred simmered below the surface, ready to boil over at any moment. They never mentioned Robert or Glynnis. Dougal carried out his duties and Struan accepted the situation.

Now, the boy returned.

Dougal would have been furious at the thought of Robert taking over the duties he'd held, but he would not know now. He would most likely die before Robert arrived, without ever knowing the boy was even here.

What would he be like? In spite of the fact that Duncan had sent reports and invited him to visit, Struan had not laid eyes on the boy since he left. He was a gangly thing, all legs and arms, back then. Thin, his manly growth yet to happen. What would he look like now? Would more of his mother's or father's features show through? The clan may know him without a word being spoken in his behalf.

He was almost a year older than Sandy. Well, at least training him for a stewardship would keep him from expecting more than his due. As a natural son, he could inherit if Struan and the clan elders chose him, but that was unlikely since a legitimate heir lived and breathed.

He glanced at the bed where Dougal lay dying. Struan now deeply regretted that he had never forced the issue between them into the open and had never explained his actions of the past to his steward, and his former friend.

"Sometimes just saying the words out loud will help yer conscience."

Moira, it sometimes seemed to him, could also read thoughts—or guilty minds.

"It will do no good, Moira, he canna hear me."

"Ye'd be surprised what he could hear, mayhap wi' his heart and no' his ears. If ye speak from yer heart."

Struan ran his hands through his hair. So many years gone, so many kith and kin gone without time to speak from the heart.

"Make yer peace wi' him as ye did wi' Edana. 'Tis time, Struan." Moira gathered her things together in a basket and left the room, closing the door behind her.

Struan walked to the bed and sat on the chair next to it. He leaned over and placed his hand on the other man's arm.

"Dougal, old friend, I hiv some things to be telling ye."

And the laird spoke from his heart for the first time in a long time.

chapter 4

B*reaking through the last barrier of trees that blocked his* view, Robert reined in and dismounted his black stallion. Dunnedin lay before him, the village spread out to the other forest, the castle and keep in front of him.

Eight years.

Not a day passed in those years when he did not think about returning. He never knew why he wanted to return—there was nothing here waiting for him.

Dougal made it clear the night of the argument that Robert was no longer his son. His actions in the next weeks were the proof—Dougal shunned him and threw his few meager belongings out of the room they shared in the keep. The insults were the worst. His chest tightened with the memories of the words flung at him in anger.

Bastard son of a lying whore.

At first, he thought it couldn't be true, the accusations about his mother, dead all those years. But the look on the laird's face and his lack of denial about his affair with Dougal's wife told the truth well enough.

Robert remembered waiting, waiting for Struan to say more after admitting by default to his fathering Glynnis's child. He had held his breath, fisted his hands, and waited. The laird looked at his wife and legitimate son, and then at him.

Please, please, please.

He'd offered a silent prayer to the Almighty, one that He chose to ignore at the time. 'Twas not meant to be, then or now. Nothing in Struan's message even acknowledged their true relationship.

And, of course, Robert couldn't forget that his half-brother had married the MacNab heiress and the marriage was about to bear fruit. There was no need in the clan for recognition of an additional son—an heir and another on the way protected the future of the MacKendimens.

Robert pulled on the reins of his horse and began walking towards the castle gate. A rock sitting in the pit of his stomach told him that this was probably not a good idea, no matter how much time had passed. Well, if he was lucky, Dougal was beyond expressing his hatred.

What about Struan? This had to grate on him—asking his true son to return to take over the duties of the man everyone in the clan thought was his father. Would anyone know the truth? How would he be treated now? Did they even know of the rank and power he held in the clan MacKillop? He may have started out as a steward, overseeing supplies for the castle, but his fighting and strategic abilities soon led him to the higher role of castellan.

Coming back to take over Dougal's duties was a step down for him and he knew that Duncan thought he did it only because of the family ties involved. He was not certain if Duncan had been told the truth about him or not. The only one at Dunbarton Keep who was privy to his side of the sad story was Ada. And she told no tales.

"Come, Dubh, 'tis the dragging it out that makes it worse." He rubbed his stallion's nose and mounted in one jump. The horse snorted steam into the frigid winter air and pawed at the dirt. "They'll no' see Robert Mathieson, castellan of Dunbarton, walking into Dunnedin like a common beggar."

He wrapped his heavy cloak and his pride around him and sat up straight. Taking a deep breath, Robert squeezed the horse's sides, urging him into action. He steeled himself to expect nothing from Struan or the clan. When his time of duty was over, he would return to the MacKillops and be welcomed.

He did not need the MacKendimens.

Some of the faces looked familiar to him as he walked up the steps to the main floor. A few of the warriors, a few of the women. By now, Struan knew of his arrival. What would he say? What would he do? Once he arrived at the doorway to the great hall, Robert stopped and looked around the room. It looked the same. Oh, a few newer tapestries hung on the walls and freshly built tables and benches were set out near the raised dais. A woman's touch was apparent throughout the hall—surely the daughter-by-marriage had had a hand in this. Robert knew of Edana's death now four years past.

His presence caused some whispering through the hall. Robert dropped his sack in the back of the hall and walked forward. He smiled at the curious as he passed them and strode confidently to the dais. The laird awaited him at the steps.

His father.

Struan looked no different from the last time he'd set eyes on him—tall, strong, with thick graying hair, weathered face. Eight years without change. Robert locked gazes with him and could not look away. Struan extended his hand in greeting and Robert grasped it with all his might.

"Robert," Struan's voice seemed to quiver, "welcome back to Dunnedin."

Not "Welcome home." So this was the way of it? Tension twisted his stomach. Robert should have known not to expect more.

"Laird," he said, as he tilted his head in as much of a bow as he was ready to offer. "Ye look weel."

"Aye, lad, I am. But all those around me are failing."

"So it would seem."

"Come, Anice, meet Dougal's son." Struan said it seamlessly, no stutter, no hesitation. The pain tightened like a tourniquet around his heart. *Dougal's son.*

He turned to watch the girl approach. Well, she was really a woman but her face looked so young. Vibrant red hair fell loosely around her shoulders, framing her pale face. Huge, fearful green eyes peered at him when she finally raised her face. She looked too young for the swollen belly she carried. Too young for the sadness that emanated from her. Too young for the fear she wore in her eyes. A wave of sympathy passed through him—mayhap the pregnancy was wearing on her?

She reached him and Struan and stopped, just out of their reach. When he took a step closer to take her hand, she backed up a step. Another step, and she matched it in a bizarre backward dance. Finally, he nodded and smiled at the poor thing and waited for Struan to complete the introduction.

"Anice, this is Robert Mathieson, Dougal's son." Struan looked at Robert and nodded to Anice. "This is my daughter-by-marriage, only daughter of the MacNab, the Lady Anice."

The pain increased in his heart with every mention of *Dougal* and *son* but there was no end in sight.

"Anice haes been here for five years and haes served the clan weel."

Struan smiled at the girl, who had lost even more color with the introduction and who did not look pleased at this turn of events.

"Breeding haes been hard on her and, for her safety and the babe's, she canna carry on as she haes since yer faither was struck down."

Ah, so 'twas the breeding that caused her problems. He smiled sympathetically at her; he had seen many women carrying bairns at Dunbarton and the problems that came with it. Anice turned away but not before he saw the tears forming, filling her eyes. For herself? The babe? This was stranger than he expected.

"She haes prepared a room for ye and will assist ye in yer duties until ye hiv a feel for them yerself."

Robert wanted to laugh. A "feel for them"? He knew a steward's duties like the back of his hand. He had trained and served for three years at Dunbarton, until the laird had recognized his greater abilities.

"Anice, will ye show Robert the room ye chose and then take him to see Dougal?"

The girl nodded at the laird and looked at him. Robert smiled at her, trying to lessen the strain, but it was for naught. "This way." Her voice was barely a whisper, as though she did not have the strength to get out more. He nodded and followed her lead.

"Robert," the laird called out, "join me at table for the evening meal. And ye, too, Anice, be at table." When he would have protested, Struan continued, "I want no argument from either of ye. Be here." Then Struan strode across the room and was gone.

Robert turned back to Anice and gestured for her to go. Following her to the back of the hall, he picked up his bag and then continued behind her to the curving staircase leading up one of the towers. He hurried to her side and offered his arm for the climb, but she waved him off and gathered her skirts. She didn't want him there and refused his help, that much was plain to see. But why? They reached the third floor and she was puffing and blowing. He again held out his hand to her, but she backed away as fast as she could.

"My lady, let me help ye." He offered his arm again.

"Dinna call me that. I am no' yer lady. I am Anice." She backed up to the wall and looked near to fainting. He was tempted to pick her up and carry her, when her body relaxed a bit. After taking a few deep breaths, she spoke. "I beg your pardon, Robert. I would prefer to be called by my Christian name if you don't mind." Her voice was soft, with but a touch of Scottish lilt to it.

"But ye are entitled to be called 'lady.'" He could not think of any woman who wouldn't want to be afforded all the privilege her rank of birth and marriage could give her.

"Just Anice is fine. The clan knows my wishes and follows them. I would appreciate it if you could as well while you are with us."

"As ye wish, my . . . Anice." She stepped away from the wall and went in the direction of the passageway. "If it is too difficult for ye to show me to my room, just tell me which chamber ye readied for me."

"Nay, I am fine now." She rested her hand on her belly and

moved it in a circular path over the mound. "When the babe moves, it is sometimes difficult to breathe. Here"—she pointed to a nearby door—"this is your room." She pushed open the door and let him enter.

The chamber was spacious and, other than the huge bed, devoid of furnishings. A small hearth, an extravagance for Struan, was built into one corner and vented outside by a metal hood built into the wall over it. There were freshly woven rushes on the floor and he could smell herbs in the air. He threw his bag in an empty corner and took his heavy winter cloak off and hung it by the door.

"I will have a chest and table brought in for you. I wasn't sure . . ." She hesitated.

"Sure what?" He probed for an answer.

"Where you would work. There is a small chamber on the main floor near the kitchen. That is where I keep the records and do most of my work. I was not certain if you would rather work here or there."

"It would seem more efficient to work nearer to the supply rooms and kitchen. I will follow your example." She sounded as if she knew what she was doing. Usually the lady of the castle supervised in an advisory way, but Lady . . . Anice seemed to be a practiced steward.

"Is this chamber to your satisfaction?" She wouldn't meet his glance—her eyes darted around the room from her position by the open door. He then noticed she had not even entered the room.

"Aye, Anice, 'tis a fine room. Do ye think ye could find me some clothes to put in that chest? I brought only what's in that bag, I'm afraid, and what's on my back."

"We always have extra clothing available; I will find some for you." She paused and her gaze roamed over his body.

Robert put his hands on his hips and turned once in a circle. When he faced Anice again, he saw the deep red hue spreading up her face. She was blushing! Well, 'twas a far better thing than looking so pale all the time.

"Weel, can ye tell my size now?" he teased her, smiling at her bashful expression.

"Ye are almost the same size as Alex. There are still some things I made for him that should fit you."

"Alex?"

"He is . . . was . . . a distant relative who . . . ah . . . stayed here the summer before last. I'll look in the linen room to see what's there." She rubbed her hands on her tartan skirt and cleared her throat.

"Whatever ye hiv will be fine wi' me. Beggars canna be choosy."

"Do ye wish to see yer faither now?" She took a step back into the hallway.

"Aye. But, ye dinna hiv to take me, just tell me the way."

"He is in the sickroom on the floor below us. Turn into the right-hand corridor and it is the third door on your left."

"Thank ye, my . . . Anice, for all of this." Robert gestured at the warm, clean room.

"It was no problem, Robert. I hope your stay is a good one for you."

"Ah, Anice?" He didn't want her to go. She had changed before his eyes from a scared child to a capable woman. Who else could she be? "Would it be possible to get some food and drink afore the evening meal? I hiv been on the road most of the day wi'oot breaking my fast."

"Oh, Robert," she gasped. "I completely forgot to offer you some refreshments. Please, pardon me while I see to them."

She started to leave so he grabbed her arm to keep her. The tensing of her whole body in reaction to his grasp surprised him into releasing her. She shook off his touch like a dog shaking off water after a swim in the loch. As she stepped away, she pulled her heavy shawl around her shoulders in a protective motion.

"Nay, do no' hurry. I will come to the hall after I see . . . Dougal."

"Very well, Robert. I will have something ready for you at the high table."

"I would rather eat in the kitchen . . . if ye dinna mind?"

"I will have it ready in the kitchen, then." She nodded to him again without meeting his eyes.

Realizing that she didn't mean to move from her spot, he walked past her back towards the tower steps. He slowed his pace on those steps, dreading what was to come now. If he was lucky, Dougal would not wake while he was there.

She walked to the next room and sank onto a small bench, her legs turned to jelly. The babe started his kicking and marauding in her belly, so she put her hand on top of the motion and waited for it to pass. Leaning her head back, she rested it on the cold wall and closed her eyes.

How did she think she would ever be able to work next to this man? At least she knew those in the clan already; she had done most of her growing up here with them. Struan, Calum, Brodie. Even the younger ones didn't bother her so much anymore. But this man!

She saw his form from where she sat by the hearth in the great hall long before she could make out any details. Tall, muscular, flowing wild black hair. The rest of him was finely formed, the arms and legs of a warrior, not a steward. He was built as Alex MacKendimen had been built—strong muscles, long legs, but not as big and bulky as Brodie.

But his eyes! When Struan called her over closer, his eyes drew her attention even before his form. They were like the eyes of a great hunting cat—slanted at the corners, but an icy blue color, when she would have expected green or even yellow. And they sparkled every time he stumbled over her name. *My . . . Anice.* Shivers pulsed through her at the warmth in those eyes and deep voice as her name became almost a possession when he said it.

And his sharp glance missed nothing as it took in everything, everyone in the room. She was certain she saw pity in his eyes as he looked at her.

One day, not long ago, she would have enjoyed meeting someone like this, someone from another place, like she was. Someone to talk with and enjoy. But her husband had ruined that for her in one short night and the days and weeks that followed. Now, even the thought of being near the newcomer made her heart race—and out of fear, not excitement. Her duties, such as they were, revolved around this man. Mayhap once she started helping him in his duties, she would lose some of the fear.

The babe quieted in her belly and she pushed off the wall and back onto her feet. She would meet him in the kitchen after he visited with his father. Poor man, returning under such sad circumstances. Walking to the hall, she made her way slowly down the steps to the main floor. She would see to his comfort as her last official duty before Struan made his announcement at supper.

What would happen to her without her work to keep her going? Days and days of endless worrying? Worrying about the babe? About whether and when Sandy would decide to come home again? She could not spend the remaining weeks of her pregnancy that way. She must find something to do, to keep her mind from being overrun with fear. Something.

chapter 5

The seer was on her way back to her cottage when the call came. It chilled her even more than the biting winter winds that swirled around her. She quickened her step; the pull on her strengthened and tugged her homeward.

Entering her home, she went without delay to the hearth and knelt in front of it. The flames grew and became tongues of many colors. She closed her eyes and cleared her mind of distractions, waiting for the wisdom that the Fates had called her to receive. She opened her eyes and gazed at the wild flames.

Scenes appeared before her—two women screaming in childbirth, one dark, one fiery. A man screaming in death—his life's blood pouring from many wounds. Another sinking peacefully into death's grip. Fear. Terror. Pain ripped through her body, in her belly, between her legs, blood everywhere. An old woman in her stead. A babe, twa, no, four babes? A bairn's peaceful sigh, sucking at his mother's breast. Quiet.

Finally, the vision faded in her mind. The pain and fear disappeared and understanding took root. She sat back and pondered what she had seen and her role in it.

She had plans to make before the things she'd seen were

upon her. The Fates were calling her once again into the fray of the clan and she had no choice but to obey. She offered up a prayer that all would end well, but she knew that some would live and some die.

'Twas always the way of it.

chapter 6

The door was open. He could see no one inside the room except for the figure on the bed. Robert stepped in and drew a breath at the sight of the ailing man. He walked the few paces to the bed and stared at the man who had once been his father.

Dougal's withering body lay unmoving on the small bed. Well, he did not move other than the shallow, barely noticeable breaths that raised and lowered his emaciated chest. Robert could not believe that this was the same person who had cared for him. Dougal's face already had death's mark on it—the bones of his skull showing clearly, skin shrunken and drying.

He thought that eight years had prepared him for this but when he tried to speak, he found his words stuck in his throat. He mouthed the word but could not say it. Tears filled his eyes at the memory of the good times . . . and the bad, with this man. In the end, it was just a hoarse whisper that no one could have heard.

"Da?"

Dougal gave no sign that he had heard the word, the voice, the plea. Of course, Robert thought, he was too near to death for this to make any difference. He turned and left the room, not certain of how he felt or what he thought about Dougal. He only knew that his heart was not so hardened and unmoved as he'd thought, as he'd sworn, as he'd planned it would be.

If he had looked back and watched closely, Robert would have seen the reaction. Dougal's eye opened, his lips moved, and his throat tried to force words out. But, Robert had not glanced back.

As he scanned the crowded hall, Robert recognized many faces from his wee years in the village and the keep. He nodded to them as his gaze and theirs met. His plan was to visit the village tomorrow to renew acquaintances and view the upkeep of the people.

They waited now for Anice's appearance at table. Struan did not look pleased at this small defiance shown by his son's wife.

And where was his half-brother? Robert remembered Duncan returning to Dunbarton, after attending the wedding here this past autumn, without the usual stories of wedding foolery. It must have been a subdued ceremony, for Duncan had seemed hesitant to talk about it at all. At first, Robert thought it was because Duncan knew the uncomfortable truth about him. But later, it was clear that something had happened and no one talked about it.

When Anice entered from the side door and made her way to the dais, he heard Struan's loud sigh. Anice obviously wished to avoid this meal with him and he wondered why. He pulled back the chair next to his and rose to greet her.

"We were waiting on ye, lass, as I said we would." Struan's voice was gentle but his reprimand was clear.

"I beg your pardon, Laird"—she nodded at Struan and then looked at him—"and Robert. I was detained abovestairs." Her face flushed with the lie she told.

Robert held his laughter as Struan cursed under his breath, something about women and stubbornness. Anice sat and placed a linen napkin on her nearly nonexistent lap. He reached out and filled the wooden platter they would share—a few slices of mutton, a leg and breast of capon. As he reached for more, she spoke to him.

"Robert, please serve yourself."

"Are ye no' eating?" He looked at the bare spot in front of her. Only a goblet of cider sat waiting for her.

"I have eaten already."

Struan slammed down his mug of ale, splashing it onto the embroidered table linen. "Anice, I told ye to join me at table."

"And I am here, Laird. I was hungry earlier than my norm and thought I should eat to appease the babe." Robert watched as her hand moved to her belly in that unconscious touch of breeding women.

Struan's face softened at the mention of the babe. Anice was good, very good, at making Struan dance to her tune. Robert watched with interest as she proceeded to turn the subject and the tone of the conversation. Now was as good a time as any to ask about the father of the babe under discussion.

"Tell me, Anice, when will yer husband return? Will he be here for the birth of the babe?"

He was not prepared for the response to his question. He swore every drop of her blood drained from her face in a brief moment, leaving her complexion a ghastly gray. Her mouth opened, but no words came out. Her back went rigid and her eyes glazed over, seeing nothing. Then she slumped forward, missing the table only because of his quick intervention.

Within seconds, the high table was the scene of quite a commotion—servants clearing a path, Anice's maid barging her way through to be near her lady, the laird of the clan bellowing orders. He sat, holding the wee lass in his arms while they argued around him.

"Firtha," Struan called out, "she's done it yet again. Robert, dinna fear. 'Tis just the breeding that does this to her. It will pass quickly."

"Aye, Struan, I can see she's passed out yet again." The maid shook her head over the sight of the unconscious girl. She began calling out her own orders to those nearby. "Jean, has Moira left for the village? Get some cool water and cloths and . . ."

She broke off her words when Robert finally took action on his own. He stood, gained a better hold on the lass, and carried her from the table. It seemed the logical thing to do. The lass needed to be made comfortable in her bed to recover from this spell. Although Struan tried to blame this "spell" on the breeding, Robert knew the real reason. The mention of her husband and the question of his return sent her spinning into a faint.

Fear.

He had glimpsed sheer terror on her face for but a moment before her entire being froze. An unprotected second that showed him clearly there was more going on here than just a hard breeding.

He walked through the hall, holding her securely in his arms. Even at this stage in her pregnancy, she weighed no more than a child herself. He took the steps without strain and stopped on the third level. He had gone to her room today to thank her for the food he'd found waiting in the kitchens and the clothes he'd found lying on his bed in his room. She was one step ahead of him all day and had not been in the room, but he knew now which one was hers.

As he stepped toward the door, her maid pushed around him and opened it. She guided his steps to the bed and helped him ease Anice onto it. Another young woman followed a few steps behind with fresh water and some cloths. He stepped away from the women and walked to the door.

"Thank ye for aiding my lady, sir. We will take care of her now." The tall woman nodded at him, dismissing him.

"Does this happen often?" he asked, looking straight in the maid's eyes. He waited for a lie.

"Aye, it does more now than before. 'Twas one of the reasons Struan sought ye out at Dunbarton."

"Ye seem to ken much about what happens here."

Servants usually did. Ada could tell him more about the goings-on at Dunbarton than any of the family. And tell him faster and more accurately. Mayhap this woman could tell him more.

"I take care of my lady, sir. Nothing else matters to me but her well-being." Firtha stood straight and tall, making her point and her role here very clear.

"Is that well-being in danger?" Robert persisted.

The two women leaning over the bed startled, just a bit, but enough that he saw it. They exchanged a glance before both looked at him.

"Struan awaits ye in the hall. Ye should join him there . . . now." Firtha was ordering him from the room.

Making enemies in this room would gain him nothing in his time here. Strategic retreat was the best course and he made one. Nodding at the women, he turned to leave.

"If there is anything that she needs, will ye call on me?"

He meant it as he said the words. If the lass needed protecting, he would see to it. Her struggle here had touched another part of the heart he'd thought was long dead. If his half-brother didn't have enough sense to be here with his wife and see her through this, well, Robert felt the bond of kinship for her. He would help if he could.

Firtha nodded and then turned back to care for the woman who was dwarfed by the size of the bed. He followed the path back to the hall and Struan . . . and more of the riddle.

"W*eel, is she resting?" Struan asked as Robert took his* seat again at the table.

"Aye." He nodded as servants placed hot food before him. "Her women are taking care of her now."

Reaching to take a piece of the savory-smelling capon, he looked directly at Struan. "Does this happen often to the lass?"

"More lately than afore. I fear there are problems wi' her breeding." Struan broke off a chunk of bread and dipped it into the pool of juices on his trencher. "That is one of the reasons I called ye back to Dunnedin."

"There are more?" Robert waited to see what the laird was willing to reveal.

"I thought ye would want to see yer father afore he passed on, of course. And, the clan will need a new steward. I thought ye might be the one for it."

Robert had wanted to know and now he did. Struan had no

intention of claiming him, of acknowledging his rightful place in the clan. He was willing to use him for the good of the clan but would not give him a place within it.

Eight years and no contact should have been enough to wash his heart clean of any longing for being accepted. Eight years of making his own way, of finding his own supporters and family of a kind. Eight years.

But, somehow, just word from the clan had rekindled the longing he'd thought was dead. The sight of Dunnedin had continued undoing his resolve to expect nothing. And hearing the familiar voices and noises of the village and the keep awakened the desire to be part of the clan where he'd been born and raised.

For naught.

Struan would play out the game forever, never admitting his mistakes, never paying for them. He shook his head.

Well, if there was one thing he'd never been called, it was stupid. He would not start now. Tamping down the feelings that struggled to rise to the surface, he shook his head again—this time in refusal. He wanted it all or nothing.

"Nay. Ye will no' be the steward of the clan as yer faither was afore ye?"

Struan's face never flinched, his eyes never narrowed. There was nothing in his expression or voice that would have told another of his cold-hearted deception. But Robert knew, and he pressed the point.

"Is that all yer offering me, *Struan?"* He waited and watched closely. The answer given now was just as important as the one denied eight years ago.

"That is all I hiv to offer ye, lad. Will ye stay on as steward?"

Robert kept his expression blank and pulled his emotions under a tighter control. No one would see his longing and his bitter disappointment. He would serve out his last duty to the clan MacKendimen and go back to those who offered him more. Make a life for himself there, since none would exist here.

"Nay, *Laird,* I canna stay here. I hiv a place waiting for me at Dunbarton wi' Duncan."

"And ye would refuse yer own clan?"

"My own clan? I hiv no clan of my own. My *faither* was a distant cousin whose family was taken in by the MacKendimens, but he was never welcomed as a part of it."

"Robert, ye are putting too fine a point on it. This is yer home."

"Nay, this is where I was born. My home now lies wi'in Dunbarton, my future wi' the MacKillops."

"That is yer decision?" Struan asked once more.

"That is the only decision I can make." Robert stood, wiping his hands on a napkin, hungry no more. "I will begin my *duty* on the morrow when Lady Anice feels up to showing me around." He threw the linen square on the table and turned to leave.

"Anice," Struan mumbled.

"Pardon?" Robert waited, hands clenched into fists.

"Anice. She wants to be called 'Anice.'"

Robert turned back to face his father but Struan would not meet his eyes now. "Why?"

"Why what?" Struan was evading the real issues between them.

"Why does she no' want to hiv her title used and why did she pass out at table?"

"She has her own reasons aboot her name and I respect them. The fainting was due to her breeding."

"And yer son? Where is he?" The word almost stuck in his mouth. *Son.*

"Sandy, as *he* now wishes to be called, is back in London wi' the king. As he haes been for over six years." Struan's tone told him not to push further, but he could not help himself.

"Shouldna he be here wi' his wife as she births their bairn?"

"'Tis as the king himself orders. 'Tis no' my place to refuse a request of David the Bruce." There was not a hint of submission in Struan's voice. This was more than a request of the king.

"Secrets, Struan? More secrets?"

Robert saw the flash of anger in Struan's eyes at his accusation, then it was gone.

"Nay, no' secret at all. The king gave leave for Sandy's wedding but recalled him immediately to his side in London.

And remember, Robert, everyone haes secrets, even the MacKillops who ye think so highly of."

"Weel, ye keep all of yer secrets then and be glad of them." Robert turned and walked away, down the steps and through the hall.

Damn Struan, and damn his secrets to hell.

chapter 7

The next day dawned cold and clear, and Robert took ad- vantage of the unusually fair day to visit the village. Childhood friends and happy memories beckoned him, without Anice's guidance, to the still snow-covered cottages outside the keep. He stood, his breath making clouds in the frigid air around him, looking down the narrow pathways between the crofts.

It looked so much smaller to him now than it did all those years ago. His feet moved him without thought to the gated fence in front of one of the houses. Robert swung open the gate and walked up the well-trodden path to the door.

"Och, laddie, 'tis aboot time ye visited yer old friends." The feminine voice had not changed in eight years. The body making that voice certainly had.

"Robena, did ye really think I could forget ye?"

A woman with wild brown hair and an ample bosom pulled him into an embrace. The breasts were new since last he'd seen her, and so were the hips and shapely legs he observed as she pulled him inside the house.

"Ye've grown into a fine-looking mon, Robert Mathieson.

Yer no' the skin-and-bones lad who left here too many years ago. Ye hiv filled oot nicely." Robena's eyes roamed his form and he grew hot under her appreciative gaze.

"And ye were more lad than lass and stuck up a tree when I saw ye last. And look, now ye hiv bubbies and hurdies that any mon would love to touch."

Her hands went to her breasts and hips and then covered her mouth as she laughed. Robena had been his friend many years ago—a gilpie, a lass acting more like a lad. She had kept up with him and his other friends as they fought and swam and explored their world of Dunnedin.

Robena had also been his first woman. They had kissed and touched each other, imitating what they'd seen in her mother's cottage—just to see what was what. Their innocent gropings and feelings had turned to inexperienced passion and exploration. That had ended when Robert discovered the truth and left the clan.

"Can ye stay, Robbie?" She took his hand and pulled him closer to the fire.

"Aye, I can."

At his nod, she helped him remove the cloak around his shoulders and hung it by the door. He watched her thin skirt sway over her hips and around her legs as she walked to the hearth and added more peat to the fire.

"Yer maither?" Robert looked around the room and saw three other doorways leading off to other places.

"She passed on near to five years ago." The smell of apples wafted through the small room as Robena poured cider from a stone jug into two battered cups and heated them with a poker from the fire. Handing him one, she continued, "She caught a fever and there was nothing to be done."

"So, ye took over her place in the clan?"

"Aye. It seemed the right thing to do. 'Tis for certain no' a hardship for me. I ken most of the men and they treat me weel enough." She made no apology for what she did; he could hear that in her voice.

"Ye hiv enough to eat and enough clothes to keep ye warm?" He looked at her bare feet. Robert did not want to think of his friend as deprived; he would help her now that he was steward here.

"Och, Robbie, I dinna wear clothes most of the time. Or hiv ye forgotten what I taught ye those years ago?"

They shared a laugh and Robert lost the last remaining bit of tension about meeting her again. They were still friends. Robena sat down on the stool next to his and took his hand, entwining their fingers.

"Struan provides for the clan in good times and bad. I hiv enough, we all do."

"Tell me aboot Brodie—is he still here?"

"Aye, he's here and married Rachelle MacMunn. Do ye ken her?" Robena took a drink of her cider without releasing him.

"Tall? Thin?" Robert searched his memory for a Rachelle.

"She may no' 'ave lived here when ye left. Her maither, a MacKendimen, brought her back here from the Borderlands when her faither died. 'Tis no matter if ye dinna ken her—ye will meet her soon enough. They married last spring."

"And Brodie?"

"I think he is away on the laird's bidding. I havna seen him around the village in weeks."

"Weeks?" She nodded her reply. A trip at this time of year? In the uncertain weather and traveling conditions of the changeable Highlands? That did not make sense to him.

"What can ye tell me aboot Sandy?" Her fierce shiver at his question said more than her words ever could.

"He came back some months ago to marry Anice and then left right after the wedding." He didn't miss the look of disgust on her face.

"And?" he probed for more.

"And, good riddance to bad rubbish." Robena lifted her hand from his and stood, clearly ending the topic of conversation. "So, Robert, how long do ye stay in Dunnedin?"

"For as long as it takes to find someone else to fill and train as steward. Then I'm back to Dunbarton." Robert stood and walked to the door.

"And what is waiting for ye there? A wife?"

"Nay, I hiv no wife awaiting my return."

A frown drew her sable brown eyebrows together. "Then why do ye return to Dunbarton?"

"My life is there—I am castellan to the MacKillop at that holding. I came h— . . . here only to see to Dougal's last days and to help Struan until someone else can take over."

"Weel, Robert, my door is always open to ye while ye are here."

She stood on tiptoes and braced her hands on his shoulders. He knew what she wanted and he gave it without hesitation. He, too, was curious about the feelings remaining between them. Her lips were warm and she rubbed them against his. He opened his mouth slightly and moved over hers, slanting his head to make the touch easier. When she responded by parting her lips, he slipped his tongue inside and tasted her more deeply, thrusting slowly, then more quickly. She moaned and he brought his hand up to the back of her head and held her closely. The kiss deepened and went on and on and he knew she enjoyed it as he did.

He let the many emotions run over him—kinship, comfort, remembrance, passion, longing. His body started to respond in kind to her movements against him. As much as he'd like to stay and continue this reacquainting, he had much to accomplish this day. There would be time for this later. Lifting his head slowly, he gazed into her eyes. No whore's trickery there—she was moved by their kiss.

"Weel, Robena, I fear I maun go now. I will be back at another time."

"Aye, Robert, ye do that."

He put his cloak on and pulled open the door. Leaning down, he kissed her lightly on the lips in farewell. He had to know; the question burned in him.

"Do ye like doing this?" Robert glanced around the cottage.

"Most times, I do, Robert. 'Tis no' a hard life for me."

"Will ye promise to tell me if ye want to change from it?" The least he could do for a childhood friend was to find her a new place if she need it. No one in Dunbarton would know her and she could start over there, if she wanted.

"I will, Robert. I promise."

She reached up and kissed him again as he backed out the door and pulled it closed. He stood up, straightened his cloak, and walked to the gate. Without looking, he stepped onto the path and into Anice.

Anice stumbled as Robert's body knocked into hers. The icy ruts beneath her feet, coupled with her ungainly size and shape, made it difficult to remain upright. He reached out to grab her, to steady her. The men of the clan knew not to touch her, even in passing, but Robert did not know yet of her abhorrence to being handled.

Her body tensed in response to his handhold on her forearms. Without thinking about how tenuous her position was, she shook off his grasp. Her sharp and sudden movement away from him caused her feet to slip out from under her and she fell to the ground. Only his quick action kept her from landing hard on the frozen ground.

"Weel, my . . . Anice, 'twould seem that I save ye again from injury." His eyes twinkled as he pulled her up from her seat upon the frozen ground.

"Aye, Robert, it does seem that I owe you my thanks for last eve and for this."

Anice pulled her hood back onto her head and straightened her cloak. Her heart thundered in her chest and her breaths were labored. She stood still, trying to calm her body's reactions to both the fall and the touch.

"Are ye weel today?" Robert took a step back from her and passed his glance over her from head to toe. Warmth spread through all the places his eyes touched. "Ye still look pale."

"Aye, I feel much better today. Firtha told me that you rescued me from my faint at supper. 'Tis sorry I am that you had to see that."

Anice looked at the ground, searching for a safe place to step. She needed to get to Moira's cottage, needed to get someplace safe to think about what she had witnessed. She had seen the kiss exchanged by Robert and one of the village whores. It should not have bothered her. She knew quite well that men sought out the comforts and pleasures of the flesh regularly.

Pleasures? Mayhap that was not the correct word to apply to it, in her opinion. Robert's seeking a whore shouldn't matter.

But it did.

It left her unsettled inside. He didn't seem the kind of man to run off to a whore as soon as he'd arrived. Well, she'd been wrong before about men, so . . .

"Struan told me it happens more and more?" Robert offered his arm. She ignored it and took a careful step towards Moira's.

"'Tis the babe, Moira says. She and Struan are two old hens, clucking about me."

"They worry about ye, Anice. Aboot the babe and ye as well."

The babe. 'Twould the babe always come before her? She knew the answer before the question even finished forming in her mind. Aye, the babe, quite possibly the heir of the clan. Never for herself, only for what she could give to the clan.

Shaking her head, she roused herself from her reverie. 'Twas her place. There were expectations on women in her position—marriages to join clans, money and land to support them, and children to inherit them. No one could ever say that Anice MacNab, now heavy with a babe who could be the MacKendimen heir, did not do her duty to the clan. Once, though, it would be nice to feel safe and secure and wanted for who she was, not what she could give. But, who was she?

Anice rubbed her belly as she walked carefully down the narrow path. The sun peeked in and out of the clouds, never warming the frigid air. Robert matched her steps, obviously shortening his longer strides next to her waddling ones. It must be the babe making her so maudlin and weepy lately. And the fainting. Struan ordered her to see Moira often, so she was on her way there now. Was he also going to Moira's?

"I mustn't keep you from your duties, Robert. You do not have to accompany me. I am quite well now." She drew to a stop at the crossing of the paths in the village. The path away from the village center led to Moira's. Now that he was done with Robena, she knew not where he was headed.

"I would like to see Moira also, Anice, if you'll but lead the way."

"You want to see Moira? Oh, to ask about your father, I'm sure. Or do you also know her from your growing up here?"

"Also?" Robert looked at her, questioning her with his gaze. He blinked and shook his head. "Ah, so you saw me at Robena's. 'Tis true, I knew both Moira and Robena afore I left the village those years ago."

She felt silly; heat flooded her cheeks at her unseemly curiosity. It should not matter who he knew before and who he did not. Who he visited, who he . . .

But it did.

"I was not sure," she stammered out. "You left a few years before I came, so I know not who is familiar to you and who is not. Not," she added, "that it is my business to pry."

"Ye are no' prying, Anice. Curiosity is a normal thing. Actually, from what I heard in the hall last night, there are a few new families who I dinna ken." He paused and held out his arm again. "Come, let me help ye in yer walk to Moira's and ye can tell me who is new to the village."

He was not going to allow her to refuse. The moment dragged on—his arm extended in the space between them. She waited for him to lower it, but he did not. She waited for him to simply start walking, but he did not. She waited for him to say something, but no words came. She saw no way out of this without an explanation . . . which she would not give.

Finally, she took a deep breath and placed her hand as lightly as was possible on his forearm. The long sleeve of his tunic and her leather gloves kept her hand from contact with his skin. It was . . . bearable. He lowered it slightly and waited for her to choose a path. She turned and nodded to the right.

"I understaun that Brodie is wed to a woman from the Borders? Her name is Rachelle?" Robert broke into the silence with his question.

Good. Small talk would ease the racing of her heart and help her to think about anything but the strong arm beneath her hand and the man it belonged to.

"Rachelle's father's family came from the Borders. Her

mother moved there when they married. When Rachelle's father died, she and her mother returned."

"How long hiv they been married?"

His question seemed innocent enough, but her traitorous body shook at the thought of another woman under the physical power of a man. And a huge, strong one at that. No. She forced her fear aside. Brodie was a good man. A good man, she repeated to herself.

"'Twas last year, in the spring. Were you friends with Brodie?" Anice kept her eyes trained on the path before them.

"Aye, we were. A small group of us caused havoc wherever and whenever we went!" His laughter came out loud and deep. She glanced at his face as he continued. "Hellions, we were. Brodie, Ramsey, even"—he nodded his head back towards the way they had come—"even Robena."

"Robena? The whore?" Anice bit her tongue as the words slipped out. Robert had just identified the woman as one of his friends and now she'd insulted her. Friends? With a lass? Unconventional, to be sure. Anice stared in puzzlement over Robert's acceptance of a woman within his circle of friends.

"She may be a whore now, but back then she was more lad than lass," Robert explained. "She could keep up wi' us at most everything we did. Running, fishing, hunting, even wrestling." His face brightened as he spoke of the happy memories.

A pang of jealousy at his belonging to the clan rippled through her. Anice remembered the wanting to belong, in her own clan as a wee lass and then in the MacKendimens when she fostered here. But at her mother's side, she was training to go elsewhere and when at Dunnedin, she *was* from elsewhere. A heaviness crept over her heart and she shook her head at the dark feelings.

"I ken yer disbelief, but ye should ask Brodie aboot Robena's head-lock and watch his reaction. 'Twill be a sight to behold, I assure ye."

She allowed him to misunderstand her head-shake.

"Will Rachelle misunderstand my question of him? I would not want her to think wrongly of him." Asking about a whore's wrestling with her husband could give the wrong impression and Rachelle's kind acceptance was something that Anice did not wish to jeopardize.

Robert laughed out loud as the realization of what the question would sound like became apparent to him. His eyes sparkled and deep dimples appeared in his cheeks.

"Yer right to hold back on the asking of it. Rachelle may no' ken about our younger days and misunderstaun the remark."

Anice drew to a halt at the end of the path. Moira's cottage stood before them. Larger than most of the other dwellings, it stood on the edge of the barren and frosted forest. Wide plots of ground, lying fallow for the winter, were arranged to the side and back of the house. Faint wisps of smoke escaped from an opening in the thatched roof and curled when touched by the colder air outside.

"'Tis Moira's cottage," Anice said, nodding her head at the small building.

"'Twas her maither's afore her as well," Robert added. "Weel, shall we visit her for a wee bit?" He looked over at her.

"She is expecting me, but you will be a surprise for her."

"No' much surprises Moira if she has grown to be anything like her maither."

"Struan says her healing and her visions are stronger than her mother's ever were," Anice answered. "You knew her mother as well?"

"Oh, aye. The guidwife Glenna healed many of my injuries wi' her remedies, potions, and dressings."

"Injuries? When you were younger, you mean?"

Anice gazed at him while her mind thought back to his more uncovered form. No evidence of past injury marred his figure, his face, his gait. And what kind of wounds would a young boy suffer? Aye, he was tall and well-muscled now that he was grown. Also obvious was the fact that he worked physically in his position at Dunbarton. But being a steward was different from being a warrior, like Brodie. Warriors were constantly injured, stabbed, beaten. Warriors were strong and powerful . . . and could be dangerous when angered. Sandy had been trained as a warrior once, all those years ago. . . .

"Anice? Yer face has lost all its color. Come, let's make our way to Moira's door and she can see to ye."

She nodded and sagged against him, something she'd sworn not to do. Even the slightest thought of her husband sapped her strength and sent daggers of fear through her. Moira knew her fears. Moira would help.

chapter 8

The door opened as he half-carried Anice the last few steps down the path. He could feel her strength draining with each moment. Moira would know what to do for her since he was convinced it was due to the pregnancy.

"Anice? Are ye ill, lass?" Moira moved back into the cottage and allowed them entrance. Robert walked Anice over to the fire and sat her in the chair that was already there. Moira had been expecting her.

"She began to faint as we approached yer door, Moira. Can ye help her?"

His stomach knotted with unexplainable tension as he waited for Moira's assessment. Was this really just part of the pregnancy or was it something more? As he watched Moira loosen Anice's cloak, he tried to pinpoint when the change had happened. Ah, yes. It happened when the talk turned to injuries. But why should that upset her? Mayhap, she'd been injured as a child and treated by a healer? Or mayhap her husband had been injured?

There it was again. Could it have been thoughts of her husband? The fainting at dinner was definitely linked to Sandy.

Was this day's also? But it made no sense at all to him. 'Twas surely a riddle waiting to be solved.

"Thank ye, Robert, for bringing Anice here." He looked up to see Moira gaze on him.

He nodded in acknowledgment. "'Twas no problem since I was on my way here as weel." He took off his cloak and hung it on a wooden peg by the door.

She had called him by name, she must remember him.

"Aye, Robert, I ken who ye are. Ye hae truly grown to be the son of yer faither." The woman's eyes seem to glow as she spoke. He shook his head at that crazy thought. Could she know the truth?

"He must favor his mother then, Moira, for truly I see none of Dougal in him at all."

He was so intent on Moira's words and gaze that he'd forgotten about the witness to their exchange. Anice sat up straighter now, looking back and forth, from him to Moira.

"I've been told that my eyes are her eyes. No' the color, but the shape of them." Their color, he knew, was a trait passed among many in the clan and even called MacKendimen blue. Their dyers and weavers were even able to duplicate it into one of the patterns they wove into the thick woolen tartans.

"I wouldn't know, she passed away long before I arrived here. And, Moira, you are too young to have known his mother."

"Aye, Anice, ye hae the right of it. None of us kenned his maither, but we all ken his faither." Robert's eyes narrowed as he watched Moira's guileless expression. Were her words a deliberate attempt to expose his true parentage? If her visions *were* stronger than her mother's, she knew the truth already. Mayhap this was her way of letting him know that she shared his secret?

"Let me see to the lass as we talk, Robert." Moira left Anice's side and went to the long table at the other side of the room.

Robert glanced around at the dark interior of the cottage. A drying rack hung low over the table; herbs and plants of different colors and sizes were tied to it in bunches. Jars, jugs, and containers of all sizes filled shelves on the wall next to the table. Moira stood before her supplies, choosing several from the lowest shelf. Pouring, measuring, and stirring, he watched as the healer brewed a potion for Anice.

Moira approached the fire and, wrapping her hand in the edge of her plaid skirt, she drew a large pot from over the flame. Ladling a small amount of heated water into the cup she held, Moira stirred the ingredients and held the brew out to Anice.

"Sip this slowly, but drink it all down, Anice."

"You are using that voice again, Moira."

"Aye, but will it work on ye now that ye ken it?"

"Aye, it will. For now."

Robert watched the exchange between the two women. He knew what Anice meant by "the voice." He remembered Moira as a lass of ten and two years using the voice to give orders to men many times older than herself.

"Robert, will ye help me by removing her boots?" Moira pointed at Anice's feet as she walked back to the worktable, carrying the pot of water with her. He knelt in front of Anice, pausing as he saw her stiffen at his approach.

"May I, my . . . Anice?" He would never get accustomed to calling her by her given name. Too many years of too many "my lady's" went before her strange request not to call her by it.

Robert looked at her face and waited for a response. An instant of fear flashed through the widened green eyes and was gone quickly, making him doubt that he had truly seen it. Then, realization struck him.

She feared being touched

His thoughts went back to each of their meetings. Each time he observed her, she held herself separate and apart, never allowing others close. She would not allow him to help her climb the stairs and when he took her arm in his room to stop her from leaving, she tightened. She stiffened when he tried to assist her in walking the path here.

Was it just his touch, as a stranger, as a man beneath her station, that caused the fear in her eyes? No. She withdrew from everyone but her maid and Moira, even maintaining a distance from Struan. Another clue to the riddle of the Lady Anice MacNab, unbeknownst to her, his sister-by-marriage.

"Go ahead, Robert," Anice said in a quiet voice. He lifted

one foot and leaned it on his thigh, unlacing the straps that held the boot in place. After loosening it, he pulled it from her foot and placed it near the hearth to dry. Robert did the same with the other.

"Here now, Robert." Moira held out a mug to him. "Drink this, it will warm ye."

He stood, took the mug, and stepped away to give Moira room near Anice. Walking around the room slowly, he observed the two from a distance. Moira drew off one stocking and exposed a swollen foot, ankle, and lower leg to his view.

Puir lass, as Ada would say. She was not handling the carrying of the babe well at all. Moira scooped a small amount of ointment from a jar next to her and applied it to Anice's foot and leg, rubbing it in slowly. He watched as Anice's head dropped back against the chair and her eyes closed. The tension in her body lessened with each stroke of Moira's knowing hands.

In a voice too soft for him to hear, Moira plied Anice with questions and listened to the responses. She smiled at several things Anice said as she continued her massage. Finally, the room grew very quiet and Moira wiped her hands on her apron and lifted Anice's legs gently off her lap. Moira stepped away from her seat and propped Anice's feet up on the cushion. Signaling him with a finger to her lips, Moira approached Robert, and he waited for her to come near.

"Does this happen much?" he whispered as he gestured towards the sleeping woman.

"Nay. 'Tis only recently that I could get her to come here."

"Why?" Robert asked. It made no sense for Anice to avoid the person who could offer her the most comfort for her physical ailments.

Moira took her time in answering, moving to the other side of her table and cleaning up some of the recently used ingredients first.

"She stays close to the keep."

"Ah, her duties keep her there." Robert could understand how busy Anice would be in her duties as steward since Dougal's illness.

"Nay, her fear keeps her there."

"Fear? Fear of what? Or should I ask of whom?" Robert

waited to hear who would dare threaten the Lady Anice in a way that kept her a prisoner in the keep.

"Robert, I can say no more. 'Tis Anice's story to tell if she wishes ye to ken." Those were almost exactly Struan's words, too. He would not pry any further now, but somehow he would find out the truth of this.

"Can ye tell me of Dougal's condition?" His irritation forced sarcasm into his tone as he asked.

"Of course I can speak of Dougal." Moira gave him a patronizing smile that matched her tone of voice. "He is a mon standing at death's door and waiting for it to open. He doesna hae much time left on this earth."

"Does he suffer as he is?" Robert remembered the sunken face and body of the man on the bed.

"Nay. I give him a broth that eases pain. He does try to speak occasionally, but spends most of his time drifting between consciousness and sleep."

He thought of other questions, but the tightness in his throat trapped any more words. Robert nodded at the healer.

She placed her hand over his. "Make yer peace wi' him now, Robert. Dinna waste time and hold back things which maun be said between ye."

"But, Moira, he is atween sleep and unconsciousness. How will he hear my words?" His voice was barely a whisper even now.

"He will hear wi' his heart, Robert, no' his ears. Fear no', yer words will be heard."

He nodded again and she moved away, busying herself with chores. Moira was right—'twas time to speak to Dougal of things that had passed between them. Even if Dougal couldn't hear them, the speaking of the words might lift his own burden.

Robert blinked several times to clear his hazy eyes and looked at Anice's still and sleeping form. It was then he noticed that the furrow between her eyebrows had eased. Her face looked even younger without the mark of worry upon it. Somehow, it didn't seem fair to him that a lass of but ten years and seven should wear such a serious frown. Her responsibilities wore heavy on her slight shoulders.

Well, his presence would lift some of the weight she carried and give her the time and strength to deal with the difficulties of her carrying. He would make his peace with Dougal and uphold his bargain with Struan until she birthed the bairn. Then, commitments fulfilled and a new steward in place, he would return and take his place of respect in Dunbarton with the MacKillops.

Anice stirred, her eyes blinked open, and she looked in confusion at her surroundings and at him. Based on what he now believed about her, Robert fought the urge to go to her, allowing her time to clear her thoughts.

"Och, ye are awake already, lass?"

"Would seem so, Moira. 'Twas not long enough for you and Robert to catch up on your gossip?"

Robert smiled at Anice. "Oh, aye. 'Twas time enough to reacquaint ourselves. Are ye ready to go back?"

He watched as she shifted in the chair and slid her feet to the floor. Before her bare feet could touch the packed-dirt floor and without thinking of his newfound understanding, he sat in front of her and lifted them back up. Anice gazed at him—wide-eyed and mouth-opened.

"All of Moira's hard work will be for naught," he started to say. Then he felt the shiver move through her body and into his hands.

He glanced at Moira for guidance but she looked away, leaving the problem, literally, in his hands. Anice began to pull her feet from his grasp. Robert tightened his grip, not allowing her to move.

"Here now, Anice. If you twist like that ye will end up on yer arse on the floor. Stop it now."

He immediately regretted his raised voice but he feared she would turn topsy-turvy on the not-so-sturdy-looking chair. Without letting go of her feet, he repositioned them on the other bench and stepped back. Then he released his grasp.

"Moira, I think ye should help Anice wi' her stockings and boots." A smart man knew when to remove himself from a bad situation.

Moira approached and he moved towards the door to retrieve his cloak. Within a few moments, Moira replaced Anice's stockings and slid the boots on, lacing and tying them snugly against the cold and moisture. He could not understand the feeling of regret he felt at her refusal of his touch. Robert knew for certain that it was not his touch alone that bothered her but the knowing of it did not ease the strange ache that settled in his chest.

Anice stood and straightened her skirts and replaced her heavy cloak on her shoulders. Moira whispered to her the entire time, sometimes more insistently than others. Robert waited for Anice to draw nigh before opening the door. He held out his arm to support her steps and waited for her to place her arm on his. After another brief but still noticeable hesitation, she did.

They had taken but a few steps down the path from the cottage when Moira called him back. He hastened to her, leaving Anice at the gate.

"Robert, I hiv need of a favor from ye." She pitched her voice low but continued to smile at Anice as she spoke.

"Anything I can do for ye, I will, Moira. Ye hae but to ask." Part of being steward was solving problems, big and small. That was one of many talents he'd developed in his years at Dunbarton.

"Once there is a break, a true break in the weather, summon yer companion from Dunbarton."

Images of flowing blond curls and enticing feminine curves flashed before his eyes. He could feel the heat enter his cheeks and other parts of his body as memories of his times with Helena entered his thoughts.

"Companion, Moira? Of whom do ye speak?"

"No' the one who warmed yer bed, mon, the one who has the healing touch."

"Ada? Summon Ada here?" How did she know of both Helena and Ada?

"Aye, the old one. Her skills will be of need to ye in the spring. Bring her as soon as ye can."

"Moira, why?" Her request was strange since her skills far surpassed anything Ada could do. And certainly no one in Dunnedin would request another healer when Moira was among them.

"I canna say for now. Just do it, Robert." Moira motioned him back to Anice. "Tell the lass I want to see her back in twa days." She waved two fingers at Anice. "Twa, no more."

Anice was still shaking her head at Moira when he reached her at the gate. Their walk back to the keep was brisk and quiet. Once inside the stone building, Anice was met by her maid and escorted up the stairs, leaving Robert to watch her escape. He was no closer to understanding Anice now than when he rode in through the gates. He shook his head and realized that the same was true about most men and most women.

chapter 9

"Come in, Anice."

Robert stood and motioned her into the small room. It seemed much more filled with him in it. In spite of his presence in the keep and around the village over the last weeks, she was not comfortable having him this close to her. Pounding within her chest, her heart beat a bit faster and harder with every moment this close to him. As if he sensed her unease, he moved back away from the table and turned the chair for her, motioning to her to sit on it. And, if she'd learned nothing in his first weeks here, she had learned how stubborn he could be. She sat in the proffered seat.

This room had been her safe haven. She'd retreated here many days when the fear and depression almost overwhelmed her. There was safety in closing and locking the door, and losing herself in the columns of words and numbers, in the books that recorded the clan's history and day-to-day supplies and plans. By forcing her mind to focus on the numbers and letters she wrote, she also regained control over her thoughts and over her life.

Now, this intruder took control. Nay, not intruder. *Visitor.* She glanced over at him as he pulled a small bench from under the table and sat next to her, moving closer so that he could look over her shoulder. Wiping her damp palms on her skirt, she smoothed it over the growing swell of her belly and took a deep breath.

"Have you found something wrong, Robert? Your message sounded urgent."

"Nay, Anice. As I told ye the first time we reviewed these accounts, the books are as they should be. I asked ye here to beg a favor of ye."

This was not what she'd expected to hear from him. Questions about her methods of record-keeping, certainly, but begging a boon from her, nay, not that.

"What do you need from me?"

"Weel, I hiv looked over yer work in keeping the clan and keep's records and I am impressed with yer thoroughness." She felt the heat rise in her cheeks, that old pride and satisfaction at a task well done forced her to sit up straighter. "Ye," he continued, "are much better at keeping the books than I am. And . . ."

"And?" She turned to face him. She dared not hope that he was leaving already. Then, a momentary flash of disappointment left her puzzled at her true feelings in the matter of his presence or absence.

"I would be beholden to ye if ye would continue to keep these records." He pushed the pile of books closer to her. "'Twould take but a short amount of time each day and I will do all the work involved. . . ."

"Just the books?" This request pleased her deeply. It would give her something to fill her time, something to focus her thoughts on, something to ease her worries.

"Aye, just the books. Struan haes asked that I oversee some chores aboot the grounds and in the village and I can do that if ye'll see to them." Robert placed his hand on the closed account books on the table and stared at her. His eyes were so unique, so unlike anything she'd seen before. He was waiting for her decision, one she'd made the moment his request was clear.

"Of course, Robert. I can handle keeping the records for you."

"Good," he said, patting the cover of the record books and

standing up next to her. "Ye are much better than I at doing this and 'twill give me a chance to get outside a bit more."

His impending departure from the room startled her. "Do you mean for me to begin now? This day?" She could see that he chafed at the bit, like a horse recently broken to it. Being cooped up in the castle was obviously not to his taste or style.

"Aye. Would ye begin this day? If ye hiv no other pressing business?" He was backing his way out the door already. His actions surprised her and Anice felt the urge to laugh at his boylike anticipation of escaping chores.

"Aye, Robert. Go, be about your other business. I am willing to do this for you." She stood and waved him out the door.

"I thank ye, Anice." Robert took several steps towards her and, without warning, placed his hands on her shoulders, lifted her to her feet, and kissed her forehead. And, just as quickly, he turned and left the room.

The shock struck her within moments, as if the movement of the air caused by his exit had been a fist instead of a slight breeze. A deep gasp tore from her lungs and she waited, waited for the terror and panic to follow.

But, it did not. Surprise. Complete confusion. But nothing like the anguish she usually felt at the touch of another. Especially a man's touch. Dropping into the chair behind her, Anice pulled a few deep breaths into her lungs. It took more than a few minutes for her racing heart to calm.

Looking around the room, Anice spied the pile of notes that Robert had left on the desk next to the record books. Numbers and letters in nice orderly rows and columns would help her focus. She pushed the loose hairs that curled around her face away, tucked them behind her ears, and bent over the tabletop. In a short time and with a bit of concentration, she was lost in the duties she'd carried for months before Robert's arrival. She could not tell how much time had passed when she heard Firtha's voice from without.

"Anice? Are ye here, lass?"

"Come in, Firtha," she answered. "I am nearly finished my work."

Firtha entered and, with the raise of one eyebrow, questioned her without words.

"Robert requested my help, Firtha. He has other duties that

Struan has assigned and he asked me to keep the records for him." She knew from the softening in her maid's eyes that Firtha could hear the happiness in her voice.

"And ye hiv agreed? But of course ye hiv." Firtha reached over and took Anice's hand, patting it lightly. "Ye hiv wandered around this drafty place for weeks since he came, with too much time and too little to do except worry."

"Have I truly been that terrible to bear?" Anice smiled at the concerned look on Firtha's face.

"Oh, aye. Ye snarl and moan at one and all. Why, even Struan's most feared warriors give a wide berth around ye these days . . . and it haes little to do with the size of yer belly."

Anice smiled, even though she could hear a thin bit of truth below Firtha's comments. She had not given up her responsibilities easily; she'd fought hard and worked even harder to earn them and fulfill them after Dougal's illness. Having Struan simply remove her and place Robert in her stead had stung her, threatening to diminish the small amount of pride she still had in herself.

"I am sorry, Firtha, if I have made your life difficult." Anice offered a small smile, this one coming somewhat easier than her last one. She'd not felt capable of smiling or joy in many days, nay, many weeks.

"So, are ye done yet? Are you ready for some food?"

Anice sat back in her chair and stretched her arms over her head. She'd hunched over too long and her body let her know it. Even the babe in her womb responded by rolling around inside as she leaned back away from the table's edge.

"I think I would truly like a walk right now. The day looked promising this morn. Is it still?" Since this chamber did not share an outside wall, she could not tell if it was light or dark, clear or stormy outside.

"Oh, aye," Firtha replied. "Come, I'll fetch yer cloak before we go."

Anice closed the record books, straightened her writing supplies, and pushed her chair closer to the table. Following Firtha through the keep, it was just a short time before she left the chill of the hall and stood in the bright rays of the sun.

Wrapping her cloak tighter around her shoulders, she breathed the cold, crisp air deeply into her lungs.

After deciding to stay within the castle's walls, she and Firtha circled the keep in a brisk walk. She felt better, clearer-minded, and more in control than she'd felt in weeks. And she had Robert to thank for it.

He spit out a mouthful of dirt and pushed his hair out of his face. 'Twas his own fault and no one else's. He should have known that Brodie would grow up and be bigger than him, even as he was back when they knew each other. Well, he'd started this, he would finish it. Rising swiftly from his crouch, he leapt up and tackled Brodie. Aiming at his waist, Robert hoped to unbalance his opponent and take him down. His maneuver worked, but he crashed to the ground along with his childhood friend. Brodie must have realized the battle was over for he lay back on the cold, hard soil of the practice yard and let out a loud raucous laugh.

"I enjoyed that, Robbie," Brodie said as he climbed to his feet and extended a hand out to him. "'Tis glad I am to hiv ye back with us."

"Was there no one to give ye sport these eight years?" Robert rubbed the dirt and sweat off his clammy torso with a piece of plaid and accepted a dipperful of water from a lad with a bucket. Stripped down to his trews, he enjoyed the air cooling his body after his bout of wrestling.

"A few hiv tried, my friend, but none hiv done as weel as ye."

They laughed once more together and Robert gathered his clothes from the ground. Walking towards the perimeter of the practice yard, he spied Anice and her maid approaching on the path from the keep. He quickly tugged his shirt over his head as they came to a stop on the other side of the fence.

"My . . . Anice," he stuttered, only now noticing how pale and breathless she was. "Are ye no' weel?" Unthinking, he reached out to touch her cheek and felt a flush of embarrassment as she backed away from him, leaving his hand awkwardly in the air between them. He really would need to remember not to get close to her and he needed to not stumble over her name each time he said it. Anice. Anice was quite a simple, plain name.

"I am well, Robert. Brodie, 'tis good to have you home again." Anice looked at Brodie and smiled. It was not much of one, but more than Robert had yet seen on her.

"'Tis good to be home, Anice." He watched as his childhood friend colored under Anice's attention. "Hiv ye been to see Rachelle while I was gone?"

"I fear not." A silence followed her brief answer as Brodie obviously waited for more and Anice obviously was not giving it. Robert cleared his throat and Brodie finally spoke.

"Weel, then, both ye and Robert will need to stop by as soon as ye can. Robbie, ye maun meet my wife while yer here."

"I would like that," Robert answered.

"Anice, you should not stay out in the cold much longer." Firtha's comment was clearly an order to return inside.

"Oh, aye, Firtha," she mumbled. "Brodie, I will visit with Rachelle soon. Robert." With a nod at him, she turned and walked with her maid back to the keep. He did not miss the maid's mouthed words of thanks over Anice's head.

"What was that aboot?" Brodie wrapped his plaid over his shoulders.

"I asked Anice to keep the books for me."

"Did ye now? I am certain that pleased her. Why did ye do that?"

"Struan has asked me to oversee some tasks in the village and so I asked her to take care of the records for me."

"And your real reason, since I ken that yer duties in Dunbarton included much more than books and buildings?" Brodie had discerned some of his reasons already.

Robert leaned up against the fence that surrounded the practice yard and adjusted his own plaid. His own investigation of Anice had led him to believe that she needed something to occupy her time. That she sank deeper and deeper into worry and unhappiness as the babe's birth approached. And for a reason he could not yet name, he had wanted to help her, to give her something to do, to lift her spirits. He'd had no idea that the simple assigning of a task would have been the thing that made her smile.

"Anice needs to keep busy while she waits for the bairn."

Brodie simply grunted in response.

"Why isn't he here?"

"Who?"

"Ye ken—Alesander. Or should I call him 'Sandy' as Struan said he wishes to be called?" Robert couldn't keep the sneer out of his voice.

"Believe me, we need him not now that he haes done his duty to the clan." Disgust and disdain filled Brodie's voice, too. Mayhap he would tell Robert more.

"His duty? Oh, ye mean marrying the MacNab's daughter and getting an heir on her? Aye, he's done that, but what aboot being here while she bears that heir? Or training with his own clan instead of traipsing around London with the king?" Robert cleared his throat once more but this time spit on the ground. Even just talking about his half-brother made his mouth bitter.

"If ye hiv no[2] found out yet, Robert, the clan is just fine wi' him being in London wi' the king." Brodie stood away from the fence and faced him squarely. "'Tis a fine thing ye did for Anice, asking for her help."

Robert laughed. "'Tis selfish, plain and simple, my friend. I hate to keep the books and long to be outside."

Brodie nodded in farewell. "I maun see to Rachelle now. I hiv been away too long already. Come for dinner one night soon?"

"I look forward to it, Brodie. And to meeting yer lovely wife."

Brodie trotted off towards the gate and village and Robert watched with a sense of envy. Brodie was going *home,* to a place and a person who waited for him. A pang of wanting, so deep and strong that he could not breathe, shot through him. He leaned back once more, relying on the fence's strength to keep him on his feet. Just once, for just one moment, he wanted to feel the comfort of a home. Catching a glimpse of the very pregnant Anice entering the keep, Robert spit once more on the ground. So long as Sandy lived and was heir here, there was no place for him.

• • •

*She concentrated on taking one step at a time. She concen*trated on the amount of air that passed into her chest. She even concentrated on Firtha's inane chatter as they walked towards the keep. But none of that could calm her now.

He was a warrior.

Although not as large as Brodie, he was as muscular and as strongly built as any of the MacKendimens she'd ever seen. Watching in horrified fascination as he and Brodie wrestled, she was stunned into near panic by his strength and his ability to overpower someone much bigger and stronger than himself with his deft moves. Once again she was reminded of Alex, the distant relative of the clan who had visited last summer and who had been mistaken for Sandy due to his close resemblance. Alex had fought with Brodie as well, but at the time she was pleased by his prowess and manly form. The anticipation of being held by him had been welcome . . . then.

One thing was clear—he was not a steward. Those muscles did not come from lifting barrels and chests of spices and foodstuffs. That strength came from working with other warriors, testing and being tested in contests of might and endurance. Years of such training to reach the level of skill he had obviously reached.

As she placed one foot in front of the other and nodded in spite of not hearing her maid's words, she knew that he was much more than a steward, a caretaker of the clan's goods and grounds. Did Struan know the extent of his abilities and skills? Struan was ever-vigilant about anything affecting the clan so she doubted that he did not already know of Robert's other talents. Mayhap that was why he had asked him to take care of other tasks outside the keep.

Forcing a breath deeper inside of her, she tried to wipe from her mind the image of Robert, naked to the waist, deep in contemplation about his next move against Brodie. His face wore such a fierce and dangerous expression that she doubted she would ever forget it. And she must not.

She must not ever forget that within any man was a core of unpredictability, when anger or lust or even fear could redirect his strength against an opponent, an enemy, a wife. She must not ever forget the hardest lesson she'd learned in her life.

Never trust a man.

The next month passed by quickly for him and for the clan. Taking advantage of some unseasonably clear weather, repairs were made and even some new buildings begun. The people of Dunnedin knew that more storms would reach their village before the spring finally claimed victory over the harsh winter.

Dougal sank closer and closer to death; even Moira was surprised that he clung to life as long as he did. Robert visited daily, most of the time sitting quietly or reading next to the man who raised him. Memories of the years before Dougal discovered the truth of his parentage filled his mind during these quiet times. Before the bitterness took control, Dougal had been a doting father to him, proud of his every accomplishment and milestone of growth. Now though, few words spoken and few truths revealed. Then one day, as the skies above grew darker and heavier with a coming storm, Dougal gave up his thin hold on this life and moved through death. Even after months of preparing for Dougal's passing, Robert was not certain what he felt for the man who died and the man who he buried among the others in the MacKendimen graveyard.

Anice waddled and grew even bigger as her time approached. The dark circles under her eyes also grew and made her look even more haunted, more vulnerable. To what or whom, he could only guess, since no one in the clan ever spoke her husband's name in her presence. He stopped as well, after those first few times, since he had drawn his own conclusions about the state of their marriage and the imminent birth.

As Moira had directed him to, he summoned Ada from Dunbarton. Robert still did not understand the need for her to be in Dunnedin, but no one argued with Moira when she turned that look and that voice on them. His old friend found a place among the old ones of the clan and was accepted quickly.

But the air was filled with a spark of anticipation, as if a scent of danger were in the wind and everyone smelled it. A certain wariness filled the people of Dunnedin and the clan waited for the reassurance of the spring, and the birth of the clan's heir. And true to form, in what seemed to be an attempt by nature to keep the coming events at bay, a series of violent early spring snowstorms rolled through the mountains and covered the village and keep.

chapter 10

The *icy blast of air that forced its way through the small* opening she'd created took her breath away. 'Twas difficult to believe that spring approached at all when the weather took this turn. Leaning against the door with all the weight she now carried, Anice closed and secured the latch to keep it from blowing open.

"Here now, Anice. Come away from there before ye freeze."

Startled by Moira's voice, she turned quickly to face her. Moira sat some distance away, in front of a blazing fire. And with her was the old woman Robert had brought from Dunbarton. Ada, that was her name. Nodding at Moira, Anice walked to where they sat. A chair and stool awaited her there.

"Och, now, lass. Here, ye should be sitting afore the warmth wi' yer feet raised. We hiv a place ready for ye." The old one spoke and her soft tone of voice washed over Anice like a warm and welcome embrace. She'd spoken to her but a few times and the experience was always the same.

"Thank you, Ada." She smiled as she sank onto the wide-armed chair with its cushions. "This spring storm is colder and wilder than I ever remember seeing in Dunnedin these last few years." Anice settled into the most comfortable position she could find and allowed the two women, the two healers, to raise her feet onto the bench in front of her.

Moira sat back and picked up some mending from the basket at her feet. Anice reached out to Moira and took what she offered. Sewing and mending was something she could do and her size did not interfere. Actually, her large belly even made a convenient shelf for her to rest her arms on. After a few minutes of stitching, Anice noticed the two other women exchanging glances.

"I was aboot to seek ye out, Anice," Moira started. "I hiv some news and wanted to share it wi' ye myself."

Trying to maintain her calm, Anice waited for this news. It could not be good, for there was an air of nervousness about both Moira and Ada.

"First, I am expecting a babe of my own, sometime near Michaelmas Day."

"Truly, Moira? You do not even show yet!" Anice glanced at the woman's small stature and then took Moira's hand in hers and patted it. "You feel well?"

"Now who is clucking like a hen?" Moira laughed. "I am weel and Pol is strutting around as though he accomplished a feat unknown to mon!" The women laughed together for a few moments.

"There is more news?" Anice knew, she could feel that there was more to be told.

"I hiv told ye aboot my sister, Margaret."

"She married a Montgomery from the Borders?" Anice asked, while nodding her remembrance. Margaret was a year older than Moira and left Dunnedin shortly after Anice's arrival there.

"Weel, she is carrying once more and is verra near her own time. The pregnancy haes been a difficult one for her and wi' her losing two bairns afore this, we fear for her and the babe she carries now."

"Is there anything that can be done?" Anice did not think anything but prayers could help and, being so close to her own delivery, she did not want to think too much on it. But Moira's words were leading to something.

"I couldna be wi' her the last two times and I promised her

I would be there wi' her for this birth. Pol and I leave in the morn for her village on the Borders."

Anice stopped sewing and stared at Moira. The unstoppable terror seeped through her. Tremors crept up her back as though someone had walked on her grave. Anice could not identify what she feared, or put into words her objections; she only knew she could feel the fear taking control of her. Moira was her link to safety and she needed her there.

"But, Moira," she stammered. "The weather is dangerous now."

"Aye, Anice, 'tis no' the best time to be leaving the safety of Dunnedin, but I maun." Moira took her hand and clasped it tightly. *"I maun."*

"Will ye . . . ?" Her voice gave out even trying to ask. Her throat tightened and her breaths turned to gasps.

"Here, now, lass," Ada said. The old woman took Anice's other hand and wrapped it inside her own two. The woman's warmth battled with fear's icy hold. "I ken ye fear what lies afore ye in yer own time. I will be here while Moira travels to her sister's and back again. If ye hiv need of me, I will be here for ye."

The heat in Ada's hands began to travel up her arm and into her body, forcing terror's grip to loosen. Soon, she could breathe again and the clammy sweat on her brow lessened. Ada's words and touch soothed her, calmed her, called to the reason within her. Anice hated this. She hated the powerlessness she felt when the terror within pushed its way out and took control of her body and her life. There was something within the old woman that offered her comfort and gave her strength. Mayhap her presence would indeed get her through in Moira's absence.

Moira released her hand and smiled at her. Anice relaxed as much as she could against the chair, trying to let the rest of the tension flow from her.

"Ada has some healing talents, Anice. And she kens many of my recipes already. 'Tis why I had Robert bring her from Dunbarton."

"But Ada arrived weeks ago, Moira. Why have ye said nothing until now?" Looking at Moira, she knew that the seer had already known what was to come. What else did the woman know?

"I hiv only seen bairns being born, twa boys and twa girls," Moira answered without the question being asked.

"Four babes? But how?"

"Either one of us will give birth to twins or someone has no' shared their news wi' us yet. . . ." Moira's eyes twinkled as she spoke. She knew more than she would reveal; her "wisdom" was never completely shared with others and Anice was certain that Moira held some knowledge closely, even now. Moira stood and nodded to Ada.

"I maun make my way back to my cottage and prepare for the journey ahead. Anice, ye should get acquainted wi' Ada for a bit. I will no' see ye afore I leave in the morn so I give my farewell now."

"God go with you, Moira. I will keep your sister in my prayers," Anice said.

"That's a good lass," Moira told her. "I will be gone but a few weeks and be back in plenty of time for the birth of yer wee one. Dinna fear."

Moira gathered up her basket and sack and walked toward the kitchens. Anice was so puzzled by the expression that had entered Moira's gaze as she promised to be back in time, that she missed Ada's words.

"Pardon me," Anice mumbled. "I did not hear your question."

"Tell me aboot yer own maither. Did she give birth easily? How many did she bear?" Ada asked.

"Um, only one. I am my mother's only child."

Ada began to talk and Anice's gaze found Moira still making her way to the kitchens. Finally, she realized what bothered her about Moira's words, or rather her expression.

Moira lied to her.

Moira knew that she would not be here for the birth and so had brought Ada here from Dunbarton. Moira knew and she lied about it.

That was so unlike Moira. The seer was straightforward in her manner and had never lied to her, at least not as far as she could tell. So why had she done so now? Or had she? Was she seeing more here than truly existed? Mayhap this was exactly as Moira had said—Moira needed to leave and Ada would be there in her stead. And Moira would be back for the baby's birth.

The babe was not due for weeks and weeks, close to two months probably. There was plenty of time for Moira to return to Dunnedin. Taking a breath in as deeply as she could, she tried to let go of the real fear that lay under everything else in her life. 'Twas not bearing the babe that worried her—her mother had had an easy time of it giving birth to her. 'Twas not facing the pain and uncertainty of the birthing, no, 'twas facing the uncertainty of the time after the birth that scared her witless and breathless. For once she gave birth to the heir of the clan—and she knew with unswerving confidence that the babe she carried inside of her *was* the heir the clan hoped for—she would once more be at the beck and call of her husband.

Even though Struan had promised that he would protect her, even though he swore on his position as laird, she knew that little could be done to keep her husband away if he chose to come home and claim his rights once more. Oh, she did not doubt the truthfulness of Struan's intentions, but what father would act against his own son when the clan stood to lose? And that was what caused her nightmares. And what caused this powerful terror to take control of her and destroy the person she was before.

Anice tried to listen to Ada's prattling tales about mothers and bairns, but 'twas difficult to turn her thoughts from those dark times once she dwelled on them. She had attempted to come to some understanding of her actions and to some acceptance of her inner weaknesses, but she'd not been successful in the months since her marriage. At times, it was easiest to believe what Sandy had told her that night—that her shameful behavior towards the man who had impersonated him deserved to be punished. And as her lawful husband and the one most shamed by her actions and open preference of another man, he was the rightful one to deliver the punishment he saw fit.

But, and mayhap due to her inordinate pride, she found that his brutality towards her only spurred her on to question his behavior and not her own. She knew of no other man in this clan or her own who had ever beaten a woman the way her husband had beaten her. Surely she would have known, since little or nothing remained a secret for long within the closeness and intricate pattern of relatives of the clan. She'd witnessed disagreements and even some hands raised against wives by boorish or drunken husbands, but none could approach what hers had done to her.

Had Sandy's feelings of rage diminished towards her in these last months? Did the news that she was pregnant please him at all? Would he come home for her lying-in? Would he stay to claim her again and again as he'd threatened on their wedding night? His words—*until parted by death*—had echoed over and over in her mind. Was her death the only way to avoid him?

She shook her head and shifted in her seat, made even more uncomfortable by her long time in one position and the direction of her thoughts. Ada must have misunderstood her gesture, for the old woman continued to sew and talk at the same pace as before.

She was not the same hopeful, willful girl that she'd been before her wedding. That one believed only in the good men could do, and in her own ability to handle anything that came her way and challenged her. The Anice she was today understood more about the ways and dangers of men and about the amount of courage and strength you needed to face the life that scared you witless and breathless, on your own with no help from anyone else. She knew that in spite of his promises, Struan may not be able to protect her. Moira would not be the protection she needed either. She would need to find her own way in this.

Sighing, she realized that Ada had stopped speaking and was watching her now. Had she given herself away? Had she spoken out loud? The mixed expression of sympathy and concern on the old woman's face convinced her that she must have said something.

"I can see by the look on yer face that my words have stirred yer fears rather than quieting them and sorry I am for doing that," Ada whispered as she took Anice's hand once more.

"No, Ada. 'Tis not your words that stirs fears. I fear I am

tired of being in this chair, tired of being held prisoner by this storm, and just plain tired." Anice handed the material she still grasped to Ada and pushed herself up and out of the once comfortable chair. "Here comes Firtha now to help me up to my chambers."

"Are ye ready to retire yet, Anice?" Firtha asked as she reached them.

"Aye, I think a rest would do me some good right now. Ada, thank you for your kind words. I appreciate knowing that you are here if I need you." Anice smiled at the woman who seemed to glow under her praise.

"Good rest to ye now, my lady."

"Just Anice is fine, Ada. My name is Anice."

The words came out on their own, since she was so used to uttering them in response to someone using her title. If her darkest truth were known, she would be scorned by all; even her babe could be taken from her. She could be abandoned and even put aside by her husband for the grievous sin she'd committed and still not repented. Although she could not bring herself to utter the words in confession, she humbled herself before God and all by taking from herself the honorable position that title and marriage placed on her. She did not deserve to be honored among the clan. She was a sinner. She was just Anice.

"All right then. Have ye a good rest now. Ye and the bairn surely need it."

Anice turned and followed Firtha out of the great hall and up the stairs leading to her chambers. Now she worried that thoughts of Sandy and his return would keep her from sleep. Entering her rooms, she smiled as she caught sight of a steaming mug sitting next to her bed. Moira had promised a "soothing brew to aid yer rest" and this looked like it. After undressing and slipping beneath the covers, Anice lifted the cup to her mouth and sipped it slowly, enjoying the warmth and sweetness as it moved over her tongue and she swallowed.

"Moira said ye will sleep after ye drink that. She said no' to allow ye to walk around unaided." Firtha smiled and took the empty mug when she finished. "'Tis no' good to see a pregnant woman swaying on her feet like a drunkard, she said."

"My thanks to you for looking over me, Firtha. I do not know what I would do without you."

Feeling the sleepiness creeping into her limbs, Anice slid down and pulled the covers up to her neck. So much faced her in the days ahead. And now she had to be strong for not only herself but also the babe who depended on her. The bairn must have sensed her thoughts for he began to shift within her, pushing and stretching and testing his strength. He? Smiling as she drifted towards sleep, she realized she only thought of the babe as a boy. A son. Her son.

A son to live for and to love and to hold precious as none had held her. She would, she could, endure anything for the babe that lived within her now. He had saved her months ago. He had pulled her out of her walk in darkness and given her something wonderful and untainted to love. Something, someone, who was her own and no one else's.

Her son.

chapter 11

He spied the messenger as the man approached the keep. Stepping back into the shadows, he watched as the courier from England, wearing the royal insignia of the House of Plantagenet, dismounted his horse and strode into the building. The others in the entourage simply stayed on their mounts and waited. Robert was tempted to follow him in, but decided instead to bide his time and keep watch.

Within minutes, the courier was back, this time racing down the steps and mounting his horse without a moment's delay. A glance at his men was all it took for them to follow him out of the yard to the gate. The whole thing occurred in such haste that Robert would not have believed it if he had not witnessed it himself. Now he would go inside and see what news this courier brought from England. In the pit of his stomach, he knew it could only be about one thing, one person. His half-brother Sandy must be returning to Dunnedin.

A sense of urgency filled him and he entered the keep, knowing even then that the direct approach would gain him nothing. Turning down one hall, he headed for the room he, or rather Anice once more, used as a workroom. It was off to the side of the hall and from there one could hear anyone on the dais if they were not guarding their words. He softened his steps as he came closer and listened for Struan's voice. The emotion in it was clear, although the low tones belied it.

"I told him no' until the bairn was born and now he does this?"

Struan's face was like stone; Robert did not remember ever seeing him this angry. The laird stood, turned to the clansman next to him and whispered something that Robert could not hear. The man—Iain?—nodded and left without a word. After taking a mouthful of whatever brew filled his cup, Struan looked at the group of elder clansmen seated around the table, one at a time.

"I promised her protection through this time. I canna break my word when given as laird."

"Were ye daft then, Struan, to ever promise such a thing? A mon haes the right . . ." The grizzled old man, on Struan's left, let his words drift off as Struan glared at his challenge.

"I do whate'er I maun to protect the future of the clan MacKendimen. And right now, the future of this clan lies in the belly of that woman." Struan pointed over their heads, in the direction of the chambers above.

"But Sandy is yer son. He is yer heir, the tanist of the MacKendimens. He was chosen by the laws of the clan, by this verra council, and stands as our next laird." Struan's opponent would not lessen his stance at all.

Robert moved closer. Struan stood a bit taller and, if such a thing were possible, his gaze became even more fierce.

"But I am yer laird now and she haes my protection until the bairn is born safely. I will no' allow him to touch her until then."

"And after the birth, Struan? What will ye do then?"

Robert waited with the rest as Struan considered his words. 'Twas obvious that Sandy was some kind of danger to Anice and that Struan had made promises to her. What had Sandy done to engender this kind of fierce protection from Struan?

"They were joined by God in front of this clan and her own. 'Twould be against God and clan to interfere in the business of a mon and his wife."

The group seemed to release their held breath at the same

time. Some crisis had been averted, but Robert was not sure of the nature of it. The men rose and pushed back from the table, the discussion clearly at an end. The distastefulness of it was obvious in the way the men moved quickly to leave the dais and hall.

Struan mumbled something as he waited alone. Robert strained to hear the words.

"Until parted by death," 'twas how it sounded. *Until parted by death?*

The words so startled him that he left his place and took several steps towards Struan before realizing it. The click-clack of his boots on the stone floor surprised both of them and he found himself staring into Struan's icy gaze and unable to think of a word to say.

"What is yer business here, Robert?" Struan stepped to the table and took the seat reserved for the laird.

"I saw the messenger and came to find out the news."

"The messenger and his information do not concern ye. Now, go aboot yer tasks." Struan lifted the cup to his mouth and drank deeply until none remained.

"What concerns the clan MacKendimen concerns me." Robert would not back down from this. For months Struan had treated him like a lackey, an errand boy to be ordered about at the laird's whim. If he was to carry out his duties, he needed to know the happenings of the clan . . . and the reasons behind such occurrences.

"I think no'. Ye are here as a visitor, only until Anice regains her strength and can oversee the new steward. Do no' expect more than ye are due here, boy."

Robert could not see; the furious haze that filled his vision blocked everything in front of him. His heart pounded at such a rate and loudness in his own ears that he wondered how it stayed in his chest. All he wanted, all he craved was one word of welcome, one word of acceptance and he would stay and make his life here. Every day of working in the clan and the need to stay and be part of his family seeped deeper and deeper into him until he recognized it for what it was. Now, that one desire, that one need, was crushed once more by the only man who could fulfill it.

"Expect more than I am due, Struan? We both ken the lie

of those words. We both ken that I should expect and be due much more than yer willing to offer me."

"Robert, no' now. I canna argue this wi' ye now." Struan waved him off and stepped to one end of the table.

"No, no' now? Then when, Struan? We both ken that ye hiv no' made any attempt to talk the truth of our bond in these many weeks since I arrived." Robert approached him, knowing only that he had to confront his father. "Ye hiv allowed me to work for the clan, plan for it, prepare for its needs, and yet ye willna call me as one of yer own."

He stood before Struan, arms on his hips, chest swelled out in anger and challenge as he waited for some acknowledgment. Struan pushed back the chair nearest him with such force that it fell backwards, crashing loudly on the wooden floor of the dais. The few men and women working in the hall paused in their chores and turned towards them. In spite of an audience, in spite of the rational part of him that screamed caution and calm, Robert forced his words out through gritted teeth.

"I . . . am . . . yer . . ."

"Brodie!" Struan interrupted. "Come quickly, for I hiv an important task for ye to do and it maun be done with haste." Waving at Brodie as he made his way to the front of the room, Struan whispered a warning to Robert. "In spite of yer beginnings and in spite of how highly ye hiv risen within the ranks of the MacKillops, ye ken ye hiv no place here. None then, none now. Dinna expect more or ye will face disappointment."

If Struan had buried a *sgian-dubh* deep in his chest, the pain could not be worse. Robert staggered back a few steps and struggled to control his rage and hurt. His head spun with all the seething thoughts, and the urge to strangle Struan at that moment grew until he could almost not control it. He turned on his heels and ran full-tilt down the steps and past Brodie. If Brodie tried to say anything to him, he did not hear it, for the roar of anger filled his ears and his being.

Even the icy wind, still howling days after the storm had moved on, did not slow him, nor did his lack of a protective cloak. He needed to get away. He needed to get his anger under control for it did him no good. A ride would tire him but he dared not approach Dubh when his rage was this strong. Needing a place and time to sort out his thoughts and set up his plans and priorities, he trotted through the gate and towards the loch off in the distance.

His eyes burned but whether with tears caused by the icy gusts or by the blow from Struan, he did not know. Tilting his head down, Robert continued his run. Soon, the resistance of the wind and the freezing air slowed him to a walk. As his pace slowed his thoughts quickened.

Why had he even let himself believe for one moment that he could return to Dunnedin and his clan and be accepted? He was usually a man who displayed a good measure of common sense, but the rawness of his confused emotions overcame any attempt to think rationally about his father, and about his father's refusal to acknowledge him.

Something else lay at the core of his feelings. Something darker and stronger than the need for recognition. Robert wanted . . . he wanted everything that his brother had. Everything his brother ignored through his absence and stupidity. He wanted the clan to know him as a member of the same MacKendimen blood. He wanted to take his rightful place as eldest son of the laird. He wanted to be accepted as tanist by the elders of the clan. And, if he were honest with himself, he wanted her.

Anice. His brother's wife. But as usual, Sandy and his get would always stand between him and what he wanted most in his life.

His steps slowed and he took in deep breaths of the frigid air. His thoughts turned back to Anice. Did he want her simply because she was his brother's wife? Did he covet her along with all that his brother owned? His brother's position and status?

Yes. He did. He wanted everything that Sandy had. It should be his; he was older, he was better. He was here, carrying out many of the duties that should be Sandy's. He even looked after his brother's wife. And he wanted her for his own.

He'd seen many different aspects of Anice in these last months. She could be a strong woman in control of home and hearth one moment and a weakling needing succor the next.

Her green eyes could blaze with anger or lately even happiness, or look vulnerable and full of emotion. Robert had many times fought the urge to draw her close and comfort her or to offer her encouragement as the days of her pregnancy became more and more difficult to bear alone.

He realized that part of him wanted her for the woman she was and another part of him coveted her as his brother's wife. Ironically, the very reason he wanted her was the very reason that would forever keep them apart—even if Sandy died, marrying her would be forbidden. She would be forever his sister-by-marriage if his true heritage were known. So a marriage between them would be sinful in the eyes of the church.

Robert let out a rough laugh at the quandary that existed for him. He wanted to be recognized as Struan's son for all that he could gain rightfully as that and yet that recognition would put out of his reach the one thing he craved most in Dunnedin. Anice. His brother's wife.

'Twas truly a situation where no good would come of his wanting. How many times did his hopes have to be crushed before he would give up and go back to Dunbarton? How many times could Struan ravage his dreams of a life among his own clan before he stopped opening himself up to the hurt? As a warrior he knew he could not win with this strategy. And he did not have enough strength to keep the wanting and desire for all his brother possessed within and not show it to those around him.

The chill finally seeped in and his skin erupted in gooseflesh. Shaking his head to clear his thoughts, Robert pulled the end of the plaid he wore from under his belt and threw it over his shoulders and head, gathering the edges close to keep out what cold he could. Looking about to gauge his location, he realized that his steps had taken him close to one who could offer him some solace no matter who his father was. And, with his innermost feelings in an uproar, he would seek the simplest of comforts in the arms and warmth of a willing woman. Following the well-worn path to her door, he knocked and waited for her welcome. Her smile as she opened her door confirmed that he could depend on Robena for a few hours of pleasure, pleasure he hoped would bring a certain measure of forgetfulness.

Later, as he buried his hardness within the warmth she offered and relinquished much of his frustration and desire, his thoughts still drifted to the one he could never have beneath him. The one whose name he almost called out as he reached his peak. The one whose haunted eyes begged for comfort and protection.

Anice. His brother's wife.

chapter 12

Now the rains came—first in briefs bursts, then in torrents. The snow and ice washed away and was replaced by a deep layer of mud throughout the bailey and even into the village. She'd long since given up trying to make her way anywhere but in the keep. If she were honest, the weather gave her the excuse she thought she needed to spend most of her time curled up on her bed.

Oh, no one would comment directly to her, but the clanspeople had become reticent about speaking to her. The many abbreviated conversations were obvious. Too many times lately, when she entered rooms or came upon people in hallways, their discussions would abruptly stop and only their stares would greet her. She searched her mind over and over for a reason or something she perhaps had done unintentionally to give insult, but she could remember nothing. So, 'twas easier for her to take refuge in her chambers and blame the pregnancy and the rains.

And just as she avoided most contact with them, none sought her out. Messages were passed through Firtha. Rarely in the last week had she seen either Struan or Robert, although Robert had tried to meet her in the workroom behind the great hall. The pains in her back had forced her to cancel that and a new time had not yet been chosen.

What was most confusing to her was the sense of fear that permeated the keep these last few days. A few times she had even seen glances of pity shared by some of the cleaning women when they were at work in her chamber. Pity? Mayhap because her time approached and they knew the pain and danger she faced. At first, that was exactly what she thought, but yesterday the expressions became even more blatant and she recognized the looks she was given. Definitely pity.

The need to walk a bit grew stronger so she maneuvered herself off the bed and slipped on some soft shoes that still fit her swelling feet. Treading carefully across the freshly laid rushes, she tugged open her door and quietly walked down the stairway to the main floor. She was not certain what she would do there once she arrived, but she knew that the workroom was her goal. It was late, almost midnight as near as she could tell, and the hallways were deserted, the great hall quiet and empty.

She pushed open the door and lit the lamp that sat on a high shelf in the wall. Glancing at the table, she saw that many papers had been left for her. Stretching first, she sat down and began to organize the work. In a few minutes, Anice found herself lost once more in the record-keeping needed for the clan.

"I thought ye haid forgotten our agreement these last days." Robert's voice broke into her concentration and she smiled.

"I did not forget, Robert. This weather seems to make my aches and pains grow until I feel like doing nothing but stay in bed."

He laughed and the richness of it filled the room and sent tremors deep inside of her. Working with him had lessened the fears that had showed themselves to her when she had witnessed his fight with Brodie. The sheer power and strength he'd exhibited had scared her silly for a long time but his manner around her was always gentle. She had to talk herself through the first minutes anytime they met, but the fear was lessening.

"Some would say that women in yer condition deserve to

be pampered abed." He pulled a stool over closer to the table and sat. "But some would say that only hard work will prepare ye for the time ahead."

"Tonight, with the rain pouring down and the winds howling, I favor the pampering." She closed the book she was working in and pushed it away.

"What brings ye here, then, when a warm chamber and comfortable bed awaits ye abovestairs, Anice? Does Firtha ken yer whereabouts?" She knew by his laugh that her guilt showed on her face. She chuckled with him.

"Come then, if yer quite finished, I will escort ye back to yer rooms." He stood and held out his arm, much as he had the second day on their trip through the village.

She hesitated, not because of fear this time, but because the thought of staying and talking to him appealed to her. She reasoned that it was simply to catch up on all the goings-on she had missed these last few days.

"If you have a few minutes, mayhap now would be a good time to discuss the questions you left for me here?"

She pointed at a list written on a parchment scrap that he had left on the table for her. He sat down and pulled in closer, looking over her shoulder at the note.

"I hiv time now, if yer no' too tired?"

She laughed at the light sarcasm in his tone and shook her head. "I think now would be just fine."

Anice was not sure how long they had worked when the commotion in the great hall interrupted. The noise passed easily through the wooden wall that separated them. Loud voices came closer and closer to the dais, which sat a few yards from them in the other room. She looked up at Robert to see his reaction. He was staring at her in the same way.

"'Tis true, Struan. He is but a day's travel away from here and says nothing will prevent his homecoming." Brodie's voice was easily recognized.

"Lower yer voice, mon." Struan's harsh whisper was easily heard. "I dinna want her to ken. She haes enough on her mind wi' the birth approaching."

Shock filled her as the subject of his words became clear to her. Unable to break from Robert's gaze, she was also certain that Robert knew what this meant. A wild tremor wracked her whole body as the knowledge sunk into her mind. Sandy was on his way to Dunnedin. Blinking quickly to clear her vision, she recognized the look in Robert's gaze—guilt and pity. He knew! They all knew! And that was the reason for the sympathetic glances over the last days.

She stood, locking her trembling knees to keep her up, and turned to leave. She had to talk to Struan. But more words stopped her. Robert's words.

"Anice, ye should stay here. I will go get Struan for ye."

He stood to go, but she shook her head. Struan had promised, he had promised she would be safe until after the babe was born. On his honor as laird. He had to keep her safe . . . *he had to.*

Her chest felt tight, as if ropes were being pulled harder and harder around her. She could not breathe. Forcing her feet to move, she took one step then another towards the door and into the hall. Her lungs refused to pull in the air around her and lights twinkled on the edges of her vision. Faster and faster she moved to find Struan. Sweat beaded on her forehead and face as she entered the hall and made her way up the steps to the dais. Gasping now, she reached the table and leaned against it.

The men saw her and silence filled the cavernous room. Brodie, Iain, Struan, and the others, she saw them all. She heard Robert come up behind her but her eyes could focus on no one but Struan. Panting once more as a strong pain pierced her side and belly, she screamed out his name.

"Struan! Ye gave me yer word. Yer word as laird. Please, ye maun tell me I am safe."

Another pain tore through her and her vision blurred. Rubbing her hand over her eyes to clear them did not work. Anice looked at Struan and he would not meet her gaze. Struggling for breath, she reached out to him. He had to help her. He'd promised. He'd promised. At his refusal to look at her, she knew the truth. Sandy was returning now. Oh, dear God, no!

Darkness began to close in on her now. The sounds of the men in front of her lessened to quiet and all she could hear was the blood rushing through her veins and her heart pumping. The light in the room dimmed from farther back in the hall, up towards the dais, until she was not sure she could see anyone. And just as her legs crumpled under her, she heard an ear-piercing scream fill the room. Clutching her belly, she stopped fighting and fell to the ground.

Her last thoughts were of the Lady Anice she had been—she would never have screamed like that.

Chaos erupted at her collapse. Robert had been standing close enough to her to cushion her fall and prevent injury to her or the babe within. Men and women of the clan rushed into the room after her scream. He lifted her into his arms, ready to carry her to her chambers, and noticed Firtha making her way to the dais. As he positioned Anice in his arms, he felt the wetness in her gown and fear filled him. Could this be the bairn coming now?

Struan called out orders to some of the men and Robert realized he was planning to leave the castle now. Robert decided to take Anice to her room and let the women tend to her. They would know better what she needed than he ever would.

"Struan, I would ride wi' ye. Give me but a moment to take Anice to her rooms." He started to walk down the steps.

"Ye stay here, Robert. I hiv the men I need."

"Struan?" Robert stopped and turned to face him. "Will ye stand by yer word to her?"

"Ye question my word?" Struan's face darkened with rage but Robert did not care. Anice would need to know she was safe from whatever danger Sandy represented to her.

"In her stead, aye, I do."

"'Twill be as I promised her. Now, take her and see to her. And see to Dunnedin until I return."

Torn between arguing with Struan and the seriousness of Anice's condition, Robert delayed but a moment before walking quickly through the hall. The growing wetness seeping through the gown underneath her terrified him. Either she bled or her birth water had broken—neither a good sign. He'd seen this before in Dunbarton and the outcome was never good. At least Ada was here. The old one had much experience in delivering babes and her presence would be of benefit to Anice.

"Firtha, fetch Ada to milady's chambers," he barked out as he passed the woman.

In a few minutes, he entered the room and placed Anice on the bed. She'd made no move since that god-awful scream in the hall and whether that scream was due to the pain or to the news of Sandy's return, he did not know. He knew only that the sound of it nearly shattered his heart as she cried out her fear. What could his brother have done to engender such terror in his wife? As he positioned a pillow beneath her head, he realized that no one ever spoke whatever had happened between the two of them. That was very unusual, since secrets never seemed to stay that way within the closeness of the clan. They did it to protect her, he understood that now.

The sounds of swishing garments and the low voices behind him informed him that Firtha and Ada had arrived. They were followed by several other women and he suddenly felt very out of place. He would turn over her care to those who knew what to do..

"Ada, she is wet underneath. I felt it as I carried her up here." His words were almost whispered but the impact of them was not.

"Dear God in heaven," Firtha cried out as she ran to her mistress's bed. The other women in the room crossed themselves and mumbled prayers under their breath.

"Go, now, Robert, we will see to her." Ada patted his arm as she walked past him. "The lass is in God's hands now."

"And, Firtha?" He waited for the woman's attention before continuing. At her glance, he said, "Tell Anice when she awakes that Struan honors his word to her. Ada? Call on me if there is anything I can do."

The words did not encompass the feelings within him at that moment. His stomach clenched in fear and anger for her situation. Many, many women died giving birth, and sometimes the bairn died as well. 'Twas the most dangerous thing a woman could do in life. His own mother had died giving birth to him. Would she die now? His throat burned and his eyes stung at the thought. Clearing his throat, he turned at Ada's nod and left the room, leaving Anice in their care.

Making his way back to the lower floor, he looked for anyone who might have heard the whole exchange and might know where Struan and the other men went. No one was there. The room was empty as when he had passed it on his way to the workroom earlier. Even though no announcement was made, Robert knew that word of Anice's condition was even now passing from one to another throughout the clan. In a short time, all in Dunnedin would be praying for her and for the safe delivery of the bairn she carried.

He entered the workroom and grabbed a woolen cloak from a peg on the wall. Wrapping himself in its length and pulling the hood up, he left the keep to check on the guards. Struan had left Dunnedin in his care and he would make certain that all was well before he retired for the night.

Jagged streaks of lightning criss-crossed the sky, lighting the bailey with an unnatural green-gray glow. Robert leaned down and fought the wind with his every step. The weather seemed to reflect the chaos of the clan this night. In spite of his plaid, he was soaked through when he reached the guard tower on the wall and he was dripping when his inspections were complete. Seeking his own chambers, he pulled off his wet clothes and put on dry ones, wanting to be ready if needed.

Kneeling on the floor next to his bed, he offered his own prayers up to the Almighty for Anice and her bairn. Once done, he lay on his bed and awaited news from either the women or from Struan. It would be a long night for the MacKendimen clan.

B*olting upright, his senses immediately alert for signs of* danger, Robert leapt from the bed. Realizing that dawn's light did not pour through his small window, he knew it was not day yet. The sound that waked him did not repeat itself, but he knew in an instant it had been Anice . . . screaming. He pulled open his door and walked down the hallway to her chambers. Robert tapped lightly on the door and it was Rachelle, Brodie's wife, who answered his knock.

"Rachelle, how does she fare?" His height over her allowed him to peek inside the room. Dimly lit, it was hard to see much from his position.

"She is no' weel, Robert. I fear for her and the bairn," Rachelle replied in a low whisper.

"May I see her?" Robert wasn't certain what he could do, but he wanted to see her condition for himself. Rachelle looked behind her and waited for permission from the others within. Once it was granted, she quietly tugged the door open and let him pass.

Robert held his breath, not really knowing what to expect. He had been present at only one birth and that was when a MacKillop woman had suddenly given birth on her way to the mill. He happened along and witnessed it—amazed at how quickly it all occurred. The woman was up in a short time, carrying her new one back to her cottage. The woman had given birth to five others in the same manner, with relative ease and apparently little or no pain. But Robert knew that was not often the case. Keeping his steps soundless, he approached the side of the bed.

Anice lay in a fitful sleep, her brow covered with sweat. They had removed the gown she wore before and now she was dressed in only a nightrail, its pale color only made richer by her ghostly complexion. Without thought, he reached out and touched her cheek. Her eyes opened and garbled words poured from her mouth. He bent over to listen more closely when he noticed that her gaze was feverish and glassy. Nothing she said made any sense.

"Is the bairn coming?" he asked, not looking away from Anice.

"Aye, Robert. 'Twas the birth waters ye felt on her dress," Ada answered.

"But the babe is too early. Will she . . . ?" He could not say the words.

"'Tis too soon for the bairn but we canna stop it. Moira's brew worked for a short time, but the pains hiv returned and much stronger than afore." Ada's explanation sent cold shivers of fear down his back.

"Does she ken what is happening to her?" Anice looked senseless to him. Could a woman deliver a babe like that?

"She is between sleep and wakefulness, Robert. She comes to, struggles with the pain, and then falls back to this." Ada held out her hand, pointing to Anice. "'Tis almost like she is trying to keep the babe inside."

Firtha leaned around him and wiped Anice's forehead and cheeks. More mumbled words flowed from her. Firtha straightened the bedclothes and pushed Anice's hair back from her face. Even he could see this would end badly.

"What can be done? Is there nothing or no one that can help her?"

Before anyone could answer, Anice clutched at her belly and began to writhe on the bed. Her face was contorted in pain, her jaws and mouth clamped shut in a horrible grimace. After a minute of struggle, she let loose a loud keening cry that made his stomach turn. There must be something he could do for her. Standing there, a witness to her anguish, he felt the sweat run down his own back. He was a man. He was a warrior. He could bear this kind of pain and face it, survive it. She could not.

"We maun make her give up her struggle and work with the pains. If the bairn is coming, it maun come for good or bad. At least she might live." Ada looked to him for an answer.

"How can ye do that? Do ye hiv some brew that will bring her back to her senses?" Their expressions were answer enough. "Weel then, how do ye plan to do it?"

"Will ye speak to her, Robert? Mayhap yer words will bring her out of this stupor," Firtha suggested.

"*My* words? But ye hiv been wi' her for years, Firtha. Surely she will respond to you. . . ." Robert ran his hand through his hair. He knew now why the birthing room was no place for men. He could fight his enemies and win but he had no idea how to bring Anice through this struggle.

"Speak to her, Robert. Please? She haes told me of yer kindnesses to her in these last months. She would trust yer words," Rachelle pleaded softly with him.

He nodded and they moved away to allow him closer. Kneeling at the side of the bed, he leaned in towards her. Reaching for the cloth that Firtha used on Anice's face, he dipped it into the bowl on the table and squeezed it out. Rubbing it lightly over her forehead, he began to call her name, first in a low voice and then more insistently. Tapping her cheek, he called her once more.

"Anice. Anice. Ye maun awake now."

She roused a bit, opening her eyes and trying to focus on him. Shaking her head, she started to moan.

"Struan, ye promised." Her voice, made husky by screaming, had taken on a more pronounced lilt, losing some of its blandness. "Will ye stand by yer words?"

He looked from one woman to the next, trying to figure out the right thing to say and do. "She thinks I am Struan." Did she see the resemblance or was she just incoherent? Did he look like his father that much that she could mistake them?

"Go wi' it, lad. Say anything she needs to hear. If she continues to fight, we will lose them both," Ada urged him on.

"I will stand by the words I gave ye, Anice. Ye hiv my protection." His throat tightened as she grasped his hand and raised her head, looking straight into his eyes but never recognizing the man who was before her.

"But only till the babe is born? Am I only safe till then? Can ye no' help me when he returns? Please," she begged in a gasping whisper and tightened her grip on his hand, "please protect me."

Although he knew he was speaking on behalf of Struan and that Struan would make no such promises, he agreed to her request. Even while he spoke the words she thought came from Struan, Robert wanted to be the one who offered protection to her. Deep in his soul and in his heart, he knew he wanted to be the one for her. And so, without any effort, a part of him went into his words.

"Ye hiv my protection, lass. Until the bairn is born and after. As long as ye need it, I will give it."

"I am safe then?" Anice stared into his eyes and he almost believed her to be awake. "The bairn struggles to come now. I am afraid."

"Ye are safe, Anice. I will keep ye safe."

She relaxed at his assurances; her face lost its terrible tightness and her breathing became more regular. She believed him. Or rather, she took Struan's word of her safety. He loosened her grasp on his hand and moved away so that the women tending her could move closer. Another cramp came upon her then for her breathing became more labored and she reached down to her belly once more.

"There now, lass. Work with the pains, let the bairn come," Ada soothed as she and Firtha lifted a few layers of bedclothes from Anice. "Blow out through your mouth when the pain is at its worst. Dinna hold yer breath."

Robert took one look at Anice and knew this was not going to end soon. Convinced that she was in the care of those who knew much more than he did, Robert stepped away and turned to leave.

"I thank ye for yer help, Robert," Firtha offered even as she tended to Anice.

"Call on me if ye hiv need."

He left quietly so as to not disturb them and walked back to his room. The sounds of people stirring for the day reached him from belowstairs. It would be an even longer day than it had been a night.

chapter 13

Would it never stop? Anice fought to open her eyes as another wave of pain sliced through her and centered on her core. The room was a blur around her; she could hear whispered voices and knew others were there, but did not know how many or who. And, after focusing her attention and strength on surviving each contraction that came, she could not care.

"Anice . . . sip this. 'Twill ease yer pains."

"Ada, is that you?"

She licked her dry lips and then did as the old woman ordered. The brew tasted warm and sweet and slid down her throat effortlessly. She could not remember how many times Ada had made her drink this or that, or cajoled her into pushing one more time. It seemed that now that she made the decision to push this babe out, he'd decided not to come. The pains still came, each one stronger and longer than the last, but the babe had not. Even in the stupor she existed in right now, she knew that something was wrong.

"What time is it?"

Anice knew that this had all begun long after dinner but had no idea how much time or how many days had passed.

Dim light entered her rooms now; the curtains would keep back most of it anyway.

"'Tis nearly noon, Anice."

Noon? So if *he* was a day's travel from Dunnedin yesterday evening, he was only hours away now. Did Struan travel to meet him even now? What could he say? Mayhap, he was going just to escort Sandy home. Struan promised she'd be safe so she must leave it in his hands and concentrate on delivering her son.

"Will he come soon then?"

"He? Who do ye speak of, lass?" Ada's warm hands lifted the hair away from her face and straightened her pillow again.

"The babe . . . my son," she answered.

"Being a mon, he is taking his own sweet time," Firtha said. Soft laughter filled the room for a few moments, a change from the tension there. "Do ye think this will be a boy, Anice?"

"I know it, Firtha. 'Tis the heir of the clan I carry."

Silence greeted her words and she knew not if it was in disbelief or in acceptance, but no one argued with her. She shifted herself on the bed and tried to push herself up. Arms behind her helped her to sit, and pillows were positioned to support her.

"'Tis hard to say how much longer this will take, lass," Ada finally answered her question. "A first birth can take many hours, even days."

"But 'tis too soon for him. This should not happen for many more weeks."

Neither woman answered her unspoken question—would the babe live? Anice knew that no one could promise her that. She only hoped that her endless prayers to the Almighty had been heard and would be answered.

"Come now, Anice. I think that walking will do ye some good. Here, now, let us help ye."

After a few minutes of rearranging and changing nightrails and brushing hair, Anice put her feet on the floor and stood. Her legs wobbled beneath her and it took much support of Ada and Firtha to hold her up. Taking a step at a time, she made it over to a chair just as the next pain hit. Listening to her helpers, she blew her breath out hard as the cramp increased and increased, until she thought she would scream. Just as she reached her limit, the pain subsided and she could breathe once again.

"'Tis a bit easier sitting here than lying in bed," she said.

A sound across the room caught her attention and she looked up into Robert's eyes. His skin was a bit sallow and his cheeks bore the growth of at least a day's beard—that he had not shaved, as was his manner, was obvious. He swallowed several times as though trying to speak.

"She is awake now, Robert," Firtha said.

"Aye, I can see as much. How do ye fare, my . . . Anice?"

She could not think of how to answer so she just nodded.

"I will check back wi' ye later, Ada," he said as he backed from the room.

"Men!" Firtha laughed. "They dinna mind being part of the fun of the making a bairn, but they dinna want to be near at the work of the birthing." Ada joined Firtha for a moment, but they both stopped when they looked at Anice. Firtha remembered the origins of this bairn, 'twas there plainly on her face, and Ada must have guessed for 'twas on hers as well.

The next hours passed as the last one had; the contractions grew stronger each time, followed by shorter and shorter respites between. She sat, she stood, she walked as they ordered, for she could not keep any sensible thoughts in her mind. Different women attended her as well, Rachelle and some others from the clan came and went, bringing in food and drink and fresh linens from time to time. But even in this time of need she could tolerate no one's touch but Firtha's and Ada's. And when Rachelle revealed that she too was carrying, Anice ordered her from the room for fear that her pain would frighten the woman too much.

Robert did come back and at shorter intervals and for shorter visits, if that was possible. He never said much, just stared at her for a moment and, when assured all was moving forward as it should, he left. She had some bit of memory of him being in the chamber with her, she could almost hear his voice, but Anice did not think it really happened.

Then, at nightfall, the bleeding began. At first, Ada and Firtha exchanged glances and reassured her that all was well.

Now, though, she knew by their expressions and guarded words that all was not. After submitting to their probing and touching in places she would rather not think about, their faces said it all. The babe was not coming. And the bleeding was increasing with each contraction.

Soon, with her strength gone, she no longer could remain sitting and had to lie in bed as she faced each ensuing wave of agony. Knowing that her chances of surviving this were lessening with each tormenting pain, Anice let go of her control and screamed out her anguish.

The sound of her scream echoed through the halls and rooms of the third floor and through his soul. How long could she survive this? His visits to her chambers only made it clearer—Anice and the babe would die this night. He did not consider himself a particularly religious man—oh, aye, he did his duty and followed the rules of the church, but his conversations with the Almighty were few and far between in actuality. He had spoken to Him more this last day and night than in the last ten years of his life, and all for her.

Moira could have prevented this or, at the least, eased Anice's way through the birth. But she was not there. Leaving Ada in her stead had not seemed a bad thing to do since the old one had some healing skills. Now it looked as though Anice and her babe would die because of Moira's absence.

He shook his head as he walked slowly down the hallway towards Anice's chamber. Moira must have known this would happen. Her wisdom would not have failed her in such an important matter of the clan. Why had she chosen this time to leave? He knew about Moira's sister and her problems, but this just did not ring true to Moira's commitment to the MacKendimens. Something in this was wrong.

He grasped the door's knob and turned it. Part of him feared what he would find within, but he had to see to her as Struan ordered. The scene before him in the room bore out his worst fears. Anice lay still on the bed; he stared at her chest and could barely make out the rise and fall of it. Ada gathered a pile of bloody sheets and tossed them into a basket at the foot of the bed.

"'Tis over?" he asked, not truly wanting the answer. Tears burned his eyes as he waited.

"I fear the lass haes little time left now."

"The babe was too early to live?"

"The babe haes no' turned the right way to be born," Ada answered. "She is bleeding and the babe is stuck."

Firtha sobbed at Ada's words, and if the truth be told, he felt like joining her. He wondered if Anice could hear them as she lay in her stupor. He fought the urge to gather her in his arms and hold her close.

"We hiv tried to turn the bairn, but my hands are no' strong enough and Firtha canna hold her down."

"Is there no one who could help ye in this? Other women who know how to deliver babes?"

"None," Firtha whispered through her tears.

"Hiv ye pulled a newborn colt from the mare, Robert?" At his nod, Ada continued, "Mayhap ye could do this."

Robert reeled back. Never did he expect to hear that. "Are ye daft, Ada? A horse and a woman are different things. And I am neither husband nor faither to her to touch her in that manner."

"Aye, Robert, different, but in this, the same. If that bairn is not freed from her body, it will tear her apart and then die. It is tearing her even now. And we lose them both. Ye would let her die wi'oot even trying?" She waited as he thought on her words.

Could he do this? He had only handled her in the briefest and most innocent of touches but this would be the most invasive touch of all—reaching into her and pulling the babe out. He knew of her aversion to be touched at all, especially by men in the clan. If she survived, how would she react to knowing he had been inside of her? If she survived? How could he be so stupid? If he did not try this, she would not live past this night. After a moment's hesitation, he nodded to Ada.

"Tell me what to do."

Firtha and Ada moved quickly to get Anice prepared for this attempt. Another pain came upon her, but as weak as she was now, she only made a low groaning sound as it built within her and then passed. And they were ready. Moving her gently so that her feet were nearer to the end of the bed, Ada and Firtha peeled back the sheets and lifted her night-rail, pulling it up to her belly. With one on each side to hold her legs back and support her, he dared to look for the first time.

This was unlike any time before and he swore any time after. He leaned down and slid his hand between her thighs, an action done many times to other women in the past but never again with such an intent. The path inside was looser and wetter than he knew it could be, but it made his reach in easier. How could a woman ever fit snugly around a man again after giving birth? And yet, he knew that they did, just as Anice would. He shook his head against such thoughts now.

"When ye touch her womb, ye will feel the babe's shoulder in the canal. Ye hiv to push that back inside and guide it to turn." Ada's words were matter-of-fact so he concentrated on the task before him. Sliding his fingers around the soft joint, he tried to guide the babe back, but a contraction started and all of the pressure and blood came in his direction.

Anice shrieked again, this time long and loud, sending icy tremors down his spine. With his hand where it was, he could feel the sound vibrate through her even as it echoed through the chamber. He waited until he felt the pulsing within her womb stop and then tried once more to push the babe back inside. Placing his other hand on her belly he applied some pressure against another part of the babe, trying to turn it.

"The head would be best, Robert, but the feet—both feet, mind ye—would work as weel," Ada directed as he struggled within the tight confines to move the babe without hurting Anice even more.

A commotion outside in the bailey drew his attention away for a moment and then he felt the babe spin a bit to one side. His fingers encircled what he thought was the bairn's head and he tried to guide it into the birth canal. His grasp slipped once more, then once again, until he finally had the slick babe in his hand. Anice's moan was a signal to that which he already felt inside: another contraction was beginning.

"Dinna let go, lad, or we'll lose him," Ada called out as she and Firtha struggled to hold Anice. "Hold tight till it passes and then bring him out."

Robert followed her instructions, holding as best he could onto the small head within Anice's body. Loud voices now filled the hall outside her chamber but Robert tried to ignore them, waiting for the chance to reposition the babe. As soon as the cramping lessened, he tugged the head down and pressed on her belly to keep it in place.

The door crashing back into the wall wakened her with a jolt. Anice looked into his eyes and he saw that she recognized him. Too intent on his task to break from it, he did not turn to see who entered.

"This is no' the time or place to deliver a message. I will see ye downstairs in the hall when this is done," Robert called out to whomever was behind him and leaned over to block the intruder's view of Anice on the bed.

"Robert!" Anice screamed as the babe's head finally slid from her womb.

"He is dead, Robert!" the messenger yelled out.

Robert did not understand his meaning, since the babe was even now following his hand into the birth canal. He turned his head to look at the man in the doorway.

"Who is dead?"

"Sandy. We found him dead in the forest."

There was a moment of utter and terrifying silence, followed by Anice's scream. Whether 'twas caused by the news or her babe's motion, he did not know. He watched as she arched her back, screamed again, and pushed with all her might, filling his hands with a rush of blood. Then the babe was there. And Anice collapsed back on the bed, unconscious.

Drawing the little body down and out, he watched as Ada came over and lifted the tiny babe, a boy, from his hands. He was purple and covered in blood and there was no movement at all. Had they been too late, then?

Ada wrapped a cloth around the boy and briskly rubbed

the babe between her hands. Not sure of what she was doing, Robert could only stand and watch. Realizing that the messenger still stood in the doorway, he questioned him.

"Where is Struan?"

"Struan is bringing Sandy, er, Sandy's body home. He is but a few hours behind me," the man replied.

"Fine, then. Tell the women downstairs to prepare for their arrival. I will follow ye down shortly."

Once the door was closed, he turned back to the bed. Firtha had moved to take the babe from Ada.

"Is he . . . ?" Robert could get no more out.

"The bairn lives. Not as hearty or hale as we'd like, but he breathes." Robert nodded, glad that his efforts had been successful. Or had they? He stepped closer as Ada tended to Anice's unmoving form.

"And . . . ?" His throat constricted so much that he could not say her name.

"She is still alive as weel. She will need time to recover from the blood loss. If the afterbirth comes as it should, she haes a good chance."

He did not even want to ask how and when that would happen. This was closer to a birth than he wanted to be. Ever.

"I need to see to Struan's return. If ye hiv no more need of me?"

He found a basin of water in front of the hearth and rinsed the blood from his hands as best he could. He would wash more later after arrangements had been made. The two women were busy and he left without another word, closing the door behind himself.

It was as he walked down the steps to the main floor that he realized the irony of it all. Now that Sandy was dead, the only person who stood in his way to recognition was Anice's bairn. The same son he had just safely delivered with his own hands. He laughed out loud at vicarious fate, but said a prayer of thanks to the Almighty. No matter what happened to him, at least Anice was safe.

She was safe.

And Sandy was dead.

• • •

Alesander Struan MacKendimen, God rest his soul, heir to the MacKendimen, was killed during an attack by brigands on his way home to be present for the lying-in of his wife. One arrow did the job, in his back and through his chest. None of his English cohorts saw who shot the arrow or even from which direction it came; they only knew that Sandy lay facedown in the mud when his father arrived to "escort" him home.

They laid him to rest in the family graveyard on the side of a hill two days later. Many remarked on the way that the sun finally broke through and shone brightly on that morning. After the strange snows and thunderstorms, the morn was as it should be on a day in April. 'Twould be a fine spring and even summer ahead of them, according to the old ones who read the signals of nature.

Since his wife would not be able to attend services for several weeks and since the priest arrived just after the storms ended, the decision was made by the laird to bury him as soon as possible. And so they did—with a lack of the usual fanfare one would expect for the heir of a clan.

The priest's other duty in Dunnedin was to christen the new heir to the clan, Craig Alexander MacKendimen. With the bairn's difficult birth and uncertain future, his grandfather insisted on a quick baptism and Father MacIntyre obliged. The good father also agreed to kirk Anice so that if she did not recover, her soul would be ready for death. A busy few days for the only priest in the area, but he left Dunnedin feeling that the living and the dead had been well served by him.

Lady Anice, now widowed, did not leave her childbed for two full weeks, her chambers for another two. Her recovery from the difficult birth was slow and one of the women of the clan helped her to nurse the bairn, for once he decided to survive, he thrived and grew, quickly overtaxing his mother's ability to make enough to keep him satisfied. Once back from the borders and her sister's lying-in and birthing of twins, Moira made fortifying potions for Anice to aid her in regaining her strength.

Her behavior was exactly what it should be for one who had just lost her husband—once recovered, she even had a mass said for his eternal soul. She attended that mass and carried her bairn with her. No one in the clan who had witnessed her marriage to Sandy those months ago would have been surprised to discover that she prayed a mass of thanksgiving while the priest prayed one for the dead.

chapter 14

Robert opened the door to the workroom and entered it. Connor followed close behind as he always did when they were within the keep. Outside, Robert could escape his young assistant, but inside they were rarely separated. Connor took his new position quite seriously and behaved as though on a holy quest. Once seated at the desk, Robert looked over the papers listing the stores of the keep. At least Connor was diligent in his duties, for the list was more organized than he would have ever done himself. The man would make an excellent steward in a short time.

"So, Connor, what other changes hiv ye to suggest this morn?"

Robert said it facetiously but knew his assistant would have several more ideas about doing things differently than before. Since Robert's strength lay in other areas, he was not offended at all by the man's changes. In fact, there were more than a few he planned to take with him on his return to Dunbarton.

He was glad for the man's help, but part of him did not want to face leaving. Not that he had any choice in whether to stay or go—Struan had announced Connor's appointment as steward-in-training at dinner a few weeks before and the matter was set. Only the timing remained undecided, and that depended on Anice's continued recovery and her ability to take over as chatelaine once more. Mayhap the end of summer and Michaelmas would find him back in Dunbarton.

He could not seek her out, so he contented himself with occasional sightings of her as they both made their way around the keep. He knew that she ventured farther and farther from her chambers as both she and the babe recovered from their ordeal. Although the babe was brought to the great hall with some regularity, even fed by a maid in front of the hearth, Robert had not gotten a close look at the newest addition to the clan. No words had been exchanged about his part in the birth and he was never certain of what explanation Struan had received on his return to Dunnedin. Robert could surely understand a hesitation on Anice's part to disclose his intimate involvement. Not many men participated in the birth of their own bairns, let alone reached inside a woman not their wife to help the babe out.

Their work was interrupted by a knock on the door. Connor opened it and, as if called by his thoughts, there was Anice standing in the hallway. Rising from his seat, he waved her into the room.

"Anice, 'tis good to see ye." He smiled as he pointed to a chair. "Come in, sit wi' us a bit."

As she sat, he could not help but notice the glow of her skin and the softness now in her form. The pregnancy and childbirth had taken her to death's very door, but motherhood clearly favored her. Her flaming red hair was pulled back and tied but loose wisps of it framed her face. The circles under her eyes when he first met her were gone and she smelled of something elusive, something wonderfully comfortable and appealing.

"Can you still smell it then? I thought I had washed it all out," she said, turning her head to sniff her shoulders and hair. "Bairns tend to spit up at the worst times."

Robert laughed, realizing he'd been a little too obvious in taking in her scent. And he noticed that Connor was well aware of his open appraisal of her.

"I canna smell anything, my . . . Anice. I mean, if the bairn left his scent on ye, 'tis no' noticeable at all." He still stumbled over her name. "So, are ye returning to yer work then?"

"You are being kind, Robert. A person cannot wear as much of a babe's leavings as I have been and not smell of it."

Her voice was replete with contentment; she was not angry or upset at all about being the target of her son's refuse. And then she laughed and he knew that it was the first time he'd ever heard her do so. The sound of it filled the small room and brought yet another smile to his own face.

"I am not quite ready to take over all my duties yet," she answered. "So, Connor, Struan tells me you will be our new steward then?" she asked, turning her attention to the other man.

"Aye," the man mumbled out.

"And he haes some wonderful new methods of record-keeping to show ye," Robert added.

"Well, Connor, if Robert will not stay with us, then I am glad to have you in his stead."

Robert's words stuck in his throat. If he would not stay? Struan had given him no other choice and had never even asked him to reconsider after Sandy's death. Seemingly intent on getting rid of him, Struan had even appointed Connor without any counsel from him.

But what good would come from staying? 'Twould be no time at all until his parentage was out in the open. He saw the open speculation on the faces of some of the elders in the clan on those rare occasions when he and Struan stood together. He even caught himself in some of the same expressions as Struan. No, no good would come from his staying.

Robert was drawn back by Connor's stammering answers to Anice's questions. As he watched, an even darker blush crept up the man's already ruddy face as Anice smiled and inquired after Connor's wife and child. He realized as he watched her that this was an Anice he had never seen before—self-assured, confident, and comfortable. And there was no fear haunting her eyes or manner.

"Connor, if you do not mind, could I speak to Robert alone?"

Connor mumbled once more and backed out the door before either he or Anice could say another word. Robert laughed at the soon-to-be steward's discomfort around Anice.

"Do ye always hiv that effect on men?"

"Actually, Robert, I used to do that to most of the men in the clan." Although her voice was filled with laughter, he sensed a deeper truth. At his frown, she continued, "Oh, aye. The Lady Anice could be quite formidable in her displeasure."

"And did ye enjoy being the formidable Lady Anice?"

She laughed and rose from her seat. "Oh, aye. I did enjoy having the clan and the servants at my beck and call." She stepped to the door and then faced him once more. "Now I find myself at the beck and call of that wee tyrant upstairs. How things have changed."

He shared a few moments of laughter with her and waited to discover the reason for her visit now. Her glance moved to the wall that separated the workroom from the dais of the great hall and he knew she was remembering, as he was, the night a few short months ago when she found out that Sandy was on his way back to Dunnedin. The joy in her expression dimmed just a bit before she smiled at him.

"Would you walk with me outside, Robert? The day is clear and sunny and I would like a few words with you." Her gaze fell back on the wooden panel and he heard her unspoken words—*where no one can hear.*

He gathered and secured the parchments on the tabletop for his attention later and then stood. He followed her into the hallway.

"I must check on the bairn first. Can you meet me next to the practice yard?"

Robert nodded, completely baffled but incredibly interested in her purpose. As he watched her walk away, he was once more struck by this new Anice and by the vitality she emanated now. He turned and walked out to the practice yards to wait.

His wait turned into longer than he anticipated; almost a half hour passed before he sighted her coming from the kitchen door into the yards. He'd bided his time by giving some directions to the men training in the yard closest to the path where he stood. Robert joined in the cheering as the two teams of warriors faced one another with swords. He pivoted just as she approached and was surprised to see her carrying the babe in a sling.

"The piglet decided 'twas a better time to eat than sleep," she said, stroking all he could see of the bairn's head within the plaid fabric. "Forgive me for keeping you waiting, Robert."

"I understaun that this is the way of it wi' bairns, Anice. My suggestion is to get used to it." He leaned closer and tried to see the boy's face.

"Here now, you have not seen him since . . . his birth, have you, Rob?"

Between the sight of her holding the babe and the familiar shortening of his name, Robert's breath caught. She lifted the babe, Craig, out from his protective cover and held him up before them. A dense thatch of hair a few shades lighter, but red nonetheless, covered the babe's head and his skin carried the same paleness that his mother's did. The little one scrunched up his face and even he, without knowledge or experience of children could tell, was about to cry when Anice gathered him back in her arms to soothe him. A few moments of cooing and soft touches and the bairn was once more staring at the world from his woolen cocoon.

"Would you care to hold him, Robert? He is really quite strong now and he grows bigger every day."

Robert backed up a few steps and held out his hands to wave her off from her intention, but Anice was not paying attention to him. A moment later he found a squirming bundle of babe in his hands. Craig, who had just found comfort in his mother's arms, decided he did not like teetering in Robert's hands and let out a yelp as he sought a more comfortable position. Afraid he would drop the babe on the ground, Robert began to shift his hands beneath the small body, trying to get a better hold of him. He was met by Anice's laughter.

"Nay, Robert. You must support his head and the rest of him, too. Like this," she said as she guided his hands into a better hold. The bairn did not like it any more than he did and let his mother and all those within the yards know it with his scream. Finally taking pity on both of them, Anice lifted the babe into her arms and placed him on her shoulder, patting his bottom and doing that soft cooing again. She looked around them and walked off in the direction of a patch of shade nearby. He followed, still wondering at her reason for asking him to meet.

She sat on the ground and laid the babe down on the plaid she used as a sling. Robert remained standing next to them, watching the men in the yard, though he would rather have been staring at this new Anice.

"They're to marry," Anice said. Robert followed her gaze and saw her maid, Firtha, walking with the eldest of the blacksmith MacInnis brothers. "Ramsey asked her months ago, but she told him she would wait until the babe came." A sigh of frustration and something else escaped her. "Now, they make their plans."

He was puzzled by her reaction. "Is there some problem with them marrying?"

"Oh, nay, Robert. She came with me from my home already widowed. I doubt she ever thought to marry again until Ramsey began wooing her. I wish them both much happiness." Her words may have said it, but there was no warm wish for happiness in them.

"But that is not what you wanted to talk about, is it?" He decided to wait no longer.

"I have not had the opportunity to thank you properly for your help with Craig's birth." She paused and looked up at him. "Not many know the extent of your help, so I did not speak of it within. But I know that you saved my life and my son's that night." Her words now were filled with emotion.

He crouched down closer to them. "I did nothing that anyone would not have done to help."

What could he say? He had thought about that night and his actions over and over since it happened. He truly did only what he knew was needed. He only realized the irony of his actions later. But he believed that even if he'd had word of Sandy's death ahead of time, he could not have done anything differently. Robert knew deep in his heart that he had separated Anice the woman from Anice his brother's wife even before that night. And, although he might have hated his brother for all he had within the clan, Robert did not feel the same about Anice. He would have done anything to save her. In the end, he could only nod at her words of thanks.

"I do not remember much of that night beyond the pain and fear, but Firtha and Ada, before she returned to Dunbarton, both sang your praises." She reached out and laid her hand on his knee. "Thank you, Robert. For being there, when and where most men would never be. And for what you did."

A shock moved through him as he realized this was the first time she had ever touched him of her own accord. The hairs on his thigh tingled as her hand rested there. Other parts of him also reacted to the touch, parts best not involved in thoughts of his sister-by-marriage. He stood and her hand dropped to her lap.

"Ye are most welcome, my . . . Anice."

Even as he stumbled yet again over her name and title, he thought that maybe it would be best to keep clearly in mind those things in their lives which separated them. She was a lady, the daughter of one earl, the daughter-by-marriage to another, and mother to one who would be as well, when her son inherited the title. He was the bastard half-brother to her dead husband. She would always be the Lady Anice and he would be the outcast.

'Twas better to know his place in all this than to let himself hope once again for more than his father was willing to allow him. But, instead of her recovery and expected return to her duties overseeing the clan cheering him, it made it clear that his departure was nearer at hand than he would like.

"If that is all . . . ?" He saw that his coldness hurt her feelings but it would be easier this way for all concerned. "I will take my leave then. I have many duties to see to before dinner." He nodded at her and turned without hesitation.

A clean break, a quick retreat would be the wisest course. But could he do it? Could he push her away even as his heart and his body wanted to pull her close and hold her forever? The irony was not lost on him this time either, for now that Struan had set things in motion for his departure, he had found reasons to stay.

Anice. His brother's wife.

S*he closed her eyes and lifted her face to the rays of the sun* that streamed through gaps in the shady canopy of the tree.

The clan's life went on around her as she sat and enjoyed her few moments of rest. The piglet, *her son,* she thought with a deep sense of fulfillment, slept next to her, blissfully unaware of anything save that his belly was filled. Letting the cool breeze move over her, Anice sat and listened to the activity around even as she tried to discern when she had insulted Robert.

Only bits and pieces of memory existed in her mind about those nights and days. The words through the panel in the workroom had seeped into her consciousness before she ever really heard them and the next thing she remembered was standing in the great hall challenging Struan. A thick darkness covered her memories from then on, as if she were looking through a heavy fog at the people around her. Struan's voice—or was it Robert's?—promising something . . . she could not hear the words now but the feelings in those words reassured her. Firtha, Ada, Rachelle, they were there too, caring for her and the babe.

The one occurrence that was clear as the crystal goblets she'd brought with her in her dowry was Robert's face as he turned the babe within her. Although she surely would rather not have been awake during that painful and embarrassing process, she could even now see that same fierce determination on his face that he'd worn when she witnessed his fight with Brodie. But, when directed at her, his efforts were gentled and his touch careful and measured. And successful. She opened her eyes now and glanced down to check the babe who was making sucking sounds even now in his sleep. The wee piglet.

So, how had she insulted Robert when she'd meant to express her undying gratitude for his actions? Was he angered by her delay in speaking to him? Surely, he knew how near to death she had been that night. And how long her travel back from death's door had taken. 'Twas just yesterday that she took over the full nursing of her son. And just three days past since she ventured into the yard and bailey outside the walls of the keep.

She had tried to look for him several times but when she did come down those few times for meals in the great hall, he was elsewhere. Robena the whore's name had been whispered about and she decided she would ask no further about him or his whereabouts. And Struan had warned her that, following his involvement in her son's birth, for her to seek him out or spend more time with him than their duties demanded would be extremely inappropriate, especially considering their different stations in life. And there was the fact that men simply did not take part in the process of birthing a bairn, let alone reaching in *there* to pull one out. She shivered, the tremors making gooseflesh rise on her arms. No, men did not. But Robert had and she thanked God for it every morn and eve in her prayers.

So, what had she said? She thought over her words and then remembered touching his leg as she spoke. The heat of a blush moved up through her face and she touched the warmth in her cheeks as she realized she had placed her hand on his knee. Part of her was horrified at her action and another part was elated. Anice knew that her touch had been an innocent one, to emphasize her words of thanks. But not long ago such an expression would never have happened—it would have required her deliberate action and she simply would not have done so.

But that Anice was gone. She had faced death twice and survived and that knowledge alone gave her the strength to live and change. Gone was the fear that she'd lived under for the last two years, since Sandy returned the first time for their marriage. She had lived for a year with the fear of what was to come and then these last months trying to recover from it. Then she almost lost her life and her bairn when news of Sandy's return and then his death reached Dunnedin.

She was lucky to be alive and as she let out more of the old Anice, the Lady Anice as she called herself to Robert, she found she could enjoy life again. Smiling and laughing had become part of her once more. She grinned as she even remembered raising her voice this last week to several of the servants. But far from being bothered by it, they looked surprised then beamed at her reprimand. It felt good to be free of fear.

Anice leaned down and adjusted the covering over Craig, tucking the loosened end under him to hold him secure and keep him warm. Even on a summer's day, the air was chilly here. Smoothing down his little crest of red hair, she touched a soft kiss on his forehead.

"I will take care of you and your clan, my wee MacKendimen," she whispered. "At least until your own wife is chosen and begins her duties."

She would take over her duties and carry them on until Craig was grown and laird himself. Then she would pass those responsibilities on to Craig's wife and train her as she should be. Anice would never marry again; she would not need to now that she had done her duty and produced this heir to the clan. She would be content in her life as mother to the heir and as chatelaine of Dunnedin, caring for the people, and overseeing the village.

Anice straightened her skirts and lifted her son onto her lap. Still sleeping, Craig made soft gurgling noises as she placed the sling around her and then placed him within the sturdy folds of plaid. She cradled him while she regained her feet and then let his weight sink into the carrier. Turning back, she felt refreshed by her time out of the keep, but she was still troubled by Robert's response to her thanks.

Walking towards the kitchen door, she decided that she would have to show her gratitude to him before he left to return to Dunbarton and the MacKillops. Since he was so obviously uncomfortable with her expressing her thanks, she would have to figure out how to thank him in other ways. And the ripped sleeve she'd noticed in his tunic gave her an idea.

chapter 15

She knew, not from her own experience on the subject, but from the many ribald and candid comments from the women of the clan, that the physical joining of a man and woman could actually bring some amount of pleasure to both participants. She suspected the same from her own vague memories of the tingling anticipation that had filled her once long ago when she'd thought that their distant cousin was really Sandy. And she even knew from the way men pursued women and from the well-worn path before her, that men sought those pleasures more often and with more vigor than women did. Somehow, though, knowing that could not explain her sense of betrayal and disgust as she watched Robert take his leave of the village whore.

Anice was on her way back from an early morning visit with Moira when the door to Robena's croft opened and Robert stepped onto the path. Still laughing and sharing some words of parting, he nodded to the woman inside and pulled the door closed behind him. He had not been in the great hall for dinner or after, so it was obvious even to her that he had spent the night here.

She stepped back into the shadows of the tree-lined path

until he had made his way towards the keep and then she approached the cottage. Anice had thought that early in the morning would be a safe time to visit the woman, never considering that one of her customers would be there after a night's . . . activities. Pushing open the low wooden gate in the stone fence surrounding the house, she walked up to the door and knocked.

"'Tis much too early in the morn for . . ." The woman's words trailed off as she realized who had come to call on her. "Pardon me, milady," Robena said with a slight curtsy, "are ye looking for . . . someone?" Anice noticed the hesitation.

"No, I was actually trying to visit when you had no . . . visitors," Anice offered as an explanation. "I did not want to see anyone." She glanced at the path where Robert had been a minute before.

"Och, so ye saw Robert here then, did ye? Did ye want to speak to him?" The woman leaned out of her doorway to look in the direction Robert would have taken. "Should I fetch him for ye, milady?"

"Nay. Please do not," Anice said, placing her hand on Robena's arm. "'Tis you I've come to see. May I enter?"

Robena nodded, backing away and pulling the door open as she did. Anice entered the small cottage, not quite knowing what to expect. Everything there looked as it did in any of the other crofts in the village: there was a table, some benches, and the dirt-packed floor was neat and tidy. If she'd thought that some sign of the woman's sins would be present, she was mistaken.

Anice noticed the slight trembling in Robena's hand as she pointed to one of the benches. Was she afraid of Anice? Anice walked slowly to the seat and lowered herself on it.

"I hiv only cold water from the spring or some cider to offer ye, milady," she said with another curtsy.

"Cider would be fine, Robena. Then please sit."

After a minute of gathering cups and pitcher together, the woman sat across the table from her. Robena poured two cups full of drink and then waited for Anice. When Anice did not begin immediately, the woman stood nervously.

"If this is aboot Robert, milady, I assure ye I hiv no' visited him in the keep. I follow yer orders, milady. I swear I do. I only go to the kitchen door and never inside. Never inside."

Robena's trembling had grown to shaking as she stood fidgeting and never meeting her gaze. Anice remembered giving the orders that no whore from the village should ever enter the keep or be in her sight. Sighing, she waited for Robena to look at her. Then she motioned for her to sit.

"No one has said that you have, Robena. If you . . . *see* Robert, 'tis your own affair and not mine. I have come to ask you something."

"Me, milady? Ye hiv to ask me something?" The woman's complexion took on a paler shade.

"Is there anything that you need? Anything that you are lacking? Clothing? Food?" Anice glanced around the croft looking for clues. "Someone to bring you peat or wood for the fire?"

Robena followed her gaze and looked around her home. "Nay, milady. I need nothing. Truly."

"I have realized that, although I see to the needs of everyone else in the clan, I have been remiss in seeing to yours."

"Mine, milady?" Robena whispered.

"Aye. I have never asked after you or made certain that you were well fed or clothed. I apologize for that now." At the sight of Robena's mouth, dropped wide open in astonishment, Anice continued, "So, do you need anything from the keep's stores or supplies? Any help to make your cottage fit for the next winter? Anything?"

Robena's mouth opened and closed several times but no words came out. The woman's surprise was not lost on Anice. She knew that this action, approaching the village whore in the woman's own cottage, was out of the ordinary. But her decision to try to make the rest of Robert's stay in Dunnedin comfortable had led her here. Robena finally shook her head in response and Anice rose from her seat.

"If you find you have need of something, see me for it."

"But, my lady . . . ," Robena began to argue.

"Oh, aye, I see the problem. I will not refuse you entrance into the keep so long as you do not shame any of the married women before the clan. Keep your attentions on the unmarried men and you are welcome to join in the meals at the keep, if you wish."

Believing she had accomplished the task she'd set out to do, Anice walked to the door. One thought did bother her. Well, there were many things she did not understand about Robena's choices but one thing that she truly wanted to know. Reaching the door and pulling it open herself, Anice turned back and saw that the woman still stood by the table.

"Do you enjoy this?"

The words hung there in the air between the women; neither one misunderstood the question.

"My lady," Robena said as she moved closer, "yer husband was a man who gained pleasure from the pain of others. He enjoyed inflicting pain and watching others in the giving of it."

Anice's breath stuck in her chest—this was not what she'd expected to hear from the whore. How did she know this about Sandy? How could she? Oh, dear God!

"You? Did he . . . ?"

"Aye, but I'd already had enough men to know that most are no' like that. Most take pleasure in pleasure. And those men are the reason I do enjoy what I do for them, wi' them."

Anice shook her head, unable to force any more words out. Sandy had spread his destruction far and wide. Stepping into the sunshine, Anice took a few steps and Robena called to her.

"Thank ye for yer kindness to me, milady." Robena curtsied again.

The tears rapidly filling her eyes blocked her vision, so Anice simply nodded in the direction of the voice and then turned away. She'd had no idea that Sandy had attacked Robena before their wedding. Of course not, she thought. No one would have mentioned his behavior if it involved a whore.

Stumbling down the path, she knew where she had to go. Following the lane away from the keep, she made her way back to Moira's cottage. Surely Moira would tell her what had happened. When she reached it, she banged on the front door. When she realized that no one was inside, she walked around to the back. When Anice left here earlier, Moira had said she'd be working in her garden. Sure enough, she found the healer kneeling between rows of plants, gently turning the soil with her hands.

"Why?"

Panting and unable to catch her breath, Anice waited for Moira to acknowledge hearing her question. When it was obvious that Moira was biding her time before responding, Anice spied a bench under a tree nearby and collapsed onto it. Moira continued and finished the row she was working on before standing and dusting the dirt off her skirts. Pausing to rinse her hands in a bucket of water, Moira came to stand before her. Now in her sixth month, Moira's belly protruded as her own had done some months ago. But where fear and apprehension had ruled Anice's pregnancy, joy and contentment were clear in Moira's face and deportment.

"Why, Moira? Why?" she asked again.

"Ye are asking several questions wi' yer one word, Anice. Why did he rape her as he raped ye? Because he chose to. Why did I no' tell ye of his actions? Because ye were no' ready or able to hear of them." Moira paused for a few moments. "Let me ask something of ye. Why did ye go to see the whore?"

Anice winced at the harsh sound of the word. Somehow meeting Robena face-to-face and talking with her had changed her perception of the woman. And, added to the comments of the women whose counsel she valued, she felt that mayhap she had also done this woman wrong in the past. . . .

"She is Robert's friend."

"Is that what men call them now? Friends?" Moira's voice was strange, almost as though she were taunting Anice with her questions.

"Regardless of whatever else they may do together, he calls her friend. I was simply looking for ways to thank him for what he did."

"So you made arrangements wi' the whore to do what? Tup him?"

"Moira, stop this," Anice said, waving her hand in front of her. "In looking for ways to thank Robert, I thought to aid his friends, if they needed it."

"And did she?"

"Nay, she says she needs nothing that she does not have."

Moira walked over to the bench and sat beside her. "And that is when she told you about Sandy?"

"Nay," Anice answered, shaking her head. "I asked if she enjoyed what she does with men and she said all men are not like Sandy was." She clasped her hands as she remembered the moment when she realized what her late husband had done. "Then I knew, Moira, I knew what he had done to her."

"Aye, he and his friends used her badly."

Anice could feel the blood drain from her face. "His friends, too?" she whispered, shuddering at the thoughts that raced through her mind. "Was she beaten?"

"No' the way he did ye, Anice, but she will never be able to bear children."

"Oh, dear God in heaven!" she cried out. "If that bastard was no' dead, I would hiv to kill him wi' my own hands." She heard her voice slip with the emotion behind it. When she realized *what* she had said, she gasped. Then she heard Moira laugh.

"Oh, lass, 'tis glad I am to finally hear that from yer lips." Moira took her hands and closed her own around them. "Ye hiv lived first in fear and then in guilt over what he did to ye. Ye blamed yerself for his abominations. 'Tis good to see and hear yer anger at him for what he chose to do."

"But, Moira, 'tis wrong to say that." Anise could feel the weight of her guilt once more. Had she brought Sandy's behavior on herself by her own? If that was not a sin, then surely her attempts to end her own life had been. She would pay for that the rest of her life and probably her soul would pay for eternity.

"If Sandy attacked ye and ye were a mon, ye would hiv challenged him and killed him on the field." Anise nodded in agreement. "But, because yer a woman, ye dinna hiv that choice. Ye maun bear what yer husband seeks to give ye—be it good or bad. Dinna allow yerself to be fooled into thinking that just because ye maun bear it, 'tis right and just."

Anice reeled at the words. She had carried her guilt so long, it was difficult to let go of it. For now, she would try to accept what both Moira and Robena had said and leave it at that. She had much to think about.

"I hiv much to do this day, Anice. So, if ye dinna need me . . . ?" Moira stood and began walking to the door of her cottage.

Anice rose from her seat and waited for her wobbly legs to gain strength. She, too, had many duties to carry out this day, the first of which was to feed the babe who was probably even now screaming out his hunger. She walked briskly back to the keep, but could not stop herself from staring at Robena's cottage as she passed by it once more.

The commotion began in the back of the room and spread slowly to the front, gaining his attention. He sat at the end of the table on the dais, as far away from Struan as he could get without leaving the table. And far enough away from Anice that he could breathe without detecting the scent that clung to her these days. 'Twas not of babe as she suspected, but of whatever herbs she added to her bath. He could smell their fragrance in her hair whenever she walked by him. He snorted, disappointed in how he'd allowed things to change so much.

The last weeks had been hell—pure and simple hell for him. It seemed that Anice was invading his life more and more each day. Even as he drew back and tried to keep his thoughts and desires under control, she pushed her way in. His room had been refurbished: first a new mattress had appeared and then clean, sweet-smelling rushes covered the floor of his chamber every few days. His meager assortment of clothing had grown and those pieces which were fraying or torn were now repaired and cleaned. If he did not sit to eat with them in the hall, a tray of food appeared in his room later.

The worst part of it was that she did not understand the impact her actions were having. He had it from a good source that she was doing these things to show her gratitude for his actions the night she had the bairn. And, even though he knew her motives were certainly innocent, it did not stop the wanting from growing within him once more. He was more the fool than he thought was possible.

Robert searched through the room for the reason behind the wave of murmuring and saw the cause. Robena had entered the hall. Not once in his months in Dunnedin had she ever done so; she had told him that Anice would not permit her within the keep. Now, there she stood in the doorway. He looked over to Anice to see what she would do, now that she had been openly defied before the clan.

Anice motioned to one of the servants standing behind her and whispered some instructions to him. Robert was impressed that she would handle this discreetly. Tales of her temper, not seen for months and months and now reasserting itself, had been shared with him and he did not want to see his friend humiliated here before the whole clan. Those attending dinner were not going to allow this to be handled quietly, for all eyes and ears followed the servant's path through the hall to where Robena stood. And to their audible surprise, instead of leaving after the servant delivered the lady's message, Robena followed the man up to the front of the room and stood before the table.

Anice did not look angry at all as she looked down where Robena stood. Robert held his breath, as did many in the hall, waiting for Anice's words.

"So you have come to the hall after all."

"Aye, my lady," Robena answered and curtsied to Anice.

"Do you have a place to sit?" Anice looked at the tables below theirs and then back to Robena. "No one you can eat with?"

A gasp moved through the crowd. This was unheard of—the lady inviting the village whore to join their company. Outside the presence of Anice, the villagers granted her a grudging acceptance; no one went out of their way to hurt or harm or harass her. Most of the women even spoke freely to her. But Anice, the Lady Anice, had long ago forbidden this woman, his friend, from entering.

"I think that they fear ye, milady, if they let me sit wi' them." Robena's soft voice carried far due to the eerie silence around them. More murmuring filled the room as the people waited for Anice's reaction to what could be considered an insult from Robena.

"You are most probably correct, Robena." Raising her voice, Anice continued, "Robena is welcome in the keep and at meals. Find a seat for her now."

Robert watched in stupefied muteness as there was some shifting at one of the tables and a space opened on the bench next to it. Robena smiled at Anice and walked to the seat as though this were something that happened every day. Soon the meal continued and he looked back at Anice. Why? Why had she done this?

"'Tis true, then? Ye had words wi' the whore today?" Struan's gruff voice was low enough not to bring attention but loud enough for all at table to hear. Robert then noticed that Struan had aged considerably since Sandy's death—his skin had lost some of its healthy color and his hair was now more white than gray.

"I did visit her, Struan. We had matters to discuss." Anice's voice was even and calm, but he could feel the tension rising between her and her father-by-marriage.

"'Tis unseemly for ye, the daughter of an earl and maither to another, to be calling on the village whore, Anice. Remember yer place, lass." Struan motioned for the tray of meats to be brought and he pulled a small bird from it. Tearing into the roasted carcass, he said, "Ye are a lady and maun keep yer distance from those no' worthy of yer attentions."

Although the subject was Robena, Robert felt certain that Struan spoke about him. Anice's many kindnesses had not gone unnoticed by the older man. He met his father's gaze without flinching.

"I assure you, Laird, I do not plan to consort with whores. This was something I needed to do. I will remember my place." Anice nodded and lowered her eyes to her plate, but that did nothing to ease the rigidity in her posture.

"Ye are a good lass, Anice. Ye hiv done yer duty weel by the clan."

There was an odd tone to his voice that made Robert look once more at Struan. The laird simply nodded to Anice and turned his attention back to his plate, leaving Robert to ponder the meaning behind his words. A little while later, Struan stood and pushed back his chair.

"The elders meet wi' me this eve in the solar. Anice, would ye hiv some ale brought there before we begin?" At her nod, he added, "And make certain we are no' disturbed."

Anice leaned back in her chair and motioned to Connor,

who was standing off to one side. In a seamless effort, no words were passed yet orders were given with nothing more than the wave of a hand and the nod of a head. Anice was clearly back in her position and back in control of all that went on within the keep. And, good God, how she reveled in it!

He realized that she had spent a good portion of her life in charge or in training to be in charge of Dunnedin. That she and Struan had long ago worked out a system between them for handling the duties each one was responsible for. Now that she was completely recovered, she was stepping back into the place she had made for herself.

Once Struan left the table, the servants began clearing away the dishes and cups. Robert looked among the people for his friend and found her in the midst of a lively discussion where she sat. Deciding to find out the reasons behind Anice's actions, he moved to the seat at her side, now vacated by Firtha.

"She is so much the outcast here, it does my heart good to see her included. I thank ye for yer kindness to her."

A blush began to color her neck and face. She smiled at him and then seemed to struggle to find the words she wanted. Finally, she spoke.

"I went to see her because of you, Robert." The surprise must have been clear on his face for she looked away and continued her explanation. "I have been looking for ways to show you the gratitude I feel for your part in saving my son's life." She paused for a moment. "And my own life as well. I knew she was your friend and offered her whatever she might need to make her life a more comfortable one."

"What did she ask for? This?" Robert looked over to where Robena was seated.

"Nay. She asked for nothing. I told her to come to me if she did and then realized that my own words would keep her away. So, I said that the keep would be open to her as long as she did not ply her trade among the married men while here."

"And ye did this for me?"

A frown filled her face and her brows gathered close together. He knew she was thinking of some personal darkness for it was there on her face clearly.

"I went to her because of you and then found I owed her a debt of my own." Anice shook her head and then looked at him. "I have tried today to understand that she does her part for the clan as much as anyone else does here. I cannot condone it, but I am trying to accept it and to accept her. She is entitled as much as any MacKendimen to share in the bounty we have. Now," she said, standing from her seat, "I am finished discussing her and need to see to my wee tyrant above."

He rose next to her and waited for her to leave the dais. Another look was exchanged between her and Robena, which he did not understand at all. Well, if Anice would say no more, that was fine. He knew that Robena would tell him all he needed or wanted to know. She stood and left her bench, accompanied by one of the younger warriors. She would be busy for some time with the bairn so he left the keep and walked the perimeter walls to clear his head. But, the crisp air and brisk pace did not help him that night.

*The fog swirled down the paths and surrounded the cot*tages in its surreal grasp. A nearly full moon added its light to the landscape, but the rays could not penetrate to the ground. He walked among the shadows, down a familiar lane until he reached his destination. No lamp or fire burned within, so he quietly opened the door and entered. The fire was banked for the night and the first room was empty. He moved soundlessly until he found Robena on her pallet in the second room. Pulling off his plaid, he lay down next to her and fitted his body to hers. He covered them both with the woolen length and settled behind her for the night.

They'd begun sleeping together a few nights a week some time ago, each one wanting the pleasure of holding someone close. Rarely did it move beyond this for them now because even though she was willing, he grew uncomfortable with their sexual liaisons. Now, Robert knew she was awake, for as quiet as he could be, she stirred at the least sound or movement within her cottage. She moved against him, making herself more comfortable now that he had settled down.

"The Lady Anice owes ye a debt?" His words were whispered, since his mouth was so close to her ear.

"Does she say so? I ken of no debt owed to me." Robena let out a loud sigh and scrunched down into the cocoon he'd made around them with his body and plaid. "Truly, I would rather if we didna talk aboot it."

He waited for another few minutes to pass and then tried again—he would know the details before morn.

"She maun feel particularly beholden to ye for something to change her own orders about ye eating in the hall."

"Rob, if I tell ye this, will ye never mention it again?"

He hesitated, now not certain if he should pursue this knowledge or not. Every instinct in him screamed of impending bad news. "Aye, I promise this will be the end of it."

"Sandy returned to Dunnedin filled with anger. He was furious at Struan for delaying his marriage and sending him to England. He was furious at Anice for the part he thought she played in the delay and for what he thought had happened while he'd been away those years with King David." Robena paused but he did not interrupt. "He and his Sassenach friends came here looking for some fun, as they called it, two nights afore the wedding."

He tried to remain still, but he could not stop the tensing of his muscles. He shifted, trying to maintain a relaxed position around her. "And?" he asked, helpless to stop himself now.

"Weel, I hiv had some rough ones afore, but they were no' here for pleasure. Moira did what she could to patch me up afterwards."

Pure rage built within him. Sandy again—and at the center of someone else's torment. He tried to force his breaths in and out slowly but it did not help. As a warrior he knew not to let anger control him, but lying here listening to Robena's calm recitation of her terrifying ordeal was more than he could bear. She turned in his embrace and massaged his arms. Then, reaching up, she touched him on the cheek.

"And this is why I hiv never mentioned it to ye. Or to anyone."

"What injuries did ye hiv?" She hesitated and he squeezed her. "Tell me."

"Rob. I am weel now. Truly. Moira did her best for me and all is weel."

An underlying current of sadness tinged her words and he

knew deep in his being that all was not well. And he knew also that until he knew the full extent of it, he would keep pushing for the truth.

"Robena, tell me what ye hold back from others. I am yer friend."

She snuggled closer to him and tucked her head against his chest. If he had not been this near to her, he would never have heard her words. And then, once he did, he wished he had not.

"I canna ever hiv bairns of my own, Rob."

Wave after wave of emotion passed over him and he struggled not to show her anything but the comfort she needed. The roar within him grew until he wanted to pummel his dead brother with his own fists. An arrow in the back was too good a death for the likes of him.

"How could ye do this again? How could ye take men to yerself after he did that to ye?"

She lifted her face to him and, by the light of the moon streaming in the small window in her chamber, he saw the tears running down her cheeks. "But what else can I do? Although a few of the men would be willing to marry me to gain children, now I canna even offer that. Whoring is all I have left."

"Here now," he said as he gently wiped the tears from her cheeks with the pads of his thumbs and stroked her hair back. "I want ye to ken that I would strangle him wi' my bare hands if he were here."

"Oh, Rob. Ye could no' harm yer own brother, even for me."

Now he did stiffen, nothing could have prevented it. She knew?

"Aye, I ken that ye are Struan's son by Dougal's wife. I kenned that the night ye left Dunnedin. And ye would no' be able to hurt Sandy if he were alive now. Ye are too honorable."

"I dinna feel honorable right now," he confessed. He knew his time was ending here and it would soon be time to go. Mayhap she would go with him back to Dunbarton. Could he offer her marriage? He was not certain of that, but he knew they could live together comfortably.

"Will ye come back wi' me to Dunbarton when I go? We

can wed there. . . ." His words drifted off; he was not sure of what to say.

She pulled from his embrace and sat up next to him. "I dinna hold ye responsible for what yer brother and his friends did to me. Ye ken we canna marry."

"Why no'? Struan doesna want me here and, unless he acknowledges me as his son, I hiv no place in the clan. Listen, Robena, I canna promise to love ye, but I would marry ye and care for ye."

"And I canna marry ye if ye dinna love me." She smiled a terribly sad smile and touched his cheek with the back of her hand. "I would want it all wi' ye, Rob. Or nothing. And ye canna offer me yer love when ye stand ready to give it to someone else."

He would have objected, but she covered his lips with her own. When she drew back from the kiss, she turned and lay close to him once more, tucking the plaid around them. What could he say? She was correct—his love was for someone else. Someone who would never know of it.

When the night was quiet around them again, she whispered something to him.

"I appreciate the comfort we share and yer offer of marriage. I thank ye, but I canna take more than what we share already here."

He held her as she fell asleep, her breaths becoming deeper and more even. And he knew he would not sleep this night as he thought over the truths he had learned. Truths about his brother, about Robena, and about Anice. And his role in all of this.

chapter 16

"H*iv mercy, Rob! There is none left to oppose ye now.*"

Brodie held up his hands in surrender from the place where he'd landed in the dirt. Only a warrior of his size and strength would be able to laugh after being pummeled into the ground before his own men. Robert stepped back from his opponent, panting from his own exertions.

Reaching down, he pulled Brodie to his feet. Once he released his friend's hand, he looked around and saw that Brodie spoke the truth—the had challenged and beat every one of the men who were assigned to the training yard this morn. Those few who were just lately watching the exercises would not meet the dare he knew shone forth in his gaze. Finally, he accepted that his attempts to wear himself out with battle were going to be unsuccessful yet again.

As he accepted a dipperful of water from one of the young boys assisting the weaponsmaster, he heard Brodie ordering the men to gather their supplies and meet outside the gate in one hour's time. Then Brodie joined him near the fence. For a time they were both silent, then Brodie turned and looked him in the eye.

"To what purpose do ye wear yerself into the ground?"

"What?" Robert asked.

"Ye ken of what I speak, Rob. Ye hiv been taking on all who would fight ye day in and day out for these last three weeks. I want to ken why."

"So I can sleep at night." That was just the beginning of the reason, Robert knew, but as much as he was ready to admit.

"I would think that Robena would be willing to tire ye out in a much better way." Brodie winked as he spoke. "Really now, this is more about rage than about wearing yerself out. And I fear ye may do injury to yerself or the men in this attempt to work out yer rage on them."

His anger rose quickly. "I wouldna harm any of them, Brodie. Ye should ken that much about me." A few broken noses and some bruises were all the suffering he'd inflicted so far, and one of the broken noses had been his own . . . twice.

"'Tis aboot yer leaving, is it no'?"

Of course it was about leaving. Leaving without being acknowledged, leaving without being accepted, leaving without her. For he could not gain one without losing any chance of the other. If named as Struan's son, even his natural one, he could take his rightful place next to his father. But that would remove Anice from him, for neither the church nor she would accept marriage due to their degree of affinity.

If he pursued Anice, there was even a chance, a very big one, that Struan would reveal his parentage just to stop them. Marriage to him would place her son under his authority and Struan definitely wanted the babe in his control. For the inheritance of the leadership of the clan was determined not only by birth, but also by abilities and the vote of the clan elders.

"Aye, 'tis aboot just that," he finally answered.

"Hiv ye decided when to return to Dunbarton?"

"I leave in three days."

"Ye dinna sound as though ye want to go."

"Weel, Brodie, I dinna hiv my choice in the matter. Struan haes made his announcements and to say otherwise would be to call the laird a liar," Robert said as he turned once more to face his friend. "And that is something I am no' willing to do before the clan."

"So, ye will hiv yerself beaten to a pulp and then leave wi'oot ever asking Struan if ye can stay?"

"Ask Struan? Me? I should, what, get on my knees and beg for a place in his hall?" Robert could barely speak the words. His blood pounded through him and he clenched his teeth against the sound of it. "Ye ken the truth of it, Brodie. Ye ken that he should be asking me to stay. And now that Sandy is dead, 'tis an even better time, a better chance for him to speak the truth of it before all."

"I ask again, hiv ye had these words with him? Hiv ye spoken since Sandy's death?"

"Nay. I've no'. Struan is either too busy to speak to me or someone is always around him." At Brodie's skeptical glance, he continued, "Or he is at Sandy's grave."

"Mayhap that is the perfect place to hiv this out at last."

He could not, would not, go to that grave. After hearing Robena's words, he feared that his rage would get the best of him and that he would desecrate the burial place. "'Tis over, Brodie. I hiv a place in Dunbarton; one that I hiv made for myself. I just hiv to let go of the anger I feel aboot no' being able to stay and make a life here."

"Can ye do that, Rob? Can ye leave it all and move on wi' yer life? Do ye even ken what ye want for yerself?"

"I want what ye hiv—a wife, a home, a bairn on the way. Not much more than that. And until Struan's summons, I was contented to find that wi' the clan MacKillop. 'Twill be enough once I return and get back to my life and duties."

That was it, he told himself. A year ago, he was preparing to make that kind of life in Dunbarton. Ada had warned him not to raise his hopes and expect more from Struan. It would have been so much easier if he had listened to her advice. Now he stood with his dreams crushed and ready to leave the very people he wanted to be with and the place that he wanted to be.

Brodie clapped him on the back and laughed. "Weel, if ye dinna hiv Moira reset that nose of yers, none of the MacKillop lasses will hiv ye." The discussion was at an end.

Robert wiped the blood that still dripped from his twice-broken nose. He would see Moira and then begin preparations for leaving. Firtha and Ramsey married in two days and he would depart the next day. Since the summer's end approached, it would be the perfect time to go. If there were such a time.

The ceilidh *to celebrate Firtha and Ramsey's vows was the* first since Sandy's death and Craig's birth so Anice chose to sit and watch the dancing. With the bairn on her lap, she sat with some of the other mothers and laughed over some of the antics of the dancers as they passed in a circle. Tapping her feet, she bounced Craig and talked to him as the music grew louder and louder. Then, with a yell, it was over and the men and women walked away chatting and laughing.

Since Ramsey was already father to three children and Firtha a widow herself, there was none of the embarrassment at the comments and suggestions offered to the newly married couple. Although she would go to live in his cottage, Firtha would continue to serve as Anice's maid and companion. That arrangement would change soon because Anice had no intention of keeping Firtha at the keep when she would be needed to care for Ramsey's children and for him as well. A wife's place . . .

It was good to see her cousin Wynda, who had traveled to be there for the festivities. Her parents had not come to Dunnedin. Indeed, she had not seen them since her own wedding and had no expectation of seeing them soon. She had lived so long with the MacKendimens that the MacNabs were part of her distant past. She belonged to Dunnedin now.

As if Anice had called her name, Wynda approached and sat next to her. Accepting her offer to hold Craig, Anice passed the babe to her and stood. A drink and some food would be welcome about now. She had missed the main meal nursing Craig and the noises her belly made told her it was time now to feed herself. Spotting Struan in his chair on the dais, she climbed the few steps to see if he needed anything. Some of the men and elders sat sprawled around him, but he had such an expression of loss and sadness on his face and in his eyes that he looked alone even within the group.

She'd never spoken to him of Sandy's death and he'd so far not brought the subject up with her, but she wondered if his son's death was the cause of his change in appearance and health. There was but one way to describe him now—Struan had grown old since Sandy died.

"Struan? Have you the need for anything? Drink? Food?" she asked as she approached. "I am about to serve myself something from the tables and would bring you something."

He blinked a few times and then looked at her. It was then she noticed the parchments in front of him on the table. They bore her father's seal. She walked closer, trying to get a better view of them, but he took notice of her curiosity and folded them together and tucked them inside his sporran.

"Nay, lass. I hiv what I need here," he said, lifting his mug for her to see.

An outbreak of laughter in the back of the hall caught her attention. She saw Robert arm-wrestling at one of the tables. Rachelle and Robena and a small group of men stood nearby cheering him on in his efforts to best Lachlan, a huge bull of a man who served as captain of the guards and who seldom lost such contests. She would like nothing better than to run down and join them in their amusement but several things stopped her.

Struan had been very clear in his feelings about her keeping to her place where Robert and the others were concerned. Also, this was Robert's last night in Dunnedin and she did not want to interrupt him and his friends. Well, that was not exactly true—she wanted to speak to him, to spend some time with him discussing his plans.

There was a part of her, deep inside and well-controlled, that wanted to ask him to stay, to work with her for the clan, to continue the only comfortable relationship she ever had or could imagine having with a man. She did not understand the animosity between Struan and him, but Struan made it clear that it was not something he would discuss.

And forcing the issue was not appropriate since the laird made all the decisions. Lady Anice knew her place and kept to it. So now she watched Robert's activities from the distance and knew that he would likely leave without exchanging so much as a word of farewell with her.

Her attempts to thank him had met with varied success. Robena was now a familiar face in the hall and her behavior was never a problem. He was leaving with a full array of clothing that fit him and was in good repair. The unexplained black eyes and broken nose she could do nothing about. Even when she asked others how he got them, she never did get a clear explanation.

"He would not stay?" she asked as Robert stood and raised his arms, the obvious winner of his challenge.

"He canna stay."

"He cannot? I do not understand, Struan. Surely you could find a place for him here. His skills are apparent in dealing with the warriors and overseeing the guards."

"He wants more than he can ever hiv here, Anice. If I asked him to stay on, 'twould bring problems for the clan." When she would have answered him, he motioned her off with a wave of his hand. "Ye dinna ken all that I ken aboot this, Anice. Remember yer place and leave the clan's affairs to those who can make those decisions."

She felt the heat rush up into her cheeks and looked away from him. Stepping back, she turned to go. The embarrassment of being dismissed by Struan in this manner, and when the others at the table clearly heard his words, drove her away.

"Anice," he called as she made her way down the steps.

"Aye, Laird." She did not turn back to face him.

"Meet me in the solar in the morning after ye break yer fast. Yer father haes sent me word of something he wishes ye to ken."

"I am not busy now, Laird. We could . . ." She turned to him now.

"Nay. The morn will be soon enough. Enjoy yer maid's celebration and see me in the morn."

A sense of foreboding filled her with wariness. What could her father have sent word about that it should not come directly to her? He knew she could read and write; there was no need to use an intermediary. Struan had made it clear that he would see her in the morning, so she decided she would retire early with the babe. Mayhap sleeping would make it go faster.

She reclaimed Craig from her cousin and took him to the

chambers they shared. It took a bit of time to calm him down from the excitement of the hall, but soon Craig was tucked in for the night. Anice climbed into her own bed and, after saying her nightly prayers, pulled the covers up and tried to sleep.

She wished she could blame it on the noise from the celebration below, but it was quiet here on the third floor. She lay in bed, listening to the wind outside her window, listening for sounds of the babe moving in his cradle nearby and even listening to the sound of her own breathing. The keep settled down for the night and she was still awake.

Anice tried pacing her room to make her relax enough to sleep. It did not work. She checked and rechecked Craig, almost hoping that he would stir and give her something to do. He had just recently begun sleeping through the whole night so he slept on, blissfully unaware of the tension gripping her. Finally, on her tenth trip to the window, she saw the lightening of the sky telling her that dawn approached.

Craig woke as the sun did and she changed and fed him and then prepared herself to meet with Struan. Her stomach was queasy with anticipation so she did not even try to eat. The great room was nearly empty, a testament to the rejoicing and drinking that took place here last night. Then she noticed Struan enter the solar, at the same time she saw Robert carrying his sack towards the doorway.

"Robert," she called out, "a moment of your time please?"

He looked as though he would refuse her, but nodded and waited for her to approach. He let his bag slip to the ground and adjusted the sword at his side and the plaid thrown over his shoulder. This close, his face looked worse than it had from afar.

"You are leaving? Now?" she asked. A lump suddenly formed in her throat.

"Aye, my . . . Anice. I thought to stay until harvest, but Struan assures me all is weel in hand now." He looked at her shoulder, he looked at her hands, but he would not look her in the eye.

"So, you would leave without a word of farewell, then?" She tried to lighten the moment by teasing him. It did not work. His expression grew even darker.

"I did no' think it wise to seek ye out. Struan haes made himself clear aboot yer place as a lady and mine as the son of the steward. Let us just say it now and I will be on my way."

"Well, then," she said, smoothing her sweaty palms against her skirt. "Godspeed go with you then, Robert. And once more, you have my thanks for all you did for me and my son." Tears began to fill her eyes and she blinked trying to clear them. This man had saved her life and her son's and was now simply leaving forever.

"Yer gratitude warms my heart, Anice, and will stay wi' me forever," he said in a voice also growing rough. He bowed to her and then picked up his sack and turned to leave. He mumbled something else but she could not understand it. When she would have asked him, she saw Struan standing in the doorway of the solar, waiting for her. She stood motionless for a moment listening to the sound of Robert's boots on the stone floor before attending to the laird's business.

Struan stood within the solar, near the large hearth on the far side of the sunny room. The windows in here magnified any rays of the sun that they were favored with and the room was bright on most days. She walked to where he stood and waited.

"Sit, lass," he said, pointing to a chair.

She did so and waited once more as he paced from the hearth to the table and back again. He carried the parchment she'd seen last evening—the one he would not let her get a look at.

"Yer faither and I hiv been working for the last few months on an agreement. This is what he sent me and bade me to speak wi' ye aboot now."

"Speak to me? About what, Struan?"

"Yer marriage to Sandy and then birthing Craig haes sealed an alliance between our clans, Anice. Ye ken?"

She nodded. That was exactly what her marriage had been—a contract between Struan and her father. Each one gained an ally, each gained clear passage through the other clan's land as well as some property that had been exchanged. She gained a husband, she thought as an uncontrolled tremor raced through her, and Sandy gained a wife and heir. She could not be sorry that he was no longer here to enjoy the fruits of his labors.

"But, yer faither needs to seal a bargain wi' the MacLarens, his neighbors to the north. Since yer marriage is over wi' Sandy, God rest his soul, he haes begun negotiations wi' the MacLaren for yer marriage to his eldest son."

Her mind fought believing the words he spoke to her. 'Twas simply not possible. She was a MacKendimen by marriage and her son would one day be laird here. She was a MacKendimen now; her place was secured as mother of the heir.

"Ye will hiv at least a year before this comes to pass, Anice. There's plenty of time to wean the bairn and see to his upbringing. The MacLaren heir haes just lost his own wife and willna be looking to marry until at least next summer. Plenty of time to work out the details and prepare for yer new life."

The room grew dark around her as she realized he spoke the truth of her father's plans. Chaos filled her thoughts and she was unable to speak as the completeness of these arrangements horrified her. They were marrying her off once more, taking her babe from her, and giving her to another man as wife.

"No' my babe," she whispered. Shaking her head, she began backing away from him. He matched her step for step and shook his own head.

"Nay, Anice. Let me explain."

"I am a MacKendimen, Struan. How can ye do this to me? Have I not done everything ye asked of me? I nearly lost my life twice for ye and this clan. How can ye . . . ?"

"Shush now, lass. There is plenty of time to think this through and come to accept the wisdom of yer elders. The babe will be weel taken care of. I will protect him and raise him as I did his faither."

"You will, Struan?" She turned and paced back and forth. "Will ye raise him to be the monster his father was? One who must be sent away in order to protect those in the clan? One who ends up dead in the mud with an arrow in his back?"

She gasped as she finally looked at Struan; his expression had turned to stone with her accusations. Struan staggered towards her and she thought her life was over. Pure rage filled his face and he raised one hand and he grabbed her blouse with the other, pulling her closer. She threw up her hands to protect herself but the blow never came.

They stood frozen there for what seemed like an eternity. She closed her eyes and could hear the wheezing breaths in his chest as he regained control of his temper. Finally, he released her and she stumbled backwards and onto the floor. Getting up on her knees, she crawled to where he stood and touched his boots.

"Please, Struan. Do not let my father do this. I beg ye for sanctuary here. As the mother of yer heir, I beg ye for help." She rubbed at her eyes and pushed her hair back from her face. "Please, Struan, please let me stay."

She felt his hands encircle her arms, pulling her to her feet. Once she had regained her balance, he let go and moved away.

"Ye are the only heir to the MacNab and the king himself haes given permission for yer faither to pursue this new alliance. I wouldna oppose ye if ye asked, and the MacLaren and his heir agreed, to keep the bairn wi' ye for some months after ye marry. If it will help ye settle in a bit easier, 'tis the least I can do for ye."

Stunned by the cruelty he offered as aid, she simply turned and walked away. Completely unable to accept any of it, she stumbled through the great room and up the stairs to her chambers. Iseabel, her new maid, stood as she entered and began to prattle about the babe. Anice did not stop her but did not hear her words either. Her mind was racing with too many emotions to listen to inane chatter. Her life was at stake once more and she needed to figure out a way to thwart these arrangements of her father's.

Finally, she took the babe in her arms and ordered Iseabel out of the rooms. Anice placed him up on her shoulder and walked to the window. Rocking back and forth, she just held on to him and searched her mind for a way out of this. But, as Struan had reminded her many, many times these last few months, she was a woman and not the one to make decisions about what happened to her or anyone else in the clan. Even her son, the one who almost cost her her life, was not hers. He was a MacKendimen, under the authority of the laird of his clan.

And she was a woman, under the authority of whichever man claimed her, be it father or husband. She should know her place.

chapter 17

He was being followed. He was certain of it now. The hairs on the back of his neck had started tingling just before sundown and now as he set up his camp for the night, he knew what that sign meant. As he watered Dubh in a stream off the path, he thought about what he would do.

Stars already filled the clear summer sky as he found a sheltered place where his horse could graze. Robert hobbled him with the reins and prepared a plain meal of oatcakes and cheese from the supplies he'd brought with him from Dunnedin. There was an abundance of food available in the forests and glens of both the MacKendimen and the MacKillop land and neither laird begrudged his people the use of those resources. He could have tracked and killed any number of small birds and game, but he had no interest in working that hard for his meal. A few oatcakes and he could retire until morning.

Well, he could have if he had not caught sight of movement far behind him on the path. Now he would need to discover who was following him. This far off the drovers' lanes, he did not expect to find any of the clan or their cattle. Most were still in the summer grazing lands to the west of

Dunnedin and would not return until the summer was done. Brodie's men had just traveled to one of the temporary villages carrying supplies meant to last those who watched over the cattle the rest of the season.

Robert ate his meager meal and waited for the moon to hang lower in the sky to cover his movements through the woods. Soon, he checked his weapons and, with sword in hand, began stealthily creeping through the trees. Careful not to make noise, he made his way for many yards until he saw a small Highland pony tied to a tree. Searching nearby, he saw a figure on the ground, tucked beneath the branches of a low tree and rolled in plaid. In the dark, he could not make out anything more of the person or the plaid. Unfortunately, he lost the element of surprise that should have been his when he stepped on a large branch and the crunching crack of it breaking traveled through the night.

He froze and waited to find out if his shadow had also heard the noise. The quick movement of the figure assured him that his mistake was heard. With a mumbled curse, the figure jumped up and, still wrapped in the length of wool, ran off towards the path. Robert followed, cursing his stupidity under his breath. Within a few strides, he had caught up with his quarry and grabbed for the tartan material that now dragged behind. The person lurched and went down, first on their knees and then, with a muffled cry, they stumbled onto the ground.

It was the babe's cry that shocked him. Robert stood, his mouth open in disbelief, listening to the squealing infant. He approached from behind and used the point of his sword to prod the person. When they did not move, he used his booted foot to turn them over. Even in the dim light, he knew Anice's face. And he knew Craig's cry, which now grew in volume and strength. Kneeling beside her still form, he lifted the babe from his place within his mother's embrace, placed him up on his own shoulder, and then he checked Anice.

A bruise already swelled on her forehead; she must have hit her head on the ground or a rock as she tumbled. Seeing how she had cushioned Craig's fall, he knew that had been her concern. He tapped her cheek but she did not respond. He sat back on his heels and tried to figure out what had happened.

Why in God's holy name was she following him in the forest? Why was she camped out here, with her bairn, alone, this far from Dunnedin? None of this made sense and until she regained consciousness, none of it would. The babe finally quieted, sucking lightly on his thumb. When he had fallen back to sleep a few minutes later, Robert laid him carefully next to Anice on the ground. He traced his path back to her resting spot and gathered the few belongings he could find and led her pony back to her.

Checking to make certain the babe slept, Robert placed a blanket over the horse's back. He found the sling she used to carry the bairn and put it around his neck as he'd seen her do. Once everything was ready, he lifted Anice from the ground and laid her over the horse, adjusting her as best he could. Then he placed the babe within the cocoon of plaid and led the pony back to his own camp.

Walking slowly so that she wasn't jostled, it took a while to reach it. Once there, he spread his own plaid on the ground and laid the babe once more on it. Lifting Anice carefully off the pony, he cushioned her head as he laid her beside the bairn. He found his waterskin and tore a piece of a linen shirt in his bag to clean her forehead. The swelling concerned him, as did her lack of response when he tried to rouse her from her stupor. Doing what he could to help her, he realized he would have to wait for his answers, for he could think of no reason that would force Anice into the forest at night with her son.

The chill grew stronger and the babe began to stir in his place on the ground. Robert knew he needed to keep both mother and son warm so he tucked another blanket over Anice and lay the babe close to her. Taking a place on the other side of the babe, he moved closer to them, sharing the warmth of his own body. His stallion nickered and then settled, now content with the pony's position nearby. Soon, the only sounds were those of the forest surrounding them and the soft breathing noises of Anice and her son. Sleep would not come to him, so Robert lay watching and listening until the sun broke over the horizon.

• • •

H*e did not know which woke him first, the wetness that* pooled on his chest or the smell of the liquid that now seeped into his shirt. Mayhap it was neither of those, but the screeching sound the bairn made in his ear when he too felt the uncomfortable coldness due to peeing in his napkin. Whichever it was, it brought Robert's short time of rest to an abrupt end. He rolled away and lifted the soggy babe away from Anice, hoping to keep her dry. Standing, he knew he needed to change the linens, but really had no idea how to do it. He found Anice's bag and searched until he found some dry ones and another gown.

He moved quickly to get the babe warm and dry and then pulled off his own soaked shirt. Tugging a fresh one from his saddlebags and pulling it on, he picked up and held the little one in his arm. Moving off a bit from where Anice lay, still apparently senseless, he lifted the edge of his shirt and relieved himself in the bushes.

"Ye see, wee one? 'Tis much easier to lift yer kilt and piss on the ground." Robert laughed for a moment at the babe's disgruntled expression. "Ye will learn soon enough to stand and do this rather than soiling yer own clothes." Finished, he carried the babe back towards Anice. "'Twill be much easier when ye wear but plaid and shirt and no' these gowns and linens."

The babe met his gaze with one of serious study and Robert laughed once more in amusement. This was the first look he'd had at Craig since that day in the yard and the babe had grown considerably since then. What had Anice called him? Oh, aye. Piglet. And that's what he looked like with his plump cheeks and belly. The tuft of hair that stood straight up on his head gave claim to his mother's coloring. Tired of staring at him, the babe began searching for his hand and the wet sucking noises warned Robert of his next impending problem. How and what would he feed the bairn?

He walked back over to where Anice lay and sat down next to her. Taking advantage of the babe's fascination with his own fists, Robert tapped her gently on the cheek. She had not moved much at all through the night, but her breathing now changed and she began mumbling words he could not understand. Calling her name, he tried to rouse her.

"Anice? Anice? Ye maun wake now. Come now, Anice, Craig is hungry and needs ye."

The mention of her son's name seemed to work, for her eyes fluttered and then opened. At first her gaze was empty but then she blinked several times, focusing on the trees above her. A loud groan filled the air as she reached for and felt the large lump on her head. Then her complexion turned ghastly and she began to gag. He helped her to sit up quickly, knowing just what was happening. Holding her shoulders, he supported her as her stomach reacted violently to her head injury. Robert had seen this many times when a man was knocked out while fighting. Dizziness and vomiting usually followed as soon as the person awoke. Anice was suffering the same. When it subsided, he guided her back to the blanket.

Before Robert could ask her any of the dozens of questions that filled his mind, Craig erupted into a sobbing cry that told them both of his hunger. Anice clenched her arms over her chest and her face was filled with embarrassment—her body was answering the babe's call for food and the milk leaking from her breasts quickly dampened her blouse. Turning away once he settled Craig on her lap, Robert built a fire so he could prepare them a meal. A few minutes later, he returned to her with a cup of watered ale. Although she accepted the cup with mumbled thanks, she would not meet his gaze. It was obvious to him that she was avoiding explanations, so he thought to start the conversation for her.

"Once the babe is fed and ye are feeling stronger, I will escort ye both back to Dunnedin."

Her terrified sob echoed through the forest around them and caused the babe to let go and scream his own displeasure and fear at being disturbed. His gaze was drawn to the babe, who settled down quickly, and to the intense sounds created by his tiny but hungry mouth on her . . . breast. He did not intend to look there, but he could not stop staring. As his mind filled, unbidden, with images and desires, welcome or not, he forced himself to his feet and away from her.

"Finish wi' the bairn and we will talk," he called back as

he walked over to the horses. Leading them to the stream, he watched as they drank their fill.

Robert berated himself for his foolish reaction to Anice nursing her son. He'd seen many women doing that and never thought twice about it. Mothers fed their children, and when mothers could not, or would not in the case of most noblewomen, a wet nurse did it for her. So why did the sight of that wee bairn sucking at his mother's breast make him breathless? Because, and he realized the deep truth of it even as the thought came to him, he wanted to be the one at her breast. Sucking for the pleasure of it, sucking to make her ready for him, to make him ready for her.

He shifted as he stood, feeling that part of him that ached to be inside her grow as his thoughts continued. Moving his gaze to the cool waters passing by did nothing to abate the fierce desire he felt for her now. This power she had to steer his thoughts to things he could not have was uncanny. He'd thought that leaving would end it. Now, she was here and all progress he'd made in his first day away from her was gone.

The horses raised their heads, indicating their thirst was quenched, so he led them back to his camp. Anice now lay on the ground, facing away from him. He walked nearer to her to check on her.

"Anice? Are ye weel?"

"Aye," she answered in almost a whisper.

"Haes the lad finished?"

"Nay, Rob. I grew too dizzy to sit up and hold him. This way works better for both of us." She looked over her shoulder at him as she spoke.

"I will hiv some porridge ready for ye soon—do ye feel up to eating?"

"Aye. Something in my belly sounds good to me now. In a short while?"

He nodded and went back to the small fire a few yards away. Taking out his cooking pan, his bag of oats, and his waterskin, he heated some water and added oats to it, cooking it until it formed a loose mix. He scooped the first batch into his cup and ate it. Once Anice had finished with her son and laid him on the plaid next to her, he made another batch and took it to her. She shifted to her side and nodded to him. He moved away once more and cleaned the pan and secured his supplies back in his saddlebags.

The tension began to build within him as he quenched the fire and finished all the tasks he could possibly do without finally talking to her. His horse was ready to leave. All he needed to do was to discover the reason she was here and when she would be ready to return to Dunnedin. He sat down on the ground near the remnants of the fire and waited. Soon only the babe's soft cooing and hiccups could be heard.

Anice slid back until she reached a place where a tree supported her back while she sat. Something was wrong with her ankle, she could feel how stiff and swollen it had become, but she would not think about that now. Leaning her throbbing head against the trunk, she wondered how to begin. How could she explain the madness that had sent her out into the wilderness to find him and seek out his help? He had already done so much, even though his displeasure was clear in every move he made and word he said. She suspected that he and Struan had not parted well and Robert was in haste to return to a more welcoming place.

"Did you offer your protection to me that night that you helped in Craig's birth?" she asked.

The memory of his words had come back to her as she stood in her room, rocking the babe and desperately trying to come up with a way out of her predicament. *Ye hiv my protection, lass. Until the bairn is born and after. As long as ye need it, I will give it.* She had mistaken him for Struan in her confused state of mind, but she knew the words had come from Robert. A clear image of his face and the memory of the sound of the words on his lips filled her.

"Anice, ye thought I was Struan. Ye were near to death." He dragged his hands through his hair as he spoke. "I said what ye needed to hear."

Then it was as she thought. She was doomed now to lose her son and all that she'd known and worked for these last many years. And, if this MacLaren heir turned out to be anything like Sandy, she would probably lose her life as well.

One wife of his was already in her grave—who knew the how or why of it.

She looked at her son as he lay near her, trying to catch the tiny dust motes in the air in his little fists, and fought to retain the control she could feel slipping. Pulling in a shaky breath, she tried to form the words she needed.

"Then you cannot help me?"

"Help ye in what, Anice? Protect ye from what or who?" His gazed drilled into her. He would expect answers from her. Would hers stir him to reject the wishes of his laird's? Or would he follow in the blind obedience of most men? He stood up and began pacing in front of her as she tried to form her explanation in her mind.

"Struan and my father have made a plan together. 'Twould seem that I still have some value as my father's only daughter. He even now negotiates a contract with the MacLaren to wed me to his heir."

Robert stopped and looked at her, his shock clear in his eyes.

"But ye hiv already married and ye hiv a son."

"Oh, aye, a son. A son who will be left behind to be raised by his father's family." A ragged sob tore free from her. "Struan has offered to let me keep him for a few months after my marriage to help me settle into my new life."

"When?" he asked.

"Since the MacLaren's heir has just lost his first wife, they will wait until summer next to finish the bargain." Sarcasm filled her voice. "Struan assures me that should be sufficient time to wean him and see to his care." She nodded at Craig, who had fallen asleep. Her little piglet, content and with a full belly, snored lightly, unaware of the turmoil around him.

Robert stopped and looked at her. "Are ye certain ye understood this? Are ye certain that this is a deed done and no' some idea being chased around?"

Part of her wanted to scream in disbelief. Did he think she was some lackwit who could not follow a discussion?

"'Tis difficult indeed to misunderstand when someone tells you that you are to be sold to the highest bidder and you must leave your son behind when you go." Her voice rose in exasperation, "Even some dim-witted man would have no problem with such a thing."

His chagrined look tempered her anger. Then she realized she was yelling at the one man who could help her. She held her head in her hands and waited, hoping some of the throbbing and dizziness would lessen. It did not.

"I beg your pardon, Robert. And the answer is aye, Struan said that these negotiations are already under way." She closed her eyes once more and leaned back against the tree, willing unsuccessfully that the pain would lessen.

"What help do ye think I can give ye, Anice? Yer own father and yer father-by-marriage seek out this alliance." He looked at her, expressionless. She did not know how he felt about this. Would he help?

"I am running away."

His mouth dropped open in shock and for a moment they just stared at each other. Then he began to laugh, in deep loud guffaws that filled the air. Craig stirred a bit and then went back to sleep. Finally Robert stopped and looked at her again.

"Women like ye do no' run away."

She stiffened at his words. "Women like me?"

"Aye, my Lady Anice. Ye were married to the next MacKendimen laird and ye gave birth to another. Ye are highborn and valuable. And ye carried Struan's heir away from Dunnedin? Ye think he'll no' come looking for ye?"

"He never sought his son's killer. Why would he seek us?"

Robert stared at her without answering and she read in his own eyes the same doubts about Sandy's death that she had. Never had a word been spoken of it between them, but doubts about the circumstances were there.

"Just because of that—ye took his grandson and his only heir. He will follow ye to the ends of the earth to regain Craig. And he may verra weel kill ye for doing it."

The blood left her face and she swayed, putting her hands on the ground to keep from falling. His words terrified her. Did she really face death if and when Struan found her? She had not considered that possibility because she thought that if she found Robert, she could convince him to help her.

"Please help me," she whispered.

He walked over and crouched down next to her. Lifting her chin with his hand, he forced her to look at him.

"The only way I can help ye is to return ye to Dunnedin and help ye come up wi' a tale about yer leaving that is no' so far-fetched that Struan canna find some way to believe it."

She shook her head. That could not be the only way out of this.

"If ye make this into some foolish woman's fear, Struan may be convinced to allow it to pass wi'oot further punishment."

"This cannot be the only way. Robert, I cannot lose my child. I cannot!"

He stood and walked away. He stood some yards away from her, staring off into the forest. He was thinking, she could see that in his expression. He talked without facing her.

"Then ye maun negotiate for yerself. Even as ye beg forgiveness for this lapse in judgment and swear to be a dutiful daughter and wife to the MacLaren heir, set yer own terms. Since boys are fostered out anyway, ask that he be wi' ye until that time. Struan can send someone as a guardian for the boy to live wi' ye and see to Craig's upbringing and care."

"But I am his mother, I will see to—"

"As a woman, ye hiv no standing when it comes to this."

His words took her breath away. No standing? She had carried and borne him, almost at the cost of her own life, and she had no say?

"Anice, I ken this is no' what ye wanted to hear but this is the only thing ye can do." He finally looked over at her.

"I cannot marry him."

There. It was out. She'd spoken the words that showed her true fear. It wasn't about losing the babe. She would lose her son as Robert described in a few years anyway. As the heir, he would be sent to the home of one of Struan's allies to grow and learn and forge relationships and bonds among that clan. The basic terror for her was once again being under the control of a husband.

She had just accustomed herself to the freedom she thought she'd earned as a widow. Now, the life that she thought lay before her was gone and another one, not of her choosing, faced her.

"Hiv ye met him?"

"Who? The MacLaren's son?" At his nod, she answered, "Aye, I met him at my own wedding. He came and brought his wife wi' him. Have you?"

"Aye. He haes come to Dunbarton often. I hunted wi' him and his brother several times."

"What do you think of him?" Mayhap Robert could give her some indication of what she would face if she returned and did as the dutiful daughter should. Not that she would. . . .

"He seemed a fair mon, no' too quick to anger or boastful. I never saw him drink to excess. And I never saw him abuse his horse or those who served him."

"He does not abuse his horse or servants? And that is supposed to give me hope for a good union with the man?" She tried to make senses of his words. Men saw things in such a strange way.

"'Tis important indeed. Sometimes the true measure of a mon can be seen in how he treats those who cannot answer back."

"And his wife? How did he treat her? As good as his horse? Not so good as the servants?" The sarcasm was back in her voice, much as she tried to control it.

"I did no' see him wi' her." When she started to glare at him, he held up his hand. "But I do remember him speaking highly of her before she took ill."

She was probably going to have to content herself with his slight recollection of Angus and his wife. She did not remember the woman; she had met her but once and they were among many visitors who attended her wedding. It did not matter. If she returned to Dunnedin and her father's control, she would marry where he said whether the man be righteous or another monster.

"I cannot go back, Robert."

"Ye maun. There is no other way." He stood his ground in the argument and in front of her. "Anice, what were ye thinking, to do such a foolish thing? I thought ye were sensible."

He shook his head and looked at her with an expression of disappointment. And his disapproval hurt her in some way. She had not thought. She could not. She was in such a panic that she had simply acted. Her only thought had been to escape, and then she'd remembered that he was heading northeast to Dunbarton. His words promising protection had come back to her and she knew only that if she could find him, he would help her. Mayhap she could find shelter in some convent or with another clan.

"I did not think this out. I panicked and ran."

"Aye, ye did no' plan weel either. For if no' me on the trail, ye might hiv run into who knows what. Ye would be fair game for anyone who found ye. That surely would be a fate worse than marrying the mon yer father chose?"

It was over. Her only chance of escape was really not a possibility. She had dreamed it, created it within her own mind, and then pursued something that could never happen. She brought her knees up and leaned her head down on them. Thankfully the babe still slept, for she had not the strength to deal with him and his needs at this moment. Taking a deep breath, she tried to calm herself. Tears flowed freely now and soon the sobbing cries broke out. She did not even try to stop them.

"Here now, Anice. Take this and wipe yer tears," he said as he pressed a cloth into her hand. "Yer head must be paining ye terribly and I hiv no' even done anything to help ye get cleaned up."

A wet cloth followed for her head. As the coldness of the stream's water pressed against the bump on her forehead, it did soothe some of the pain. A few minutes later, another icy compress replaced the first. Mayhap it was the cold or the dampness, but very soon Anice realized that her body had needs to be seen to. She lifted her head to see where Robert was.

"Robert, I must . . ."

"Here, let me help ye to yer feet. Ye can see to yer needs near the stream." He nodded his head off to the left. Reaching out his hands, he took hers and gently pulled her up.

The forest spun around her as she tried to get her balance. Her stomach clenched and she thought she'd be sick all over Robert, but it calmed a few seconds later. Her ankle, however, had been twisted in the fall and would not hold her weight. She gasped at the pain.

"Yer head?"

"Nay, my ankle. 'Tis twisted. I fear I cannot walk on it."

She sat back down and he crouched once more in front of her with his hands outstretched. Anice held out the injured part and braced herself as he touched it. His fingers were warm and strong as they pressed around the joint, seeking a break in the bones. He moved it within his grasp to see how it functioned. Soon he put her foot down. She let out the breath she did not know she held.

"I feel no broken bones and the swelling, though painful, is no' severe. Here, let me help ye to the stream and I will bind it for ye after ye finish there."

It took more time than she thought it would to get there, take care of her needs, clean up, and then return to the campsite. Robert had assisted her in getting there, but left her alone for privacy. She stumbled along, putting most of her weight on the uninjured ankle, to find Robert holding Craig up in the air and mumbling at him. The babe's response was to drool on him. She felt her strength waning as she finished changing Craig. She was about to take his soiled clothing to the stream to wash it when Robert stopped her.

"Yer color has gone pale, Anice. Why do you no' take a short rest before we leave?"

"Leave?" She felt light-headed at the very thought of going back.

"Since we are closer to Dunbarton, I thought we should go there and send word back to Struan. There is a hunter's croft not far into MacKillop land where we can stay the night and reach Dunbarton sometime tomorrow." He looked at her, apparently waiting for her agreement.

"If we must. . . . If there is no other way. . . . ?" She prayed to the Almighty that one of them would think of some other way.

He just grunted and moved away. She lay down and brought her son near. Soon a plaid was thrown over them and covered them against any chill in the shade on this summer's day in the Highlands. Craig would need to eat again in a short while, but she should be able to rest for a while. Mayhap that would help the throbbing in her head and the aching in her heart.

chapter 18

If she'd cut his heart out with a spoon, it could not have hurt any more than it did now. Every word, every glance, every plea she begged of him, tore into his soul and left him in shreds. Even now, it hurt to glance over at her as she rode next to him and see the defeat and desperation in her eyes.

But what choice did he have in this?

Struan would be out searching for her as soon as her absence was noticed. He had his own suspicions about why Struan never pursued Sandy's killer, but he could not let this go. It would not take long before Struan began to suspect that they might be together. And what he'd told her was true—she could be killed for what she'd done.

Robert looked overhead, trying to gauge the setting sun's position and how much time they had left to reach the croft before dark. It had been difficult for Anice to sit on her pony because of her head injury. He had offered to take her up before him but she refused. Now he was about to insist or they would face another night in the forest.

He forced himself to look at her once more. She cradled the babe within the sling in front of her. Craig's behavior had been most accommodating so far; he'd slept and ate or he'd lain within his plaid wrapper lulled into compliance by the soft rocking motion of the pony's walk. He would be ready to eat soon and Robert hoped that Anice's endurance would not give out yet.

He slowed Dubh down to come next to her. She looked over at him with the same fearful expression he'd seen so many times during her pregnancy. Seeing it again reminded him of how much he hated it.

"Come, ride wi' me." He held out his hands to help her over.

"Nay." She shook her head to emphasize her refusal.

He simply leaned over and lifted her and the babe onto his lap. She turned to rock in his arms, not moving, not resting back against him even when he urged his stallion forward. The feel of her in his arms was simply too much to ignore. He urged her with gentle motions to lean back. Her exhaustion must have won the argument for a few minutes later, she did rest against him.

"We can get to the croft much faster this way, Anice. I dinna want ye and the babe wi'oot shelter tonight. From the feel of the wind, a storm is coming our way."

She nodded but said nothing. With her positioned on his spread legs, he could hardly breathe. 'Twas not her weight that caused it of course, but the thoughts that ran rampant in his mind. And his body responded. The ride was both heaven and hell.

T*hey arrived at the croft just after sunset and not a moment* too soon. Robert had no sooner watered and fed the horses and placed them in the lean-to behind the croft, than the skies opened and poured down rain. The small cottage would offer them shelter and some measure of comfort against the weather for the night. He could go to the keep tomorrow and get some additional supplies and food.

He put some peat in the small hearth and, with a flint, finally got it burning. Once that was started, he set out to make up a sleeping area for Anice and the babe. Using a wooden pallet in one corner, he spread out the several blankets they had between them and then offered it to her with a motion of his hand. She had stopped speaking to him or the babe several hours ago. Walking slowly over to the platform, she lifted the babe out and laid him on the makeshift bed.

Robert busied himself with the food while she changed the babe once more. Some stores of flour and oats were sealed in stone jars up on a shelf and he helped himself to what he needed. This cottage was kept stocked at all times for any of the clan who traveled or hunted in the hunting grounds nearby.

He held out his waterskin to her and waited for her to drink her fill. She'd told him that she needed more to drink since she was nursing. So, each time he thought of it, he offered something to her. If her milk dried up now, it would be disastrous. Their meal was simple—more porridge, more hard cheese, and some watered ale. He was exhausted and longed for sleep but he wanted her and the babe to settle down before he did. Part of him suspected that she might try to escape in the night, so he planned to sleep in front of the door.

For now, he stood in the doorway and listened as the rain poured down around them, on the trees and the bushes and onto the ground. He tried very hard not to listen to the noises of the babe behind him, feeding once more. He tried to force the images of that from his mind, to no avail. This would be another long and restless night.

Soon, she and Craig lay huddled together under several layers of wool, protected by the tartan's weave from wet and cold. He spread another on the packed-dirt floor and blocked the door. Robert was certain that sleep would not come, but soon he felt his body relaxing into it. Then her voice sliced the silence.

"He thought I'd given myself to someone else before him." Robert did not understand her meaning.

"Who did?"

"Sandy. Two years ago, we were visited by a distant cousin who looked enough like Sandy to be mistaken for him." Her voice lacked any emotion or variation and it frightened him. "Alex MacKendimen," she said with a sigh, "was the heir that the clan wanted, but could not have."

"Who was he, Anice?"

"Moira said he was a distant cousin who came here with

his leman, Maggie. I do not know the whole of it, but he left here after several months and we never saw him again."

"And Sandy thought ye'd given yerself to him, believing him yer betrothed?" He heard the rustling of the covers as she moved on her pallet. He thought she now sat up but 'twas so dark he could not tell for certain.

"No matter who tried to tell him or how many times they reassured him, he claimed I was a whore and would pay for humiliating him before the clan with my disgusting behavior."

"What did Struan do to protect ye? Surely he—"

"He sent Sandy back to England for a year to try to calm his anger down." She paused and he waited for what he knew was coming. "He came for the wedding in even more of a rage for being held off."

"Anice, ye dinna hiv to speak of this."

"But I do, Robert. You must know why I cannot return and put myself under another man's control. I would rather . . ." She stopped and he could hear that her breathing had grown ragged. When it calmed, she began again.

"He beat me first and then forced himself inside of me before I even knew what happened. My struggles seemed to excite him and he did things to me and forced me to do things I had never even dreamed possible between a man and woman. He said over and over that my behavior with Alex was the reason for it. And he told me that he would do this any time he wanted since I was now his wife."

He gagged listening to her haunted words. He wanted her to stop, but part of him knew she needed to say the words. He forced himself to remain quiet.

"He punished me when I gave up fighting. He even threatened to share me with the men he'd brought back with him from England."

The same men who had brutalized Robena the night before the wedding, he thought.

"And over and over he told me that this would be my fate with him. To be taken as he wanted, to be beaten at his whim, to be shared whenever I did not please him. Until parted by death, he said. Just like in our vows. *Until parted by death.*"

His forehead was clammy with sweat and he sat up. His stomach rolled and lurched now, sickened almost beyond his control. He would have killed Sandy dozens of times over if he'd been alive. For Anice, for Robena. How could Struan have stood by and let this happen?

"Firtha found me the next morning when Sandy left the room and called Moira and Struan. Moira saved my life, but I did not want to live, facing that kind of hellish existence with him. So, a few days after that I decided that I would separate us by death and I cut my own wrists."

He could not help the gasp that was torn from him by her words. Dear God in heaven, she had tried to end her own life? That was the gravest sin a soul could commit. The church even taught that it was worse in the eyes of God than killing someone else. Killing could be justified in many circumstances, but not taking one's own life. Those who committed suicide were buried in unblessed ground, exiled for eternity from all who they loved in life.

And his monster-brother had driven this innocent young girl to such a fate. He hoped Sandy was burning in the everlasting fires of hell right now for all the destruction he caused during his life.

"Firtha found me again, but it was only when Struan pledged his protection of me that I decided to try to live. Those weeks are cloaked in darkness for me; I do not remember much of them at all."

She took a long deep breath in and let it out slowly. He could not breathe easily.

"'Twas when I found out that I was with child that I grasped at life and tried to function once more within the clan. But the carrying was more difficult. Moira said the damage he caused inside me was to blame for the hard pregnancy."

Robert immediately thought of what Sandy's damage had done to Robena as well. He could only imagine, nay, he could not even begin to imagine what his brother had done or why. Another wave of cold sweat poured over him and he got to his feet, knowing what was about to happen.

"You needed to know the truth of why I can never marry again. I have never been able to bring myself to confess my sin and I could not in good conscience enter into marriage with a man who did not know the truth. The most frightening thing to me even now is that I know that I would rather end my life than go through that horror again."

He pushed open the thin wooden door and ran out into the still-raging storm. The sting of the frigid downpour could not calm his rage. He ran until he could run no more and then bent over and vomited up the contents of his stomach. The dry heaving continued for many minutes until he could no longer stand. He sank to his knees in the mud and waited for his body's reaction to Anice's words to cease.

Soon he could breathe again and he sat back on his heels, allowing the rain to stream over him. Drenched through to the skin, he felt the biting drops and the weight of his plaid as it sopped up the moisture, but he could not gather enough strength to take cover.

Anice's description of Sandy's behavior and attack had seared him. Unwilling to hear it and unable to ignore her voice, Robert could sense the desperation that she felt. It was not so much in her words as in the complete lack of emotion. She recited the events of her wedding night as though she'd watched it happen to another person and had not suffered the blows delivered by her husband.

His brother.

A shiver wracked his body, whether caused by the rain or the horror, he did not know. And what could he do now that he knew? Could he return her as he'd planned to when he first found her? Although he knew that Angus MacLaren was a decent man and that no one spit on the ground and crossed themselves when his name was mentioned, he realized that was not enough to bring Anice any sense of security for her future. And, could he take her back knowing it was to give her to another?

Robert leaned his face up and let the rain wash over it once more. Filling his mouth and spitting out the vile taste within it, he rose to his feet and tried to gauge his location. He'd run along the muddy trail, so he began the walk back to the croft. The storm lessened as he trudged slowly, following the path in the darkness, and when he reached the small hut, the rain had lessened to a drizzle. He unwrapped his plaid and wrung out as much of the water as he could. Hanging it over the ledge of one of the windows, he tugged the sodden shirt over his head and did the same. Trying to be as quiet as possible, he opened the door and crept to the pile of wool he'd left on the floor.

He wrapped himself in one of the covers and lay on his back listening to the sounds of the night return as the storm moved on through the glen. Rain dripping from trees into puddles, the cries of the birds of night echoing in the air, and the soft snoring of mother and child filled the croft. He thought over his choices. He actually had none—he had no place in this decision to barter her off to another clan for property and power. By the laws of God and king, her father could do as he wanted with her now that she was free from her marriage. And Struan was within his rights as laird of the MacKendimens to keep his grandson and heir with him when she left.

But knowing they could do this did not diminish his own belief that it was wrong. If not the deed, then the timing of it. He felt certain that if given enough time, Anice could reconcile herself to marrying again. Many women did after becoming widows; even her maid and friend Firtha had. With sufficient time to adjust and to witness the good marriages around her and to familiarize herself with the man who would marry her, Anice could tame her fears.

Time, however, was the one thing Anice did not have. He knew that once she and the bairn were known to be missing, Struan would have men searching for her. He would send to the summer shielings in the grazing lands, he would search all of Dunnedin and the surrounding areas, and he would send messengers out to his allies with word of her disappearance. Robert was certain that those messages would reach the MacKillop before he did.

Turning to his side, he tried to fall asleep even as his thoughts still churned away in his mind. The one thought that seemed to dominate was that he had no standing in this. His obligation was to return her to her clan and their decision of her future. Complicating that clear duty was the knowledge that she had lost all bargaining power she might have had with this rash move. Even as he suggested she negotiate with Struan to keep her son, he knew that it would not happen now. Craig would be stripped from her and given to some other woman to care for and Anice would be taken, forcibly if needed, back to her father—all for defying those who had the right to control her life.

And, if her words were true, that would send her back to the only option she thought she had. She'd tried once to end her life and he doubted not that she would try again. Especially, he thought, if her son was taken from her. He shuddered at such a sin. How could he bear it, knowing he'd brought her to it? Letting out a long frustrated breath, he searched his mind for a way to help her. He knew he was the only one who could. But how? How could he get her out of this situation with her life and her ties to her son intact?

chapter 19

The soft voice and loving words sounded like a song. He smiled, still in that time between awake and asleep, and listened, without letting her know, as Anice talked to her son. There were no words he recognized in what she said, but the babe did not seem to mind. Craig focused on her mouth as though he understood every sound she made. Then the croft was filled with his laughter; small giggles shook the babe's body and made Robert want to laugh with him. Anice just smiled and leaned down to kiss Craig's forehead. When she looked up, their gazes locked.

The nasty bruise drew his attention—its color and shape looked lessened since yesterday, but it must still have been painful. Set on her white skin, it increased the paleness of her complexion. His gaze drifted over her face and neck and down to the opening in her blouse. It was obvious she'd been nursing her son for the laces were loose and it hung down on one shoulder, exposing more than that to him. Startled by a burp from the babe, he looked up and saw that she noticed where his eyes had been looking. She tugged on the laces, bringing the edges of the blouse together and removing that creamy shoulder and breast from his inspection.

Clearing his throat, he sat up, ready to apologize for his wayward glance. His body had reacted quickly and he dared not stand up for fear of exposing himself to her. Settling the folds of the plaid more securely over certain places, he nodded a greeting to her.

"I hope we did not wake you, Robert. Craig is at his most pleasant in the morn." Her voice was light, but no smile filled her face now.

"Och, nay. I rarely sleep past dawn. 'Twas the light of day that woke me." He looked around for his saddlebags and a shirt, but could not find them. And he did not want to rise in the condition he found himself in now.

"Here, Rob," she said as she stood up in front of him. Limping slightly, she took a few steps to the small table and handed him his bag. "You still have two clean shirts in there."

"Are ye certain ye should be walking yet, Anice? Ye twisted that ankle just a day ago."

"It is sore. But I can walk if I take it slowly. And the wrapping you did yesterday surely made it feel better."

She lifted her skirts slightly to show him the ankle was still wrapped. The last thing he needed right now was to see a peek of her shapely legs. His body was already afire and that just made him even hotter. He shifted his position, trying to figure out how he could stand without horrifying her with his physical reaction.

"I must . . ." she stuttered, pointing to the woods. "Can you watch Craig for just a few minutes or should I take him?"

"Dinna be foolish, Anice. Ye canna carry him and attend to yer needs. Leave him wi' me." She nodded and he continued, "There is a stream some yards right through that gap in the trees. Ye may want to wash up there, but hiv a care. It may be swollen from the storm."

She nodded wordlessly at him, picked up a sack that, judging from the smell, held some of the bairn's soiled clothing, and took it with her. Once she was out of sight, he let go of his covers and stood. He wanted to blame his erection on the morning. He woke with one most mornings even if sated when he went to sleep. But, in truth, he knew it was her. Holding her on his lap yesterday, and the feel of her rocking against him, had made him hard for most of the ride. Seeing that glimpse of shoulder and breast and leg was enough to make him more uncomfortable.

Robert was dressed in a few minutes and then went over to where Craig lay, playing now with his toes and jamming his fist in his mouth. It was interesting how babes could look so carefree one second and then so needful the next. He took advantage of the quiet contentedness to organize his bags and Anice's and come up with a list of supplies and food they would need if they remained at the croft. He was still not certain about what to do, but returning her to Dunnedin or even to Dunbarton immediately was not part of it.

When he saw her hobbling back through the trees, he went out to help her. Taking the wet clothes from her, he offered her his arm for support. She hesitated for a second and then held on to him as she made her way back to the croft. She reached for the clothing but he stopped her.

"I will see to these, Anice. Ye maun rest." She'd pulled her hair back and bundled it tightly at her neck. The severity of the look simply emphasized her injury.

"Robert, I am fine."

"The dizziness is gone?" He scrutinized her closely.

"Aye. Other than an ache in my head when I tilt it, I am well."

As he spread the babe's clothing out on some branches, Anice went inside the cottage. He realized he'd never even spoken of how she'd been injured.

"'Tis sorry I am aboot yer head. I did no' ken that ye were the one on the ground or I would've approached ye differently."

Anice came out with Craig on her hip. "And I was asleep when you came near. I knew you were close by but the noise frightened me awake. I did not know it was you."

"Why did ye no' simply catch up with me on the road, Anice? Dear God, when I think of ye and the bairn spending a night alone wi'oot cover or protection, I . . ." His words drifted off.

She patted the babe on the back and shrugged. "As I said, I panicked, Robert. I did not think at all. I did not want you to find me until I was far enough not to be returned to Dunnedin."

He could see her eyes beginning to fill with tears and her efforts not to let it show. He hung the last gown over a branch and turned to her.

"I maun go to Dunbarton today. I want ye to stay here. . . ." She began shaking her head even before he finished. "Ye came to me for help, Anice. Let me try to find a way for ye in this."

She grabbed his arm with her free hand. "Robert, I cannot go back."

"Ye may hiv no choice in this."

She dropped her hand and turned away from him, rocking the babe.

"Ye maun trust me for a day, Anice. I will see what messages Struan haes sent out to his allies and see his intent from those."

"But the MacKillop is one of his friends."

"Aye, but the MacKillop will listen to me first. I need yer word that ye will be here when I return."

Anice turned to face him and her face wore that defeated expression once more. He hated it. He hated what he might have to do. She met his gaze and nodded.

"Let's see to a meal and then I'll be on my way. The sooner I get there, the sooner I can return here to ye and the babe."

The next hour passed quickly as they each carried out tasks that would organize them for the day; they refilled their waterskins, prepared a meal, saw to their animals, and then ate in silence. Soon, he put on his sword and mounted his stallion and headed for Dunbarton. He could not look back.

S*he watched as he rode away. She kept her eyes upon him* until she could no longer see him moving along the forest path. Her son cooed and gurgled in that language of babes and had no cares in the world. Perched on her shoulder, he raised his head and looked around as though he knew something or someone was missing from their world.

Would he miss her when she was gone? Although she'd like to convince herself that he knew her as his mother, the reasoning part of her understood that he would seek nourishment from whomever provided it. And when he was old enough, he would call someone else mother.

Her breath hitched as she tried not to cry. Craig was very sensitive to her mood and since he'd been so accommodating so far on the wild adventure, she did not want him to become upset. She just did not know what to do.

Mayhap this was God's way of punishing her for not confessing her sin. She may not have taken her own life, but a part of her would die if they took the babe from her. Or was this punishment for some other shortcoming—her inordinate pride years ago when she first came to Dunnedin? Her refusal to submit to her husband's demands? She would not presume to know the mind of the Almighty. What could she do?

Anice thought of her choices. She could run away again, from here, without Robert. She could return and try to come to her own agreement with her father and Struan about keeping the babe with her when she married. She could simply return and submit to the wisdom of those in charge of her life. Or she could finish what she started on that night long ago when faced with the same kinds of choices she had now.

Craig was dozing off to sleep, so she gently laid him down on the blanketed pallet and tucked the covers around him to keep him secure. His newest trick was to roll from his belly when waking and she wanted to make certain he was safe. She walked outside and into the scattered sunlight within the canopy of trees.

She knew that she had only until the time when Robert returned from seeing the MacKillop to make her decision. Once back, he would prevent her from her one choice and if her suspicions were correct, he would be forced by honor and obedience to the clan to take her back, whether she wanted to go or not. So, she thought as she paced in front of the small hunting croft, she had until sundown.

Could she live now that her dreams of raising Craig within the MacKendimen clan were shattered? Could she live without her son? How would he fare if she were not alive to keep watch over him, even if from afar? And would they tell him the truth about his mother's death?

Too many questions filled her. Too many possibilities, and not enough freedom to choose the one she wanted, faced her.

Sundown was not far enough off to make these weighty decisions.

He dismounted in one movement and waited as a stable-boy came to take Dubh from him. Robert greeted many as he strode into the keep and up the familiar stairs that would take him to the main floor. It felt good to return here. The sights and sounds, even the smells welcomed him back to Dunbarton. After asking for the laird, Robert was directed to the solar and walked there briskly. This needed to be handled correctly in order to keep events under control and Anice safe. He knocked and entered when one of Lady Margaret's servingwomen opened it for him.

"Lady Margaret, how do ye fare?" he asked as he bowed before her.

"Ah, Robert lad, ye are a sight to behold after a long absence. It does me good to see ye returned to Dunbarton. Tell me," the laird's wife asked, "did the MacKendimen treat ye weel?"

"No' as weel as I hiv been treated by ye, my lady." He winked at her, which he knew would make her laugh. Lady Margaret had always held a soft spot in her heart for him and he knew that she had interceded on his behalf many times during his stay there.

"Then 'twould serve them right for ye to stay here wi' us, lad."

"Margaret, leave Robert be. He's been on the road for two days and is probably thirsty and hungry. Welcome back." Duncan MacKillop offered his hand to Robert and grasped his in a firm hold. "'Tis good to see ye back."

"Laird" was all Robert could say. He was somewhat overcome by the warmth of the welcome and knew once more that his place here was secure.

"Margaret? If ye are done here, may I speak wi' Robert in private?"

Lady Margaret gave her husband a knowing look and motioned to her entourage to gather up their things and follow her. In a few minutes and after a flurry of skirts and women, Robert was alone with the MacKillop.

"Some surprising news haes come from Dunnedin, Robert. Did ye ken that the Lady Anice and her child are missing?"

"Missing? From Dunnedin?" Robert repeated the words, not daring to look Duncan in the eye.

"Aye. Struan haes sent out searchers and messengers, but no trace of her could be found. He thought that she might hiv accompanied ye here."

Robert shifted on his feet and walked to a small serving table under the window. Lifting up a pitcher, he offered it to the laird and then poured each of them a cup of the ale. He did not want to lie to Duncan. The man had been more than fair with him and offered him more than his own father had in life. To lie to him would be to break the bond between them and Robert could not do that.

"Laird . . . Duncan . . . give me a day to bring her to ye. That is all I ask."

He handed Duncan one of the cups and finally gathered enough courage to look him in the face. Duncan wore a wistful expression; there was not the anger he expected to see. Neither did he see disappointment or disapproval there, for which he was deeply grateful.

"Why a day, Rob?"

"She was injured and needs time to regain her strength before facing the repercussions of her act."

"Did ye take her from Dunnedin? I got the distinct impression that Struan thought so from the tone of his message." Duncan swallowed deeply from his cup, but his gaze never left Robert.

"She found me on the road. I had nothing to do wi' her leaving."

"Weel then, fine. I sent the messenger back to Struan and told him I would send word if we found the missing lady and babe. Tomorrow would be soon enough to find the lass."

"Thank ye, Duncan." Robert drank the last of his ale and put the cup back on the table.

"Do ye hiv need of anything to aid the lady? Does she need a healer perchance? Mayhap Ada can give her injuries the care they need . . .?"

Duncan's voice took on a strange tone. Robert felt as

though he were telling him to seek out Ada for some reason. Not for her healing abilities. For something else.

"I will ask Ada for help, Duncan. Thank ye for yer indulgence in this."

Duncan slapped him on the back and walked towards the door with him. Stopping a few steps away and letting Robert go on without him, Duncan stayed in the solar. Robert was almost out the door when Duncan's words reached him.

"For a moment there when ye came in, I felt at least a score and five years younger and thought my good friend Struan was here to call on me."

Robert turned and looked at the MacKillop.

"The resemblance is there for anyone to see, Robert. If they look closely enough."

Duncan smiled and chills passed over Robert's skin. Gooseflesh was raised everywhere as some of the implications of Duncan's words sank into his mind. He knew the truth? Before he could ask any of the dozens of questions that raced within his heart and head, Duncan nodded and closed the door, effectively stopping any discussion of his revelation.

Robert left the solar and headed for the kitchens; someone there would know Ada's whereabouts. Once in the cooking area, though, his stomach began rumbling loudly at the appealing smells and aromas surrounding him. Several of the servingwomen offered him food and he sat down and accepted the well-cooked meat and hot bread from them. Two days of oatcakes and porridge had left him deeply hungry. He finished quickly and asked for some food to be packed for his trip back to Anice and made arrangements to pick it up as soon as he talked with Ada.

Walking through the yard, he approached the small stone chapel where he was told he would find the old woman. Stepping into the cool darkness within, he saw her sitting on a bench near the altar. Other than the two of them, the chapel was empty.

"Are ye waiting for a priest?" he asked quietly as he walked up the center aisle.

"Nay, boy, I was waiting for ye. 'Tis good to see ye returned." She stood and gathered him within her embrace.

Since she was so much shorter than he, her head lay on his chest.

"Ada, I hiv missed yer counsel these last months in Dunnedin. How do ye fare?"

"I am weel, Rob. How is the Lady Anice?"

He could feel the blood drain from his face at her question. He moved back away from her and sunk onto a stone bench. "How did ye ken?"

"Ah, lad. 'Twas plain to me that ye were in love wi' her already when ye saved her and her bairn. When I heard she was missing from Dunnedin and kenned ye were on yer way here, I just thought she would be wi' ye." She paused and looked at him. "Am I wrong then?"

"Ye are most likely wrong aboot how it all happened but ye are right that she is here." He looked at her. "She left on her own, running away from her father and Struan's plan to marry her off to the MacLaren heir."

"Angus MacLaren?"

"Aye. Struan would keep her bairn and she would marry Angus. Next summer if everything is worked out between them."

"Angus is a fair mon. Would he force himself on the lass, do ye think?"

"Ada, I dinna ken what part he has in this. I dinna even ken if he wants to marry her. I only ken that Anice panicked, took her son, and left Dunnedin wi'oot Struan's kenning or permission, once she heard the news. She caught up wi' me on the road here and begged my help."

"And will ye give it?"

Robert let out a breath. That was the question that he pondered most of the night and during the hours it took him to reach here. Now he knew the answer.

"Aye, I will. I dinna ken how, but I want to help her."

"Is there a way to stop the betrothal? Mayhap that would give ye time to come up wi' some way of helping her. Mayhap ye could speak to Angus and ask his cooperation in waiting to wed her until she is ready?"

"After what Anice told me last night, she will never be ready for another marriage."

"'Tis a shame that," Ada answered. "For I can only think

that a marriage to someone else is the way to stop the one she doesna want."

"She would never agree. She lives in absolute fear of submitting to a husband." Robert shook his head. There was no one he could think of who was both suitable and safe for Anice.

Ada sat next to him and looked at him. She did not speak for several minutes and then she smiled.

"She would no' fear marrying the mon who saved her life and her bairn's."

"Are ye daft, Ada? She is my brother's wife. Even if she would agree to it, we canna marry."

Robert leaned back against the cold stone wall behind him and closed his eyes. The longing within him threatened to overwhelm him. Marrying her would be his fondest desire. To live with her as husband and wife would fulfill the dreams he had hidden for many months. But his connection to Struan and Sandy made it impossible. For a woman could not marry her dead husband's sibling, even one who was illegitimate. His choice of her, and the place within the clan he would gain through acknowledgment, was as impossible now as before. And wishing it to be done could not make it so.

"She is yer brother's widow. The old church teaches that 'tis a mon's responsibility to care for his dead brother's family. 'Tis a long-held custom, Robert, one still honored and even practiced by many here in Dunbarton."

"But Anice doesna practice the old church, Ada. Nor would Struan or the MacNab recognize the marriage. I fear 'tis just folly to believe it could be the way." He tamped down the longing and knew it would never work out.

"Do ye love her, lad?"

He nodded, unable to speak the words.

"Would ye hiv her as wife?"

Again, he nodded.

"Then seek out Faither Cleirach before ye rule this as something impossible. Hear his words and decide." When he would have argued, she added, "She can consent to the marriage and not ken that ye and Sandy were brothers. Mayhap that would soothe yer mind."

"Ye are suggesting that I deceive her into marriage?"

"Nay, no' that. Just tell her that Faither Cleirach will hear yer vows wi'oot the posting of banns or the witnesses. Ye can be married before she returns to Dunnedin and ye can face Struan as man and wife."

"And will he?" He must be crazy to even begin to let thoughts of this into his mind. He could only blame it on his desire and love for her.

"Are ye willing to give up yer dream of being named as Struan's son?"

She brought up the worst of it. He would need to forget about being Struan's son, and the one who should be heir, in order to have her. For although there may be a priest willing to hear the vows and declare them married, forcing his true identity on the clan would be asking for trouble. Her father could seek an annulment if he knew the truth. So, he could hope to one day take his place among the clan as the son of the laird, or he could marry her and keep his secret forever.

"If she will hiv me to husband, I will."

chapter 20

The sound of hoofs moving down the now-dried path woke her from her sleep. 'Twas still twilight outside, due more to the season, she suspected, than the time. She stood and gathered a plain shawl around her shoulders against the chill. She stayed back in the shadows of the doorway until she could see who approached. From the size and shape of the man on the horse, she knew it was him. Robert had returned and now she would know her fate.

He drew up close to the croft and pulled the stallion to a halt. Jumping to the ground, he loosened several sacks that were tied to his saddle and carried them inside. She reached out to take them from him.

"Food for us, Anice. I am hungry and certain that ye maun be as weel. I will see to Dubh and be back shortly."

She could only nod at his words and watch him walk out of the cottage. Food? How could she eat with her life hanging in the balance? Men were so strange; their stomachs and their cocks seemed to control their lives. One appetite or the other had to be satisfied almost every waking hour of each day. 'Twas a wonder to her that they accomplished anything at all besides eating and tupping.

Anice opened the sacks and checked inside each one. Finding some roasted pigeons and bread, she placed the food on one of the wraps on the table. She found a round of yellow cheese and added it to the rest. She pulled a bench closer and sat. Robert entered a few minutes later, carrying more supplies and two skins.

"Good, ye found the candles," Robert said, pointing at the few tallow lengths she had used to light the cottage. "I forgot they were usually stored here when we arrived so late last night. How is the bairn?"

"Asleep for the night."

He simply grunted and seated himself opposite her. Tearing off a chunk of bread, he stuffed it in his mouth and followed it with a mouthful from one of the skins. Her stomach tightened with every passing moment. Was he going to eat a complete meal without telling her anything? She stared at his movements as his hands went between the food and his mouth. After a few times, she slammed her hands on the table and stood.

"Is something wrong, mil . . . Anice?"

"Wrong? I have been sitting here all day waiting for you to return with a plan and you eat?"

She realized her tone of voice too late to stop it. But instead of anger, Robert's face lightened at her words. She frowned, thoroughly confused.

"I thought ye might be hungry after three days of nothing more than oatcakes and water. And ye had this set out and ready for me. Are ye no' ready to eat then?"

She tried to tamp down her impatience—he had been on the road all day while she stayed here resting and caring for the bairn. Once she had realized that she no longer had the courage or desire to take her own life, a sense of anticipation had grown within her. Surely there was some dread mixed in with it, since she did not know if she could convince her father and Struan to let her keep the babe with her, no matter who they married her to. She hoped that Angus would be accepting enough to allow his new wife to bring her bairn with her to their home. Any number of things could go wrong, but she knew now that her focus must stay on keeping her son.

She shook her head. "Robert, truthfully, I could not eat a bite. My stomach rebels even at the smell."

He stood at her words and wiped his hands on the napkin holding the food. "Come then, let's step outside and speak."

She looked over at her son and then back at him.

"We will stay close enough to hear him if he haes need of ye."

Robert opened the door and Anice followed him through. The night sky was clear and the half moon shed its beams over the forest. A light breeze added a chill to the air and Anice gathered her shawl closer around her shoulders. He walked a few paces away from the cottage and stopped near the path. She held her breath and waited for his words.

"I spoke wi' the MacKillop and he haes given me until tomorrow to 'find' ye."

"Find me? But I am right here."

"I couldna lie to him. He told me that Struan's messengers had reached him and that Struan believes ye are wi' me."

"Why?"

He blew out an exasperated breath at her. "Who else left Dunnedin at aboot the same time as ye? Are ye daft? Ye never go to the shielings in the summer so he kenned to look for ye wi' me."

"Oh."

She could say no more than that. She had never left Dunnedin since she arrived there at age twelve. She had explored the boundaries of keep and village, but never out to the summer shielings where the clan took the cattle for summer grazing. The shielings were primitive cottages, not unlike this one. She preferred having some comforts about her and those were found in the keep.

"I ken, ye didna think aboot yer actions when ye left." She nodded and he continued. "There may be a way to avoid this marriage to Angus MacLaren and keep yer babe." He paused and the tension grew as she waited for his pronouncement. "Ye maun marry someone else who will agree to stay at Dunnedin."

Her body quaked at the thought of wedding any man. And there was no one suitable for her to marry within the MacKendimens, no one of rank or title suitable for the daughter of an earl and mother of one who would inherit such a title at becoming laird. If one had been available, her father would have pursued that match to keep his alliance with Struan a strong one, rather than looking elsewhere. Angus's father, the current MacLaren, stood high in the respect of the community of the realm that guarded Scotland's interests while King David was still a hostage, but he ranked as an earl as well. It was a good match if a marriage of equals was being sought.

"Even if I could make myself submit to a husband again, and I am not certain I could; there is no one suitable for me, Robert. Surely you see that?"

"Marry me, Anice."

The world stopped at that moment. Everything around her went silent and then her ears filled with a buzzing sound that grew louder and louder until she could hear nothing else. Robert wore a grim expression on his face now, probably insulted by her reaction or lack of it. Marry him? The son of the steward? How could she? And even if she could, how would it work? The noise subsided in her ears and she knew she must answer him.

"How, Robert? Struan would never . . ."

"I will deal wi' the laird, Anice. Leave that to me."

"And my father? Who will deal with him?" She twisted her hands together and turned away. Her father would not stand for this. Even if they could find a priest who would marry them without her father's permission, he could seek to have her marriage annulled.

"Again, I will see to him as weel. I can handle all of this, but only if ye will hiv me to husband. Will ye?"

His voice had softened on those last words—they sounded like a plea rather than his earlier statement. If she brushed aside all her concerns, the minor and major ones that came to mind immediately, it still came down to the question of whether she could put herself under a husband's control. Robert was asking her to do that of her own will; her father and Struan would force her to it, will-her or nill-her. Even as the terror inside fought its way out, she knew that all men were not the same. If she had believed they were, she could never have left the security of Dunnedin to seek Robert out on the road for help.

He was different. He was safe. Could she accept him as husband and submit to him in all things? *All things?* She grimaced as she faced him and, from his reaction, she knew he'd seen her look.

"I am not certain that I can yield all of me to a husband, Robert, even if that husband is you." There, she'd said it. He needed to understand that she could not be a wife to him in the true sense of the word, for she could never willingly submit to the physical attentions of another man. If she married, her husband would have to take his marital rights without her consent or cooperation. She shuddered at the very thought of lying with a man in that way.

He approached her and put his hands on her shoulders. Months before, she could not have tolerated such an action, but now it simply sent chills through her. His face was in the shadows now so she could not tell his mood or his reaction to her words. They were a challenge of sorts, since no wife could deny her husband anything he wanted. Both God's laws and the clan's upheld a man's right to everything a woman brought to the marriage—her body was included along with any property or gold she brought and any children she produced.

"I am no' the monster yer husband was, Anice," he whispered. "I would no' take that which ye canna give freely to me."

"You say that now, Robert, but once the deed is done . . ." Once the vows were taken, he could do as he willed.

"Ye came to me because ye trusted me. Ye brought yer son to me because of that trust. I am telling ye that ye can accept my word now. Once married, I will no' force myself on ye. Other than a few kisses, ye will no' bear the brunt of my attentions." He let go of her and stepped back.

"Kisses?" She swallowed deeply at the thought of his kisses. She remembered the one between him and Robena that she had witnessed his first day in Dunnedin. How would it feel to have his lips on hers? Could she stand it? She raised her fingers to her lips trying to imagine it.

"For appearance's sake, Anice. We maun look married for

this to work. If Struan and yer father suspected otherwise, they could press for an annulment."

"You give your word?"

"I hiv said so," he said on another exasperated breath. "Ye question my honor when ye doubt me this way." He stood with his hands on his hips, looking every inch the warrior. His words, his very stance, were now a challenge to her. Could she accept his offer even though there were more uncertainties than guarantees? Did she have another alternative that would save her life and keep her son with her?

Nay. They both knew this was the only choice she had.

"Aye, Robert. I will have you to husband."

He grunted at her acceptance, turned from her, and walked away in the direction of the stream. She was not sure what she had expected his reaction to be, but this was not it. A part of her thought he might use one of those occasional kisses to seal their agreement and she had felt a tingle of anticipation move through her. Obviously, he had not thought the same thing.

She stood now in the silence of the night alone and listened to the sounds of him moving through the bushes in the distance. Anice knew somehow that he was not coming back soon and decided to wait for him within. The food on the table still waited and now she found she had an appetite. Tearing oft a piece of the roasted pigeon, she bit into it and savored the cold yet flavorful meat. She wondered if he would return to join her in this meal.

H*e cursed himself all the way to the stream. He truly was* a fool a thousand times over for agreeing not to . . . have her. He burned inside out with the need to touch her, taste her, fill her, and now he had given his word that he would not? He smacked his head with his hand and cursed his foolishness out loud this time.

"A bloody buffoon! How could I hiv been so god-awful stupid to agree?"

He reached the water and almost walked right into its rushing current. 'Twould serve him right to end the night in its icy depths. And mayhap it could help the constant state of erection he'd lived with since she found him on the road. A lot of good it would do him now; he'd just promised not to touch her. Her pale face with its look of haunted vulnerability had led to his downfall. He'd taken one look at her and knew the problem.

Now he would have to live with his promise. And he knew deep within that this was only the start of the trouble he faced now that she had consented to marry him. Once the vows were taken, they would go to Dunbarton and then back to Dunnedin and Struan's wrath. Well, at least he had some information that he could use to stop Struan's protests. For Robert had recognized Dunbarton's new fletcher that morning. One look at the man and Robert realized that the arrowmaker and Sandy's death were connected. A few well-placed questions and Robert knew the truth of the link between Struan and his son's demise.

That would be enough to stop Struan. For how long, he did not know. He would take the time to build a marriage, one that Anice could hopefully find some measure of happiness in. But, the question he could not answer was why he was doing it. Yes, he did love Anice in his own way and he wanted to protect her. It was the origins of his feelings that led him to guilt. He did not know, he could not say, how much of what he felt was for her or for the sense of triumph over his brother it brought him. It was not the noblest of beginnings, but he promised himself that she would never know by word or deed that any part of him wanted her simply to best Sandy. He could also not deny that part of him wanted her for the position it brought him to within the hierarchy of the clan. For as her husband, he would be guardian of the next laird and in place should something befall either Struan or Craig.

Without even being recognized by Struan as his son, Robert would gain all that he desired by marrying Anice. And, since the MacKendimens still chose their chieftain by the selection of the elders and not the primogeniture that the lowlanders and Sassenachs favored, he had time to demonstrate the skills and abilities he had honed over the years as castellan for the MacKillops. Struan was old and Craig was very, very young and many things could happen to an old man or a bairn in the years between one or the other being laird.

He knelt beside the rushing rivulet and splashed the cold waters on his face and arms. Scooping some in his hands to drink, he felt the rumblings in his belly and realized that he never had eaten the meal he'd brought back with him. Robert trotted back to the croft and entered quietly, not wanting to disturb the sleeping babe or Anice if she'd retired for the night. He saw her bending over and picking something up from the floor next to her pallet.

"I forgot aboot the food. Hiv ye eaten?"

She gasped and straightened before him, keeping her hand hidden in the folds of her skirt. "Aye, Robert. I waited but you did not return."

"'Tis weel that ye went on wi'oot me, Anice. What is left?"

"I did not eat much, really," she said, pointing to the food still remaining on the table. One candle still burned to light his way around the cottage. "There are still two of the pigeons and most of the bread and cheese."

He noticed that she slipped her hand into her pocket then out again empty. What did she hide from him? He walked to the table and sat, pulling the food closer to him.

"Ye should get some rest now, Anice. Tomorrow promises to be a trying day for ye."

"I could not sleep without hearing from you about your plan. Is there a priest to marry us? Does the MacKillop know what you are doing?"

"I spoke at length wi' Faither Cleirach today and he will hear our vows."

"Without banns?"

"Aye," he said as he tore some bread and cheese off the loaves. "And wi'oot witnesses."

"Robert, how can that be? No priest would do this." She stood nearer to him and her voice was filled with the beginnings of panic.

"A priest of the old church will." Father Cleirach practiced the ways of the older Celtic church. A small but faithful following still worshiped at his stone church in the woods outside Dunbarton. The good father had confirmed just what Ada had told him—'twas his duty to care for his brother's widow and her child. He urged him to follow the way of the Bible and shelter Anice from those who would harm her. If the cleric had been surprised to hear his story, he never showed it.

"There is one here? I did not know any still lived in this area." She walked over, took the refuse away from the table, and threw it in the hearth.

"Aye. He haes lived here all his life and Duncan respects him and his ways." He sensed there was something she wanted to ask. "What is it, Anice? What do ye hesitate to say?"

She took a few shaky breaths in and out before she spoke. "Did you tell him . . . ? Does he know . . . ? About my trying to . . . ?" She could say no more, but he watched her rub the inside of her wrists as though they itched or hurt.

"I didna share yer sin wi' him, Anice. 'Tis yers to hold wi'in or confess."

She nodded and turned away; he heard her let out the air in her lungs. Before he could say anything else, she faced him once more.

"How can you marry me when you know the sin I carry on my soul? Will I not damn you as well with the evil inside me?" She stood motionless, waiting for his answer.

"And how can ye marry me wi'oot kenning mine?" He reached over for her hands and was pleased when she did not pull away from his grasp. "We are all sinners, Anice. And we all try to make our way in this world. 'Tis the trying that I think matters the most to the Almighty." And he would pray that she never discovered his deception or his dishonest desires for her and what she offered. She simply bowed her head for a moment and then lifted her hands from his.

"What did ye hide from me in yer pocket?" He suspected but wanted her to tell him.

Anice stopped where she was and slipped her hand inside the pocket and drew out an object. A small dagger. It was an eating knife, but she planned another use for it. She would not meet his eyes.

"Hiv ye decided no' to, then? Am I the lesser of two evils?"

"'Twas all I thought about most of the day, Rob. At one

point, I even decided to carry out the deed before your return. But I could not go through with it."

"Why no'?" He needed to know what stopped her.

"I realized that the Almighty had saved my life twice and mayhap I should not be questioning his gift. And"—she looked up and met his gaze—"I trusted you to find another way."

This was a good sign to him. She trusted him. The ordeal of the next several days would be a bit easier now that he knew.

"Faither Cleirach would hear yer confession, if ye so desired, before the vows."

"I thank you for your consideration. I will think on it."

He turned and looked at the babe, sleeping peacefully on the pallet next to her. "Ye should get to bed; we need to leave at first light if we want to be at Dunbarton by the evening."

She looked as though she would argue with him or ask another question, but she stopped and nodded. He turned and wandered over to the table, purposely keeping his back to her to grant her some measure of privacy as she prepared to join her son on their bedding. Wrapping the remainders of the food tightly in cloth, he stored everything away for the night. He gathered his plaids and spread them out in front of the door and, seeing that Anice was settled, blew out the candle remaining alight.

Soon, the sounds of the night filtered into the croft and Robert felt himself closer to sleep. Her voice broke into the quiet.

"Why do you do this, Robert? Why saddle yourself with a wife who does not want to be one?"

He clenched his teeth shut and fought not to let words pass his lips that would show him for the fool he'd been already this night. They were there, at the ready, the words, the declaration that would change everything that stood between them. He swallowed several times and then came up with a response he thought was suitable.

"I hiv my reasons, Anice. Dinna be concerned aboot them now."

Robert waited for her to question him. He almost wished it to see if the spirit he'd seen in her earlier was true. Part of the reason he did this was so that he would never have to look upon that expression of desperation and fear on her face again. If nothing else came of this exercise in madness, he would be pleased with the results of his gamble.

chapter 21

S*he was once more a married woman. In spite of her* promises to herself and her attempts to prevent it, she was now under the power of one man. She shivered and looked ahead at her husband, whose stallion led the way down the road to the village and keep of Dunbarton. Robert had helped her onto the saddle, then gained his own seat and taken off at a brisk trot; her pony could do nothing but follow along behind. She felt just as her mount must—out of control and out of sight.

Robert said it would take a few hours to ride back to the village. Her bottom told her that it had been long enough without a break but she hesitated to call out to him. The easy-going disposition that he'd displayed to her while living in Dunnedin was gone and an irritable, grunting man had replaced him. She remembered similar complaints from women she knew who'd married, but never dreamed the transformation took such little time.

Mayhap she did release a groan for he turned in the saddle and looked back at her, lifting his hand to block the sun's light while studying her without a word. Anice tried to smile demurely at him. She was not successful for he turned his horse and approached her slowly.

"If ye can make it awhile longer, ye can take yer ease in the comforts of Duncan's keep."

Rather than saying something rude, she simply nodded to him.

"Is the bairn weel?" He brought his horse side by side with hers and peered into the carrier she'd fashioned once more to carry the babe without using her hands. For some reason, her skin tingled as he stared past her breasts and at her son. He began to reach inside the sling as if to touch his head and she leaned back and out of his reach. His gaze moved to hers in a questioning expression.

"He sleeps now. 'Tis easier to manage him this way while traveling."

"I did but seek to check him, no' to wake him." He directed his mount away from her and turned to lead her once more.

"Robert," she called out softly to him.

"'Tis weel, Anice. We are both exhausted and out of sorts from the last few days. 'Twill be much easier for all of us when we reach the keep. Come." He motioned her to follow with a wave of his hand. She allowed her pony to trot along behind his the rest of the way without comment or complaint.

Not much time had passed when the lush growth of the surrounding forests began to thin and the road widened to a size that would accommodate several horses riding side by side. The path climbed a rolling hill and then the village came into sight, like Dunnedin and not.

A sense of excitement filled her even in her exhaustion because this was only the third village she'd visited in her lifetime. Once she'd thought and dreamed of traveling all over Scotland, to Edinburgh and David's court with Sandy since he was apparently high in the king's favor. David's capture and imprisonment in England had changed those dreams. In spite of her preparations and training in the customs and languages of the English and Scottish courts, Anice had never once stepped outside of Dunnedin since the day she entered it.

As they drew closer, people called out greetings to Robert. Warriors raised their hands to him, workers nodded to him, and, she was bothered to notice, the women all offered exceptionally warm words of welcome. Observing him from a few paces behind, he unhesitatingly accepted them from one and all. Here was the man she remembered from Dunnedin, the one who had such an amiable manner and smile for everyone. Then, as if he realized she was there, he turned and drew her to his side.

"Ye should be riding next to me, Anice. Come, the keep is just ahead." Robert nodded to the left and she turned to look.

Dunbarton rose against the sky, larger than Struan's keep and darker in color as well. She stared as the structure grew as they approached. Robert controlled her pony so she could simply gawk at the size and splendor of it. They crossed over a stone bridge leading through a portcullis and into the main yard. Every manner of activity filled that place—people coming and going from the building, animals being herded, horses ridden and led. The sounds and sights had begun to overwhelm her when she heard Robert's name being shouted. Blinking to regain her control, she turned to see who called to him.

A tall, hulking figure came from among the people towards them. His hair was completely white, but he did not look to be as old as Struan was. What she noticed most about him as he came closer was the terrible scar that slashed down the right side of his face and the look of kindness in his eyes as he returned her gaze.

"Robert! Welcome back to Dunbarton! Is this Lady Anice wi' ye?" His eyes twinkled even as he asked his question and as his glance moved back and forth from Robert to her. She knew that the MacKillop recognized her. It had been over a year since she'd laid eyes on him, but she sensed that not only did he know exactly who she was, he also knew why she was there.

Robert dismounted and gave the reins to a stableboy, who took control of them and led Dubh away. From the way the boy patted and spoke to the stallion, she saw they were old friends. But then, Robert had lived here for more than eight years, so this was more a home than Dunnedin to him.

Robert did not wait for her to climb down. He lifted her from the pony's back and placed her on her feet. Luckily his hands did not leave hers right away, for she stumbled after so long a time in the saddle. As Robert steadied her, the babe let out a muffled shriek between them. A commotion nearby drew their attention.

A short woman, shorter than Anice was herself, pushed her way through the crowd to the side of the huge man. Anice would not call this woman fat, but she did carry a comfortable layer of natural padding that gave her a very soft appearance.

"Here now, husband. Did ye look at the puir lass? That bruise on her forehead needs tending and she looks nigh to fainting. And," she asked as she peered over at Robert, "did I hear a bairn's cry?"

"Aye, Lady Margaret," Robert answered as he stepped back. " 'Tis Lady Anice's son making himself known."

Anice unwound some of the sling and exposed Craig's head with its tuft of bright red hair to them. Lady Margaret let out a cry.

"Come, Duncan. Let us move inside where the mother and babe can rest." The lady did not wait for the laird to move at all—she simply wrapped her arm around Anice's shoulders and pulled her away from Robert. Before she could be drawn away completely, Robert spoke.

"My lord, my lady. Before they leave, may I make known to ye once again my wife, the Lady Anice MacNab?"

Everyone within hearing distance stopped and stared without any measure of discretion at them. The laird and his lady exchanged glances and Anice saw the hint of a message passed between the two.

"Lady Anice, welcome to my humble estate," the MacKillop said, bowing before her. "Is it true then? Hiv ye taken Robert as husband?"

Anice curtsied even while she remained in Lady Margaret's grasp. "Aye, my lord, Robert and I exchanged vows this day. He is my husband now."

Some tremor rumbled through the crowd and the clapping began and grew louder. Soon all around her were applauding and tears filled her eyes when she realized the meaning of it. Robert's clan of the last eight years, those whom he'd trained, and trained with, were expressing their approval of his marriage in their own way.

She turned her head and found that Robert and the laird

were now exchanging glances. The Lady Margaret tugged her along towards an archway off to one side. Looking to Robert, she saw him nod and smile at her, so she walked along, not resisting the guidance of the laird's wife.

Soon she found herself ensconced in a huge wooden tub filled with fragrant steaming water. A young woman, handpicked by Lady Margaret, came to the room and took Craig from her. The lady insisted that she give over his care for the night to the wet nurse. When Anice protested, she was assured of the competence and caring that he would receive. As the real exhaustion of the last days set in, she found the idea of bathing and sleeping very appealing.

From then it was all a blur of activity around her and for her, as she was bathed, her hair washed, and clean clothes provided to her. Lady Margaret circled the room, calling out orders in a soft but firm voice until all of her needs had been seen to. Then as quickly and quietly as it all began, everyone left the room and she collapsed onto the cushiony mattress of the rope bed. It would feel heavenly to sleep on a real mattress instead of the hard pallet or unforgiving ground of the last several nights.

Although a tray of food sat on a table next to the bed, she could not gather the strength needed to eat. So she climbed onto the bed and pulled the layers of warm blankets up to her neck. Within a few moments, she felt herself drifting off to sleep. Just before she could let go, a thought tickled at her mind. She tried to focus on what concerned her, but it was difficult to do so as she lay in her comfortable cocoon.

It was something about how the MacKillop had asked about her marrying Robert. She had called him husband before the whole crowd; everyone had heard her words. Now why did that seem so significant? She would have to ask Robert when she saw him next.

"P*oor dearling! To be dragged over hill and glen in that* condition. Robbie, I thought I raised ye better than that."

She may have been small, but the Lady Margaret packed a powerful punch. It landed in his stomach and he blew out sharply from the impact of it.

"I dinna drag her! She ran away to me." How was it that women never listened to the important parts of the story and made up their own endings? "I brought her here—is that no' enough to make ye happy?"

His foster mother muttered again as she walked to the other side of the solar where the wet nurse was just finishing feeding Anice's little piglet. Now Craig lay upright on the girl's shoulder, peering around the room as if he knew what went on there. Margaret adjusted the bairn's coverings for the tenth time and rubbed his head. He knew then and there that he had made the right decision in bringing Anice there. If he had doubted Duncan's cooperation, Margaret had more than assured that things would go well for them now.

"Where hiv ye put her?" Robert asked. He looked at the laird for an answer, but Duncan shrugged and nodded at his wife, who was playing and cooing with the babe.

"In yer room, of course," she answered in a singsong voice as though speaking to the babe. "Where else do ye think I would put yer wife, ye daft mon?"

He had not remembered her to be so insulting before he'd left for Dunnedin. He shook his head and looked to the laird for guidance. Another shrug was all the help he got from that one. Craig, however, was enjoying her voice and her antics and let out one of those laughs that began at his feet and shook his body. Something tightened within his chest as he listened to the two of them.

"I need to wash up." It seemed that everyone else was being looked after but him.

"The tub is set up in yer room," Lady Margaret answered without looking at him. All Duncan offered was another of his infuriating shrugs. "Anice was asleep before I left the room the first time. If ye hiv a care"—she cast him a warning glare—"she will stay asleep while ye bathe."

Robert crossed his arms and narrowed his gaze at her. Duncan's silence in this was a puzzle. The laird knew exactly what he had done in asking Anice if Robert was husband to her. Robert knew it even as the words left Duncan's mouth. From the expression that passed between laird and lady, Margaret understood the significance of it as well, even if she was not privy to all the reasons.

Even if the wedding before the priest of the old church was not upheld, something almost as old and respected would bind him and Anice together . . . for at least a year and a day. For in calling him husband and declaring it before the crowd, Anice and he were handfasted, by his words and hers. The laird and lady knew it. The crowd of old friends among the MacKillops knew it. He knew it.

Anice apparently did not.

It must be a dream, she thought as she snuggled even deeper under the covers. She felt clean for the first time in days. A soft bed lay under her, caressing her in its warmth and comfort. Her son was being cared for while she rested. Robert was . . . ? She could not remember where Robert was. She stretched and rolled to her side, moving the covers aside and repositioning herself. It was the sound of the water splashing that forced her eyes open.

She'd found Robert, and dear God in heaven, he was getting a bath not four feet from where she lay. And he was naked. Not four feet from where she lay. Her breath caught in her throat at the sight of him so close and so . . . wet. Intimidated by his nearness and size, she gasped, inadvertently drawing his attention.

Robert leaned back his head and groaned out loud. He shifted his body, drawing his long legs up to his chest. The tub that had been luxurious to her did not accommodate his much larger size and longer limbs.

"Lady Margaret will hiv my head if she finds out I woke ye," he complained. Pounding his fist into the water, he groaned once more as water splashed everywhere around the tub.

"You did not wake me, Robert. Truly. I was shifting and heard the water."

She tried not to stare at him, but this was her first sight of him this undressed. The water made his skin glisten in the fire's light and she had the most absurd impulse to touch where the drops ran down from his shoulders and onto the wide expanse of his chest. His hair was slicked back and even the growth of many days on his face looked clean. Suddenly, the covers that had warmed her just minutes ago in sleep were too heavy and too many now and she wished she were alone so she could throw them back and cool off.

"I will leave," he said, beginning to stand in the tub. Holding on to the sides, he pushed himself up and then stopped as if he finally realized she would see the rest of him.

"Nay," she called out, afraid of what she might see if he stood now. She started to get out of the bed, but the glimpse of the sheer nightrail she wore stopped her. "Robert, I will turn over this way"—she turned away from him—"and you can finish your bath." She faked a yawn and patted her mouth at the end of it. "I am so very tired I will be back to sleep in no time at all."

"Are ye certain I am no' disturbing ye?"

"You are not," she answered as she turned to face the wall. She lay down and pulled the covers high up onto her shoulders. Even as hot as she was, she would not lower them until he was gone.

He grunted in that low tone she'd heard several times over the last days. Did that mean he would finish? Well, she was not turning back to find out what he was doing. She would stay in the bed until he was gone.

"Ye will no' tell Lady Margaret, will ye?"

She wanted to laugh, but his voice was filled with a kind of grudging respect for the wife of his laird. "Do you fear her?"

"Oh, aye! She has fists of rock and a tongue that will slash a mon to bits."

"Then I will protect you from her wrath," she said. He grunted once more and then began to splash around in the water, obviously finished his bath. She added another word to let him know that the realization of what they had done before the clan was sinking in.

"Husband."

chapter 22

She knew.

He did not think her a fool, but he did think she had been too exhausted and overwhelmed to notice the words that Duncan invited her to say. Her words sealed their bargain and, although Struan and her father might seek annulment of the church ceremony, the handfasting bound them together for a year and a day. And it could only be broken by one of them. Now he could think of nothing to say to her in response to her call.

He resumed his bath even as she lay under the covers listening. He smiled as he remembered the blush that crept up her neck and face when she looked at him sitting in the water next to her. Her mouth had dropped open and she looked at him with unashamed interest. Robert fought the urge to call her from under her tent of covers even now as he stood to climb out of the tub. She was treading a thin line between curiosity and terror now and he did not want the expression on her face to turn to fear at the sight of him naked. It would ruin his own esteem to see dread in her eyes as she looked upon him.

Once he was dressed again in plaid and shirt, he tied his

hair back and sat on the corner of the bed to replace his boots. He heard her squeal and then saw her peek her head out.

"Ye can come oot now, wife. I am dressed." He stood before her as she pushed the covers back and took in a breath of the cooler air.

"I can see that," she answered in a snippy tone. He arched a brow at her.

"Is there something amiss?"

She slid back and sat against the wooden headboard, never taking her eyes from him. She lifted a single layer of linen up to her neck, effectively blocking the view of her breasts he could see through the sheer nightgown she wore. A gift from Lady Margaret no doubt in anticipation of their wedding night this evening. She must have seen the path of his gaze now for she arranged her hair over her shoulders like a curtain. Anice probably would not have done so if she knew how the sight of those fiery red tresses inflamed him even more.

"Was the handfasting part of your plan?"

He crossed his arms and faced her. "No, but Duncan thought it would help to strengthen our cause."

"He knows? What have you told him?" Her voice reeked of condescension, like a lady to a servant, and he took offense to it. His glare must have warned her off. "I bet your pardon, *husband*. I thought you would keep your plan, our plan, secret. The more who know, the more of a chance of Struan and my father finding out before you want them to." She ended her words with her head down where he could not see her expression.

"I would rather ye ask me the questions ye hiv than to throw out these darts of anger and sarcasm, Anice. We maun find a way to deal wi' each other fairly if we are to live together as mon and wife."

Robert wanted to smile, but fought to keep it from his face. The infuriating, haughty Lady Anice still lived inside her and with his help, she would come out once more. He did not favor either her behaviors—the sarcastic remarks or being spoken down to as though he were a servant. He took them as a good sign that she was still a fighter and would not back down now as they moved step by step closer to what they both sought. Together.

She looked up at him and studied his face intently. He met her gaze and waited for her words. Anice nodded at him.

"I have never been a wife, Robert. I do not know the way of it." Her voice trembled as she shared her fear with him.

He realized the truth of her words. She and Sandy had married but shared only the debacle of a wedding night. Anice knew more about living with Struan and accommodating his wants and needs than those of her own husband. He fought to control the shudder that passed through him as he thought of what might have happened if Sandy had returned to Dunnedin seeking an obedient wife. May his depraved soul burn in hell for eternity, he thought even as he smiled at her.

"And I hiv never been husband to any woman, Anice. So we will need to learn of it together. . . ." She gifted him with a tentative smile, one that held such promise that he felt his chest tighten from it. "Now, Lady Margaret was hoping you'd be rested enough to join us at table for dinner. If she finds that I woke ye and kept ye up wi' talking, she will have my b— . . . head." He stood and turned to leave. Her voice stopped him.

"Robert. A question, please?"

He looked at her and waited. That becoming blush reappeared on her face and she looked uncomfortable about asking him something.

"What is it?"

"If I come to dinner, will they . . . ? I mean to say, will I . . . ?" She looked at him as though he could answer the question she could not get out.

"Just say it, Anice."

"Must you kiss me in front of them?"

Of all the things he thought she'd ask, that was one he'd not thought of. Did he have to kiss her? Nay, but now that the question was asked, all he wanted to do was kiss her.

"Aye, wife. 'Twill be expected of us as newly married to celebrate our union wi' a kiss or two."

"Two?" she whispered. He could not tell from her widened eyes if she was pleased or horrified by the possibility.

"As I said when we made this bargain, lass. A kiss now and then for show. Only for that and only when needed, of course."

He waited to be struck down for the liar he was. He would have kissed her for days on end if she'd allow it. Her naive belief that he could be satisfied with those few simple expressions of affection was so far wrong he wanted to burst out in laughter. But he knew that he would have to break her in just as he did any terrified filly—soft touches, soft words, and the necessary time.

"Could you . . . ? Do you think . . . ?" She stuttered over her words and twisted her fingers in the sheets and she would not meet his glance. He walked closer to the bed and lifted her chin with his hand. Looking at him now, he smiled to reassure her.

"Anice? Just say it."

"Would you kiss me here so I know what to expect at dinner? I do not want my fears to embarrass you in front of your friends and the laird."

He was deeply touched by her consideration and he admitted to himself that it was genuine. But under that concern he also recognized some amount of curiosity and longing to kiss him. He thanked the Almighty that there might be a glimmer of passion yet left within her.

Still holding her chin in his hand, Robert leaned forward and touched his lips to hers. Her soft intake of breath told him that she was fighting her own fears in allowing him this. Robert opened his eyes and found her staring at him as he drew closer. He did not break from her stare.

He controlled his own hunger for her and did nothing more than move his mouth gently over hers. Once, twice, and then again, he pressed against her mouth, never allowing his tongue to slide inside and seek hers within. He did not want her to be afraid. He hoped she would learn not only to tolerate his kisses, but at some time to want and welcome them.

He lifted his head and looked down at her, awaiting her reaction. She barely breathed, but then neither did he. An innocent kiss and yet its effect on him was so powerful. His body reacted at her first request, surging, full and ready beneath the hastily wrapped plaid. But it was his heart that was now even more engaged that before.

"Weel? How was that?" he asked as she continued to gape at him without speaking.

"'Twas fine, Robert. Thank you for showing me what to expect."

He grunted, not knowing what else to say to her. Her polite acceptance was not what he'd hoped for, but 'twas all he was getting at the moment. Straightening his belt and plaid, he walked to the door without looking back at her. He truly feared his actions if her lips looked fuller or if her eyes were passion-glazed because of his kiss. He might run back and dive onto the bed, taking her down into the soft mattress and covering her with himself. It would end any hope he had of a gradual acceptance of a physical relationship.

Opening the door, he walked quietly out and pulled it snugly into its frame. It was only later, after a run-in with Lady Margaret over waking Anice from her rest, that the truth of the experience hit him.

They'd shared their first kiss. If the laughter that bubbled forth from him confused anyone in the hall when it happened, he neither cared nor worried. 'Twas their first kiss.

Every space at every table in the hall was filled and the level of noise made her wince as they approached the entrance. This room was also larger than the one at Dunnedin, as were the keep and the village. Duncan had spared no expense or comforts when building his keep, for she spied glass windows in many of the higher rooms and even some carpets on the floor. The design of the keep was also very different from Struan's. To her surprise, she was escorted through an enclosed courtyard before entering—the keep was built around it, giving a measure of privacy and protection to those who wanted or needed it. And she discovered that the private solar on the second floor was the size of a small great hall!

Luckily her hand lay on Robert's forearm and he guided her steps for she knew if he did not, she would stumble in her nervousness. Could she, could they carry this out? She had tossed and turned in bed after he'd left, thinking about the bargain they'd made and how it would affect not only the lives of her and her son, but also the rest of the MacKendimen clan. And how would her father react at the news that she had defied him and married the son of a steward instead of the son of an earl? In spite of Robert's assurances that he would handle those concerns, the tremors shook her and she was unable to hide them from him.

"Easy now, Anice. No harm will come to ye here."

He patted her hand as he whispered the words. The warmth in his big hand seeped into her frozen one and she did try to let go of some of her tension as they walked into the hall. But the sound of his name being shouted by hundreds of people caused her to shake. She would have turned and fled if not for his hold on her hand.

"Ye rule over the hall in Dunnedin wi' ease, Anice. Dinna let this rattle ye."

He was correct, of course. From the time she'd been old enough to speak, she'd been trained to rule and run the keep and the people of Dunnedin. This was really no different. She could do this. Taking a deep breath and letting it out, she walked by his side through the hall as people shouted to him and greeted him on their way to the dais. He assisted her up the steps and guided her to her seat next to Lady Margaret. As she sat, she watched Robert accept warm and hearty welcomes from the other men at the table. She nodded to Laird Duncan and then noted the resemblance between him and a younger man at his side.

"Our eldest son, Jamie," Lady Margaret said, as she pointed to the younger man. "Duncan's brothers, Ian and Logan, and his uncle Malcolm join us."

Anice nodded at each of the men as Lady Margaret named them. Although their faces were all roughened by age and life and two of them bore the same type of scars that the laird did, ones gained in battle no doubt, their expressions were not cruel or hard. Their eyes sparkled with a sort of joy of life and their affection for Robert was evident in the greeting they gave. A few minutes later, Robert sat next to her. A serving boy came forward and filled both of their cups with wine. She waited as Robert exchanged a few words with the boy.

"Young Kevin has progressed weel in my absence," Robert announced as she watched the lad color under his praise. "And he haes grown a foot more in height and put on at least a stone in weight, thanks no doubt to Lady Margaret's care." Robert raised his cup in salute to the laird's wife.

"Here now, Robert," Duncan said as he rose from his seat. "Our good wishes should be for ye and the Lady Anice." Turning to face the hall, Duncan held his cup aloft and waited for quiet. "Raise yer drinks and voices for Robert and Lady Anice on the occasion of their marriage." Duncan turned to them and nodded. "Much happiness and much prosperity and much fruitfulness do we wish them this day!"

She tried to raise her own cup to her lips, but the attention and her nervous shaking prevented her from doing so. To her surprise, Robert covered her hand with his and raised their hands and her cup to her mouth. She took a sip and met his eyes over the rim. His smile made her breathless; she could almost believe from his actions and his expression that this was more than an arrangement between them. As she swallowed she realized that he did this all to put on a brave face to the people who had raised him. She would do as much for him since his plan would save her and keep her son with her.

Once she sipped, she let him guide the cup to his own mouth and watched as his lips parted and he drank deeply of the wine. Lost in staring at his mouth, the sound of hundreds of fists pounding on the tables throughout the hall finally broke into her reverie. Startled, she looked around at the expectant faces of those seated nearest and then back at Robert. He smiled and leaned closer, whispering to her as he did.

"Yer pardon, Anice."

She looked at his eyes and saw the softening in his gaze. Ah, so the time had come to play the married couple. After the brief kiss in their room, she felt prepared to face this now. She lifted her face to his and waited. In an instant, she knew she was wrong, completely wrong.

His hand slipped behind her head and drew her closer. She felt his fingers tangle in her hair even as his lips touched hers. Unlike the kiss already shared, this one was filled with a passion she did not expect. His mouth was hot on hers and soon she felt his tongue touch her lips. She gasped and he slipped inside to touch her there. Held close by the hand on her head, she waited, a bit terrified by the feeling of him inside her there and by the feelings that rampaged through her. His tongue touched hers and she tasted the sweetness of the wine they had shared. Anice sighed as he titled his face and the kiss deepened.

She lost track of time and of the company around them as his mouth claimed hers. Instead of fear, Anice felt something within her tighten and tingling waves moved through her from her stomach and into her breasts and then deep inside to the very core of her. Memories of another kiss, one filled with passion, one shared with the impostor years before, filled her thoughts. The raucous yelling and cheering finally grabbed her attention and Robert's, for he lifted his mouth from hers and slid his hand from her head. Looking around the room and then at her, he claimed one more quick hard kiss from her and leaned back smiling.

Anice blinked, trying to reclaim her wits, for she was certain he'd stolen them from her. Her breathing came fast and hard as though she'd run the length of this hall and back again. Most unnerving to her, however, was the continued pulsing that made her quiver inside.

"Yer pardon, Anice," he whispered to her as he offered her the cup of wine, now refilled by the young page nearby. "I didna plan to overstep the bounds we set." She could only nod as she drank deeply of the wine, hoping it would calm her racing heart.

Duncan rose once more and called out to his people. "Here now, bring out the food. They will need to build up their strength for the night ahead, from the look of it!"

She felt the heat burning in her cheeks as all those around them cheered and clapped once more. And her lips still felt swollen from Robert's kiss. Lady Margaret must have noticed her unease for she drew her into conversation as the servants began bringing out large platters of food. Looking down at her hands on her lap, Anice wanted to run from the room. As if he had heard her thoughts, Robert leaned over as he placed some food on the plate they would share.

"I am sorry aboot that, Anice. Now that we hiv given them what they wanted, they should leave you in peace."

His voice calmed her fears. One look at his face, full of concern, and she knew she had nothing to worry about. Robert understood their agreement and would stand by it, even if they had to put on these displays from time to time to appease the people who knew him. She had no idea if the same type of behavior would be needed to demonstrate their relationship to Struan and the MacKendimens. She nodded at him and then turned to answer Lady Margaret, who asked a question about Craig.

The rest of the meal progressed smoothly and her stomach calmed enough that she was even able to eat. Knowing that Robert would abide by her limits made things much easier. So much so that when Lady Margaret took her hand to lead her and the other women off to prepare her for Robert and the night ahead, she did not tremble.

chapter 23

"*Does she ken?*"

Duncan's voice cut through the welcome silence of the private solar. The hall had grown too loud for him and the laird had invited him abovestairs to share a cup of wine before retiring. It was obvious that Duncan wanted to speak to him now that the ladies had left the hall for their chambers.

"What?" Robert turned to face the man who was more a father to him than his natural one. Duncan had taken in a scared boy those eight years ago and turned him into an accomplished man, and he had done it with a sense of humor and a concern usually reserved for one's own children. "Does she ken what?" he repeated.

"That ye really did this because ye love her and no' for any other reason ye may give as an excuse."

"I did it to . . ." He could not complete his words. His reasons were now so jumbled in his mind that he could not unravel them. Robert looked at Duncan, helpless to explain the whole of it. Duncan poured more of his favorite wine into Robert's cup and nodded.

"Ye may hiv begun this as a way to get from Struan what

he would no' give ye freely, but that is no' why ye do this now."

"'Tis worse than that, Duncan. Truly worse," he confessed as he sat down in a chair next to the table where Duncan now sat. "I wanted her because she was Sandy's wife." He put the cup down on the table and, leaning over, ran his hands through his hair. Holding his head, he rubbed his temples, trying to ease the tightness there.

"Coveting yer brother's wife? 'Tis surely a grave sin. Did the good Faither Cleirach give ye penance for that?" He could hear the laughter, completely inappropriate for the discussion, in the laird's voice.

"How much do ye ken?" Robert asked, lifting his gaze to meet Duncan's.

"All of it. Mayhap even more than ye ken yerself."

"Then why do ye support me in this?" Duncan frowned at him. "Do no' deny it, Duncan. Ye hiv pushed and pointed me in directions I would no' hiv taken since the day I arrived here. If ye are Struan's oldest friend and staunchest ally, why do ye do it?"

Duncan stood and walked over to the hearth, staring into the flames for a moment before he spoke. Without turning his head, he answered.

"Because I can tell right from wrong and he wronged ye deeply. I dinna ken his reasons, and they maun be clear to him, but I dinna agree wi' what he haes done to ye these last eight years."

"But, Duncan, if ye back me in this folly, it could bring war between the MacKendimens and the MacKillops. How can ye risk such a thing . . . ?" Robert could not say the words but they hung between them in the air. *For me.*

"Is it folly, lad? To right a wrong? To do what I can to give ye back the place ye should hiv within yer family? And to help the lass who has suffered in her own way because of the same mistake by Struan? Is that so foolish?"

"She haes no idea," he said, answering Duncan's original question.

"Of yer feelings or motives for marrying her? Or do ye speak of the rightful place ye deserve within the MacKendimens?" Duncan walked to the table once more and sat across from him.

"All of those things and more. And I hiv no' the courage to tell her."

"She haes the courage to hear the truth from ye, Robert. She haes faced down a demon and lived through it. Surely a tale of love would be less frightening than that?"

Robert looked across the table and snorted. "Is there nothing that ye dinna ken?"

"No' much," Duncan said with a laugh. "And what I dinna ken, the Lady Margaret does."

"Do ye share all wi' her? Even this knowledge?" He was not sure that he wanted his and Anice's story known by anyone but the laird, Ada, and the priest. Duncan stood and walked around the table to Robert. Reaching out to him, the laird grasped his hand and pulled him to his feet.

"I learned many, many years ago that 'twas definitely less painful to simply tell that woman what she wished to ken, rather than struggle to keep things from her. Aye, Robert, she kens as much as I do aboot ye and yer lady wife." Duncan put his arm around Robert's shoulders and guided him to the door. "And ye hiv her formidable support as much as ye hiv mine."

"Even if it brings war?"

Duncan laughed now and put his hand on the handle of the door. "I hold thrice as much land and that many more warriors than Struan can call to face me. He may be a stubborn old mon, but he is no' stupid. Mayhap my backing will cause him to think aboot his reasons for treating ye as he haes and to consider his options once more for the good of his clan."

The laird pulled open the door and stepped into the hallway.

"Now, ye had best get yerself to yer room before Lady Margaret comes looking for ye herself."

He turned and held out his hand. Duncan took it and pulled him into a hug.

"My thanks for all ye hiv done for me, Duncan."

"'Twill be thanks enough if ye tread carefully as I taught ye and settle this between ye and Anice and ye and Struan."

Robert nodded, for he could force no words from his tightened throat. He was touched beyond belief at Duncan's support for him and Anice. He turned and followed the corridor to his room. Not knowing what to expect, he knocked. He took a deep breath and tried to let the wine he'd drunk in the hall and in the solar calm his ragged nerves. He felt like a bridegroom after the ceremony today and the celebration tonight, but he knew that no bride's welcome awaited him this night.

"Come," her soft voice filtered through the door and he pushed against it.

The soft glow of many candles lit the room and the smell of freshly laid rushes reached him where he stood. He inhaled their aroma and recognized the full and powerful scent of roses. Lady Margaret had worked her wonders on the room after they'd left for the meal and she had turned it into a wedding-night bower for them. If she knew the truth of their situation, then why had she done this?

"She said that every bride and groom deserved such a start to their marriage." Anice's voice traveled to him in the quiet and he finally found her in one corner of the room. "I did not have the heart to tell her the truth."

"I hiv a feeling that she kens the truth of it anyway, Anice."

"She does?" At his nod, she continued, "Then why carry out this farce?" Her head tilted towards the petal-strewn bed and the decorated room.

"The Lady Margaret is ever hopeful. She wants to believe that the best will happen, even from the worst of beginnings."

He stepped further into the room and pushed the door closed behind him. At least he would not rest among vermin now that the laird's wife had cleaned the chamber. A bed of blankets on fresh rushes before the hearth would be more comfortable than many other nights he'd spent on the ground or on cold stone floors. As he walked closer, he realized that she held a bundle on her lap. Craig.

"I had to feed him, Robert. I missed two other feedings, and the pain of it . . ." Her words faded as she tried to explain it to him. He did not mind if she nursed the bairn here, 'twas her room now as much as his. "Lady Margaret tried to convince me to let the wet nurse see to him this night, but I needed to. . . ." Her one hand moved to her chest and she pressed it against her breast.

"If ye dinna feed him, 'tis painful then?" Robert thought he understood this situation. Like cows if not milked, he thought and he winced as he realized his wife would not be complimented by such a comparison.

"Aye."

He knew now that her clipped response told of her embarrassment on the topic. And since he did not want to dwell on the shape or size or hardness of her breasts, he changed the subject.

"Will he sleep wi' us here?" He looked around the room and spotted a cradle near the bed. The decision had been made already.

"It is up to you, Robert," she said as she rose from her seat in the corner. Lifting the babe to her shoulder, she patted his back until he let out a loud burp. "Once the piglet is fed, he will sleep anywhere."

He smiled at her name for the babe. She could have asked him for anything and he would have granted it while looking at her like this. The sheer nightrail trailed on the floor and her hair hung down in waves over the plaid she wore as a shawl. The red and gold shades of her tresses were lit by the fire and even her skin glowed from it. The bruise on her forehead was fading even now and would be gone before their return to Dunnedin.

All he could think about was unwrapping her and making love to her before the fire. He wanted to see the blush steal its way up her breasts and onto her neck and face. He wanted to kiss and touch every part of her and he desperately craved her touch on him. And mostly, he wanted her to return his kisses. Return them with vigor and wanting and of her own choice. Sighing, he realized that he was only fueling his own lust and for naught. Nothing but his own discomfort and sleeplessness would come from letting his desires get out of control.

She must have thought his sigh was one of displeasure for she walked to him and reached out in supplication. "Robert, truly, it will be as you wish. Lady Margaret said to call and a servant would take him to the nurse's chambers for the night. I do not wish to disturb your rest."

"Anice, ye misunderstand. If the bairn sleeping wi' ye will ease yer own rest, then keep him here. The bed is big enough for the two of ye."

Her eyes widened and she looked from him to the bed and back again.

"Where will you sleep?"

"There," he said, pointing at the spot in front of the hearth. "'Tis many a night I've slept on worse. Wi' a blanket or two, it will be just fine."

She looked at him in frank disbelief and then turned and placed the babe in the center of the bed. Opening one of the storage trunks, she pulled out several thick blankets and began to arrange them on the floor.

"Here, Anice, give them to me."

"'Twould seem to be the least I can do for you, Robert." She layered the blankets and took a pillow from the bed and placed it for his use. "This would not seem to be such a good bargain for you, Robert. I cannot imagine what there is in it for you."

At that moment, with his body's desires raging and his mind warring with his wants, he could not think of anything good in this situation either. Mayhap the morning would bring a clearer mind and a swim in the loch outside the village would ease his lust. Then he could understand why he had come up with this hellish torture called a marriage in name only and why he had entered it of his own free will. He finally just grunted at her question, and, peeling off his plaid, he lay down and wrapped himself up before the fire. He could tell a long night awaited him.

He had barely closed his eyes when the knock came on the door. It could not yet be morning, but the light shining through the small glass window told him it was. He climbed from his cocoon of covers and hastened to the door, not wanting to wake Anice or the bairn. Opening the door a crack, he saw young Kevin standing in the hall.

"The laird said to join him at the stables when ye can, Robert."

"Tell Duncan I will be there immediately, Kevin," he whispered.

"He said to tell ye no' to rush. He said there's time to break yer fast."

Turning back and seeing Anice asleep on the bed, he knew this was the perfect time to leave. She would have the privacy she needed to take care of the bairn's and her own needs and he would be able to seek out the relief of the icy waters of the loch.

He nodded at the boy and closed the door. Finding a clean length of plaid, he placed it over his belt on the floor, positioned the pleats, lay on it, and gathered it around him. He still wore the shirt from yesterday, but it would suit his needs for now. Adjusting the extra material over his shoulder, he hooked on the large brooch to hold it in place. He tugged on his boots and was ready to leave when he heard her yawn.

"Is something wrong, Robert, to take you from your bed so early?"

The morning huskiness of her voice wakened his desire for her once more and he stood and stared at her as she sat up in bed . . . in his bed. Her hair, now loosened from her sleeping braid, flowed over her shoulders and fine wisps of it encircled her face. The sun's rays beaming through the window behind her made it appear as a sparkling crown on her head and his fingers itched to move through it again as he had during their kiss at dinner. If she knew her appeal, she did not show it. Instead she tortured him further by stretching and yawning.

Her breasts, now full and ready for her son's appetite, whetted his own as they pressed against the thin layer of linen she wore. His body reacted vigorously to the enticing view she presented and he knew he had to leave before his lust overpowered his control.

"The laird summons me. I maun go now," he said as he turned away to gather his weapons and sporran.

"Now? This early? Is something amiss?"

Anice pushed back the covers, slid her feet to the floor, and reached for the plaid shawl next to the bed. Pulling it around her shoulders, she turned away from him and in but a few moments rebraided her hair. She never realized the unobstructed view of her round, soft bottom that she presented to him with her motions and although he could barely breathe, he could not look away. Memories of holding her on his lap during the ride here flooded his mind and his erection grew harder. Even the loosely hung plaid around his waist would not hide it from view.

This was, he realized in that moment, to be his punishment, his penance for his many sins. He would live in a constant state of wanting his wife who, in spite of the fact she had borne a son, was as innocent now as the day she married. She would never know the effect that her everyday movements, the way her hair flowed down her back or the sway of her hips as she walked, drove him to the brink of explosion. He was to pay for his lies and his coveting by being so near to her and yet never having and never touching her? 'Twould be a long and torturous life ahead if that was the Almighty's plan.

"I maun see to the laird's call, Anice. I will see ye later in the day."

She called out a farewell to him, but he could only grunt in response. He could not risk another look at her without also risking her seeing his current state of arousal. And, innocent or not, the sight would be difficult to misunderstand. He left, pulling the door closed behind him. A visit to the loch and then to find the laird. And, with sufficient planning, he would not see her until she was asleep once more that night.

chapter 24

"He seems to grunt a lot."

Her answer to Lady Margaret's questions caused the other women in the room to exchange knowing glances and then soft laughter filled the room. The laird's wife reached over and patted her hand in a comforting sort of way.

"He is a good mon, Anice. Give him time to adjust to yer ways."

"But my mother taught me that 'tis a wife's duty to adjust to her husband. Is this not the way of it then?"

She was confused. She knew how to wheedle what she wanted from Struan; their many years together had shown her his weaknesses and she used them as she needed to in order to accomplish her tasks and duties at Dunnedin. She somehow thought that dealing with a husband would be different from that. Anice shook her head and looked for guidance from Lady Margaret.

"Now, dear, dinna fash yerself over these matters. Ye and Robert will learn each other's ways soon enough."

"'Tis not the same, Lady Margaret. He said you knew . . ." She realized the others in the room were listening with unabashed curiosity and she could not expose the real basis of their marriage.

"Here now, ladies," Lady Margaret called out. "Please give us some privacy."

Anice watched as the women gathered up their work and left the room. She feared speaking of such private matters even with this woman, but she needed some advice. And so far, all that she'd seen of and heard about the laird's wife told her this was the person to ask.

Lady Margaret stood and walked to the other table and poured both of them some ale. Bringing it back to where she sat, the older woman sat down and looked directly at Anice.

"So, 'tis to be a marriage in name only then? No' a true union of man and wife?" Although she did not expect such a blunt question, Anice could detect no sense of disapproval in her tone.

"That is our agreement."

"And is that what ye want? Marriage to a mon who will no' share yer bed? Do ye no' crave more bairns and the happiness of a true marriage?"

Anice began to answer and then stopped. Did she want that? Years ago, when preparing for her move to Dunnedin, she had dreamed of a wonderful life, filled with children and a husband and her duties as lady of the clan MacKendimen. Her innocent imaginings were far from the reality of her life once she arrived. Sandy, whom she had met only twice before, was in England, and she spent her time carrying out Lady Edana's orders. Then after the lady's death, she took over and ran the keep as chatelaine and prepared for her wedding—the wedding that did not come until five years later. Memories of that wedding and the weeks after reminded her of what she wanted.

"I want simply to return to my duties in Dunnedin and be allowed to carry on as I did before, without the attentions of a husband." There. That explained it clearly.

"Even if that husband is Robert?" Lady Margaret sipped from her cup and looked at Anice over its rim. Anice nodded. "Then why did ye seek him out? What did he do to ye that ye would punish him in this way?"

"Punish him? I do not understand your meaning."

"Weel, lass. Ye hiv saddled him for the rest of his life wi' a wife in name only, one who will no' give him bairns of his own, one who will no' share his bed. It surely sounds to me that ye meant to punish him."

Anice reeled at her words. She had not thought of the impact of her actions on Robert's life. She had sought him out because she trusted him to help her, never dreaming of the solution he would suggest. In her desperation to escape marriage to another man and losing her babe, she had sentenced him to a life without a family to call his own.

"I did not realize . . . ," she whispered, horrified at the results of her actions.

"Can ye no' commit to him in a real marriage?" Lady Margaret's words were soft, but the question terrified her.

"I cannot. Not even knowing now the wrong I did against him." She had told him that he would have to take whatever he wanted from her, that she could not offer it to him. He knew the truth of their arrangement. Why was Lady Margaret trying to change things between them? "He knew before we married that I could not give in to him that way. That he would have to take his marital rights without my cooperation."

"And kenning him enough to trust him with yer life and that of yer son, do ye think he would take from ye? I raised him better than that, dear. Can ye no' trust him wi' yer body now that ye hiv turned yerself over into his care?"

Flashes of the night with Sandy reminded her of the horrors her body and soul had suffered. She would never be able to separate those memories and fears and hold them aside while joining physically with another man, even if that man was Robert. Shivering at the terror provoked even now by those thoughts, she stood and stepped away from the table.

"I want to check on the babe. If you'll excuse me, Lady Margaret?"

"Of course, my dear." Lady Margaret stood as Anice made her way to the door of the solar. "Anice?" Anice turned to face her.

"Why do ye think he did this?"

"Robert? I do not know. I asked him and he said he has his own reasons."

"What do you think those reasons are? Have you thought aboot it?"

"To raise his own standing? To seek the inheritance I bring to my husband? That is why men marry above their station in life, is it not?"

"That is why most men would marry someone with a title and wealth. Do ye think he does it for that?"

Anice just needed to get away—from the lady and her troubling words. She did not want to examine Robert's reasons or her own more closely right now. She just wanted to get back to Dunnedin and settle this with Struan and her father.

"A true union can stand against any and all who threaten it. There is nothing stronger. Remember that, lass."

She almost ran from the words. Craig did not need her right now; that was an excuse to leave. Anice searched for a place to be alone and found it after several tries. She discovered a small herb garden near the lower kitchens and sought some quiet there among the still-growing plants. It was not long before she was on her knees, weeding out the herbs and preparing them for the coming autumn harvest. Only the signal of her very full breasts told of how much time had passed while she toiled there. Wiping her hands on a towel she'd found among the tools, she stood to leave.

The sound of a baby crying echoed through the garden and she felt her milk let down and start to seep into her dress. Crossing her arms over her chest, she walked to the entrance, only to find Robert standing there. He carried her squalling son on his shoulder and smiled when he saw her.

"Emma was aboot to feed him when I returned to my . . . our room. I thought ye may hiv need to?" He looked at the telltale stains on her gown and his gaze seemed to make the milk flow even faster.

She could only nod and take the babe from him. Returning to a bench in the shade, she threw her shawl over her shoulders and loosened the ties on her chemise and her gown. Bringing the babe to her breast, she sighed as the draw on her nipple released the flow and brought with it some measure of relief. It was only then that she remembered Robert's presence.

"I am once more in your debt, Robert."

"The laird has made arrangements for us to leave at daybreak for Dunnedin."

"So soon?" She rubbed her hand over the babe's head as he suckled contentedly.

"Duncan sent a messenger early yesterday saying you had been found and that he would arrange an escort when you had recovered from the injuries you sustained in your journey here."

"Did the messenger tell the rest of it?"

"Nay," he said. "Duncan sent him at our approach, before anything more was kenned."

"He is a smart man." Anice recognized the tactic—Duncan said only what needed to be said and did not lie.

"I learned much from him in the years I spent here."

"And in spite of the affection I can tell you feel for him and Lady Margaret and the welcomed place you would have here, you would leave and return to face the uncertainty at Dunnedin?"

"Aye." His voice was low and he looked away as he answered her.

"Why, Robert?" She hoped for some answer to the question that Lady Margaret posed to her. She needed to gain a better understanding of what drove him to help her in this way.

"I hiv my own reasons, Anice. I told ye that before we married."

"And you will not share them with me?" His face hardened as she watched and she knew he would not.

"I will no' be at dinner in the hall this evening. There are errands I maun complete today that will keep me away until late."

Craig had stopped sucking so she lifted him up to burp him. Patting and rubbing his back, she looked at the man who had saved her life. How could this work between them when she could not give him what men wanted from their wives? A sense of depression filled her and she felt like crying. Her selfish fears had brought him into this. Her inability to obey those who were in charge of her life cost him any chance at real happiness. The only thing she could do to repay him was to stay out of his way and follow his directions.

"Very well. Would you like me to keep a tray warm for your return?"

"Nay, Anice, dinna trouble yerself. I can see to it when I return."

She placed Craig in the crook of her arm and lifted him to her breast. When she looked up she was alone in the garden with her son. And wasn't that just what she told Lady Margaret she wanted?

So, if this was how she wanted her life to proceed, why was she unable to stop the tears from flowing? Why was she filled with regret over her actions? And why did she want to beg Robert's forgiveness for entangling him in her plot?

"*Did ye speak to her?" Duncan asked his wife as she en*tered their chambers. Although Robert had left, Duncan could still see Anice sitting on the bench with her babe. And, when the wind blew just so, it carried the sounds of her soft crying to him where he stood above her.

"Aye, husband. I did as ye asked." Margaret joined him at the window and looked down into the herb garden below. "Is she there?"

"Robert just took his leave of her. Things are no' going weel between them, I fear."

"Truly? What makes ye think it?" His wife had to stand on tiptoes to see over the ledge.

"Listen."

The wind carried the sad sounds to them once more and Duncan saw tears in his wife's eyes. He took her hand in his and lifted it to his lips. Although discarded callously by Struan, Robert had been a joy to them in the time he lived at Dunbarton. Margaret had supported his decision about Robert's upbringing and training as soon as he'd made it and in spite of Struan's requests to the contrary. Neither one of them understood Struan's hardheadedness in the matter of his natural son.

"He loves her already," Margaret said, sighing.

"Can she love him, though? After what she's survived?"

"I think she can, but does no' recognize it yet. She watches him when he does no' ken and I hiv seen the interest there." Margaret turned to face him. "She needs time to get over her fears, Duncan. Then, I think they could be happy."

"Ah, time. I am no' certain that Struan will give them that time."

"He will support her faither in this, do ye think?"

"I wish I could say, Margaret. I just dinna understand his opposition to Robert. If I kenned his reasons for steadfastly refusing to recognize him, I might ken what he will do when he finds out aboot their marriage."

"Robert does no' seem worried aboot Struan?" His wife looked out once more and they watched together as Anice gathered her son in her arms and left the garden.

"He will no' tell me more aboot that, only that he haes a way to assure Struan's compliance."

"Robert would no' be the first natural son to seek to raise himself by marrying an heiress. Even the MacNab found his fortune that way."

Duncan laughed out loud and took his wife's hands in his.

"'Tis best if ye dinna remind the man of that fact. Those recently titled dinna want to dwell on how lately they came to it. Or how."

"Weel, husband, all we can do is hope for them. Now, I will leave ye to yer work." She tried to walk away, but he pulled her into his embrace.

"Wi' all this talk of the newly married and wanting and loving, I find myself wanting you, wife." He took her mouth with all the passion she still enkindled in him after all these years together. When she was breathless, he dragged her to their bed and took her down with him. Kissing her again and again, he whispered to her, "Will ye hiv me, wife?"

"Aye, husband. I will hiv ye."

Her eyes were filled with desire and even as he tugged at the laces of her gown, he offered up two quick prayers to the Almighty—one of thanksgiving for finding her and one begging that Robert and Anice could find the same thing between them. Then he was lost in the love they shared.

chapter 25

It was much later than daybreak when they were finally on the road back to Dunnedin. First, Duncan insisted that they break their fast together. A problem with the wagons they would take back put off their departure even later. Then just as he thought they were ready to leave, Anice became ill. Although it was surely her nervousness about returning to Dunnedin that caused her stomach to rebel, that explanation did not suit Lady Margaret and so he waited. Finally, after a dose of some herbal concoction that Ada and the laird's wife created, Anice's stomach calmed enough for them to leave.

They left with much more than they arrived with, for the MacKillop was generous in giving to them on the occasion of their marriage. A mare with good bloodlines to match his own stallion, clothing, some jewelry, and even some matching gold cups were included. Although both he and Anice assured them that they did not need these things, Duncan would not hear of him refusing the gifts.

So the two wagons, laden down with supplies and gifts, an armed escort of six warriors, all known to him, and two maids to accompany and see to Anice and the babe's needs made up his entourage as he returned Anice to Dunnedin. The journey progressed well, taking advantage of the warmth of the early August days and using the main road to reach Struan's keep in as short a time as was possible.

He saw little of her during the trip; he spent his time with the other men, and she stayed with Craig and the women. They spoke only when necessary and he could see and feel the tension growing within her as each mile passed, bringing them closer to their destination.

Robert wished he could share his fears with her about their future, but she was dealing with her own fears. Her eyes began to take on that haunted look and she seemed restless. He was not the only one to notice her behavior. Even Craig was off his schedule and became fussy as the journey continued. Robert realized that nothing would improve until they arrived and faced Struan with their actions. And with the knowledge he now carried with him.

After three days of traveling, Dunnedin came into view and everyone in their group came alert. In a short time, they rode through the gate and into the castle. Shielding his eyes against the midday sun, Robert saw Struan standing on the steps, watching their approach. Struan said something to Brodie, who stood nearby, and turned and entered the keep. Robert pulled up on the reins, bringing Dubh to a stop, and dismounted. Walking over to Anice's mount, he waited for her to adjust the bairn in her arms and then lifted her to the ground next to him.

Firtha's cry could be heard throughout the busy courtyard as she saw Anice for the first time. Before he could say aye or nay, the woman had Anice in her embrace and was checking her over from head to toe. Then she claimed the bairn and subjected him to the same inspection. Every little thing that did not meet her standards gained Robert a frown or stare. As if it was his fault that she had run away by herself! But before she could spirit Anice away, as she obviously planned to do, Brodie called to them.

"The laird would see ye both in the hall, Robert."

Robert nodded and offered his arm to assist her up the steps.

"Courage, lass. Here we go now," he whispered so that only she could hear.

They made their way into the keep and then up and into the great hall. Struan and some of the elders sat at the table in front of the room. Since the evening meal approached, the room was filled with people preparing the tables. Robert led her up to the front and waited on Struan. They did not wait long.

Struan stood quickly, knocking the chair he sat on over and then kicking it out of the way as he circled the table. His fury was palpable and Robert prepared himself for the confrontation to come. The laird strode down the steps and approached them. Robert felt Anice's shudder and her grasp of his arm tightened with Struan's every step. The hall quieted as the clan waited to see his response to Anice's flight.

"How dare ye? How dare ye think ye could run and take my grandson from me?" Struan's eyes blazed with anger and he raised his hand to strike her. Anice threw up her hands to protect her face, but Robert was there first. Grabbing Struan's hand, he stopped the blow in midair before it could even come close to her.

"She is my wife, Struan, and no one will touch her while I live and breathe. No' even ye."

He grasped Struan's arm and threw it back away from her. The shock of his announcement roared through the hall until everyone present had heard. Struan stumbled back a few steps and then he caught himself and stood.

"It canna be! She is to marry Angus MacLaren."

His words brought on another wave of surprise and Robert could hear whispered gasps throughout the room.

"The Demon MacLaren? Surely ye did no' plan to give her to the Demon?" Firtha's voice rose above the rest and Robert was puzzled by the name given to Angus, for he'd never heard it before. The women in the room clearly knew it for they all turned a disapproving look towards Struan, as though giving Anice to this man was a fate worse than death. And considering what Anice had already faced in her life, that was not a good thing. They actually began hissing at their laird.

"She is my wife, Struan, and no' to be part of yer plans any longer. I will take care of her and her son from now on."

"Nay!" Struan roared. Robert waited for Struan's next words and watched as his father struggled to regain control over his anger.

"Is it true, Anice? Did ye marry him?" Struan asked, his breath coming hard for him.

He looked over at her and waited for her words. Her face was a ghostly pale and she shook in the face of defying Struan. But she placed her hand in Robert's and nodded. "Aye, Struan, he is my husband."

Robert contemplated kissing her here in front of the clan as he had in Dunbarton, but decided not to push her that far. Exhausted as she was, he feared she might faint before them. He turned and instead touched his lips to her forehead.

"Firtha, take Anice to her chambers. She has no' recovered from her injuries and needs to rest now." Struan started to object but Robert cut off his words. "I will speak to ye in private, Struan. Anything ye hiv to say to Anice can be said to me now."

Struan recognized he'd been outplayed for the moment and acquiesced to his demand to speak privately. Allowing Struan to lead the way to the solar, Robert watched Firtha take Anice and the bairn out. Content in the knowledge that she was being cared for, Robert turned his attention to the battle before him. Closing the door as he entered, Robert waited for Struan to speak first.

Struan faced him from across the room and Robert looked for some indication in his expression to tell him what to expect. There was no sign of the fury that had held him sway in the hall now. Only the cool facade of a master strategist planning his next move. Robert cleared his mind and waited.

"Ye canna think that this marriage will stand? If the truth is kenned, she will disavow ye for the lying bastard ye are."

"But ye hiv sworn never to acknowledge me as yer son before the clan, Struan. If I am no' yer son, then I am free to marry the Lady Anice."

"Ye are my son, Robert. We both ken the truth of it. A marriage to yer brother's widow is no' a true marriage in the eyes of the church. It will no' stand."

Robert fought the urge to cry out at Struan's words. For the first time in his entire life, Struan had called him son. The need within him to hear those words through all the years of his exile at Dunbarton had not lessened and he felt his throat tighten with unshed tears as he let the words sink into him. Why could it not be that simple? Why did Struan say them now and not when it would have mattered the most? He pulled in a ragged breath, trying to retain his control, for losing it could be the end of this.

"Faither Cleirach married us at his church. I hiv the papers wi' me declaring us wed."

"But he is a priest in the old ways. The MacNab will no' recognize it."

"The old ways are just as accepted in the Highlands as the Roman Church, Struan. We both ken that. And an annulment will be just as difficult and expensive to get, since the Roman Church will no' take the chance of simply ignoring it."

"Ye will no' thwart the MacNab in this, Robert. He wishes an alliance wi' the MacLarens and will get it wi' Anice's marriage to Angus."

"No' any longer. She is my wife now, declared by the church and handfasted before witnesses at Dunbarton. The MacNab will hiv to look elsewhere in his clan for someone to bind them to the MacLarens."

Struan paced back and forth across the room, clearly not done but planning another attack. He stopped and faced Robert with his fists on his hips.

"If she says that ye forced her to this, all yer subterfuge will be for naught."

"Ye were the one who forced her, Struan. She ran away from yer plans to take her bairn from her and wed her to another mon." Robert crossed his arms over his chest.

"And ye mean to tell me that ye did no' hiv this in mind? Ye dinna expect me to believe that ye never wanted her for yerself!" Robert must have let his guard slip and something show in his gaze for Struan latched on to his argument. "Does she ken ye want her because yer brother had her first? Does she ken that she is as much a pawn for ye as she would be for her faither?"

"She came to me, Struan, begging my help." He strengthened his resolve not to show weakness.

"So, ye hiv no' shared the truth of yer birth wi' her? She does no' ken that ye covet her just as ye coveted yer brother's place here in the clan? What do ye think she'll do when she discovers yer secret?"

"And who will tell her? Surely no' ye, for it will mean acknowledging me to the clan." Struan opened his mouth to speak, but no words came out. "I would propose a bargain between us, Struan. For the good of the clan, of course." Struan nodded and Robert continued.

"I will agree no' to seek my place as yer son here if ye agree no' to oppose this marriage. Actually, ye will need to go further than that. Ye will need to convince the MacNab to give us his blessing."

Struan looked at him and burst out laughing. "The MacNab haes already begun negotiations for the contracts. He will no' back down from those."

"Then ye maun find a way to make him see the wisdom in making his alliance using some other woman in his clan. Anice haes a cousin Wynda who is no' yet married."

"Why would I when I agree that this way suits both of us?"

Robert wanted to pummel the man for his complete disregard of Anice in this whole business. Her needs and wants were of no account in the face of his decision. He knew that this was the way of it, but surely her sacrifices for his family should count for something, some small consideration in this. Robert walked closer and reached in his sporran for the item he'd carried from Dunbarton. Placing the feathered end of the arrow in Struan's hand, he stepped back and waited for his father's reaction.

"Because, Struan, if ye share the truth of my parentage wi' Anice or support the MacNab's pursuit of an annulment of our marriage, I will share wi' the clan the story told to me by a fletcher who left here the day after Sandy's death."

He got the reaction he knew would come. Struan looked at the arrow and then stumbled backwards into the table. His breathing became labored and his coloring turned gray. Although a laird was expected to be ruthless in his protection of his clan, most of Struan's allies would think that the cold-blooded murder of his own son was going too far. His father appeared to age before his eyes. Sinking into a chair, Struan rubbed his face and mumbled under his breath.

Robert remembered something Duncan had told him. "If the MacNab objects to my marrying his daughter, ye may want to remind him of his own climb to wealth and title by kidnapping Anice's mother and keeping her against her will until she was pregnant. I am certain he does no' wish his daughter to ken the truth of her beginnings either."

When Struan said nothing more to him, Robert turned to leave. This extortion was distasteful to him, but necessary to ensure Anice's safety here. A part of him wished that Struan could have just accepted him and accepted the marriage without argument. And another part of him still wanted the acknowledgment that he had just forsworn away. Stopping at the door, he asked the question that still haunted him.

"Why no' me, Struan? Why could ye no' accept me as yer son?" Robert swallowed deeply, trying to prepare himself for whatever words Struan said.

"'Tis of no consequence to ye now, Robert."

"No consequence, ye say? When lives hiv been torn apart and lost? When yer son lies dead and buried and his widow is scarred for life by his depravity? Ye could hiv chosen me as yer heir. I was older. I was worthy. I could hiv done ye proud. Why could it no' hiv been me?"

"I canna say any more than that, Robert."

The feelings of the night when he discovered the truth came rushing back to him. The shocking news, the longing to be called son, the sinking despair as the acknowledgment did not come. His stomach rolled and his eyes burned with the same fury as they had that night over eight years ago. And the anguish of something precious lost to him forever tore through him once more.

He pulled open the door and ran out into the hall. He could not face anyone at that moment so he left, running to the stables and reclaiming Dubh from his groom. Leaping on his back without the use of a saddle, Robert gripped the horse's mane and steered him by hand and leg out of the yard and gate and away from the village. Giving the horse his head, Robert stared through tear-filled eyes as the trees and bushes passed in a blur. Not even aware of his direction, Robert allowed the stallion to carry him where it would as he grieved for all he had lost.

chapter 26

She spent most of the day pacing in her chambers. She waited for some sign of how the meeting between Struan and Robert had gone, but no one spoke of it. Anice had looked through the window and seen Robert racing away on his stallion. She feared what that meant to her, to them, and waited, as he'd said to, in her chambers. Surely, if Struan meant to punish her, he would do so while Robert was absent from the keep. When no one came to drag her down to face the laird, she felt some semblance of relief. She knew she would have to wait for Robert's return to gain the whole story.

The servants delivered her trunks and Robert's an hour or so later. Anice hesitated to rearrange her chambers to accommodate him. For all she knew, he was out riding to gather his courage to tell her that she could go with him back to Dunbarton but that her son would remain with Struan.

Her apprehension threatened to take control of her and she knew it was that fear and tension that made her unable to nurse Craig. She tried several times throughout the afternoon, but each time he refused to latch on and draw nourishment from her. He fussed and cried and screamed out with anger and hunger and she became more and more nervous. She was tempted to send him out to the nurse who'd accompanied her here; however, she feared never seeing him again.

The room grew quiet and Anice looked up to see Robert standing in the doorway. Searching his face for some indication of what had transpired between him and the laird, she waited for his words.

"I would like to speak to Anice in private."

The servants and Firtha looked to her for guidance. She nodded them out and watched as Robert closed the door. Craig still screamed on her shoulder, but she could almost block out the sound of his cries while she waited on Robert.

"Here now, Anice. What ails him?" Robert asked as he lifted the babe from her and placed him on his own shoulder.

"I cannot feed him. He will not nurse and he grows angrier by the minute. And I grow more and more full."

"Do ye hiv wine here?" She nodded and pointed at the jug of it on the table. Robert reached into his sporran and took out a small bundle. "Put a pinch of these in the wine and drink it. Ada said ye may need something to soothe yer nerves and release yer milk."

She looked at him in honest admiration. What kind of man would care about these things? Most men would simply demand that she turn the babe over to a wet nurse and bind herself until the milk was gone. And yet he had carried herbs with him that would calm her raging emotions and allow her to nurse more easily. Once more she felt in his debt.

She took the packet from him and added the herbs in as he directed; their aroma was savory and they added to the wine's sweetness as she sipped it. He watched her as she drank and although she wanted to shout her questions at him, she waited for him to tell her. He carried Craig around as though he belonged there and he motioned for her to get into bed. Once she leaned up against the headboard he came closer and leaned down to hand her the babe.

He smelled of outdoors and of horse and of that smell that belonged only to men. And he took care of her and her son before seeing to his own needs. Anice knew that whatever happened she would be grateful to him until the day she died. He looked up at that moment and caught her gaze. Then she looked at his mouth and wanted to feel his lips on hers. Anice saw him staring at her mouth and knew that although he wanted the same thing, he would not move first. So she tilted her face to his and pressed her mouth to his.

It lasted a few seconds, for Craig screamed out his frustration and startled them both. Smiling, Robert placed the babe in her arms and stepped away. She tugged a blanket over her shoulder and tried once more to feed her son. He turned to and fro, searching for her nipple, but he was not able to latch on due to the fullness of it. Anice reached in and massaged the nipple, expressing enough milk to soften it for Craig's mouth. He finally took hold and Anice found that she could relax and let the milk flow on its own.

Glancing up, she saw an expression of pain on Robert's face. Pain and something else. She could not understand it and when he looked quickly away, she wondered if she had truly seen it at all.

"I spoke to Struan and we will stay here at Dunnedin."

"What? Here? He gave his permission?" She tried to remain calm, for now that he'd started nursing, she did not want the babe to stop.

"He haes accepted our marriage." His voice carried no tone to tell her how he had accomplished this.

"And?"

"And what, Anice?" he asked. "Ye and yer son will remain together and we will remain wedded."

"How did you accomplish this? It looked so hopeless when I left the hall."

He paced in front of the hearth before he spoke. "I told ye that I would handle things wi' Struan and yer faither and I hiv. Let it go at that."

Anice wanted to ask more questions—she had thought of dozens while waiting for his return. However, the expression he now wore warned her off. She nodded and turned her attention to her son, now suckling vigorously at her breast.

"I would have unpacked your trunks, Robert, did I know the outcome of your talks with Struan. I will see to them as soon as I finish with Craig."

"There is plenty of time for that, Anice. I need no more than the clothes on my back today."

"How will we do this, Robert? I think you will tire of sleeping on the floor every night."

He looked at her as though he wanted to say something and then stopped himself. Shaking his head, he smiled at her.

"Duncan sent along one of those carpets ye admired so much, Anice. Laying it over the rushes will be plenty of cushioning for me."

She wanted to offer to share the bed with him; it was on the tip of her tongue and she could feel the words forming in her mouth. A ripple of fear passed through her and she stopped. Even though she honestly wanted to, she knew that it would be impossible for her to invite him to her bed. The very thought of him lying beside her during the night, even if for nothing other than sleep, left her terrified.

"'Tis just not right, Robert. I do not know how to make it right, but I can feel the unfairness of this bargain we've made between us."

"Anice," he whispered. "We maun take this one day at a time and all will be weel."

Craig chose that moment to let go and gurgle his pleasure out to her. She looked down and laughed with him and when she looked up, Robert was gone. She lifted her son to her shoulder and rubbed his back as he cooed to the empty room. Anice did not know how to be a wife to Robert. She only knew that she would try everything within her power to take care of him and make him happy with their bargain.

T*he knock on her door surprised her when it came. She* had already seen to organizing Robert's trunks in the room and had another chair moved into the chamber. Rearranging the furniture and changing the rushes made all the difference within the room and now there was space for Robert's makeshift bed to be placed by the hearth. Anice had eaten her meal there since she had not the strength or the composure to face the clan this evening in the hall. Tugging open the door, she found Moira and Pol standing in the corridor.

"Come," she said, inviting them in.

"I will wait for ye out here, Moira," Pol said in his deep voice.

"I will join ye in the hall when I am done here," Moira answered. "There is no need to wait by the door."

Anice could have sworn that Pol growled in reply. Moira looked at him and his expression did not change. With her hand on the door, Moira smiled at her husband.

"Verra weel, I will no' be long then."

Anice stared at the woman who now waddled across the room and sat on the edge of her bed. Moira was now getting closer to her time and obviously Pol was not content to let her wander through the keep alone.

"The daft mon thinks I canna see to myself now that I carry his child."

"He worries for you, Moira. I think he worries that you will face what your sister did all those times before this."

"Aye, he does. No matter what I tell him, he is happier worrying. But, he is a good mon."

"Aye, he is that. Now what brings you here at this time?" Anice sat next to her on the bed.

"Struan said ye were hurt on yer journey. I came to see to yer injuries." Moira's gazed focused on her and moved from head to toes. Standing up before her, the healer lifted her hair and pressed lightly on the bruise that remained on her forehead.

"When did he say that?" Anice asked.

"Tonight at dinner when he announced yer marriage to Robert and Robert's new duties as castellan."

"Struan did that?" Anice was surprised. From the look on his face when last she'd seen him, acceptance was the last thing she expected.

"Aye. He told us that ye were hurt during yer journey so I thought a visit would be a good thing. Did that bleed?"

Anice touched the bruise. "I do not think so. Moira, I fell and hit my head. I did not wake until the next morning. Robert took care of it for me." Moira gave her a look filled with disbelief.

"Were ye dizzy or nauseous when ye woke? Any pain there now?"

"I have had an ache in my head for days, but I do not know if it comes from the injury or from what has happened." Anice stood and walked to the hearth, not facing Moira.

"I hiv no' heard all the details yet, but 'twould seem to be an interesting story to hear."

She was using that voice again—the one she'd sworn to teach her to use when trying to make children and men obey her. Anice turned and smiled at her.

"My father and Struan were negotiating a new marriage for me, Moira. They planned to wed me to Angus MacLaren and Struan planned to keep my bairn." She looked over at the cradle where Craig now slept.

"To the Demon?"

"I heard him called that today in the hall, Moira, but not before this. Why is he named so?"

"'Tis rumored that he killed his wife for not giving him a son."

Anice shivered at the thought of another woman married to another man like Sandy. No wonder they called him a demon. And she thanked the Almighty that she had gathered enough courage to run away from that marriage.

"Do you believe the talk?"

"All rumors are made of mostly story around a few facts, Anice. I dinna ken what to believe."

"I ran without knowing that rumor. I ran because I could not face marriage and losing Craig. I did not think, I just ran."

"To Robert? And into married life once more?"

She paced before the hearth. "I ran for my life. Robert offered me protection as his wife. He said it would be only for that."

Moira did not say anything and Anice looked at her. "Did he say why he would do this for ye?"

"Only that he has his own reasons. I asked him what he will gain from this, but all he does is scowl at me when I ask."

"Mayhap he hopes for the wealth yer faither planned to bestow on yer husband? Mayhap a title from the king, as yer faither gained in marrying yer maither?"

"It could be that, Moira. I just do not know his reasons."

"Weel, mayhap 'tis best to leave it be for now. Once ye ken him better, he may explain himself to ye. The bairn is weel?"

Anice smiled at Moira. "Aye, Craig is well. And growing like the weeds in the garden. I think his first tooth may come soon."

"And the nightmares? Do they come as often as before?"

Anice frowned, trying to remember the last time the dreams came. "Not since Sandy's death. Do you have some reason to think they'll return?"

"Now that yer married again, yer fears may give rise to them."

"Fears? Now that all seems settled with Struan as Robert promised it would be, I have nothing to fear."

Moira simply stared at her in that assessing way of hers and said nothing. The sound of voices outside the room drew their attention. The door opened and Robert entered.

"How do ye fare, Moira? Ye look weel."

"I am weel, Robert," she said, glaring past Robert at Pol, who stood watching her from the doorway. "Welcome back to Dunnedin. I did no' think to see ye so soon after yer departure."

"I had no' planned to return, but plans change." Robert looked right at her as he spoke.

"Weel, I will take my leave of ye. Anice, do ye want some herbs for the pain in yer head? 'Twould be no trouble at all to get them for ye."

Anice started to answer, but another growl from Pol interrupted her. Instead of being concerned about Pol's obvious anger, Moira laughed. Pol took her hand and began to pull her from the room.

"My thanks for your visit, Moira. I will call on you if I need anything for my head."

Moira started to speak, but the door slammed before she could get the words out.

"He thinks she is being stubborn and doing too much so close to her time," Robert said, laughing. "Much like ye were while carrying Craig."

"You think I was stubborn then?"

"Oh, aye. Stubborn is a polite way of saying it."

She thought back to some of her behavior near the end of her pregnancy and realized he was right. She also realized that he had shared much of that time with her.

"'Tis just like a man to expect a sweet disposition from a woman who cannot sleep, cannot tolerate certain smells and foods, and can no longer see her feet when she stands."

He grunted and she laughed at the sound. She knew now that he did that when he knew not what to say. Robert grunted, Pol growled. Changing the direction of the conversation, Anice sat on the bed and pointed across the room.

"I put your clothes in that trunk and your belongings in the small casket next to it. The plaids you brought from Dunbarton are in that one over there, along with the ones I already had. Is there anything else you need here in our chambers?"

He looked at the trunks and then around the room.

"Nay. I will keep my weapons in the armory."

"I brought in another chair so that you can eat here if you wish. And I plan to use the antechamber for bathing. . . . At first I thought to make it into a nursery for Craig, but I am not ready to have him so far from me. If it meets your approval?"

"Anice, this is fine." He walked to the table and sat down in one of the chairs next to it.

"Or . . ."

"Or what?" He looked at her and waited. She took a breath and offered another choice to him.

"We could use separate rooms, if you'd rather not sleep in here at all. 'Twould not be such an unusual arrangement for a married couple."

She regretted the moment the words left her lips. She offered it because she did not want him to be uncomfortable sharing her chambers. But she hoped deep inside that he would not choose that way. Confused by her feelings, she waited for his response.

"Is that what ye wish? Yer own room?" His face darkened and she noticed that he kept clenching and unclenching his hands into fists on his lap.

"I . . . ah . . . 'tis truly up to you, Robert. I offered it only as a way to give you some privacy and a bed to sleep in."

He stood and walked nearer. "I think we should keep up the charade of a marriage for a bit until everyone is accustomed to it. My thanks for making these changes to yer room to accommodate me."

" 'Tis our chamber now, Robert."

"So 'tis," he answered. She watched as he checked on Craig and then he approached the door. "I hiv some duties to see to before I retire. Ye dinna hiv to wait up for me."

All she could do was nod in agreement as he left. Once the door closed, she changed into her sleeping gown and arranged his bed on the floor near the fire. Duncan's carpet would be well used.

chapter 27

The *routine happened by itself, without much planning at* all. He left early in the morning, before she or the babe rose, and he returned to the chamber after they'd gone to sleep each night. He joined her for a few meals, but his new duties really did keep him busy and outside most days and into most nights. If she minded, she never said. The only response she ever gave him was the same—it is your decision, Robert, just say so.

He never bathed in the chamber's outer room and so far, thank the Almighty, he had never entered to find her in the large wooden tub kept for that reason. Robert had enough difficulty sleeping in the same room with her; the image of her naked in that tub was more than his poor body could handle. He found it necessary to never enter the chamber until he had exhausted himself physically. At least then he could get to sleep without his mind wandering.

The fact that his wife slept just a few feet from his miserable bed and he was not welcome there ate at him. Some nights when he could not sleep, he stood next to her bed and watched her breathe. He ached to feel the touch of her lips again, to run his fingers through her fiery hair, to hear the sound of her laughter. He would even enjoy hearing her use that imperious tone of voice to him. But his wishes were for naught, for if she had somehow discerned his feelings for her, she never gave any indication of it.

Days turned into weeks and summer was almost done. The clan began returning from the summer shielings; the drovers guided the cattle back to their pens to prepare for the slaughter and preserving. Struan spoke to him as needed, but there was little else exchanged between them. Anice carried out the duties she'd returned to just before their marriage and he gradually took on more of the responsibilities for running the defenses of the village and castle and the training of the warriors.

And he knew that if something did not change between him and Anice, he would go insane. He was tempted to visit Robena, but he knew that word would get back to Anice. He valued Robena's friendship too much to risk her place, now a comfortable one, in Dunnedin. And he realized that he did not want the embraces and kisses of another woman, he wanted his wife. He cursed himself for being such a fool as to enter into this agreement with her and saw no way out for himself. He prayed, however, nightly for help in his dilemma. 'Twas Brodie that gave him the help he needed to take the first step towards her.

B*rodie challenged him to a wrestling match. It seemed like* a good way to burn off some of his restlessness, so he agreed. Now, with his face being pushed into the dirt of the practice yard, the idea did not seem as smart as it had before.

"Come now, Robbie. Ye can do better than that," Brodie goaded him on.

Robert slipped free of his hold and attacked again. He managed to grab hold of his leg and upend his friend to the ground. Pouncing on him, Robert twisted along with Brodie, keeping hold of him at each maneuver. Those watching along the perimeter of the yard cheered for one or the other with every move. Out of the corner of his eye, he saw Rachelle approach the fence.

"I was taking pity on ye, friend. I dinna want yer wife to hiv to watch yer defeat in her delicate condition."

The one moment of distraction caused by his words was enough for him to claim victory, his first over Brodie's superior skills. He jumped to his feet and hollered his joy to everyone around who could hear. Then, reaching down, he pulled Brodie to his feet and they walked towards Rachelle. It was then that he saw Anice standing next to her, red-faced from cheering and still clapping.

"I let ye win, Robbie. I did no' want ye to disappoint yer new wife."

He smacked his friend on his back and they ran over to their wives. Brodie lifted Rachelle into his arms and kissed her long and hard. To do less with his own wife would be too obvious, yet he feared her reaction if he showed the same enthusiasm as Brodie for Rachelle.

"I thank ye for yer support, wife." He took her by the shoulders and pulled her close. Dipping down to her, he kissed her mouth. The quick, for-show-only kiss he planned quickly turned into something more when she leaned into him and opened her mouth. He slipped his tongue in to taste her and held her closer as the kiss went on and on. It was as he had dreamed it could be—she did not pull back, she did not cry out in fear. Instead, he felt the tentative touch of her own tongue on his as he kept their mouths together.

His cock surged yet again beneath his plaid and, on its own, his body sought hers. Stepping closer, he wrapped his arm around her shoulders and held her tightly. He knew immediately that he had done something very wrong for she turned to stone in his embrace. Lifting his mouth from hers, he saw the old fear in her eyes. Seeking to make the end look somewhat mutually planned, he smiled and released her.

"Brodie, I think Anice just got a good whiff of me. I should wash up before accosting her again."

Brodie and Rachelle laughed, neither of them apparently bothered by the odor of fighting men. 'Twas an excuse, pure and simple, to allow Anice to escape from him without drawing too much attention. And she did so with hardly any words. Rachelle went off with her, but not before exchanging some curious looks with her husband. Robert watched with utter longing as Anice walked away.

"So, when will ye end this charade and tell her how ye feel?"

"What are ye talking aboot, Brodie?" He tried to bluff his way out of this, but Brodie saw too much.

"Come now, dinna play me for a fool, even if ye hiv chosen to act like one."

"Brodie . . . ," he growled in warning.

"Rob, I can see what is happening. Ye want her now even as ye wanted her this last month. Now she is yer wife, but something holds ye back from her. Is it her fear of men?"

"Aye, 'tis that. And was I so obvious in my lust for her that you and others noticed?"

Robert did not wait for an answer; he turned towards the armory and Brodie followed along. When they were away from anyone else, he stopped. Wiping his brow with the back of his hand, he stared at his friend.

"I saw it because I ken ye. I doubt that anyone else noticed."

He grunted.

"Most here ken she canna abide being touched, even innocently, by the men of the clan," Brodie continued. "They go oot of their way to avoid any contact wi' her, and hiv since she recovered from Sandy's savagery."

He exhaled, surprised that so many knew what it had taken him days to see. "Do they all ken what he did?"

"Oh, nay," Brodie assured him with a fierce shake of his head. "Most ken that Sandy beat her, but no one haes ever spoken of it wi' her. I doubt that even Moira haes. But the fear shows itself despite her efforts to hide it."

"Do ye ken what he did?"

Brodie did not answer right away, but spent a moment or two looking at the keep in the distance. "Aye, Rob. I was closest when Firtha sought help." He saw Brodie swallow deeply and heard him clear his throat once and again. " 'Tis a miracle that she is alive today."

If Brodie, a warrior of fierce abilities and experience, was so moved by what he had seen, Robert could only imagine the horror of it. And here he was lusting after her. How could he so callously ignore all she had suffered?

"And here I stand lusting after her and trying to force myself on her."

"Nay, Rob. Anyone could see she was involved in that kiss. Mayhap she is learning to let go of her fear?"

He shook his head at his friend. "If it were only that easy, Brodie."

Brodie gave him a questioning frown. "What hiv ye done, Rob? What holds ye back?"

"I promised her a marriage in name only. I gave my word not to take what she did no' offer on her own." Even he could hear the misery in his voice.

Brodie slapped him on the back and laughed at him. "Then get her to change the agreement—or get her to offer! Whichever is the easier quest."

Robert looked in disbelief at his friend. Easier? Neither of those choices offered much hope of gaining her confidence and trust.

"Or get used to yer hand!" Brodie roared and trotted away before Robert could punch him.

A fine friend he turned out to be—laughing at his pain and making such a suggestion. Mayhap he would ask her to change their bargain. . . . If she agreed he would make it work between them, he would make it good for her. And if she said no, then he would be free to seek relief elsewhere.

H*e entered the room without knocking and found her sitting* in one of the chairs, working to repair one of the babe's gowns. It was still daylight and he guessed she worked here because Craig slumbered in the cradle near the fire. She looked up and watched his approach.

"I would speak wi' ye, Anice, if ye hiv time?"

"Aye. Craig should sleep for at least another hour. Do you want to talk here or should I call someone to sit with him?"

"No, this is fine," he said as he sat on the other chair. "I wish to speak to ye aboot our arrangements."

"Arrangements?"

"Our marriage."

She blanched, losing all the color in her face. Her reaction did not bode well for him or their future. She twisted her fingers together and he could see her tremble.

"Do ye think we could ever hiv a real marriage, Anice?"

"Lady Margaret asked the same question of me, Robert, and I think the answer is still the same. I fear not."

"I promise to make it good for ye. I would never hurt ye. Ye do believe me, dinna ye?"

She shuddered at his words. He had his answer without her saying anything. He stood to leave. Anice reached out to him and then stopped just short of touching his hand.

"Robert. I am sorry. I tried to tell you when you made your offer."

"Aye, Anice, ye did. And damn me for the fool I am, I thought it would change as ye got to ken me better."

"I know that men seek their pleasures, Robert. You do not need my permission; however, I would understand if you sought your pleasure with someone else. I fear I cannot give you what you want from a wife."

He stared at her, but she would not meet his gaze. He walked straight out of the room, not daring to say any more to her. Seek his pleasures with someone else? As though he needed her permission.

She could see that he had been drinking for some time before the meal started. One pitcher sat in front of him and she could tell as she lifted it that it was nearly empty. Anice took her seat between Struan's chair and Robert's. He had never overindulged in wine as long as she'd known him; somehow this day was different. She knew that she was the cause.

"Kenneth?" she called out to the boy who served the head table. "Bring me a new pitcher, with water this time, please."

"Ye may drink water if ye choose to, wife, but I want more wine."

His eyes were red and she could smell the wine on his breath as he held out his cup to the page and demanded more. Would he be a mean drunk? She looked around and noticed the speculative looks from those closest to the head table.

Platters of food were placed near them on the table and she reached out to fill her plate.

"Can I fix your plate, Robert? Some food to fill you?"

"Nay, wife. I hiv no stomach for food. I wish to drink my meal."

This was bad, truly bad. She had no power to stop him from doing whatever he wished to do, be it drink or anything else. Anice decided that her best choice might be to leave and eat in her room. There was no sense in angering him more with her presence after she had refused to consider his request earlier.

"If you will excuse me, Robert, I must check on Craig." She started to rise, but he grabbed her hand and pulled her back down into her seat.

"Nay, Anice. There is no need for ye to leave, for I hiv no intention of staying here. Enjoy yer meal and yer evening."

He stood and swayed on his feet, the wine making his balance wobbly. He tripped down the steps and she held her breath, waiting for him to fall. The entire room grew quiet as he laughed his way through the hall. Then, shocking her even more, he paused in the back and plucked Robena from her seat. Dragging her to him, he wrapped his arm around her shoulders and pulled her from the hall with him.

She could not move. The muscles of her chest refused to draw in air. Her eyes burned with tears of humiliation at his actions. She blinked to try to control them, for crying in front of everyone here would simply add to her shame. Realizing that she had to leave, she rose in one movement and stepped away from the table. If God was merciful, she would escape the room before losing control.

The Almighty must have been paying attention to someone else's prayers, for she had taken only a few steps when the tears began to fall. Anice gathered up her gown and ran from the room, as much horrified by her reaction as by his behavior.

chapter 28

Someone was pounding on his head. Blinded by the light surrounding him, Robert tried to make his eyes open. Lifting his head only caused more agony and he moaned from the pain of it. He heard noises nearby that he could not identify and tried to turn towards them. His stomach rolled and heaved and he missed vomiting on himself by mere moments. Climbing to his feet, he stumbled to some bushes and aimed away as the contents of his belly were ejected.

"Ye deserve every moment of the hell yer suffering now, Rob. Every moment of it."

'Twas Robena's voice, but why did she curse him so? Forcing his eyes to open, he saw that he now knelt in the clearing next to her cottage. And it was day. And the village was waking around him. How could this be?

He struggled to his feet and entered through her small back door. Robena sat at her table, sipping from a steaming mug and scowling at him.

"Do ye hiv any idea of how much damage ye hiv done to me now? Lady Anice was kind to me and ye hiv to humiliate her and use me to do it? What the bloody hell were ye thinking?" She slammed down the mug, spilling the contents on the table and on herself.

He pushed the hair out of his face and tried to remember how he got here and what he had done. The last thing he remembered was sitting at the table and deciding that a cup of wine would help him face Anice after his disappointment. He did not remember anything after the first pitcher. Oh, dear God! Not a pitcher? He groaned once more, realizing now what must have happened.

"'Twas at least two pitchers of wine before ye disgraced her by hauling me out wi' ye."

"Please. I beg ye to tell me I did no' do that. No' in the hall wi' everyone watching."

"Aye, ye damn fool, ye did it. Now she will never allow me to step foot in the keep again. If I am lucky, I will simply be chased from the village and no' tarred like some of the other whores hiv been."

He walked slowly to the table and sat across from her. "I will no' let her banish ye for my sins, Robena."

She snorted at him. "As if ye will hiv any say in it. She is still the lady and her word aboot me is the law. Did ye no' stop to think?" She stood and went into her room, coming out a few minutes later completely dressed.

"Where are ye going?" he whispered. It hurt to open his eyes. It hurt to speak. Hell, it hurt to live right at this moment.

"I am going to beg her forgiveness. Mayhap she will see me and hear me oot."

"Nay, Robena. Stay here until I send word to ye. If she will no' listen, I will send ye to Dunbarton."

"And I would be welcomed there? A whore who took the lady's husband? I think no'."

He frowned at her words. Something did not make sense.

"Did we . . . ?" He pointed to the two of them.

"Nay, Robert. Ye were so drunk I almost carried ye here. I was tempted to leave ye in the dirt where ye fell the first time, but I couldna."

"So then Anice will understand. We did no' do anything."

"Ye are such a daft mon, Robbie. 'Tis a wonder ye hiv made it this far in life. She does no' care whether ye tupped me or no'. She only kens that ye chose me over her in front of everyone last night. Ye hiv disgraced her before the clan."

He let his head thump down on the table, hoping the pain would clear his muddled thoughts and let him come up with some solution. He would have to do the begging. It would not be right for Robena to bear the brunt of Anice's anger.

He smiled as he realized that Anice would be angry. That was good. He could deal with her fury in a way that he could not face that desperation and fear that came over her at times. Mayhap she would even yell at him.

"What are ye smiling aboot now? There is nothing funny in this, Robert."

He stood up, a bit too fast, for he had trouble keeping his balance, and laughed in spite of the pain it caused.

"Aye, I hope she is angry. 'Twill be good for her to feel that again." She frowned at him and he explained. "She haes been walking lightly around me since our marriage, waiting for me to strike oot at her. This may bring oot the old Anice, which is a good thing."

He pulled her close and kissed her on the forehead. "Ye will no' suffer for this, Robena. I promise to make it right for ye."

Then he tugged open her door and walked out in the village. Now he had to find Anice.

H*ours later, he felt like a dog chasing his tail. No one* seemed to know where Anice was. Oh, many people gave him suggestions, but she was never where they thought she would be. He'd gone from keep to kitchens, to laundry, to stables, to the village, to the smithy and on and on without ever seeing any sign of her. He'd caught on to their game early. However he went along with them, accepting it as the penance for his foolhardy behavior.

He got the message—Anice would not talk to him until she was ready to and the people of Dunnedin were supporting her the only way they knew how. So, he hid in the workroom until long after dinner. Then he enlisted the help of the wet nurse he'd brought from Dunbarton. When he was certain that Anice had retired for the night, he went to their room. Knocking softly, he waited for her to open it. She surprised him by speaking through the door.

"Who is there?"

"'Tis I, Anice. Open the door." He tried to keep his voice down and not draw any attention.

"Go find someplace else to sleep, Robert."

He wanted to laugh out loud at her words. This was the old Anice stirring.

"Open this door now, wife," he said more forcefully through the door. He knew she hesitated on the other side. "If ye dinna, I will break it down."

He heard her gasp clearly and then he could tell she was moving around the room. He pounded on the door and spoke again.

"I dinna want to frighten the babe by breaking in, Anice, but I will if ye dinna open this . . ."

He stopped when he heard the scrape of the bar being raised inside. He turned the latch and opened the door. He stepped back and Emma passed by him and entered the room. Robert motioned to Anice to stay as Emma lifted Craig from his cradle and carried him from the room. She looked like she wanted to argue, but kept silent while the servant was there.

"I dinna want to disturb the babe, Anice, and we hiv some things to discuss. Emma will care for him until we are finished."

He turned and lowered the bar into place, preventing any interruptions. She sat down in one of the chairs and glared at him.

"Why did ye lock me oot of my own room?" He stood with his arms crossed in front of the door.

"You made it clear by your actions last night in the hall that you would rather sleep elsewhere. I was simply enforcing your decision."

"That is no' what I want, Anice, and ye ken it."

"Then why did you leave with . . . that whore?" He could feel her anger bubbling out. Her tone of voice was filled with it. Once it flowed, there was no stopping it. "How dare you humiliate me in my own hall before the clan? You married me. You promised your protection to me. Is this how you give it? By getting drunk and dragging the village whore with you as you leave?" She stood and pointed at the door. "If you plan to have her, you may as well go to her now, for you will not sleep with her and then come back here."

Robert fought against the urge to laugh out loud. He knew she would not understand how happy this tirade made him. It would not solve their problems in the run of it; however, they stood a chance if she did not cower at his own anger when it happened.

"Does that no' feel good, Anice? To shout oot yer fury at me rather than living in fear?" He waited for her reaction.

She was enraged and, by God, she had reason to be. Her tears had turned to rage once she realized that he had gone with Robena to her cottage. He had asked her to be a wife and when she could not, he simply discarded her and took up with a whore. The worst of it was that she'd believed their tale of being friends. She'd believed that Robena was different. She'd thought Robert was different than other men and their boorish behavior when it came to taking their pleasures. She'd been wrong and now she was angry at how her foolishness had been exposed before everyone there last night.

"I do not understand you, Robert. Are you pleased that you have driven me beyond control?"

"Ye are no' beyond control, ye are simply too angry no' to say it. 'Tis fine wi' me if ye do. I think we will deal better wi' that rather than the constant fear ye carry." She was not fearful of him. What did he mean?

"I do not fear you. I have not been afraid of you since the first week of your stay here."

"Then why," he asked in a softer voice, "do ye walk around me as though ye wait for me to strike oot at ye? Ye did no' treat me this way before we left Dunnedin, Anice, and I would ken why ye treat me differently now?"

Did he speak the truth? Did she treat him differently? Of course she did—they were married now and he was her husband. He was not the same man who had left Dunnedin.

"You are my husband now. You are not the same as before." Saying it to him made her wince at the absurdity of it. She thought about his treatment of her and her son and realized that he had been the same kind and concerned man as before he'd left to return to the MacKillops. It was only her perception and her anticipation of the change in their roles that made her fear him.

"Hiv I done something to make ye believe I would turn on ye? Is there something I said that frightened ye?"

"Other than your horrible behavior last night?"

"Aye, other than that." His mouth moved into that enticing smile that made her stomach nervous. He stepped closer to her, yet remained a few paces away. "Would it help ye to ken that I did no' sleep wi' her? I was too drunk and hiv paid a dreadful price for my stupidity in turning to wine instead of having this talk then."

"So, you did not have her only because you could not? Now that the effects of the wine have passed, will you turn to her once more?"

"Anice, in truth, ye are the only woman I want."

Her breath caught and she could not think of anything to say in response to his claim. He stepped closer again.

"I hiv wanted ye for months now, even when I never dreamed it would be possible. And now that you are my wife, I find that I dinna want to face the rest of our lives wi' only part of ye."

"I told you, Robert . . ."

"I ken what ye said, but yer lips say something different to me when we kiss. Yer gaze is always on me, I can feel it when we are in the same place. I ken that ye are confused, Anice. Just say ye will let me try?"

Oh, how she wanted to give over to him. A part of her that had been buried deep inside was pushing for release. There was fear, fear of pain, fear of rejection, but there was a glimmer of hope and a glimmer of the passion that had lain dormant within her for years. She'd felt it once for the impostor; it had driven her to sneak into his room and offer herself to him. 'Twas only his self-control that had prevented a catastrophe that night. And the feelings, the heat, the passion lay waiting for the right man.

Could it be Robert? Was she strong enough to conquer the fear and take what he offered to her now? A true union, as Lady Margaret had said.

"I am terrified at the thought of it, Robert," she admitted. "I do not know if I can be a wife to you in this way."

He held out his hand to her and smiled. "Just take my hand and say ye will try. 'Tis all I ask, Anice, just that ye try."

Her hand moved on its own for she had surely not made up her mind to try this. But once she saw his face brighten at the sight of her hand moving, she could not, would not stop it. The least she owed him for all he had done for her and her son was an honest effort on her part. She'd trusted him with her life countless times, could she not trust him with her body now?

Her body shook as he took the final step towards her. Lifting her chin, he leaned down and touched his lips to hers. The same heat that happened with his kisses burned inside her again. Waves of fire pulsed within her and the feel of his tongue against hers made something tighten deep inside her core. With every movement, his mouth caused the heat to increase until she thought she could not take any more. When he lifted his mouth from hers, she knew she wanted even more.

His eyes were glazed and she could feel that his body was ready, and yet he did not throw himself at her as Sandy had done. She found it difficult to breathe at a normal pace.

"I want so much to touch ye. May I?" He watched her and waited, not moving until she gave him the permission he sought. His voice, now husky and deep, enticed her further. She nodded her head and closed her eyes.

His mouth covered her again and as his kiss deepened, she felt his hands glide through her hair. It was thrilling in an unexpected way and it was the last place she thought he'd touch. In a way she was disappointed that he had not touched the place she thought he would first—her breasts. They ached and swelled, almost as though she was ready to nurse, but she knew this was different. His fingers combed down through her hair and she found it strangely exciting to feel the pull on her scalp. Just when her knees felt as though they would collapse, he stopped and looked at her.

"Are ye afraid? May I kiss ye again?"

"Aye. Nay." She laughed. "I mean, I am not afraid." She did not know they could laugh while doing this and it felt good to do so. "Please, please kiss me again."

Robert leaned down but she met his mouth this time, eager

to taste him the way he had tasted her. He was close enough for her to feel his body surge each time she slipped her tongue into his mouth. It was a heady, powerful feeling to know she affected him this way. She was so intent on his mouth that she nearly jumped when his hands glided over her shoulders, pushing her woolen shawl down her arms. Then she felt his fingers trace her collarbone and his thumbs moved down onto her breasts, tickling and teasing them as he went. The intensity of his touch on her nipples was almost painful and she drew in a breath as he moved over them.

"Not good?" he asked, lifting his lips from hers just enough for the words to fit through.

"Nursing makes them sensitive," she whispered back.

"But no' here?" He touched under her breast. "Or here?" He rolled his fingers around the fullness of her and drew circles around them.

The tingling grew until she knew her breasts were swelling in his hands. His touch was stirring sensations within her that she did not know existed. She arched towards him, increasing the contact between them and bringing her closer to the hardness of him. She raised her hands to his shoulders to keep him close.

He lifted his mouth from hers and traced the same path over her neck and shoulders, however this time he used his tongue instead of fingers. Hot and burning against her skin, it moved down and down as he unlaced her gown. She thought he meant to touch her breasts in the same way, but he stopped for just a moment between them and looked at her. She could hardly breathe or focus her eyes on him; the feelings that rampaged through her made concentration so difficult. She let her head roll back as heat exploded inside of her.

His hands on her hips began to slide down once more, so slowly that she felt something within her tighten more and more with every inch of her that he touched. She felt a gush of wetness between her legs and she waited, nay, she wanted him to touch there. As he moved his hands closer and closer, and his fingers began to slip into the curls there, he kissed her neck. A moment later as his fingers slid deeper into that heated, aching cleft, he nipped at her shoulder, letting his teeth graze lightly over her skin there.

It was as though icy water had been thrown on her in that moment. Worse than that, flashes of Sandy and their wedding night poured into her mind, terrifying her with memories of his teeth on her skin. Bites and cuts and blood filled her vision until she could only scream out against them.

"No, please, no!" she screamed as she pulled from his embrace and ran to the other side of the room, backing up against the wall, as far away as she could get. Robert's face changed into Sandy's and back again until she felt as though she would faint. He approached slowly, holding out his hands to her, but her mind could not make out which one stood there before. Terror wracked her with tremors until she could not see anything at all in the room. The blackness covered over her.

chapter 29

He caught her before she hit the ground. 'Twas becoming a habit he thought gone with her pregnancy months ago. Robert recognized the terror as her face drained of blood and her eyes rolled back in her head. If he had not witnessed it before, he would not have believed the speed at which she went from awake to unconscious. Scooping up her slight weight, he laid her carefully on her bed. He drew the edges of her gown together and tied them more securely so that her breasts were covered.

After tossing a sheet over her and then a blanket, he pulled one of the chairs close to the bed and sat to wait. Holding his head in his hands, Robert took some deep breaths and blew them out. His body still hummed with the passion she'd aroused. He was hard, rock hard, but that was dwindling by the moment. The sight of her face as some memory returned to haunt her was something he would never forget. And he hoped to never see it happen again.

The pounding in his head began anew and he thought about lying down. Looking around he realized that the bedding he used was not pulled out yet. He smiled halfheartedly as he comprehended that she meant her words—he was not welcome there. Robert reached under her bed and pulled the blankets and piece of carpet out, intending to place them before the hearth. Her gasp alerted him that she had awakened.

Before he could sit back up, she had scooted back up against the headboard on the other side of the bed and had dragged all of her covers with her. Her eyes were filled with fear as she watched him. He decided to wait and say nothing until she had calmed down. Every move he made startled her, so he sat as motionless as possible on the chair. Finally, after several minutes had passed, she whispered his name.

"Robert?"

Her breathing was still ragged and her face had not regained its color. Clutching the covers like a shield to her, she pushed the hair back from her face and looked around the room. He could see the confusion on her face.

"Aye, Anice. 'Tis me. How do ye feel? Would ye like something to drink?" He began to stand until he saw her shaking increase. He sat back down and waited.

"What happened? I remember your kisses and then the blackness. What happened to me? Oh, dear God, what did I do?"

Her question ended with her voice cracking. She started to cry and it broke his heart to hear. She had tried, she had tried for him, and now her pain was so clear and visible to him that he wanted to sob for her.

"Ye did nothing wrong, Anice. Truly, the fault is mine for trying to force ye to do something ye are plainly no' ready to do. Can ye forgive me?"

"But you did not force me, Robert. I wanted to try . . . I wanted to try for you and . . ." Her voice descended into sobbing once more. "Wait," she yelled, kneeling up in front of him. "I know what it was! Your teeth! You bit my shoulder and the blood . . ."

She was nearly hysterical now, grabbing and tugging on the laces he had just tightened. Tearing the gown from her neck, she rubbed her neck and shoulders and looked at her hands. Obviously, she did not believe what she found, for she repeated it over and over until she was shaking and sobbing so badly she could no longer control her hands. Realizing that she was far past his abilities to help, he strode to the door and walked into the hall, calling for a servant. Sending the man off to bring Moira as quickly as possible, he returned to find her still rubbing her neck and still examining her hands.

"Anice, I hiv summoned Moira to help ye. All will be weel, I promise."

She rocked on her knees and clutched her hands to her chest. The only word he could understand was blood. He could only imagine, and only if he forced himself to it, what Sandy had done to engender such a reaction in her to the touch of his teeth on her skin. Robert knew without a doubt that he himself had not bitten her. His teeth did nothing more than rub over her shoulder, something that women in his past had found to be pleasurable. Some memory of some horrible act had flooded back to her in that moment and brought the terror alive in her again.

Not for the first time, he wished Sandy were alive so that he could kill him in some torturously slow way. His hands clenched to fists as he continued to watch her frantic motions. He would like to hold her securely in his arms until Moira arrived, but he feared that an embrace of that kind would scare her even more.

After what seemed to be an eternity, he heard a soft knock at the door. Anice was kneeling, still mumbling, on the bed. He crossed quickly to it and opened it for Moira to enter. Pol nodded to him and did not try to enter. Closing the door, he pointed to the bed across the room. Moira looked at him for a moment and then walked to where Anice was on the bed. Using that calm, commanding tone of hers, she asked Anice what had happened.

"He bit me, Moira. Can ye no' see the blood on my neck and on my hands?" Anice held out her hands to Moira. There was nothing on them.

"Let me see yer neck, lass. Here now, I will clean it for ye."

Robert watched grimly as Moira went through the motions of cleaning a wound that did not exist. He clenched his teeth together, all the while fighting the urge to roar out his own anger.

"He tore my skin, Moira. Wi' his teeth. He bit until I bled. Promise me ye will stop him. Ye canna let him do this again.

Struan promised me . . ." She rattled off the words, never pausing, and with an accent that he had not heard from her before. Robert realized that she normally spoke in a very unaccented, formal Gaelic, but she slurred her words now as most people he knew did.

"Sit back, Anice. I will fix ye a brew to help ye wi' the pain," Moira directed as she poured a cup of wine from the pitcher on the table and took out a packet of herbs from the leather pouch she wore around her waist. "Drink this, lass, and let it rid ye of yer pain." Moira lifted the cup to Anice's mouth and Robert watched as she drank every drop of it without resistance.

"Will ye hiv to stitch it again, Moira? Haes he torn it open?"

He shivered at her words. She was clearly in the past, reliving the days after her wedding. She did not look at him at all, focusing only on Moira. 'Twas a good thing, for he was not certain he could even speak to her. He crossed his arms to control his own horror.

Nothing could lessen his guilt.

He had brought her to this state. Oh, he had never expected something like this to happen; he truly would never want her to suffer in this way. But his lust for her and his demand that she try to be a real wife to him had caused this. He was just as responsible for her pain now as Sandy was all those months ago.

"Nay, lass, no' this time. 'Twill heal quickly enough," Moira reassured her. "Lie back now and let me fix the covers around ye so ye can get some rest. Let the brew warm ye inside, Anice."

He watched as Anice followed the healer's instructions, first sliding back and climbing under the bedcovers and then lying quietly. He watched in silence as her eyelids started to droop and some of the tension left her face. She still mumbled words that he could not understand, but somehow he knew it was better that he not. Sometime later, only the sound of her breathing, now low and easy, could be heard.

Moira checked her several times before gathering her supplies together. She made several small bundles of herbs and left them on the table. Then she turned to him.

"We thought this was past."

"This haes happened before?"

"The night terrors leave her confused and reliving some of what happened to her. It haes been months since anything like this."

Robert walked to the chair and sat down in it. He lifted one of Anice's hands and smoothed out her fingers from the fists she held. The herbal concoction must have helped for there was no resistance in her at all.

"'Tis my fault, Moira." He could not look at her as he spoke.

"I dinna believe that ye bit her, Robert."

"I pushed her too fast. I wanted her and I did no' think aboot the problems it could cause her."

"Robert, ye put too much guilt on yer own shoulders. This haes happened before and I fear it may happen again. Some small word or some small gesture of yers simply brought back the memories to her."

"But I . . ."

"Ye would not force yerself or yer lust upon her, Robert. I ken ye too weel to think that of ye. Give her some time to adjust to ye and yer marriage and things will be fine."

He let out a long breath and nodded his head. Moira was probably correct—Anice simply needed more time. He would not pressure her again about his desires.

"Now, I should go. If she wakes during the night and is distraught, mix one of these packets in a cup of wine and make her drink it. She should sleep through until morning, though, so dinna expect her to wake."

"My thanks for yer help and for coming so quickly to her aid."

"I was here treating Struan's stomach pain so 'twas no inconvenience to me."

Moira walked to the door and he rose to follow her. She stopped him and saw herself out. Robert sat just watching Anice sleep for a long time. Then he realized that he should tell Emma to keep the bairn for the night. Standing and stretching, he circled the room and blew out most of the candles before leaving.

"Robert?" she whispered. "Is that you?"

"Aye, Anice. I am here."

"Keep me safe, Robert. Please?"

He knew by the turn of her head and her breathing that she had sunk back into a deeper sleep. And he swore then that he would keep her safe even if it meant from him.

T*he sunlight shining through the window above her was a* good thing. The bitter aftertaste of one of Moira's brews was not. She pushed herself up onto her elbows and looked around her chambers. Firtha sat off in the corner with Craig on her lap, singing to him about his toes and tickling them as she sang. He obviously enjoyed it, for he giggled right along with her words and touches. Anice smiled at her son's antics.

"Yer pardon, Anice, if we woke ye?" Firtha asked when she saw her sitting up.

"I think it is time for me to rise. How far past daybreak is it?" She slid to the side of the bed and stood. A bit unsteady on her feet, Anice held on to the bedpost and waited for the dizziness to pass.

"Weel, we finished the noon meal sometime ago."

"What? And no one woke me?"

Firtha stood and positioned Craig on her hip. Coming closer, her companion offered her a cup of water.

"Robert gave orders that none were to disturb yer rest. He said ye were no' feeling weel and should be left alone. Ye look weel now."

"I feel better, too, Firtha. Is he ready to eat yet?—for my breasts are surely ready for him." Her breasts were full and hard from the length of time that had passed without a feeding.

"The little piglet will eat anytime ye offer it to him, Anice. Let me help ye to a chair. Or do ye wish to see to yer needs first since he is no' pitching a fit yet?"

"Can you keep him for a few minutes longer? Let me wash up a bit first."

Anice quickly used the garderobe and washed over the basin in her room. Many questions about last night pressed into her thoughts, but she refused to think about them now. After she saw to her son's needs would be soon enough. She was settled down, feeding her son, when Firtha gave her the message.

"Robert asked if ye would join him outside, if ye felt up to it."

"When?"

"He said I should ask ye when ye awoke if ye felt up to a short walk wi' him out in the yard. If ye do, he said to come oot when yer ready. If no', he will speak to ye later."

She did not know if she could face him yet. He must be shocked by her behavior. She remembered only patches of it when the terror came upon her and knew that she completely lost control during those times. Usually it happened at night, so only Firtha and Moira and Struan were aware of the hysteria she suffered from. But now, Robert had seen it and he must be horrified by it.

Anice did not dwell on it, fearing that thinking too much about the cause might bring it back. She hoped that Robert would not either, for she was not certain how to explain the madness to him. He had gained many more problems in their marriage than even he had bargained for; he surely knew that now. And with her inability to grant him his marital rights, he must be regretting ever getting involved in this.

"I do feel like taking a walk, Firtha. If you'll help me dress, I will meet Robert as he requested."

S*he found him standing not far from the keep, leaning* against the fence that surrounded the stableyards. The late summer breeze blew across the open expanse between the buildings and caused his hair to blow in his face. If he noticed, he gave no sign of it, staring off into the distance at something she could not see. Anice walked quietly to his side, trying not to disturb his thoughts. Although she thought he'd stiffened at her approach, he gave no sign of noticing her presence. Until Craig gurgled at the sight of him.

Robert turned and faced her then, first a quick glance then a thorough one from her head to her feet. Then he smiled at her and reached for the babe.

"Here, ye maun be tired oot from carrying him all this

way." He took Craig and led them both to a spot in the shade of a nearby tree. "Would ye like to sit?"

He held out his hand to her and she took it, holding on as she knelt down then sat on the ground. He sat down and placed Craig on his lap as though it were the most natural thing for him to do. She watched him with her son and felt such love for him that her heart felt as though it would burst. Her eyes filled with tears as she realized that she loved him for all that he meant to her. He met every need she had and never forced his own on her. He cared for her and her son through injury and illness and never asked for a return. And she loved him with everything within her.

She rubbed her eyes to hide the tears. Looking away, she took a few slow deep breaths, trying to accept the emotion she now felt within her. She could never tell him about it for he would feel even more responsible for her, but it was there in her heart.

"Are ye weel, Anice?" he asked in a soft voice. His concern nearly forced the tears to her eyes once more.

"I am well, Robert. Just some dirt in my eye, 'tis all." She wiped at them again and had the feeling that he saw through the weak excuse.

"I wanted to speak aboot last night," he started. "I am certain that ye are as uncomfortable as I am in bringing it up."

"Robert, you do not have to say . . ."

He held up his hand to stop her. "In spite of what Moira said, I feel responsible for yer . . . attack last night. I can accept that I did no' mean for it to happen, but my actions caused it."

"No, Robert, 'twas not your fault."

"I pushed ye too hard for what I wanted and did no' give ye time to adjust to our marriage."

She turned to face him. "Robert, I wanted to be your wife in all ways last night. I did. Truly."

He lifted his hand and rubbed her cheek lightly with the back of it. "I think ye did, Anice. But some part of ye is no' ready or the terror would no' hiv seized on ye as it did."

She wanted to argue with him; however, he was right—something inside was not ready. "How will I know, Robert?"

"Ye will ken the time of it, Anice. And I will be waiting for ye to come to me. I will wait for ye to take the first step. Dinna fear that I will push ye in this again."

"Another man would not be so tolerant."

"I canna answer for any other mon, Anice. I only ken that forcing ye before yer ready would make me no better than the monster ye married first. And I could no' live being that kind of mon."

No, he could not. He was honorable and kind. He put her concerns before his on a regular basis. No other man could come close to him. And he was her husband.

"Will you be in the hall for dinner or should I have something kept for you?" She had to change the subject or she risked sobbing out her love for him.

"If ye would like, I can join ye there."

"Please?" Robert looked at her and nodded his agreement.

"Now, I should take the piglet inside for his nap." She stood and reached down to him. "I'm certain you have things to do?"

He stood and straightened his plaid. "Aye, I do. So, I will see ye in the hall."

She watched as he walked away. She watched the wind blow his hair wild and the long stride he took when he moved. And she loved him more than she had just minutes ago.

chapter 30

The next week moved quickly for her. *For the first time* since her marriage, Anice felt like her old self and worked on a daily schedule with Connor. A year before she had not been able to complete many of the tasks usually undertaken in the autumn so she wanted to be prepared for the coming change in seasons. The clan, still uncertain of how she and Robert came to be married, yet unwilling to involve themselves in the estrangement between them and Struan, missed nothing.

Robert continued to work with the warriors and to improve the defenses of the castle and village. He and Struan seemed to forge some kind of understanding, for she did not notice the outward signs of their dispute. She would like to have known how he gained Struan's compliance, but feared asking either one. Anice decided to allow her husband to worry about that.

She did fret about her father's reaction to this. The fact that he had said and done nothing in response to the messages Struan must surely have sent, did make her nervous. When she tried to discuss it with Robert, his reply was the same—he would handle it.

What concerned her most however was how to take the

first step towards what she really wanted. Her body's reaction to his nearness, his smiles, his movements, told her she was ready to try. She did not know how he maintained such a calm demeanor around her, for she knew he caught her staring at his hands and at his mouth as she remembered the feel of them on her that night. The heat that surged through her at those moments was as enticing to her as he was and she searched for a way to make it happen. However, it was her uncertainty about the terror returning that kept her from taking that first step.

One evening at dinner, she looked around the hall and searched for Robena. Something tickled her mind and she thought that mayhap the woman could help answer her question.

"Robert, I do not see your friend here. Does Robena not eat in the hall?"

He choked on the food he was swallowing when she asked and it took several minutes and several mouthfuls of ale before he could speak again.

"I hiv no' seen her since that night, Anice," he said in a low voice. "I think she fears yer wrath aboot what happened here."

No words about Robert's behavior that night had been spoken since then, so she was puzzled by his comments. Robert had sworn that nothing had happened between them and she took him at his word. No one had asked how she felt about it, but 'twas obvious what they thought.

"My wrath? Why, Robert? What have I ever done to make you think I blamed her for your stupidity that night?"

She fought to keep the smile from her lips. Her words almost exactly echoed his own when he asked about her preconceived notions of him. And she waited for his reaction when he realized that she insulted him. His mouth dropped open and he stared dumbfounded at her. It felt good to tease him like this.

"Kenneth?" she called out. When the boy approached, she spoke again. "Go and fetch Robena to me, please."

When the boy had left on his errand, she turned back to find her husband still staring at her.

"Truly, Anice, she should no' bear the brunt of yer anger. I was to blame for the foolishness that night." He reached for her hand and then stopped, clearly unsure of whether he should touch her or not.

"I only wish to speak to her, Robert. And if somehow I have given the clan the idea that she should be punished, then I want to straighten that up now."

He looked as if he wanted to say more, but he took another drink of his ale instead. A few minutes passed and Kenneth entered the hall, followed by Robena. No one greeted her as they had, no one offered her a seat at their table. Instead, the sound of hissing could be heard as she moved through the room. A few men even spit on the floor as she passed by. As she came closer, Anice could see the fear on her face. She stood and walked down the steps to meet her. Robena dropped into a deep curtsy before her, but Anice grabbed her hand and made her stand.

"Robena, thank you for coming so quickly. Will you join me in the solar?"

As they made their way through the crowd, Anice asked her if she'd eaten yet. When Robena said no, she asked for someone to bring a tray to them in the solar. She knew exactly what her actions were saying to those who witnessed this. She could not allow the good that she had done in getting this woman accepted by the people to be lost because of her problems with Robert. She hoped this meeting would be enough without saying something more direct.

A short while later, after the tray had been delivered and after Robena had been assured that Robert had spoken on her behalf, Anice was ready to discuss the real reason behind her summons.

"I need your help, Robena."

"My help, milady? How can I help ye?"

Anice stood and walked over to the large window on one side of the room. This would not be easy—for either of them—and she did not know how to begin. She heard Robert's voice in her mind telling her to just say it. She smiled at his straightforwardness.

"How did you get the courage to take men to your bed after Sandy's attack?"

Anice turned at Robena's gasp. 'Twas as she feared—too personal a question even for a whore.

"Milady, are ye certain we should speak of this? He is dead and buried and I would prefer no' to think aboot that."

Anice walked to her side and knelt down on the floor. Taking the woman's hand in hers, she looked directly at her. "I think you know that he did to me what he did to you?" Robena answered her with a shaky nod of her head. "I need to get past it as you have." At her frown, she added, "For Robert."

"Milady, I will no' speak to ye of my times wi' Robert . . ."

"Nay, I do not expect you to break any of the confidences you hold from times you . . . saw him before we were married. But, Robena, I will not share him with you now that we are. No matter the state of our marriage, I cannot allow that."

She was bluffing of course and in spite of the fact that she thought that Robena knew it too, the woman nodded in agreement. No woman could keep a husband from sleeping where he would and spreading his seed where he wished. In spite of that, Anice could issue this ultimatum to Robena and hope the woman would do her best to abide by it.

Anice stood and walked to the chair next to Robena's. Sitting in it, she looked at the whore. "I want to . . . I wish to fulfill my . . . Robert wants . . ." Oh, damn, she thought, this was simply not something a lady spoke of to another woman.

"Ye hiv no' slept wi' Robbie yet? Is that the problem?"

"Aye," she whispered, now unable to meet Robena's gaze.

"And ye wish to?"

The heat stole into her cheeks. "Aye."

"Can ye answer my questions so that I might help ye in this?"

Anice glanced up and found a look of concern on the woman's face. This might work after all.

"I will answer what I can."

"Haes he kissed ye?" She nodded but Robena shook her head. "As a mon kisses his lover? No' simply on the cheek, but in yer mouth?"

Thoughts of his tongue in her mouth and the waves of heat those feelings created filled her mind. "Aye."

"Haes he touched ye? On yer breasts and there?" Robena pointed to the junction of her thighs. She could almost feel his fingers approaching that place again, and as his fingers had done, even the memories caused the wetness to seep there.

"Aye," she said a bit breathlessly.

Robena smiled at her; obviously the signs of her arousal were not missed by someone who made a living at creating that condition in her customers.

"When did the memories come upon ye? When he tried to enter ye?"

She did understand! Anice wanted to cry in relief as she knew then that Robena had gone through the same thing.

"Nay, he did not put himself inside me. It was a simple thing, a touch of his teeth on my neck."

She saw the shiver move through Robena and knew they shared another shameful experience. But if Robena could resume her activities, mayhap Anice could learn to take Robert into her body. . . . She did not need or expect to like it; she really only need tolerate it . . . for him.

"Forgive me, Robena, for reminding you. I . . ."

"Nay, milady. 'Tis fine. Let me tell ye how I managed to hold the bad memories at bay. Of course, I was already more experienced in this than ye are. I kenned that it did no' hiv to be this way."

Anice nodded. Robena had been a whore for some years before Sandy attacked her, not a virgin bride, completely inexperienced and untouched.

"I was able to choose who I would tup after that and I chose men who I kenned would be gentle and even fun. Then, when I would feel the fear gaining a hold of me, I would make sure to keep my eyes open and watch them. And if the fear came, I would think aboot the good feelings they kindled in me."

"You watched them? While they . . . ?"

"Aye, milady. Keep yer eyes open so ye ken who it is. Another question for ye, if ye dinna mind?" Anice nodded even as she thought over this approach Robena suggested. She had become confused in her terror and could not tell who was with her. Visions of Sandy's face had merged with Robert's until she did not know. Keeping her gaze on his face might help.

"Does he make ye wet . . . there?" Anice followed

Robena's eyes and nodded again, unable to admit that even now she was.

"Then if ye feel the fear beginning, just concentrate on how he makes ye feel there. Think only aboot his hands and his mouth on ye. Keep watching him."

Anice sat back and reached for the cup of ale on the table. Her face felt overheated and she could feel the sweat dripping down her back. She pulled out a linen square from her sleeve and mopped her brow.

Robena laughed at her actions. "If just talking aboot doing this wi' Robbie gets ye that way, ye will be fine."

Anice stood and Robena followed. They walked to the door, but before Anice could open it, Robena touched her hand.

"Milady? I hiv kenned him since we were bairns. He is a good mon, a special mon. If ye but give him a sign, he will take care of ye in this."

"I know that, Robena. He is waiting on me for that sign. And I do not know what to do."

"Touch him the way ye like to be touched. Kiss him the way ye like to be kissed. 'Tis simple, really."

"I will try. I owe him that much." Anice reached for the handle of the door, but Robena stopped her again.

"Ye do no' do this because of obligation, lady. I can see the love ye bear for him in yer eyes when ye speak of him."

She tried to smile, but tears filled her eyes at Robena's truth.

"And he does no' ken, does he?"

Anice could only shake her head.

"He's a good mon, milady, but more than a little bit daft if ye ask me."

Their laughter filled the solar and spilled into the great hall when she pulled the door open.

T*hey were laughing? He stood to watch the two women in* his life come out of their encounter and to see if both were unscathed. And they walked out of the solar laughing? 'Twas certainly not what he expected. He wanted to go over and find out what they spoke of, but this really needed to be settled by Anice. The hairs on the back of his neck prickled as he watched his wife and his friend approach the dais. Anice climbed the first two steps and then turned back to Robena who still stood below on the floor.

"Robena, you are still welcome to join in our meals here."

"Thank ye, milady," Robena answered as she curtsied before Anice. "If ye hiv need of me, please call on me again."

Robert could see that this was for show, to let the others know Robena was permitted in the keep once more after his indiscretion, but something else was going on here. He watched the two of them closely and thought he saw Robena wink at Anice as she turned to leave.

He remained standing until Anice was seated next to him. When he sat, he could see her eyes were filled with merriment. It did him good to see that. Too many of her days had been spent in dread and fear and he would make her laugh if he could.

He took her hand and brought it to his mouth, touching his lips gently to her knuckles. "Ye hiv my thanks once again for treating her with kindness."

"She is quite an . . . enlightening woman."

Those hairs tingled again and he wondered just what they had discussed. Anice reached over and took a wedge of cheese from the platter near him. Whether meaning to or not, she brushed against his arm. That was all the contact it took for his body to react—and react quickly and with vigor. His nightly swims in the loch were the joke of the other men, although Brodie assured him that they did not know the true reason behind them.

He walked around with an erection most of his days and all it took to put him in that state of being was one look at her, or one word, or that damned smile of hers. He'd been caught more than once lately in their room when she woke and he was forced to watch, through nearly closed eyes, as she slid from the bed. She would stand and shake her hair free of its braid before pulling it into a fresh one for the day. His fingers would begin to twitch and then his cock would harden as he watched the flimsy nightgown she wore to bed glide over the curves he wanted to touch.

Mayhap sleeping on the bare stone floor would make him

so uncomfortable that this reaction would not be possible. . . . If he thought it might work, he would try it. However, since he continued to catch her staring at his mouth, it was difficult to divert his thoughts.

She interrupted him at that point, which was probably a good thing considering the path his thoughts were taking. Another sleepless night he could do without.

"I will retire now, Robert, if you do not mind?"

He looked at her carefully. Her face was red and tiny beads of sweat lay on her upper lip. "Are ye weel, Anice?"

"I am just more tired than usual."

"I do no' mind. Mayhap ye should rest tomorrow?"

"Nay, Rob. I am certain to feel fine after a good night's sleep."

As he watched her walk away, he calculated the length of time that his nightly jog to and around the lake would take and his nightly swim. Even if he took the longer path, he could be back at a reasonable time and she would already be asleep. Mayhap he could also get a full night's sleep.

His bedding was laid out before the fire as it always was. Anice made certain that he would only have to climb under the covers and not have to fuss with the preparation of it. He closed the door as quietly as possible and walked over to check on the babe. The cradle was empty and he looked to the bed, for sometimes she took Craig to sleep with her there. He was not next to her. She must really be tired if she asked Emma to keep him tonight, he thought.

He peeled off his plaid and shirt and stretched before the warmth of the fire. His hair was still damp, for even the long walk back to the keep from the loch did not give it sufficient time to dry. As he stared into the flames, he thought he heard a noise from her bed and he turned to check on her. She coughed in her sleep and turned to her side.

Turning back to the hearth, he pulled his bedding a few feet more away and then climbed inside the layers of wool. He had just started to drift off to sleep when Anice stirred in her bed. She slid out of the bed and he frowned. She usually only left her bed to check on the babe, but he was not there.

Instead he watched as she walked towards him. When he would have spoken to her, she signaled him with a finger on her lips to remain quiet.

She stood next to him and then knelt beside him. As she leaned over, he thought to say something, but he was gifted with the touch of her lips on his. Her mouth moved on his, pressing and sliding until he opened for her. Her tongue licked over his lips and then he felt her slip it inside. The urge to grab her and take her almost overwhelmed him in his surprise. He fought to control himself and let her lead the way this night.

She deepened the kiss and he followed her motions, lip to lip, mouth to mouth, tongue to tongue. Anice moved closer and he felt the soft caress as her hair fell around him. He opened his eyes and found her looking back at him. She lifted her mouth from his and he felt her fingers tracing his lips and then his chin. She slid them down over his neck and onto his chest. Swirling them around in the hair on his chest, she moved them slowly towards his own nipples. Tingles of pleasure shot through him and he waited with a heightened sense of anticipation for her next touch.

Pushing the covers down to his waist, she explored every inch of his skin. The touch of her lips where her fingers had been sent shivers from his head to his feet and the pulsing in his cock grew even as it did. She was mimicking his actions of that night, he realized, but that did not stop the gasp when she licked his own flat nipples with her tongue. If he had thought that sleeping in the same room with her was torture, he'd been a fool. He sensed her need to control this and struggled to lay compliant beneath her searching fingers and questing tongue.

The groan that burst forth as she reached beneath the plaid could not be helped. Whether she stopped because of the sound of it or due to her own sense of reticence, he did not know. He only felt her fingers still on his skin. Looking down to see what she saw, he saw her gaping at the outline of his cock, erect and pulsing under the layer of plaid.

"Touch it through the plaid if ye dinna want to touch it beneath."

If he thought that would dull the fierceness of his arousal, he was wrong. All she did was move one finger around and over his cock and then she followed the contours of the sac and balls below it and he was lost in the waves of heat she created. He was ready to beg her for more when he felt the plaid slide down his hips and onto his thighs. He looked at her face, almost fearing what he would find in her eyes. Trying to lessen her apprehension, he smiled at her. She was killing him.

Wrapping his hands in the layers to keep them from reaching for her, he tried to breathe normally to calm down before she touched him flesh to flesh. It did not help at all.

First she repeated what she had done on the plaid, sliding her fingers over the surface of his erection and then down to the sac. Then—and he could not control the groan that escaped as she did it—she cupped her hand around him and stroked him. Another moan tore from him and she stopped.

"Nay," he moaned hoarsely. "Dinna stop."

"Do I hurt you, Rob?"

He gritted his teeth and shook his head. Satisfied by his reply, she repeated her actions again and again until he knew his seed would explode from it. He loosened his hand and grabbed hers before he reached the point of no return.

"I need to touch ye, Anice. Please let me touch ye?"

She looked confused for a moment and then shifted next to him.

"Should I lie down?"

"Lie, sit, stand, or hang from the bed, I dinna care so long as I can touch ye." He laughed at the innocent bewilderment in her expression. "How would ye be more comfortable?"

"I do not know, Robert." He detected guileless frustration in her voice; she was just as aroused as he, but did not know what to do about it.

"Come closer," he said, sitting up. "Step over here and sit down."

She frowned until she placed one foot on each side of him. He lifted her nightgown as she slid down on his lap. With her legs spread, she was open to his touch and he was to hers.

"Oh," she whispered and he adjusted her knees and brought the part of her that he knew ached closer to his hardness. "I ache," she moaned, as though she had heard his thoughts.

He touched her as he had the other night, tracing the fullness of her breasts through the silkiness of her gown. She arched again into his hands and he resisted the urge to use his mouth. Sliding his hands down to her legs, he pushed the gown out of the way and moved towards the very heat of her. Anice moved restlessly in his lap, until his fingers touched the dampened curls. Then she moaned as he had and the sound of it gladdened his heart. Waiting for her to adjust to that touch, he moved them in a bit deeper until he heard another moan. Her head began to fall back, but she opened her eyes and stared into his instead.

Robert lay back and began to move his fingers deeper within the cleft. Stroking over the wet heated folds, he watched her face for any sign of fear. When it did not happen, he slipped one then two fingers inside of her, always sliding gently in the moisture she created, never rough or fast. Her body began to follow the rhythm he set and she kept her gaze on his. She moved forward on his hips and rubbed herself against his erection.

"Help me, Robert. Show me what to do."

"Are ye sure, Anice? I would no' want to hurt ye."

"I trust you. Make me your wife now."

If he thought he could be noble at a time like this, he was wrong. His cock surged against her and he wanted to bury himself deep within her. Guiding her up with his hands on her hips, he paused for the tiniest of moments to give her a chance to stop him. She was looking at his face and not at his erection, so he pressed into her. Inch by inch, he entered her as slowly as the Almighty gave him the strength to do, praying that it would be good for her. He felt her stretch around his length and width and she moved ever downward on his shaft until he was in as deeply as he could go.

The expression of wonderment on her face brought tears to his eyes. He waited until she was accustomed to him inside of her like this and then he lifted her and drew down a bit. She gasped and then smiled.

"Do that again," she ordered. He was obviously bedding the imperious Lady Anice.

"Aye, my . . . Anice," he groaned out as she worked with him and made the movements exquisite torture to him. He was not certain, after another slide, whether he or she controlled it, but he gave himself over to the throbbing pleasure. He could feel his sac tighten and his peak approaching so he slipped his finger within her folds once more and found the little bud he knew would help her reach hers. Using the wetness that poured from her, he moistened it and then gently tugged on it. From her frantic movements, he knew she was close. He held off as long as he could until his body refused to obey and his seed gushed forward into her. He pulsed and throbbed inside her as her inner walls answered with their own waves of pleasure. Now her head dropped back and a moan resonant with sexual fulfillment echoed through their chamber.

She collapsed on his chest and soon only their labored breathing could be heard. He felt his cock slip from her body after a few minutes and he waited for her to say something. Her hair flowed over him as he once dreamed it would and he drifted off to sleep, completely contented for the first time in a very long time.

chapter 31

She felt the heat of the hearth on her legs and bottom, but could not figure out where she was. The front of her felt just as warm in spite of the fact that she was not covered in her bed. Anice opened her eyes and realized where she lay—on top of her sleeping husband. Memories of their joining flooded back to her and she rubbed her cheek against his skin remembering the heat and pleasure of it. When she tried to lift her head to look at him, she found his hands entangled in her hair. Her movements must have awakened him, for he shifted beneath her and loosened his grip on her hair.

"My pardon," he whispered in a gravelly voice. "I only wanted to touch it."

She pushed herself up on him and found the embarrassing fact that her bottom half was naked against his and her gown, soaked with milk, now grew cold in the chilly air of the room. Her nipples contracted and she gasped as his hardness grew under her once more. Anice looked at his face and found him staring at her breasts.

Struggling to get off of him, she kept doing all the wrong things and ended up losing her balance and falling on him. She felt the rumble of his laughter in his chest and then his hands were on her hips, lifting her off. With a quick turn to his side, she found herself sitting on the floor next to him. She let her gaze wander over him and she could not help but stare when she saw that his body was ready for another joining.

"Does it stay that way all the time?" She pointed and watched his hardness move under her gaze.

"Aye, Anice," he said, laughing and drawing the plaid over it. "It haes been that way for weeks and weeks."

"Is it painful?" He grunted at her. "Yer pardon, Robert. I just thought that it looked . . . uncomfortable."

"Aye," he said on a groan. "'Tis painful and I would rather if we dinna speak of it right now."

He pulled a layer of plaid around his waist and climbed to his feet. Once he gained them, he reached down to help her. The nightgown clung to her now and she needed to get it off and dry herself. She looked at his chest and noticed he was wet with it as well.

"I could not stop it. When I . . . er . . . we did that, the milk gushed out, too."

She went to one of the trunks and found what she was looking for. With a fresh gown in one hand and a length of toweling in the other, she walked back to him. With a few quick strokes she dried him off. Then walking to the far corner of the room where the light did not reach, she peeled off her gown, dried her breasts and stomach, and dressed again. Anice turned quickly at his gasp. Apparently the light exposed more than she thought. Her gaze went to the bulge clearly visible beneath the hastily wrapped plaid.

"Anice, ye maun stop looking at it," he moaned, readjusting the covering.

"Looking at your . . ."—she pointed at it when she could not say the word—"does that?"

He leaned his head back and growled out his reply. "I am trying no' to think aboot it and mayhap it will relax."

She was so intrigued by his body and by everything that had happened between them and she had so many questions to ask that she simply went on. "You cannot be serious that simply speaking about joining will keep that ready?" She pointed once more and watched the bulge move against the plaid he wore.

"Words are powerful, Anice. I will show ye how to use them, but no' now."

She felt the heat of embarrassment fill her cheeks. Her curiosity was unseemly and it obviously made him uncomfortable. She turned away and walked over to the pile of blankets in front of the hearth, intending to straighten them. Then she realized that things had changed between them. Or had they?

"Where will you sleep?"

He let out a breath and took a step closer to her. "Wherever ye say, Anice. There or in yer bed, 'tis up to ye."

She looked from one to the other place and did not know what to say to him. She wanted to touch him, but could she stand to have him close through the whole night? Would his shaft stay like that until she woke to find him pushing his way inside her? A shiver moved down her spine and some fleeting glimpse of Sandy's face entered her thoughts. Realizing what was happening, she looked at Robert and focused on his face.

"'Twill take more than just this one time to get over yer fears, Anice. There or there"—he pointed at both places—"it makes no difference to me."

She did not answer; she could not find the words to say to him. They were husband and wife now and she did not want to refuse him, but she was not certain she could stop the terrors from visiting while she slept if his body was so near hers.

"That settles it then, 'tis the floor." She would have objected or argued, she wanted to; however, she knew he could see her hesitation. "Dinna fash yerself, Anice. 'Twill take some time for us to adjust to this. I am willing to wait—so long as ye promise to visit me there when the mood strikes ye again?" He offered her a smile as he passed her. She could see he struggled to be kind.

Her love for him filled her heart. In every situation when he had a choice to make, he put her first. Torn by the love inside her and the long-standing fears that still fought for control, she could do nothing but return his smile and climb into her bed. Her empty cold bed. She pulled the covers over her and listened as he settled onto the floor.

"It did not hurt," she said to no one in particular.

First the outrush of his breath was heard. Then he spoke. "I did no' think it would."

She sat up and looked over at him, his face and form outlined by the low flames behind him. "Truly? Whyever not?"

"Once I remembered seeing the babe come forth from ye there, I feared ye would no' feel me at all."

"Oh." She had not thought about what he saw of her that night. She'd been too near death to worry about it then and had forgotten it afterwards.

He laughed and looked over at her. "My hand and my arm were inside ye, Anice. After that I did no' think my cock would find a tight fit. I did no' think ye would feel it at all moving within ye."

Mortified at his easy talk of such a personal event, she lay back down and scrunched her eyes closed, trying to ignore his chuckling.

"Well?" she called out to him. He could not expect to make such a comment and then not answer the doubts it raised in her thoughts.

"Aye, Anice, 'twas snug there for me. Ye fit around me like a falconer's glove is made to fit his hand, surrounding it wi'oot space between skin and leather. That tight." His voice ended on a sigh and she heard him shifting around on the floor.

It was then she noticed the wetness in the spot he spoke of, and how her breasts tingled again, aching for his touch on them. His words had stirred her to arousal just as he told her they could and now she lay, alone in her bed, trying to ignore the throbbing that built within her core.

"Do you think that two times might lessen my fears, Rob?"

"Two times? What do ye mean?" He sat up now as she did and gazed at her across the flame-lit room.

"You said yourself that it would take more than one time at this to lessen my fears. Mayhap we should try the second time here on the bed instead of there on the floor?"

Robert was at her side in a second, but he slowed himself as he got closer. She smiled; he was ever mindful of not frightening her. He stopped a step from the bed and waited for her signal. She slid back in the bed and lifted the covers. He held her gaze as he loosened the plaid still at his waist and let it drop to the floor. It was too tempting for her to ignore and, by his wicked smile, he knew what she would do. She moved her gaze down him to that part of him and watched as it surged in size before her eyes. Breathless, she looked back at his face.

"As ye wish, wife." He leaned forward and slid into the bed with her. And it was as she wished it would be.

They drove each other to distraction and exhaustion as she became accustomed to his body and the ways in which they could join. 'Twas quite easy, she discovered, to arouse her husband. With just a look or a glance at his groin or the slide of her tongue on her lips, she could draw that groan from him. He played the same game and she often found him waiting in dark corners for her approach. Her joy at being able to take pleasure from their joining and all that came before and after overtook her life and she found laughter once again filled her.

Robert also helped her to discover the darker fears, the embraces and touches that she could not abide. He knew never to embrace her too tightly or hold her hands behind her and that even the feel of his hand resting on her head brought on the shuddering terror. Even though the remnants of Sandy's depravity still existed within her, Robert's gentle touches and concern were helping her to lessen its importance in their life.

Each night he stayed longer in her bed, until he slept by her side the whole night through just a fortnight after their first time. She would come awake in a fright sometimes, but now the feel of him at her back soothed the fears for her.

The clan noticed the change in their relationship, as did Struan. Although he never commented on it, she caught him smiling at their antics from time to time. The smile would always turn quickly to sadness and Anice was tempted to speak to him about it. He would wave her off whenever she tried to talk with him alone about any matter.

Life was changing for her into something that she had longed for. She loved Robert—she knew that each time she looked at him or thought about him—and she thanked the Almighty every morning and night in her prayers for ever bringing him to her. She was practical enough to recognize that he did not love her back, but that was fine. He had given her his protection and she would make sure he never regretted his bargain with her.

The call came to her at the worst possible time. As she struggled through another contraction and her bairn forced its way into life, the wisdom pulled her to it.

"Firtha, help me stand," she called out to her sister-by-marriage. "I maun get to the hearth."

"Moira, yer bairn comes. 'Tis no' the time to walk now."

"Pol!" she screamed. Waiting a moment more, she called to her husband again and louder this time. Pol stood at the doorway, looking pale and uneasy, as every man did in a birthing room. "I maun get to the flames."

"She is delirious, Pol. Leave her and I will see to her."

But thankfully Pol knew the importance of what she needed to do and came to her side. Lifting her in his huge arms, he carried her over to the hearth and helped her to kneel before it. Waiting until she had her balance, he did not leave her until she nodded that she was ready. Then, taking hold of Firtha's arm, he pulled her from the room over her very loud objections.

She tried to take in the deep cleansing breath she needed, but the pain from her womb grew until she wanted to scream. Curling her body over, she waited for it to pass and hoped there was time before another began. Her daughter was impatient to be born. However, she knew from the strength of the call that the wisdom would not be ignored. The pain lessened and she stared into the flames and waited.

The visions came upon her with the same force as her labor and she watched the flames as she saw the colors and faces and scenes appear. She tried to discern the message within the wisdom as she observed them before her. Just as they began to fade, a much more powerful contraction struck her and she fell to her side.

"Pol!" she screamed.

Her husband raced in to help her and Firtha followed him into the room. He must have explained how the wisdom worked, for she was much calmer now. But Moira knew she did not have much time. The message must be delivered before it was too late.

"I maun see Struan. Please call him here."

"Moira, ye are aboot to give birth. Surely ye can speak to the laird after that?" Firtha tried to convince her.

"It maun be now, Pol. If ye dinna get him for me, I will walk there myself."

His smile told her he knew she could not do that, but he left the room and came back a few minutes later. "I sent a boy for the laird, Moira."

Caught up in the waves of contractions, she could only nod. She tried to do all those things she advised other expectant mothers to do during this process; however, the pressure of knowing the message must be delivered to Struan added to her pain and frustration. Finally, the laird entered their cottage and walked into the room.

"I am here, Moira."

"Struan, come closer. I maun share the wisdom wi' ye."

"Could this no' wait until after ye give birth?"

"Dinna be foolish. The wisdom has its own rules and its own time. 'Tis now ye maun hear it."

Waving Firtha from the room once more, she grabbed Struan's arm and pulled him close.

"I warned ye aboot yer habit of sending yer sons away, Struan, but ye did no' heed me," she whispered as another pain hit her. Gasping for breath, she pulled in nearer still. "The MacNab comes wi' his own solution."

Struan looked at her and shook his head. "I canna control the MacNab. I warned Robert this marriage would no' stand."

"Ye maun stop trying to protect the dead, Struan. Yer promises to those who hiv died are no' as important as how ye treat those here now."

"Ye dinna ken, Moira." He tried to pull free from her hold but she hung on tighter.

"I do ken, Struan. I saw it. I saw it all."

She saw the horror enter his face and knew that her visions had been true. Although she could not condone what he had done, 'twas not her place to judge him in the matter. She simply knew she had to convince him to change his mind.

"Ye refuse him because of the promises ye made to Glynnis and to Edana. They are dead and gone—and the promises wi' them. For the good of the clan, Struan, and for yer immortal soul, ye maun release yerself from the pledges ye gave."

"But I swore . . . on my word, Moira. Yer a woman, ye dinna understand."

She gasped as she felt the rush of birthing waters between her legs and another contraction forced the breath from her. Still, she would not release his arm. When she could draw in a breath, she forced out the words.

"I do no' need to understand, Struan. I *see,* and I saw what the results would be if ye continue to ignore the wisdom. Ye are the only one who can do this."

She could no longer ignore the burning stretching happening to her. She felt the bairn move down and knew it was time. She let go of his hand and called out for Firtha. Struan stood and moved towards the door.

"Struan," she called out to him once more. "Do no' fail the clan in this." Then with a scream of her own, she pushed the bairn out and into Firtha's waiting hands. Her daughter was born. A dark sense of foreboding came over her, whether due to the birth or what she knew was about to happen, she did not know. She only knew that dark days were coming for some in Dunnedin.

chapter 32

She was in the workroom with Connor, discussing some questions of the harvest and food storage for the coming winter months, when the messenger entered the hall. She could hear his heavy marching steps as they approached the dais. If Struan were still at the table, she would know the news the messenger carried soon enough. Connor began to speak, but she hushed him and waited.

"Laird," the messenger began, "I come from the MacNab."

"What is yer message?" Struan commanded.

"The MacNab is a short distance from here and comes to fetch his daughter, the Lady Anice. He asks that you make all arrangements so that they can leave before the sun sets."

Anice was stunned by the news. Why did her father think he could come and force her out of here? Her son was here, her husband was here. This was the challenge she knew would come against their marriage. Robert had always promised to handle this and now it was time. She had to find him before her father arrived.

Running out of the workroom and following the long corridor, she left through a posterior door where the messenger would not see her. Lifting her skirts, she hurried through the yard looking for any sign of him. Finally, after almost a half hour of searching, she found him in the stables. She stopped outside the stall where he was working but could not speak from her exertions. He took one look at her, handed the tools to the groom, and climbed over the fence to reach her.

"What is it, Anice? Ye look as if ye hiv seen a ghost." He brushed the hair from her face and waited for her to catch her breath.

Finally she could force the words out. "My father comes."

"Here?" He looked past her and out into the yard. "Now?"

"The messenger said he comes directly to take me home."

"Ye are home, lass." His smile did not reach his eyes and did nothing to soothe the new fears that raged inside of her. Even his embrace did not settle her thoughts.

"Rob, you said you would handle this."

"And I will. Come, let us prepare for yer faither's visit."

They walked side by side back to the keep. Climbing the stairs to the first level, they entered the great hall just after her father arrived. The large group in the hall included not just her parents, but several uncles, two priests, many servants, and even some MacNab warriors. Coming in behind them, she heard Struan call out to her. Everyone turned to watch as she approached.

Her father separated himself from his entourage and came towards them. Pointing to two of his largest soldiers, he motioned them to her side. Instead of grabbing her, they took hold of Robert. She screamed and threw herself against him.

"Is this the mon who thinks he can interfere wi' my lawful control of my own daughter?" Her father grabbed her arm, wrenching her away from Robert and into another soldier's grasp. Then without warning he punched Robert in the stomach. She screamed again as Robert bent over at the power of the blow.

"My lord?" her mother said, walking between the two men. "Should we no' pursue this in privacy? We do no' want to expose our daughter's shame to one and all."

Looking around at the gathering crowd, her father relented and she found herself dragged towards the solar. Once inside, she was taken to a chair, where she sat and waited for an explanation of her father's words and actions. Robert, Struan, and a few of the elders of the MacKendimen clan entered and stood near the hearth. Her mother's hand on her shoulder told her she would not like what was to come.

She looked to Robert as he whispered something to Struan. No longer in the hold of the soldiers, she was disappointed that he did not come to her side.

"MacNab, let the women retire and we will come to terms among ourselves."

"Nay. She will hear the truth of what brought her to this shameful reckoning. Then she will see the wisdom in my arrangements."

"Father, what shame is upon me?" she asked, looking from her father to Robert and trying to understand his words.

"Haes he told ye his reasons for marrying ye, Anice?"

"He married me to save me from your plans to take my babe and send me to the MacLarens." Her voice shook now in fearful anticipation. "He married me to protect me."

"He married ye for his own reasons, Anice. He married ye for his own plans."

"But, Father, he had no other reason to marry me. He will not use me as you plan to—for the good of our clan." She fought for control, but felt it slipping away.

"Is that what ye think, Anice? Women are used all of the time by men. That's what God placed ye here for. We use ye to secure property and title, we use ye to produce heirs for those lands, and we use ye for our comfort and pleasure. 'Tis the way of it and he does the same thing wi' ye."

"Nay, you are wrong, Father. Robert married me for none of those reasons." She turned to Robert and waited for his added denial to these charges of her father. It never came. She tried to rise, but her mother's strong hands on her shoulders kept her in the chair.

"Do ye tell her or do I?"

Time slowed down around her and she saw flashes of anger pass between the two men. Robert did not face her.

"Tell me now, Robert. Explain what my father hints at. I trust you."

"Yes," her father goaded. "Tell her how yer so-called marriage has stained her soul with a grievous sin."

She began to shake as she waited on his words. Did he

know of her sin? Or did he speak of something else? The room became silent as they waited for Robert's words.

Robert took in a deep breath and expelled it loudly. Walking closer to her, he squatted down next to her chair and spoke quietly to her. "I am sorry that ye maun hear this news told this way, Anice." He leaned closer and spoke again. "I am also Struan's son."

Anice recoiled from his words. She couldn't have heard him correctly—he was Struan's son? That would make him . . .

"Yer dead husband's brother, Anice. And uncle to yer own son. And he drew ye into an incestuous marriage for his own gains." Her father filled in the missing words. But he didn't stop there. "Do ye ken he will be heir to the clan if any harm should befall yer bairn? A nice cozy position to be in, would no' ye say? The wolf guarding the sheep?"

Robert lunged forward to challenge the MacNab, but Anice cried out in distress. It couldn't be true, could it? Did Struan know? He must if her father knew. And he kept it from her? And the clan?

One look at Robert and Struan was enough to tell her it was true. She had married her husband's brother, breaking one of the rules of God and church. How many marks could her soul take on it? Even now she was in peril of eternal damnation.

Robert said to trust him; he said she was safe with him. Was she? Was the bairn? Did he truly have designs on inheriting his rightful place in the clan at the cost of her babe's life? Nay, he would not. He could not. He had saved their lives when he could just as easily have not given her aid and watched her and the bairn die.

"Anice," Robert said as he started towards her, reaching out to grasp her hand. "Let me explain."

She pulled out of his grasp, shaking her head. "Explain? Does my father speak the truth? Did you know when we married that I was your brother's wife?" Even as she asked him, she knew the answer. It was not the lack of banns and witnesses that had him search out the old priest, it was her previous marriage to his brother. In the eyes of the church, she was his sister-by-marriage and even after his brother died, she was still beyond his reach.

"Aye, Anice," he answered in a defeated tone. "I sought oot Father Cleirach because I kenned we could no' marry otherwise."

Tears filled her eyes as she faced the end of everything good in her life. All the changes he'd brought about, all the joy, all the love.

"I did no' do it to hurt ye or yer babe, Anice. Ye will ken that if ye think about it."

"So, you did not think about the position you would hold here when you offered me your bargain?"

The look of guilt was so clear in his eyes that it hurt her to look at him. She could feel her hard-won control slipping away from her . . . control of her emotions, her choices, her life. She hadn't felt this way since that night months ago when Struan first told her of her father's plans to marry her elsewhere and to turn her son over to Struan and the MacKendimens to raise. But where Robert had been her refuge from the insanity of that night, today he was the cause.

Mayhap if she had obeyed then, this crippling pain would not be hers to bear now. And now not only did her soul carry the dark sin of trying to take her own life, but now it also carried the mark of incest on it. Mayhap if she repented and confessed her sins and promised to obey, she could be forgiven?

Blinking away the flood of tears that blinded her, she turned to her father. "What would you have me do?" She heard Robert's anguished groan and tried very hard to ignore it.

"Return wi' us and wait out the handfasting. I hiv already applied to the bishop for an annulment of this marriage on the ground of incest. Once the year and a day haes passed, we will find another suitable husband for ye."

She almost feared to ask, but forced the words out. "And my bairn?"

She thought Struan would answer; instead Robert's voice interrupted. "Struan, let her take the babe wi' her. I'm certain ye can arrange for a guardian to accompany them and see to his weel-being while he is wi' the MacNab."

Struan agreed and, with that, her entire life had changed.

Gone was the future she'd only recently allowed herself to plan. One filled with happiness and a husband she loved and the children she gave him.

She finally noticed her mother tapping her on the shoulder. Turning to look at her, she realized they were done here. Rising on shaky legs, she began to walk from the room. As she walked past him, she did not meet his gaze. Passing through the doorway into the great hall, she thought she heard him whisper her name.

T*he next days were all a blur of black and white, night and* day, to her. Her father had planned a quick leaving, but she was so overwrought she could do nothing but sob. Moira was called and came as soon as she could; the only thing she could offer was a sleeping concoction that Anice took willingly. When she was asleep, she could dream wonderful dreams where everything was not black. Robert was in them and she could ignore the reality of their situation in favor of the temporary happiness she found there. Her milk dried up, probably from the shock, her mother said, and Craig was turned over to Emma to nurse.

If it rained outside or was fair, if meals were served or not, she did not know. She only knew the misery of Robert's betrayal and the loss of all she once held dear. Her mother brought Craig to her in her room, but Anice could not gather the strength to play with her son. She was never left alone—either her mother or Firtha or one of the other women was always in the room with her. She did not know if they'd found out what she had tried to do before or not. However, she could not be bothered worrying about their presence.

The one person who she missed the most and at the same time dreaded seeing again was Robert. Part of her simply wanted to ride away without ever seeing his face again and yet another part of her wanted to throw herself in his arms and beg him to find a way that they could be together. Of course, that was impossible since he was truly Struan's son and she'd already married his other son. Even the fact that he was a bastard son did not negate the church's objection to their marriage.

How had she missed the resemblance between father and son? Now that she looked back in her memories, she could see it clearly. They shared many of the same expressions and body movements. And they were both as stubborn as sin. And what was the truth of his birth? She tamped down her curiosity. Although Robert had encouraged it, she was certain that whomever her father chose for her would not have such a liberal view of a woman's role within marriage.

Anice decided to visit with Moira and see her new babe before she left Dunnedin. She had really not had the opportunity to speak with Moira while the healer tended her and there were many things left to be said between them. Three days after her father's arrival, Anice felt up to a walk and left her room with her mother in tow, unwilling but accompanying her still. They would be leaving in two days' time, she was told by her mother. Anything that needed to be done should be.

Anice walked through the village without raising her eyes from the ground. She did not know what the clan knew of her and Robert's situation, but she could not face the piteous looks that she knew were sent in her direction. Soon, Moira and Pol's cottage came into view and she hurried her steps, seeking the shelter it offered. Knocking on the door, she entered when Moira called out to her. If she was surprised to see her, Moira did not show it. But then too, not many things surprised the seer of the clan.

"Anice, 'tis good to see ye. Come in and sit."

"Moira, may I make you known to my mother?"

"We hiv already met. Three nights ago."

Her cheeks burned in embarrassment—they'd met when Moira was summoned to care for her. Of course they'd met.

"Will ye hiv some tea?" Moira wrapped her skirt around a large kettle on the hearth and lifted it to the table.

"Should you be doing that, Moira? You have just given birth."

"I feel weel, lass. I can do as I maun, in spite of Pol's thinking that I should lie abed for days." They chuckled and she seemed to remember something else. "I maun send a message over to Pol." Anice watched as she left the cottage and, through the open door, she heard her call one of the village boys over and send him off to Pol. "Now then, let's take our ease for a few minutes. What brings ye here, Anice?"

"I wanted to talk to you before I left. I have many things to thank you for."

"Ah, lass, no thanks are necessary. I did what I could wi' the gifts I am given. To do less would be to dishonor them."

"Still," Anice said, "I wanted you to know how much I have appreciated your help and the counsel you've given me these many years. I will miss you most of all, Moira." Her eyes and throat burned with tears she did not want to shed. Of their own accord, they spilled out and ran down her cheeks.

"Here now, Anice, dinna greet. Life haes too much to offer to ye that ye should spend yer time crying." Moira reached into a pocket and brought out a linen for her to use. "Mop yer tears and come to see my daughter." Moira took her by the hand and tugged her to one of the alcoves, where a cradle lay.

"What have you named her?" Anice asked, looking at the sleeping babe.

"*Jean,* after Pol's own maither. Wi' all of Ramsey's boys, she is the first girl born to him or his brothers."

"She is lovely, Moira. Does she fare well?"

"Oh, aye. A bit of a rough start, but ye ken aboot those, dinna ye, Anice?"

She was about to ask another question when the door opened. Expecting to see Pol answering his wife's call, she turned to greet him. In the doorway, Robert stood, just watching her as she watched him.

He looked horrible. His hair was pulled back away from his face and his arms and hands were nicked by many cuts and burns. A rough beard grew on his face, where none had been before, and he looked as though he had not slept since she last saw him that day in the solar. And, in spite of his betrayal, she drank in the sight of him.

"Come, Suisan, let me show ye where I just planted some new herbs." Moira took her mother by the arm and steered her out the back door towards the gardens. If her mother wanted to object, she never had the chance.

She waited for him to speak, since he had so obviously arranged this with Moira. In truth, she could not think of one thing to say to him. And she could think of hundreds of questions she wanted to ask him at the same time. He cleared his throat and finally spoke.

"I wanted to talk wi' ye before ye left Dunnedin. I hope ye will forgive Moira for her part in this?"

She nodded, knowing words would never escape from her mouth.

"Yer faither had many things to say that day—"

"And you did not deny any of them, Robert. Is that what this is for now?"

"Nay, I canna deny the truth he spoke, Anice. But I wanted ye to ken some of my side of things. Will ye listen?"

She stood on the opposite side of Moira's high worktable from him. Keeping it between them made her feel safer. Nodding her head, she waited on his words.

"When I came here at Struan's summons, I thought he might finally be ready to acknowledge me as his son. As ye ken, he did no' and that refusal ate at me. Then watching ye and seeing how yer husband, my own brother, ignored and mistreated ye, I began to want ye for myself. Aye, at first, I admit to ye freely that ye were simply part of what he had that I wanted. I coveted my brother's home, his place, and, aye, even his wife. But as I came to ken ye, I wanted ye because of the woman ye are, Anice."

She thought she could control herself, but when faced with his words, she could not hold back the tears. They rolled down her cheeks and neck. "And the marriage? Ye did that for the position it offered ye?"

"I told Struan that I would no' seek recognition from him because it would mean losing ye and I wanted ye more than anything. I wanted to make things right for ye. I wanted to undo the damage Sandy wrought on yer body and soul. Now 'twould seem that I only caused ye more pain and suffering."

"What will you do now, Rob?" Her words came out on a sob.

"I hiv sent word to Duncan that I return to serve him if he will hiv me."

"Of course he will. Lady Margaret will welcome you with open arms."

"Robena haes agreed to come wi' me to Dunbarton."

"Truly? That might be good for her." She had to ask the question that this news raised. "Will ye marry her, Robert?"

He took a step closer and she looked away. She did not want to hear the answer now that she had asked.

"She will no' because she canna bear children, and I canna marry her, Anice, for I am already married. And annulment or no', disavowing of the handfasting or no', I took vows wi' ye and they will always bind my heart to yours."

"It cannot be, Robert. You are my husband's brother. It is all wrong."

"I may hiv wanted ye for all the wrong reasons, but I loved ye for all the right ones, Anice. And I married ye for love. Not position or power. For love."

She shook her head, she could not listen to this. Regardless of whether she believed him or not, their marriage was wrong. This could not be made right in the eyes of God and church. They could not be together.

"I needed ye to ken. If the only way for ye to find some measure of happiness is to agree to yer faither's plans, then do it, lass. Ye deserve it after what ye've suffered at the hands of the MacKendimens."

She could only move her head, for the tears completely blinded her to everything in the room. Happiness? There was no such thing in life. She rubbed her eyes, trying to clear some of the tears, when she heard him open the door.

"Anice? I hiv made certain that the bairn will stay wi' ye until he is old enough to be here wi'oot ye."

"How, Robert?"

"I told ye I would handle Struan. I just did no' plan on yer faither's anger."

"Thank you for that."

He turned back towards the door, then stopped and faced her again.

"Did ye ever think aboot . . . harming yerself again?" he asked quietly.

Startled by his question, Anice realized that she had not even contemplated ending her life to avoid what she would face now—possibly losing her son, definitely losing Robert, losing the clan she'd grown up with, and facing the uncertainty of another attempt at married life with some as yet unknown man. Her sense of confidence in herself was one thing that Robert had given back to her during their time together. She smiled through her tears and shook her head.

"Nay, Robert, not even for a moment. Besides, if you are not here to save me, I cannot risk trying it again."

He grunted and then left without another word and she sank onto the bench next to the table. Laying her head on her arms, she let out the sorrow that overwhelmed her once again.

The sound of the babe stirring roused her from her stupor. Anice looked around to find herself still alone in Moira's cottage. Turning the bairn over, Anice laughed as Jean's little rosebud mouth pursed and sucked on nothing but the air around her.

"Come, little lass. Let us find your mam."

Carrying the babe outside, she saw Moira and her own mother talking in the far plot of the garden. Walking over to them, she handed the babe over.

"Suisan, can ye take the babe inside for me? I will take my leave of Anice and be there directly."

If her mother thought it was a strange request, she never showed it. Without a moment's hesitation, she put the babe on her shoulder and walked back to the house.

"Did ye speak to him?"

"Aye, Moira, I did." She could not look her friend in the face.

"Did it help?"

"Aye and nay. It does not change anything."

"Ah, so it does no'. Weel, he asked for my help in arranging this meeting and I hope ye are no' angry at me for it?"

"Nay, Moira. How did you know where to find him?"

"He haes been working wi' Pol and Ramsey at the smithy these last few days and staying wi' Robena." She turned to go and was stopped by Moira once again. "Can I ask ye a question before ye go?" She nodded. "Did it bother ye to marry a man when ye thought he was the son of a steward? Did ye think about being the daughter of an earl when he brought his proposal to ye?"

Anice thought of what her reaction had been and remembered thinking about that exact thing. "Aye, it did at first. Then I realized it was not as important to me as feeling protected."

"I just wondered, lass. Weel, now, yer maither is probably tired of being entertained here and I am sure ye hiv many things to do before ye leave."

Moira approached her and opened her arms. Anice hugged the woman and then stepped back.

"No more tears, lass. The time for greeting is done."

"Thank you, Moira, for everything."

Anice turned and walked around the cottage and met her mother on the other side. They walked back through the village and into the castle without sharing a word of conversation.

chapter 33

She pulled a chair into the far corner and sat down on it. All alone, she watched the comings and goings of the great hall of Struan MacKendimen. It had been her home for nearly half her lifetime and she wanted a few quiet moments here before finishing packing for the morrow's journey. She had accomplished much here, first under Edana's guidance and then on her own. The keep was well tended and well run and the MacKendimens had all been taken care of while she was in charge here.

Anice watched as several of the clan's elders made their way into the solar. A short while later, more joined them there. Struan was probably sharing the whole sad story with them, for there were decisions of inheritance and decisions of guardianship to be made this day. She was surprised when she saw Father MacIntyre come out following Struan. The elders must have been asking for the good father's guidance.

She enjoyed the quiet for a bit more before returning to her chambers. Most of her clothes and belongings had been packed on the wagon that would carry her back to her father's keep. The bairn was down for his afternoon nap in Emma's room. A knock at her door drew her attention. After a moment's pause, her mother entered.

"I thought we could talk, Anice, if ye are no' too busy?" Her mother crossed the room and sat down before she could answer. "I hiv no' seen ye since yer marriage to Sandy last year. And yer letters hiv been few and far between."

"We were never especially close, Mother. I know Moira better than I do you."

"Ye left to live here when ye were so young, Anice. Mayhap I did no' ever tell ye of yer faither's courtship of me?"

The whole visit was strange and now this topic of conversation made her turn and stare at her mother.

"Nay? 'Tis quite a different tale than most ken. Most hiv heard that he kidnapped me and held me against my will, ravaging me until I was pregnant. That's no' the truth of it. We planned it together, for my faither threatened to disown me if I did no' marry his choice for me."

"What? I have never heard this."

"Weel, 'tis no' a surprise that no one shared this kind of story wi' ye. Aye, we were madly in love, but yer faither was the son of a soldier and certainly no' high enough in standing to marry the daughter of a duke. My faither had arranged a more suitable marriage for me to the heir of one of the lowland clans and he was about to announce my betrothal. We decided to run away and let out word that he had kidnapped me. We hid away for months, until I became pregnant and there was no way for my faither to refuse his suit."

"Months?" she asked, horrified and fascinated at this story of her parents.

"Weel, it took him most of that time to build up the courage to touch me. Finally, I had to do the deed, so to speak, or ye never would hiv been conceived."

The image of her brusque, hearty father unable to "do the deed" made her laugh. She had never doubted her parents' love, she had just not heard this tale of it before.

"What if your father had disowned you?"

"His only daughter? Bah, 'twould never hiv happened. Nay, he knew I was as stubborn as he and that I was willing to live in a cave to be wi' yer faither. He relented—and no' just because I carried ye."

"Well then, why?" She had to know.

"Because, under all the bluster, he loved me. And he kenned that yer faither did, too."

She thought on her mother's words as she moved from trunk to trunk, organizing her clothes and Craig's. Her mother stood and left as quickly as she had arrived and then the day dragged on relentlessly. Finally night came and she lay in her bed for the last time. The night was no kinder, for she tossed and turned, unable to sleep. The sun's rays poured through her window and she gave up the fight to rest. Every time she closed her eyes, Moira's or her mother's words echoed in her thoughts until she wanted to scream.

She dressed and saw to Craig and then broke her fast with a quick meal of porridge. The sounds from the courtyard entered her window and she looked out to see the final preparations for the journey home being made there. Her father's loud rough voice rose above it all, the frustration in the slowness of the process evident even to her listening above.

She left the room and walked down the stairs to the main floor, then out into the yard and into all the commotion. Observing her father from her place near the keep, she realized that no matter how angry or how busy he was, his gaze softened whenever it lit on her mother. Their story had made her laugh. He caught sight of her and directed her to one of the smaller carts. Emma, who had agreed to accompany her home and care for the babe, stood there already with Craig, waiting to climb in for the trip. She was about to climb in and get settled when it struck her.

Her stupidity made her laugh out loud. She dropped the bag she held and lifted Craig from Emma's arms, directing the girl not to get into the wagon. Then she went to her father.

"I cannot leave him, Father."

"Yer marriage is no' valid, lass. I will make arrangements for a better one for ye." Her mother joined them.

"Then I will ask him to live with me without the bonds of marriage."

Her father inhaled so quickly that he choked. Sputtering and coughing, he yelled at her, "No daughter of mine will live in sin wi' a man."

"Then I am no daughter of yours," she yelled back, surprising even herself at the power of the words. Robert had taught her about that power and the courage to call on it.

Her father looked aghast at her and then turned to her mother, who stood smiling next to him. "'Tis frightening to hear yer own words come back to haunt ye as my faither said they would, is it no', husband?"

She waited no longer to see what he would do, for she needed to get to Robert and beg him to forgive her for her lack of faith in him. With Craig on her hip, she walked quickly through the gate and out into the village. Following one of the side trails, she soon stood before the well-worn path leading to Robena's cottage. Once she caught her breath, she called out his name as loudly as she could, scaring Craig to tears and startling some of the children playing nearby.

She heard some scurrying inside the cottage and then the door opened. Robert stood there looking at her. She pushed open the gate and walked towards him.

"Please take me with you to Dunbarton. . . . Take us," she said, looking down at Craig.

"Anice, yer father said . . ."

"I have no father. Will that matter to you? I know it does to most men. If I come to you without dowry or name, will you have me?"

"Ye ken I did no' offer for ye to gain those things, Anice. I'm afraid I canna offer ye the protection of marriage, lass. Not now that ye ken the truth aboot me."

"Did Father Cleirach know the truth when he heard our vows?"

Robert nodded his answer. So Robert had not deceived the priest.

"Then if my father goes through with the annulment, we will ask him to hear our vows again. Or I will live with you and bear your children without the bond of marriage, Robert." She stepped closer and knelt in the dirt at his feet. "If you will have me, Robert. Please?"

He grabbed her and dragged her to her feet. "Anice, as much as I want ye, as much as I love ye, I canna let ye throw away all that should be yers. And, yer faither will no' stand for this. He seeks a suitable marriage for his daughter."

"I cannot marry someone else, Robert, for I gave you my

heart when we took our vows." Tears filled her eyes and she cried out to him once more. "For, annulment or not, we are already married in our hearts."

He recognized his own words and took her, took them, in his embrace. "Will ye regret this later? Will ye wish for the title ye give up now in order to do this?"

"My only regret would be in letting you leave here without me."

He drew her near and touched his lips to hers. Just when she would have opened to him, the crowd that had gathered around them parted and her parents, Struan, Father MacIntyre, and some of the clan elders came through.

"What is this talk of leaving, Robert? Ye canna leave," one of the elders called out to him.

Father MacIntyre approached, carrying several parchments. "'Twould seem that Struan has discovered a problem wi' the original betrothal and the old laird's will. Both refer to Struan's eldest son and heir. When this wording is used, rather than referring to the male issue of a legitimate marriage, all sons were considered, not just legitimate ones. If Struan kenned of the existence of another, older son when he contracted with the MacNab, then he entered into this agreement fraudulently. Since Robert was older than Alesander, he and not Alesander should have married the MacNab heiress. And been named tanist as is the custom here."

Anice looked in confusion at Robert, not quite understanding what had just been established. Her father interrupted.

"So ye are saying that if Struan kenned of Robert then Anice's marriage to Sandy was invalid?" Her father snorted and huffed, not used to having anyone interfere with his plans.

"Aye. And Struan has already signed a statement attesting to that prior knowledge. Although it will take some time to file the papers with the courts and with the church, it appears that Anice's first marriage was invalid. That is, of course, if Struan acknowledges Robert as his heir before the clan."

Anice did not dare to hope that everything could be settled this easily. If Struan was going to call him son, why wait until now? Why not do it earlier? How could Struan punish Robert with exile and then wait through all of this?

"No, Struan," Robert said, surprising her with his vehemence. He shook his finger at Struan, who looked very tired. " 'Tis too late to hear the words from ye."

"Come, Robert, let us speak in private. Please hear me oot before ye decide." Struan's voice was roughened with emotions.

"Anice, come wi' me? For this is aboot ye and yer son as weel."

Robert held out his hand to her and she followed him and Struan into Robena's cottage. When she shifted the babe to a more comfortable spot on her hip, Robert lifted him from her and placed him on his shoulder. She looked at Struan, but not before catching sight of Robert rubbing Craig's head and placing a tender kiss on the babe's forehead. What a fool she had been to ever doubt him.

She caught his gaze and he smiled at her, embarrassed a bit by being seen in that tender moment. Then Struan cleared his throat.

"When yer maither came and told me she was carrying ye, Robert, she made me swear never to openly acknowledge ye as mine. In spite of the love we shared, she did not want Dougal hurt by our affair. I did no' see her again as her lover and we did no' speak again until the night she bore ye and died. She begged me once again to keep yer parentage a secret to protect Dougal and I held to our bargain.

"I was faithful in my heart to Edana for our whole marriage except that brief time with Glynnis. When Edana discovered the truth, as women always seem to, it destroyed her. The only thing that would begin to heal the rift between us was my promise to never let ye inherit over her son. Alesander had been born a few months after yer birth and the fact that Glynnis had given me a son first ate at Edana. Through the years, I watched ye grow into a mon and kenned that others saw the resemblance. Somehow, Edana found out and confronted me that night over nine years ago. Once Dougal found out, he treated ye differently. I could no' openly accept ye so I arranged wi' Duncan to foster ye there."

"So you kept the promises made to everyone else and abandoned your own flesh and blood?" Anice asked. Robert looked at her in surprise.

"'Twould seem so," Struan answered in a strangled voice.

"Robert, you do not need him. Duncan will make us welcome there." She was furious upon learning the truth. How Robert had grown into such a loving and wonderful man, under circumstances like these, she could not imagine. Then she realized that Duncan and Margaret were the answer to that.

"Anice, ye hiv the most to gain or lose by his words. If he acknowledges me and yer marriage to Sandy is invalidated, I gain title and position, but yer son loses it. If we refuse his words, ye will lose title and position and maun be contented to live outside the bonds of marriage, but yer son will inherit."

Before answering, she looked to Struan.

"But what of your promises and pledges to Glynnis and Edana and Dougal? Can ye simply forswear them? Yer word will no' be accepted again by allies or enemies," Anice asked, reminding Struan of the other complications that would come from this.

"I hiv lived my life in service to this clan. Every decision I hiv made haes been made wi' that in mind. If setting things to right is best for the clan, then I will do it and let those promises rest with those who died."

She looked at Robert and saw that he was torn between wanting his father to say the words and leaving it all behind. When he looked at her, she smiled and let him know that she would be by his side no matter what course life took. He took her hand in his and kissed it.

"Do not let your pride get in the way now, Rob. Take what he offers if that is what you wish."

"And Craig's place?"

"Craig will lead the clan if it is his destiny to do so."

"Then, Struan, I will accept yer acknowledgment."

Struan grunted and turned to leave. The gesture was so much like Robert she wanted to laugh out loud at it. He led her outside, where an even bigger crowd had now gathered to hear Struan's declaration that would begin a process to right the wrongs done so many years ago to him.

He walked out before her, carrying her son, whose life he had saved, in his arms. Her heart felt so full of love she knew that the life before them would be filled with happiness.

As Struan made his announcement, Robert leaned close to her ear and whispered to her. "Hiv my children, did ye say?"

She felt the heat of a blush enter her cheeks at his words. "Aye, I think I did say something like that."

"Can I make ye my prisoner like yer faither did to yer maither?"

"Only if I can make you mine."

She looked at him and saw the promise of passion and pleasure and love in his eyes.

"I am yours, my lady Anice."

"Nay. Say it the way you usually say it. When you thought I did not notice."

"My . . . Anice." He put his arm around her shoulders and drew her close.

"Aye, my . . . Robert."

Epilogue

Ten years later

Robert leaned down and picked up a handful of dirt. Holding it out, he tossed it on the coffin and then supported Anice as she did the same. In her eighth month, she was ungainly on her feet and the slope made her steps even more precarious. Robert nodded and the boys followed their example. Craig led his six-year-old brother to the end of the grave so that the dirt would land where it should.

Struan MacKendimen, earl of Dunnedin, was laid to rest on a clear and sunny August morn after a short illness. His grave was dug next to his wife and his other son within the family plot on the hillside near the castle.

After a few others had tossed dirt in, the workers took shovels to finish the burial. Although Anice looked tired, she stayed by Robert's side until it was done. Then, with his arm to help her, she walked down the hill with him and back towards the keep. The boys ran ahead of them, already planning their next activity for the day, as children did.

"I am just glad that you made your peace with him, Robert. I am certain it made his passing easier."

"I did it for ye, wife."

"Nay, Robert. You did it because you are a good man."

"A good mon, ye say?"

"Aye. Of course, that's what Robena called you all those years ago."

"What else did she say aboot me?" he asked, already knowing the answer. His friend had become his wife's friend as well and he knew what Robena had told his wife those many years before.

"A good man, but more than a bit daft."

He laughed with her and then scooped her into his arms rather than letting her walk all the way back to the keep in her condition. As he carried his wife, the new countess of Dunnedin, into her home to prepare for the coming of their child, he reflected on how his life had been changed so much for the better by a love that had been once forbidden between them.